THE COSMIC PRINCIPLE

THE COSMIC PRINCIPLE

Developmental Edit: Quinn Nichols, Quill and Bone Editing
Editing: Britt Laux, Magic and Moons Press
Cover Design: Alexandra Purtan, Fenix Cover Designs
Book Design and Typesetting: Enchanted Ink Publishing

Content Warnings Page

Please note that this story contains themes and situations which could be considered triggering. If you aren't concerned with potential triggers, feel free to skip this page.

This book contains the following;

Foul language
Physical violence
Blaster (gun) violence
Death
Death threats
Near asphyxiation
Mentions of war
Depictions of grief

While many of these themes are only touched on briefly or shown in one or two chapters, I would never want you to risk your mental wellbeing while you're reading my book. Please be assured that there are no scenes which contain sexual assault of any kind. In addition, none of the LGBTQIA+ characters depicted are deadnamed or misgendered. I want you to feel safe as you escape into the world of The Cosmic Principle.

THE NEXUS SERIES BOOK ONE

THE COSMIC PRINCIPLE

WRITTEN BY

ABBY R. LAUGHLIN

CHAPTER 1

A cool breeze rustled Caldera's hair against her shoulders as she sat on the roof of her shuttle, irritation biting at her nerves. Fumes from the other ships idling on the flight lines stung her nose, making the air seem thick despite the night's clarity. She looked up into the blackness, beyond the personal transports that crisscrossed the sky, and examined the little white specks between the high-rise buildings of Astrum, the capital city of Tellis. Knitting her brow, she shifted, knowing she shouldn't be able to see stars with all the surrounding light. As if on cue, one of the thousands of orbital satellites blinked, proving her point.

The bright city lights reflected off the metal of her ship into her eyes, even though the Vanguard's shipyard was nowhere near the middle of Astrum. It was on the border between rapid industrialization and flat nothingness—fenced off, protected ground that no one was allowed to build on. Even so, she could still hear far-off laughter and snippets of indiscernible conversations filtering through the open air.

She squeezed her eyes shut, the propaganda speech they fed to the new Vanguard recruits rattling around in her head from when she first joined. *As members of the Vanguard of Tellis, it will be you, along with the members from the other sectors, that will save us, the inhabitants of Bersama, from total annihilation.*

She shuddered despite the balmy weather, and absentmindedly picked at the last remaining string of the once-embroidered planetary emblem over her right breast pocket—the golden crown representing Sector One that was now just a skeletal outline.

The fact that she was no longer the eighteen-year-old girl who had impulsively joined the Vanguard continued to prod her mind as she pulled her knees up to her chest.

Happy ninth anniversary to me...and what do I have to show for it? A meaningless captaincy and a headache.

"*Tch*—the people of this planet deserve better than us," Caldera muttered, gritting her teeth. She flicked through the informational displays on the flexible monitor that wrapped around her wrist and part-way up her forearm—continual body readings, current outside temperature, and area scans—until the time flashed in her face. Frowning, she pulled the device off her body with a sigh, flattening it against the cold metal beside her.

"Call Ren," she commanded, pressing her finger against the screen as it clicked into place. The monitor obeyed.

Rennick answered almost immediately, a smile stretching across his golden-brown face. "What's up?"

The call-image lifted off the screen and floated in front of her, coating the surrounding area in white light—a beacon in the darkness.

"Where are you?" she asked, though she could tell from his surroundings he was somewhere on the flight line.

"Almost there."

"We're already behind schedule."

"You want the flight plan, don't you?" he countered, holding up a small black holodeck.

Caldera smiled, unable to stop herself. "Just hurry up," she scoffed, then ended the connection and replaced the monitor on her arm. She stood up, activated her mag-boots, and stretched, her back cracking with the effort.

She began her descent, the mag-boots clicking rhythmically against the metal with each step. Taking a deep breath, she silently went through her systematic routine of cursing the king for continually sending them on ineffectual missions.

Maybe this time will be different. Maybe we'll find something—an exoplanet, a plot of land, anything—on this mission that can be used to help replenish the dwindling resources. Maybe we'll find a habitable ecosystem...

Just as her feet met the pavement, Rennick reached her.

"On top of the shuttle again I see," he said, running a hand through his short brown hair.

Caldera nodded. "No new bridge techs this time around?" she asked, glancing over his shoulder as if they might be hiding behind him.

"Nope. Just the two of us, as usual. Besides, with the number of people that board this ship and then quit as soon as the mission ends?" he said, putting a hand on Caldera's shoulder. "I think headquarters is getting the hint that no one *wants* to stay with us."

Caldera pushed his hand away. "If you're implying that it's my fault—"

"Of course not."

She started up the ramp. "I let them know the boundaries," she continued matter-of-factly, placing her hand on the airlock scanner when she reached the top.

"In kind of a...judgy way."

"I'm the captain," she said calmly, as the airlock cycled through. "I have that right—"

Rennick's expression turned hard. "And as your first officer, I think I should remind you it's just us on the bridge now."

They stepped into the ship, which was immaculate despite its age—scrubbed down to the bolts after each mission by unseen cleaning crews.

Caldera sighed as they made their way down the winding hall

toward the elevator shaft. Soft, blue light backlit the curved gray walls and floor as they passed nameless engineers and technicians who promptly got out of their way. When they stepped into the lift, the doors quickly whisked closed.

"Bridge," she commanded, and the oval compartment began to rise.

"We need a permanent bridge crew, Callie," Rennick said. He leaned against the wall and crossed his arms, his expression softening. "We're spread so thin we can barely operate."

"I know," Caldera whispered, averting her gaze, the back of her neck prickling as the doors *whooshed* open onto an empty flight deck. Four empty stations and chairs surrounded her as she took her place at the co-pilot's terminal in the center of the room and scanned her hand to begin the pre-flight checks.

Atmospheric pressure throughout the ship within normal range... Check.

All maneuverable thrusters in working order... Check.

Rail gun systems working and at full ammo capacity... Check.

"Plus—and I hate to even bring this up again—if you want that promotion to commander, you're gonna need to find a new bridge crew and your replacement for this ship."

"And yours. You're coming with me...right?"

"If you get the promotion and you get to choose your right hand, yes, I'll come with you." A mischievous smile spread across his face. "Maybe taking a ground assignment and moving into the Vanguard Headquarters permanently will keep you out of trouble."

Caldera laughed. "Yeah right. It'll take more than that, but hopefully from there, I'll be able to exact real change. I want to help the people of this planet and this captaincy position just isn't cutting it."

Rennick slid into the pilot's seat to her right and placed his chin in the palm of his hand. He stared at her as if in admiration.

"Umm... Where are we headed?" Caldera asked, changing the subject as heat rushed to her cheeks.

"We're going to the first section of the galaxy." He turned

away and inserted the holodeck containing the flight plans into the ship's system, then pressed a button on the command center.

As he spoke, a two-dimensional holographic map popped up on the screen in front of them that revealed a layout of the entire Centaurus galaxy, overlaying their flight path onto it.

How is this mission going to help Bersama?

Caldera took in a sharp breath. The first section of the galaxy was well-known to be deserted. They, along with the rest of the dwindling population of five different species, had been shoved onto the planet, Bersama—the last inhabitable, solitary planet left in the Centaurus galaxy. Images of the other four long-dead planets loomed on the screen in front of them, hovering haphazardly in space as if nothing had happened—as if over half of the population of the entire galaxy hadn't been wiped out.

Although the cataclysm had happened over a century ago—well before Caldera was born—she found it hard to look at the remnants, even if they were just computerized models on a flight plan. It reminded her that if the Vanguard couldn't find another planet, they would be alone with nowhere to turn, stuck on Bersama until the resources ran out.

The Vanguard usually didn't get orders to go to that part of the galaxy anymore. There was nothing of use there.

But that's exactly where they were headed.

"The desolate section..." Caldera muttered the nickname, shuddering as the images of the desecration flashed across her mind.

Rennick nodded, sending the details over to her terminal with a flick of his wrist.

"An exoplanet. What are we supposed to be looking for on what's basically an asteroid?" she mused, more to herself than to him, as she scrolled through the mission dossier.

"That's the thing," he replied, readying the thrusters. "We're used to vague orders, but this feels like something else."

So much for a worthwhile mission. "The king has officially lost his mind," Caldera said, slumping against the thick plastic chair, loose from years of use, causing her to lean back further than intended. *Damn it! How is this going to help me get us both off this ship?*

Rennick's lips were pursed, brow furrowed with concern as he spoke into the ship's com. "Flight tower, this is T7456, ready for liftoff."

"Acknowledged, T7456. Captain's approval?"

"Approved," Caldera replied into the com, then returned her attention to the wall of text in front of her.

"All right, T7456, you're clear for liftoff."

The ship shifted as the docking clamps released, and they were in the air. It was so quick she hardly noticed the transition. They flew in silence for a while as Rennick followed the designated flight path so as not to crash into any stray satellites, personal shuttles, or other Vanguard ships that were trying to land.

A half hour later, Rennick said, "We're about to be under thrust." He sounded the alarm so the technicians and engineers below decks knew to strap into their crash couches.

Caldera leaned back against her seat and took a deep breath, readying herself for the push. It was never painful, but she didn't like the feeling of someone standing on her chest for the five minutes it took to get into null-g. The sensation came and went, and then she and Rennick were both floating in their chairs, held down only by the straps across their chests and waists.

"This isn't even our jurisdiction," she mumbled, pulling her platinum white hair back into a short ponytail to keep it from floating around her face. "It's Sector Five's."

"The Muléus Vanguard is spread thinner than we are," Rennick replied simply. The antigravity pulled on his skin, effectively erasing the worry lines from his expression. His hair haloed his head as his hazel eyes stared into her dark blue ones.

"Let's just get this over with. Then we can move on to something that actually matters."

CHAPTER 2

Can you stop that? You're driving me nuts!" Caldera said through gritted teeth as another *ting* echoed throughout the flight deck. Rubbing her temples, she walked to the window that covered the far wall of the bridge from floor to ceiling. Specks of light flew by outside, and the rough one-g the ship had been coasting at for the last few hours only intensified her headache. She wished they were on the float again, or better yet, back on Bersama where the gravity didn't make her joints grind together.

"What?" Rennick asked. He tapped his foot harder against the metal floor, the *ting* of his boot echoing throughout the deck again.

"You're lucky you're the pilot, or I would have airlocked you five days ago."

"Only five?"

"If not sooner."

The corner of Rennick's lip lifted into a grin. "I'm losing my touch, then."

She let a smile break fully across her face. "Maybe I will space you. I can fly this ship by myself, you know."

"Oh, please." Rennick rested his elbows on his knees. "You'd get lonely."

She opened her mouth to reply—to agree with him—when the monitor next to him beeped.

"We're here," he said, all joviality gone from his expression. He turned toward the command center and carefully brought the ship to a stop right outside the exoplanet's gravitational radius.

Caldera retook her seat and looked out the window but was met with nothing but stark blackness. The exoplanet was almost completely hidden by the debris cloud that encircled it, unable to break free from the planet's gravity. She tried to catch any glimpse of the planet below whenever there was a break in the detritus, without much success.

"This doesn't look good," Rennick said, echoing her thoughts. "I assume our report is going to be pretty short."

"I agree, but take us down anyway."

"Why?" He glanced at her from the corner of his eye. "We've been ordered not to. Let's just scan it and get out of here."

"Correction. We were never specifically ordered not to land," she replied, already pressing buttons on the control panel to let the rest of the crew know they were going to touch down. "We might as well look around, and who knows? Maybe it's not as bad as it looks."

"Right... As if it's going to be a utopia down there, below a debris cloud that barely lets in any sunlight..." Rennick muttered, starting the initial scan.

Caldera strapped herself in. "I'm tired of going on ineffectual missions. We're bringing something—*anything*—back, so it can be analyzed. Bring us down."

"Bringing us down," Rennick said, easing the shuttle into the exoplanet's atmosphere.

Caldera glanced over the readings from the various atmospheric scanners. "Breathable air," she murmured.

They drifted below the thick gray clouds, jolting as they connected with the surface.

"It may have breathable air, but that's all it has going for it," Rennick said, looking out the window at what little could be seen of the desolate landscape.

Caldera chuckled as she scanned the area directly outside of their ship. Nothing. Light from the orbiting sun cut through the dusky atmosphere and coated the planet's surface in a dull gray, making it just bright enough to see. Dust and debris blew past the window and across the landscape, obstructing any view further than sixty feet.

"Let's head down to the airlock," Caldera said with a decisive nod, walking over to the flight deck door.

"Callie, are you serious? We're going out there?"

"There's no reason not to. Sure, a planetary scan will show the overall state and habitability of the exo..." She paused, looking over her shoulder at him. "Maybe if we produce actual samples, the king won't send us back here in the future."

"I wouldn't count on that. There's no telling what he'll do next," Rennick replied as they cycled through the door, the lift transporting them as close as it could to the exit.

"If he has a single functioning brain cell left, he won't," Caldera said. Techs she didn't know bustled down the hallway, wearing black flight jackets with bright gold embroidered crowns, furiously typing on their holopads as they approached the first airlock chamber.

Once inside the room, Caldera and Rennick grabbed Vanguard-issued vac-suits from large metal lockers with practiced efficiency. The suits were standard black with gray trim running down each arm, the sides of the body, and the legs. They were designed to be loose enough to slip over clothes and, with the push of a button, retract to fit the form of the body so as not to lose range of motion.

As she pulled on her suit, Caldera watched the dust-filled wind twist and turn outside through a small circular window.

"This seems...unnecessary," Rennick said, mimicking her movements.

Caldera didn't respond. When she discarded her flight jacket onto the bench beside her, she noticed a small metal box on the top shelf of her locker.

I should take those. She reached toward the box, then paused with her hand midair. An approved request from headquarters was necessary to use them. Her fingers glided over the smooth case. *If the specs are true, I could create a small crater with these— dig down deep into the ground to get more useful samples...*

Taking a deep breath, she glanced over her shoulder to make sure Rennick wasn't looking. His back was to her, and he was taking his time putting his vac-suit on, the way he did when he was stalling.

Caldera gritted her teeth and grabbed the box, opening it to reveal two thick black bands folded neatly inside. The flexible material of the outside housed the artificial neurotransmitters and miniature body-activity scanners.

They don't look like much. She ran her hand over the rough fabric and found the holes where the needles would pierce her flesh if she were to activate the device. *If I can make something out of this useless mission, they'll have no choice but to give me commandership. This will work.*

As quietly as she could, she slipped one band onto her right bicep, the other onto her forearm, and her body into the vac-suit.

Biting her lip, she put the empty box back in her locker and slammed the door shut.

"Ready?" she asked, turning around to face Rennick, hoping he hadn't seen that she'd broken another rule. "Hold on a second." Rennick grabbed two blaster pistols from another locker across the room. He strapped one to his belt and held the other out to her.

"Really? The planet is completely desolate."

Rennick readied his helmet. "Regulation clearly states that whenever personnel leave the ship onto an unknown planet, exo, or piece of land, we take blasters as a precaution. It doesn't matter the circumstance."

Caldera raised an eyebrow.

He sighed. "I didn't put up a fight when you broke a rule by coming down here. Will you follow one for me?"

A small smile curled her lip. "Fine." She took the blaster out of his hand and strapped it to her hip.

Caldera spoke into the coms once they made their way to the secondary airlock doors. "Attention. This is Captain Caldera Keane. Commander Rennick Silvera and I are going out to collect samples and investigate the planet's surface. We shouldn't be gone for more than two hours, but I need two of the most senior officers to report to the bridge to monitor our position."

"Copy that," a tinny female voice replied through the speakers. "Senior tech officers Dove Lenik and Iyan Serin reporting. Good luck."

"Ever met either of them?" Rennick muttered, glancing over at Caldera.

"No..." She locked her helmet into place, then lowered the ramp, cycling them both out onto the surface.

Wind whipped viciously at her body as she descended. Soft pieces of ash-like debris blew past her helmet, disintegrating when they landed on her protective visor. The land was barren except for minor protrusions in the distance that Caldera could only assume were mountains or giant boulders. Light from her helmet shone in thin beams toward the ground, illuminating her footfalls. A dry gravel crunching sensation echoed up her body as she took another step forward, completely leaving the familiarity of the shuttle behind.

"How far in do you want to go?" Rennick asked, his voice coming through the speaker inside her helmet.

"At least two miles," Caldera replied. She drew her weapon and adjusted the heads-up display across her helmet's visor to track their progress.

"Damn it, I knew you were going to say something ridiculous like that." As he spoke, the speakers crackled, then cut out.

Caldera took a deep breath. "I'm turning my com to manual. I suggest you do the same. That way we won't have to listen to each other's breathing." She glanced at Rennick. As he nodded, the twin beams of light from either side of his helmet bounced.

Her breath fogged the inside of her helmet as she walked, slightly obscuring her vision before the circulation system cleared it away.

Time passed slowly. Each minute lasted a lifetime as they approached a large, unidentifiable mound, which was the only break in the monotonous landscape that they had seen in over a mile. The wind never slowed or stopped; it constantly pushed against them, making it hard to walk.

"What the hell?" Rennick said, running ahead. The speakers crackled to life inside Caldera's helmet for the first time in twenty minutes. "This isn't a rock formation."

She pushed the button on the side of the helmet. "Okay... What is it then?"

"It's..." Rennick turned to face her. "It's the wreckage of a ship!"

"What?" Caldera gasped. She ran to join Rennick beside the wreckage, her mind racing through the recent reports of ship disappearances. Deep, uneven claw marks in the metal caught her eye, accelerating her heartbeat.

The land shook under their feet, knocking Caldera and Rennick to the ground.

"What the f—" Rennick was cut off by an ear-splitting screech, and the ground continued to shake violently.

Speakers crackled inside Caldera's helmet and Rennick grabbed her arm. "Callie, are you okay?" His voice was frantic as he scrambled back to his feet, dragging her with him.

"What the fuck is going on?" It wasn't until the second deafening screech that she realized her com was still on manual. She switched it to automatic and tried again. "I'm fine. What the hell is happening?" Tremors ran through the ground and up her body, making her voice waver uncontrollably.

"I—I don't know." Rennick's voice trembled, too.

The hold he had on Caldera's arm was beginning to hurt, but she was glad that he wasn't letting go. They both took wide stances in an effort to stay on their feet amid the vibrations.

"Let's go back!" Rennick yelled through the helmet as he pulled on Caldera's arm and broke into a run.

They didn't get more than a few feet before falling again.

"Son of a bitch!" Caldera yelled. "Damn it, Ren, let go of me!" She pushed herself to her knees.

The screeching stopped, and silence fell over the dusty landscape.

"Ren?" The grip on her arm loosened but was still there. Rennick was sitting, helmet facing straight ahead, arm outstretched—pointing.

Caldera turned her head slowly in the direction that Rennick pointed. When she caught sight of it, the air froze inside her lungs.

The thing was at least one hundred feet tall and hunched over on multiple limbs. Its maw was jagged, black, and empty, its skin ashen—stone-like. Despite being the tallest living thing Caldera had ever seen, it was almost impossible to tell exactly how far away it was.

The creature took a step forward, smashing boulders bigger than ships under its rocky feet. Its yellow, empty eyes fell over them and it roared, pawing the ground in agitation, preparing to charge.

The sound echoed in her ears, bouncing around the inside of her head. She raised her blaster and pointed it in the general direction of the monster. It shook in her hands. Despite their training, Vanguard members weren't soldiers, and she was no exception.

"Wait." Rennick put a hand on her arm. "Do you really think these blasters will put a dent in that thing? We have to get out of here."

"Right," Caldera whispered back. "I think we can still see the shuttle." She risked a glance over her shoulder, pleading with the universe to let her be right. An involuntary sigh of relief escaped her lips. "We need the ship's rail guns. That'll buy us enough time to get back and maybe even kill that thing."

She swallowed hard, requesting an open connection to the ship.

"I'm here, Captain!" the tinny voice of Dove said, answering immediately. "What the hell is going on?" she continued, all formality gone from her voice.

"Listen," Caldera replied, "I need you to lift off—briefly."

"I can't—"

"I'm granting you permission. The rail guns won't fire with the ship landed."

The woman hesitated. "I don't know how—neither of us do."

"I asked for the two most senior officers," Caldera said, her heart ricocheting against her ribs. "And neither one of you knows how to fly a fucking ship?"

"I'm sorry... I—"

Desperate frustration took over her body. Caldera cut the connection, then screamed as loud as she could until her vocal cords hurt, her voice echoing off her helmet and back into her ears. Rennick's body was rigid beside her.

"We're dead," she whispered.

"We just have to make it back to the ship," he countered, glancing back again and ignoring her meltdown. "The ship is small. It won't be comfortable for us or the crew, but I can get that thing off the ground in less than a minute by implementing an emergency launch."

"Okay... On the count of three, we'll run," Caldera said with a gulp, trying unsuccessfully to compose herself. "Don't look back. Don't wait for me. Just run as fast as you can to the shuttle."

"No."

"What?" Caldera looked into the tinted visor of his helmet, wishing she could see his face. "That's an order."

"I'm not leaving you. We're going together." He stretched out his hand. "That's nonnegotiable."

"But—what if..." Caldera searched for a diplomatic way to say what she was thinking, but gave up. "What if you die because of me?" Her voice caught in her throat.

"Then we'll die together," he replied without hesitation, reaching toward her.

The monster stalked toward them. Desperate. Hungry.

"All right..." Taking a deep breath, Caldera grabbed his hand. "Count down together," she said. "Ready?"

Rennick nodded.

Her heart felt like it was going to pound out of her chest. "One." She poised herself and gripped Rennick's hand as tightly as she could.

"Two," he continued, taking a deep breath.

"Three!" they yelled together, pushing off the ground and sprinting toward the shuttle, their hands clasped.

Caldera's chest heaved and her legs ached with sudden exertion. She ran as fast as she could but still felt herself slowing him down.

"We're almost there," Rennick's voice huffed over the speaker.

The roar came again as the ground quaked beneath their feet. She didn't have to look behind her to know that the thing was gaining on them. They lost their balance and hit the ground hard, separating. Caldera's helmet flew off on impact.

Without her helmet, the noise of the planet was deafening. Her lungs filled with dirty air and her hair whipped wildly around her face as she got to her feet and desperately searched for Rennick.

She locked eyes with the monster in front of her, whose gaze was trained on the interloper of its planet. It was so close that Caldera could make out the shifting and cracking of its stonelike skin as it moved. Dust tumbled down from between the creaking crevasses of the previously dormant monster.

"Callie, run!"

The voice that filtered through the open air let her know that Rennick had either lost or discarded his helmet, too. She whirled to the side, catching sight of him between puffs of kicked-up dirt and debris. He was a few feet away with his blaster drawn.

"Ren, no!" Caldera screamed.

"Get to the ship!" he yelled, and shots rang out. He was trying to draw the monster toward him. And it was working.

The mass of body and rock turned away from the ship—from her, shaking the ground. His blaster shots were ineffective. Rennick was going to die.

"No!" She drew her own blaster and leveled it at the creature, firing. It ignored her, its full attention on Rennick.

Caldera glanced down at her arm and the device she knew was wrapped around it under her vac-suit. Her breath came in short, ragged gasps.

If this thing can create a crater, it can kill a monster.

She reached down into her boot and pulled out a small knife from a hidden compartment. Then she frantically cut the right sleeve off her vac-suit, revealing the two black bands. Crimson blood trickled down her arm from where she nicked herself with the knife in the process.

The monster was no more than twenty feet away from Rennick. Its eyes blazed, mouth gaping. It crouched down on its limbs, ready to pounce, gearing up for its attack.

Another ear-splitting roar echoed through the air, the ground, her very being. The monster charged as Rennick continued to fire relentlessly.

"Ren! I'm not leaving you!" *This has to save him. It has to! If the specs are correct, all I'll have to say to make it work is...* "Activate."

The needles dug into her flesh at the command, making her flinch in pain. The band's thick black outline contrasted harshly against her pale skin. She raised her arms and faced her palms outward, thumbs touching, like the specs described.

Faint holographic symbols appeared, floating around the bands in a circle. The symbols glowed blue, turning to faint gold as the bands sucked energy from her body. She could let them charge as long as she wanted, but there was only one shot, and she had to take it.

"Fire!" she screamed, just as the rock monster lunged at Rennick. The symbols blazed darker gold at her order. Her entire body grew warm, then hot. The monster's head exploded, splattering them both with a black substance. Her vision went dark around the edges and blurred more with each passing second.

She was vaguely aware of Rennick's voice, and then... nothing.

CHAPTER 3

Blurry light came into view overhead as Caldera blinked awake. A constant beep echoed in her ears. The crash couch she was lying on shifted on its gimbals as she sat up slowly, trying to regain her bearings.

Non-reflective gray metal walls and various body scanning monitors surrounded her, beaming with blue light. Bright white letters and numbers scrolled across the screens next to her.

I'm in the sick bay.

Instead of a clean, cream-colored wrap-gown the patients were usually required to wear, she was still in her dirty, ripped jumpsuit. As Caldera removed the covers and swung her legs over the side of the crash couch, she glanced around for the attending physician before remembering they didn't have one. Due to understaffing, the entire scope of medical issues was now left to the Emergency Care System.

"Hello, Captain Caldera," a robotic voice chimed through a speaker on the wall, causing her to jump.

"ECS—" Caldera began as a coughing fit overcame her.

"I am glad to see that you're awake. I will alert First Officer Rennick to the change in your condition. Even though—"

"No," she said, finding her voice raspy and unused. "I'll tell him myself. I need some questions answered, first."

"Of course, Captain. What can I assist you with?"

"How long have I been unconscious?"

"Five days, thirteen hours, twenty minutes, and four seconds," ECS replied without hesitation.

Caldera blanched. "Five days..." She shook her head and re-concentrated. "What the hell was wrong with me?"

"Your metabolic rate was off the charts, and your Adenosine Triphosphate—ATP count—was at absolute zero. I suppose you could say that you had no usable energy left in your body."

She glanced down at her right arm. Dark black and purple rings circled her bicep and forearm like grotesque bracelets from the bands of the rail beam. Little dots from the needles adorned the bruises in four distinct spots.

"When First Officer Rennick brought you in and hooked you up to me, I immediately had to put you on life support," ECS continued, delivering the information as bluntly as ever.

Caldera let herself fall sideways, head landing on the pillow with a *flump. Ren won't be happy about that.* "I'm going to need something clean to wear."

"Here."

She looked up to see Rennick standing in the doorway. He was holding black sweatpants and a gray t-shirt with the planetary emblem embroidered on it. His voice and expression were flat. He dropped the clothes onto a chair and walked out of the room before she could say anything.

"How did he know I was awake?" Caldera grumbled while checking her vitals. All were within normal range. "I was going to ambush him on the flight deck."

"He modified one of the console screens to monitor your condition while he flew the ship," ECS said.

You could've led with that.

"But I believe 'ambushing him' would not have been a good idea... I did *try* to warn you about the modified monitors."

Caldera shot a glare at the speaker. "Okay, thanks for your help, ECS. You can shut down for now," she said, as she stood up and stretched.

"Very well, Captain," it replied, shutting off with a ping.

Caldera walked over to the garments that Rennick had all but thrown onto the chair. A pang of guilt stabbed through her chest.

He's my partner. I should have told him I was wearing the RB.

She inhaled deeply and changed into the loose-fitting clothes, letting all the potential outcomes of the upcoming conversation run through her head. None of them ended happily.

The door *whooshed* open, and she stepped into the hall, heading to the lift that would take her to the bridge. Her bare feet padded against the thin cushion of the floor, her soft steps almost silent. No one passed her on her way up to the command center.

Did Ren tell everyone to keep this level clear? No, he wouldn't do that. The techs are probably avoiding me on purpose because of my freakout—I'm sure Dove was broadcasting the whole thing for the record... Damn it, I should really try to rein in my temper...

Rennick sat in the pilot's seat, fiddling with screens and scanners as Caldera tentatively walked onto the flight deck. His back tensed, letting her know he was willfully ignoring her.

"Ren, listen..." She paused as her stomach twisted.

Rennick's shoulders slumped, and without turning around, he motioned for her to sit down, patting the co-pilot's chair.

Caldera obliged, the surge of anxiety waning as their eyes met.

"Why?" he asked, breaking the silence, his voice barely an audible whisper.

"Why what?"

"Why didn't you tell me your plans to wear the RB?"

"I—"

"Because if you had, I could've brought the necessary revitalization instruments, instead of running through the ship like a madman, trying to get you hooked up to ECS before it was too late."

"It was a spur of the moment thing. I knew you'd try to talk me out of it."

He rubbed his eyes and let his arms fall limp against the armrests before meeting her gaze. "Callie, when you do things like that...it makes me feel like you don't trust me."

"Of course, I trust you. Ren, I trust you more than anyone else on Bersama." *More than anyone in this forsaken galaxy. I...* Caldera laced her fingers together in her lap—the way she always did when she had to stop herself from reaching for his hands. *Captains and first officers are not allowed to be in romantic relationships with each other—I'd either lose my position, or one of us would have to transfer out.* She repeated the rule and consequence of Vanguard command for the trillionth time in her head. "Surely after nine years together, you know that."

Rennick sighed. "I know. Your recklessness is just irritating sometimes."

"Noted," she muttered, glancing out the window.

"Callie, you could have died. You almost did. I need you to understand... You're not just my captain, you're my best friend. I don't want to lose you."

She leaned back in her chair and faced the ceiling, hoping to hide her face as warmth rushed to her cheeks. "I do understand that, and I'm sorry for upsetting you. I really am."

"It's all right. Just keep me in the loop from now on."

Caldera nodded, gazing into his eyes. He gave her a half-smile, which she gladly returned.

"So, do you know how it works?" Rennick asked. "The rail beam, I mean."

"Well, other than the vague spark notes the king's representative gave us when we got the thing, not really."

They were both quiet for a while, watching as the empty vacuum of space flew by outside the window.

Rennick snapped his fingers. "I bet Sear will know about it. Let's ask him when we get back to headquarters."

"Good idea. I wish he was here now." She sighed, pushing away her annoyance. Sear had been reassigned to headquarters several weeks before. Though he was still their flight consultant, it wasn't the same as having him there with them.

Rennick gave her a side-long glance. "Wait... Is that why you're scaring away all the new potential bridge crew members that get assigned to us?"

"No one could ever replace Sear...or Markarian. And I'm not scaring them away."

"Fine, 'politely hinting that they're not welcome'."

"Essentially."

"The Vanguard is spread thin—most are working with less than a skeleton crew, like us. The king had to split up the most competent crews to fill in the gaps." He crossed his arms. "Honestly, you should be happy for Markarian. He got promoted to captain, and Sear got reassigned to his specialty."

Caldera sighed and stood, exhaustion creeping in. "I am happy for them. It's just... We were all together for years, and now we're not. It sucks, okay? They're our friends and we hardly ever get to see them."

"I know." He paused and a reassuring grin spread across his face. "So... You think you'll get summoned to the palace for this fuck up?"

Caldera laughed, shaking her head. "The situation isn't that bad—besides, hardly anyone gets to grace the king himself with their presence, unless you're a member of the Council or a sector leader." She motioned to herself. "And last time I checked, I was neither—just a nobody Vanguard captain." *But If I could just get off this ship, I could talk to him...maybe to all of them.*

Silence crept in from all corners, the reality of the situation sinking into her skin.

I'm definitely not getting a commandership after this... "Well, on that note, I'm gonna get some rest," Caldera said, stifling a yawn as she walked toward the lift.

"You didn't get enough already?"

"Being unconscious for five days and actually sleeping are two different things."

Rennick chuckled. "Callie, wait," he said, hastily taking a step toward her.

She stopped, waiting for him to approach her, but he didn't move. "Yeah?"

"I'm...glad you're okay."

"I—I'm glad you're okay, too." The conversation held an air of awkwardness that she wasn't expecting. "Umm, call me back when you want to switch," she said, then continued through the door and directed the lift to take her to the level her quarters were on.

CHAPTER 4

"W hat can you tell us about the rail beam?" Caldera asked, glancing over at Rennick as she tapped her fingers on the desk in front of her. She tried to ignore the lingering discomfort in her arm. Over the rest of their five-day trip home, the needle points had completely healed and the bruises around her arm had faded to a sickly yellow, but the pain was still there.

Sear, their friend and flight consultant, sat across from them. He quietly rifled through the printout of the flight record of their last trip, scanning it carefully into the computer system. Sunlight peeked through the half-closed blinds of his small closet-like office, making his orange fur glisten from under his white button-up shirt.

Caldera would have thought that he wasn't listening, but his catlike ears twitched attentively with each statement.

"I believe I can tell you a lot," Sear said. The black slits of his orange eyes expanded as he looked up at them, his face—hairless around his forehead, eyes, and nose—lit up with excitement.

"Enlighten us then," Rennick said, tipping his chair back on its hind legs.

Sear poked a claw at one of the papers. "Well, your ATP count was at absolute zero—"

"We already know that," Caldera interjected. "ECS filled us in on the what, but not the why."

Sear tapped his chin and continued to rifle through the papers. "The rail beam is experimental, but from what I have learned so far, it converts all of your body's energy into a destructive force that can be used outside the body at a specific point."

"So, the light that came out of my palms..." Caldera trailed off and looked down at her hands.

"That was presumably all your body's energy concentrated into a light beam," Sear said, scratching his thick beard with an exasperated sigh.

Caldera blew out a breath and leaned back hard against the stiff metal chair as the walls of her friend's small office seemed to close in on her. "Does that have something to do with the runes that appeared?"

"I would say so, but this is brand-new technology that I have only just begun to study. And the letters and numbers you saw were not 'runes.' That would be archaic."

"Then what were they?" Rennick questioned.

"Scientific symbols. Energy is symbolized with an E. The standard unit for measuring energy is the joule, symbolized by J. The force at which you exert said energy is the newton, and that is symbolized by the letter N. Putting it all together with the numerals you saw, the bands were simply measuring how much energy output you released."

The office fell quiet for a moment.

Caldera turned to Rennick. "Did you get any of that?"

"Barely."

"All I am saying is that, according to these readouts, you got lucky—*genuinely* lucky. From what I can tell, it seems like your device might have malfunctioned," Sear said, picking up the papers and tapping them on the table to straighten them out. "Did you not run a thorough scan of your equipment before you left the ship?"

"We—I did not, no," Caldera muttered, averting her gaze.

Sear's ears drooped. "I would also like to remind you that I would be at a loss if you got yourself seriously injured—or killed."

A grin took over Caldera's face as she glanced sidelong at him. "Does that mean you'll actually join us for a beer this time? You know, to celebrate my miraculous recovery."

The door opened, interrupting Sear as he opened his mouth to reply. A newcomer barreled into the tiny office, ducking his head as he entered the doorway. Suddenly the space felt even more cramped.

"Have time for another report?"

"Markarian!" Rennick exclaimed, standing up to greet him.

Caldera always forgot how large Markarian was until she watched the top of his head almost brush the ceiling.

"Hey, my three favorite people are all here," Markarian said with an amiable smile. As he grabbed Rennick's hand and clapped him on the back, his black curls fell into his face.

"That is usually what happens when you barge into an office during a meeting you know your friends are at," Sear said, his long tail swishing back and forth behind him.

Markarian waved his hand dismissively. "Barge? I would never," he replied with a wink.

Caldera laughed. "We were just finishing up and getting ready to go out for drinks. Wanna join us?" she asked, leaning to the side so Markarian could place his report into Sear's out-stretched hand.

"I have not yet agreed to go," Sear reminded her as he began to scan the new documents into the computer system.

"You're coming," Caldera said.

Sear narrowed his eyes. "Fine."

"And so are you, Marky," Rennick added, reclaiming his seat.

Markarian leaned against the doorframe. "Don't call me that."

"Here we go," Caldera mumbled.

"Sure, whatever you say, Kari," Rennick said with a laugh.

"Ren, I swear!" Markarian snapped, his voice booming through the tiny office.

Caldera rubbed the deepening crease in her forehead. "Will you two stop? I'm really not in the mood for this."

Markarian moved closer. "What's wrong?"

"Nothing."

"She used the damn RB," Rennick replied.

Markarian's expression went blank. "The what?"

Caldera and Rennick stared back at him, open-mouthed. Sear paused scanning in the documents, the vertical pupils of his eyes enlarging.

Markarian flicked his gaze from each set of eyes. "What?"

"How do you not know what the RB—the rail beam—is?" Caldera asked.

"Because I don't... What's going on, are you joking around?"

Rennick shook his head. "No. The rail beam is a new experimental weapon that we thought was given to all of the captains in the Vanguard."

Sear clicked away on the keyboard, his tail flicking sporadically behind him. "According to the records of the ships I currently oversee, no other captain has any record of this weapon."

"You didn't notice that before?"

"It is not something I typically scan for."

Markarian's eyes widened. "Who the hell gave you this thing in the first place?"

"Some blond guy," Caldera muttered. "He said he was a palace rep."

Sear tapped an extended claw on the table. "Well, this is... concerning," he muttered, his expression etched with apprehension. "I, too, believed all of the captains had received an RB."

"They probably just haven't finished assigning them," Rennick replied, ever the reasonable one.

Markarian stroked his chin thoughtfully.

Caldera's head spun as silence filled the office. *It doesn't matter. Nothing happened, so there's no use worrying.* She didn't want to talk anymore about their botched mission, or the RB. *Anyway.* How do you like your new position?" she continued, turning to Markarian.

"Oh, it's great. I'm in charge of a bunch of underqualified newbies running around like their heads have been cut off. Who wouldn't love that?"

"I'm sure you'll whip them into shape," Rennick quipped, leaning on his elbow.

"If they don't catch on soon, I'll probably end up with another huge scar, or worse," Markarian said, subconsciously rubbing his right shoulder down to his elbow. "These missions from the king are becoming more and more dangerous."

"You can say that again," Caldera said. The weight of his words knotted her stomach. She had known Markarian almost as long as she'd known Rennick, but all she could gather about his previous assignment—the one that had resulted in his scar—was that he refused to talk about it.

The silence of the room once again became heavy, and the only sound was the document scanner.

Rennick cleared his throat. "Are we getting those drinks, or not?"

"Can't—I have a date," Markarian said, his attitude instantly changing.

Caldera smiled, eager to move the conversation along. "Really? With who?"

"Burke. He works over in weaponry," Markarian replied, the amiable smile returning.

"Oh yeah? I know him. Seems nice," Caldera mused. She wanted nothing more than to get out of the office and down as many drinks as her stomach could hold.

"Wait, weren't you dating someone named Bryla?" Rennick asked.

Markarian waved a nonchalant hand in the air. "That was forever ago. She didn't work out. Have we really not met up in that long?"

"Sorry for not being more ingrained in your personal life." Rennick rolled his eyes.

"You are forgiven," Markarian shot back mockingly.

"There, finished," Sear said. He stood up from his desk, his body seeming to bear down on them despite his slender frame. His head completely touched the ceiling, flattening the tips of his ears. As he moved toward the doorway, his loose-fitting shorts and furry legs swished against Caldera. The bend in his catlike legs and his thick fur prevented him from wearing long pants. As he exited the room, the claws of his feet clicked on the tile floor.

"What bar do you guys want to hit this time?" Caldera asked eagerly, shuffling out of the office after everyone else.

Her friends didn't answer. No one moved.

"What?" she started, pushing her way to the front. "What's wrong..." She trailed off when she spotted two men walking toward them.

They were both a little over six feet tall, with shiny blasters strapped to their sides. They wore matching black suits, shoes, and sunglasses. A gold crown enclosed in a circle embroidered their jackets over the right breast pocket.

"Who are these guys?" Markarian asked, his voice low.

"Not sure," Rennick whispered as the men approached, stopping directly in front of them.

"Caldera Keane? Captain Caldera Keane?" the one on the left asked.

"Yes, what's this about?" she replied, hoping her voice didn't waver.

"We're here to escort you to the palace."

Oh no. Her stomach dropped. "Why?"

"You've been summoned—" He paused as if he wasn't sure if he should tell her more. "By the Council."

All of them? Caldera looked over at Rennick. She couldn't believe what she was hearing. The fluorescent lights of the hallway inexplicably stung her eyes.

I used the RB in a way it wasn't intended. But I couldn't just let the monster kill us—kill Ren...

"All right," Rennick said, stepping partially in front of her. "What's this about?"

"We were just told to retrieve her," the man continued as he removed his black glasses and glared over at Rennick. He had one brown iris and one blue. "Now move aside."

"She's not going anywhere until you tell us what's going on," Markarian insisted. He placed a hand on Caldera's shoulder, gently pulling her behind him.

As Caldera stumbled backward, the man on the right put a hand on his blaster.

Sear cleared his throat and stepped to the right of Markarian so that he was completely visible. "All we want to know is that she will not be harmed." His tail flicked from side to side in short, jerking motions.

The man blinked. "Of course not," he said flatly.

"At least tell us who you are." Rennick balled his hands into fists.

The one who had been doing all the talking sighed and rubbed the back of his sandy brown head. "We're palace security. My name is Sol Naram, and that's my brother Saro," he said, motioning with his glasses toward the silent man.

Standing behind her friends in the middle of the protective semi-circle that they had instinctively made, Caldera eyed the two mysterious men and tried to force her head to stop spinning. *I have to do something now. Before we all get arrested—or worse.*

She took a deep breath, then grabbed Rennick's elbow, causing him to turn toward her. Standing on her tiptoes, she wrapped her arms around his neck, hugging him. "I'll be okay," she whispered into his ear. Their eyes met with unspoken emotion. "All right," she said, pushing her way to the front again to face the two men. "I'll go with you."

The man named Saro spoke for the first time, taking his hand off his blaster. "Good. Follow us."

Caldera didn't look back, trying to tune out the protests of

Markarian and Rennick as she followed the men down the hall and outside the Vanguard Headquarters, where a sleek, black transport was waiting for them.

Her hair caressed her face as she stepped through the doors, the brisk wind seeming to push her away as the two men turned their backs. A homeless person shuffled away from the entrance, backing themselves into one of the many alcoves around the outer walls of the Vanguard Headquarters. They averted their gaze when they accidentally locked eyes with Caldera, as if ashamed of their situation. Dirty, ill-fitting clothes covered their emaciated body as they shivered. Unwashed black hair covered their eyes when they lowered their head.

Caldera's heart broke to witness the despair—the desperate state of Bersama's poorer citizens. It never got easier, even though it was one of the most common things to see around the city.

Ruffling around in her pockets, Caldera pulled out a few larger Tellin bills—her recently withdrawn bar money—and handed them to the skeletal person before her.

"Take care," she whispered, gently cupping the homeless person's hands in hers.

"May the universe bless you, ma'am," the person whispered, their voice smooth and strangely melodic. Glancing suspiciously over Caldera's shoulder, they quietly shuffled away.

Wouldn't that be nice?

"Come on," Sol called, holding open the door to the transport and motioning for Caldera to get in.

Caldera climbed inside and sat in the seat closest to her. Looking over her shoulder, she found it was impossible to see who was driving through the tinted privacy window. She hoped she was in a genuine palace transport, and not about to be kidnapped by the shady men.

The transport itself was beautiful. Two rows of genuine leather seats faced each other, and each one had its own armrest and temperature control. In the middle where the passengers' knees would almost touch, a small, wood-plated table sat on a skinny metal neck that was bolted to the floor.

The only person in Tellis who could afford something like this is definitely the king.

Sol got in, taking a seat across from her and next to Saro, slamming the door behind him. The vehicle jolted forward.

"Okay," Caldera said, crossing her legs, her confidence building. "It's just us now. Why don't you tell me what the hell is going on?"

The men glanced in her direction but didn't respond.

"Have I done something wrong?" she continued, trying to remember every action she had ever taken and every command given over the years.

"We were only told to retrieve you," Sol replied.

"Fine," she said, leaning back against the comfortable seat. The cushions formed around her back, making her want to close her eyes. "Then how did you know where to find me?"

Sol sighed. "You're a captain of the Vanguard. Your keycard and handprint are monitored."

Caldera gritted her teeth. She thought about how she had to scan herself to get into headquarters—how they all had to, not just the captains. "Isn't that illegal?" she demanded, narrowing her eyes.

"Not for the Council," Saro said coldly. He removed his glasses to reveal the same two eye colors as Sol. Besides a small scar on his chin, everything about them was identical.

Caldera bit her lip. "Why the Council? Shouldn't the king have summoned me first?" *If the Council summoned me, maybe this won't be so bad. I can reason with them. The king's the one making everything worse.*

Saro's eyes blazed. "We aren't authorized to talk to you. We've already said enough." He glared from her to Sol.

"He's right," Sol replied. "Please try to relax. I'm sure the Council will answer every question that you have."

Relenting, Caldera sighed heavily. Outside, the buildings streaked by as the unknown driver took them to the palace.

CHAPTER 5

After what felt like hours of riding in silence, they reached the palace—an enormous, modern, pristine brick structure, with two identical cylindrical towers reaching up toward the sky on either end. Instead of mortar, burnished metal held the bricks together, making the palace seem to sparkle in the growing night. Hundreds of windows lined the walls, with curtains covering most of them. The building sat dutifully just outside of the capital, between the borders of Sectors Four and Five.

The transport slowed and pulled through the open gates of a brick and metal archway into a giant courtyard. Lush green bushes cut into perfect squares lined the paved drive and beautiful flowers of every color sprinkled the meticulously manicured garden, split up by immaculate brick paths. Caldera's eyes moved from one section to the next, her breath catching in her throat at the sheer amount of greenery.

Following the flow of the brick paths, her gaze met the edges of the garden courtyard and the high wall surrounding the entire structure. Her heart pounded as the gates sealed her in. Aside from what could be seen of the towers and roof from the outside, the palace was closed off from public view. The only way in or out was the entrance they had just come through.

There's no running from this now. Caldera's mind raced through the rumors of people disappearing when they got summoned to the palace. *It's just hearsay.*

The transport pulled around the circular drive and stopped beside a lit-up fountain in the shape of a lion, which sat in the center of the roundabout. The illuminated palace doors lay just beyond, up a short flight of marble stairs.

Sol hopped out and opened the door for her.

"Thank you," Caldera said. She tried to steady her breathing as she stepped into the chilly night, but her heart didn't slow its rhythm. The sweet smell of the flowers met her nose, trying its best to soothe her, but failed miserably.

Sol jerked his head toward the marble staircase. "This way."

He led the way, slowing only to scan his hand, which caused the giant metal and wood plated doors to swing open. Sol and Saro kept a brisk pace as they walked through the doorway four or five paces ahead. Caldera looked around in awe.

The palace was massive. Huge archways and towering columns met them as they hurried her through the great hall. Beautiful crystal chandeliers gleaming with electric light hung down from elevated ceilings. Stone walls were inlaid with the colors of the Sector—gold and honey—with silk drapes covering the windows, blocking out the light of the two moons.

"Hurry up!" Saro called over his shoulder as they rushed down a long hallway to the left.

Caldera's boots clicked across the shiny marble floor, echoing off the walls. Her eyes moved across the palace interior; despite the obvious cleanliness and upkeep of the palace, the entire place seemed to be deserted. The walls were barren, and there were no signs of personal belongings to be found.

Does the king really live here?

"Here we are," Sol said, coming to a stop in front of a set of old-fashioned wooden doors adorned with beautiful carvings. "The conference hall. The Council is waiting for you inside."

Caldera tentatively stepped forward, grabbed the ornate handle, and stopped. "Seriously, what's going on here?" she asked, turning to look directly at them, unable to accept that they truly knew nothing.

Sol stared at her not with contempt, but with sudden, deep despair that unnerved her to the core. "Step through those doors and find out," he whispered, gesturing toward the doorway.

Before she could respond, both men strode down the hall, leaving Caldera alone outside the conference room.

She opened the doors and forced herself to step inside.

The large table with multiple chairs that she'd expected were nowhere to be seen. Instead, before her was an open area half-encircled by an enclosed, connected, high-rise wooden dais that took up most of the space. Looking down at her from their seats were the five members of the Council, one representing each sector.

They wore robes with their sectors' corresponding colors: gold for Tellis, silver for Natioh, obsidian for Sedrolla, ruby for Aelmead, and jade for Muléus. A black planetary crown emblem was embroidered over the right breast of each robe—an inversion of the regular color-coded symbol that 'common' people wore.

Caldera sucked in a breath and tried once more to force her racing heartbeat under control, her body tense as she stared up at the Council.

"You must be Captain Caldera Keane," the man in the middle of the half-circle said, his voice booming.

"Yes, I am."

"My name is Vandren," he continued with a nod. His gold robe swayed slightly. "I represent Sector One, Tellis."

"Yes, I—I know," Caldera stammered, clasping her hands behind her back to keep them from shaking.

"Oh? Are you familiar with the rest of us as well?" he asked, motioning toward the other council members.

"Well..." Caldera said, fidgeting with her fingers. "Not exactly—I only recognize you—umm, sir, because you represent this sector."

The representative from Muléus silently lowered her jade-green hood, revealing her matan features; catlike ears, sharp canines, and jet-black fur. "It is our custom to introduce ourselves upon a first meeting, regardless of the recipient's knowledge," she said in a musical voice as her emerald eyes focused intently on Caldera. She placed a dark hand over her chest. "I am Cleo, representative of Sector Five." Without hesitation, she went on to introduce each member.

Randis, Sector Two. Kex, Sector Three. Thael, Sector Four. Not knowing what else to do, Caldera bowed slightly as the names swirled in her head. "It's an honor to meet you all."

"Captain Keane, there's no doubt that you're wondering why you've been called upon," Vandren said, sitting straighter.

"I am. This was very...surprising."

"Surprising for us all."

Caldera cleared her throat, ears ringing. "Why am I here?"

"Well, I don't mean to be blunt with you, but I'm afraid there's simply no choice," he continued wearily. Solid white around his temples broke up his salt and pepper hair and made him look older than he probably was.

How can I get out of this? Caldera's stomach cinched into a knot as sweat poured down her back.

I don't have any family. Who can I call?

Ren, obviously.

Would he have enough money to bail me out?

Can I even be bailed out?

The Council's powerful enough to make me disappear.

Vandren looked at each council member as if he needed silent encouragement for the words he was about to speak. "I regret to inform you that King Quill has passed away, and according to his last will and testament, you are his heir." He paused. "It seems that you are the next in line for the throne." His gray eyes were unflinching as they stared down at her.

"What?" Caldera said, her entire body going numb. "But—I—the crown can only be passed down through generational bloodlines!"

"Yes," Vandren said, more sternly. "It appears that you are royalty, Captain."

Caldera stood still, waiting for someone to shake her awake. "I don't—I don't understand." The words fumbled out of her mouth as she desperately tried to make sense of what she was hearing.

"We'll need to test your DNA to make sure this claim is valid, and to confirm that you are indeed the right person," Vandren continued as if the news wasn't life-changing. He lifted his hand, about to snap his fingers.

I don't want this!

"No!" Caldera said, finally finding her voice. Her words echoed off the white walls and high ceilings.

"Excuse me?" Vandren laid his hand back down, his fingernails almost imperceptibly scratching across the tabletop.

"Is there an alternate option?" Caldera asked, forcing herself to remain calm as every thought raced to get out of her mouth all at once. "Is there a way to...not accept?"

"I'm sorry," Vandren replied calmly, closing his eyes. "But there is not. If the tests come back positive, you will be the new Queen of Tellis." He sighed and opened his eyes as the other council members shifted in their seats, clearly wanting to move on with the proceedings. "The kings, queens, and rulers may be in charge of their specific sectors, but we are the ones in charge of *them*," he continued, staring down emotionlessly at Caldera.

Thael, the representative from Sector Four, adjusted his scarlet robe and scoffed. The akar's five-inch horns pointed straight up to the ceiling from behind his ears. A black tattooed line began at the base of his chin and ran down the length of his neck. His rubicund skin and amber eyes were vibrant as he met her gaze. "To refuse is to commit treason," he said as he tucked a strand of long black hair behind his ear, his tattoo undulating when he spoke. "You of all people should know this. As a captain of the Vanguard, you should be well aware of the rules that govern our world."

"Thael," Vandren said, taking a deep breath. "That's no way to represent Aelmead."

Rage built inside Caldera's chest as she opened her mouth to reply.

"You'd be put to death," Kex, Sector Three's representative, interjected, her forked tongue poking out from between sharp teeth. The hood of her brown robe slid back to reveal the mossy green scales around her face, and slicked, short brown hair. Her sage green skin looked like it was absorbing all the light around her as she stared down at Caldera, her elliptical yellow eyes piercing.

"Kex!" Vandren snapped, turning to face her.

"But at least you won't have to be queen," she hissed. Her lips curled into a smile that only saurians were capable of.

Caldera's face flushed red. She wanted to jump up on the counter and punch the saurian until she started bleeding—to attack the entire Council for putting her in this impossible situation and carelessly uprooting her life.

She planted her feet firmly on the ground. "I don't want to commit treason," she replied through her teeth, balling her hands into fists.

"Wonderful," Vandren said flatly, snapping his fingers before anyone else could interrupt.

A side door that Caldera hadn't noticed before opened, and a man and a woman stepped into the room.

"This is Justle," Vandren said. "King Quill's public representative and personal lawyer."

The small blond man bowed. His bright blue eyes held a hint of recognition as he focused on Caldera.

You! "I know you!" Caldera said, meeting his gaze. "You were the one that gave me the RB—"

"And this is Aloriea, Quill's political advisor. If the tests come back positive, she'll be your advisor, too."

The tall, rail-thin woman stood still, her dark eyes narrowed as if she were scrutinizing Caldera's every move. Wavy black hair stopped just below her light brown jawline, and brown horns curled back and under her ears. The thin-strapped, light-green dress she wore reflected the light as it fluttered around her feet.

"Follow us," Justle told her softly, motioning toward the open door. "The tests are simple, but there are quite a few of them."

"We will await the results," Vandren said as Caldera followed Justle into the extra room, Aloriea bringing up the rear and closing the door behind them.

"Are they just going to wait in there?" Caldera asked as she looked around at her new surroundings—a small room modified to act as a makeshift lab. Vials, microscope slides, a microscope, and a holopad sat on top of a desk surrounded by overstuffed chairs.

"This won't take long," Justle assured her, gesturing for her to sit. "First, we'll start with the obvious test, the blood sample. Then we'll take saliva, fingernails, hair, and skin samples as well. Nothing too invasive." He smiled, his perfect white teeth gleaming.

"Seems repetitive," Caldera replied, taking a seat.

"Every test has to match with Quill's exactly, or you don't get to become queen. There can be no inconsistencies," Aloriea snapped.

Caldera jumped, startled by Aloriea's harsh voice. "Take it easy. I don't want to be the queen of the sector."

Aloriea glanced at her skeptically. "Join the club."

"Let's get this over with," said Caldera.

Justle typed something into his wrist communicator.

For fifteen minutes, Caldera sat there, getting poked and prodded. Nameless nurses transferred the results onto the holopad that lay on the desk before they shuffled out. A new nurse for every sample taken and every test ran. Justle and Aloriea observed in silence.

When the last nurse stalked out, Caldera stared at the holopad as it calculated the results, the percentage slowly ticking its way up to one hundred. The device chimed, and the results were verbally announced as soon as they were completely computed.

They were all positive.

Justle nodded, unable to mask the dejection on his face. "Well, I guess..." He trailed off, scratching his head and making eye contact with Aloriea, who looked horrified.

This cannot be happening, Caldera thought as she rubbed her eyes and rose from her chair.

"Please, stay here." Justle gripped the holopad tightly. "I'll inform the Council." He hurried through the door, leaving Caldera alone with Aloriea.

"What happens now?" Caldera asked.

Without responding, Aloriea turned on her heel and ran out of the room through another adjacent door.

"Okay," Justle said, walking back in. "If you'll—" he paused. "Where's—"

"She left."

He sighed. "Well, if you'll follow me, the Council will swear you in."

Caldera's head spun. *This is happening too fast. I need to think this through. I need to call Ren.* With stiff legs, she walked back into the conference room to face the Council.

"It seems congratulations are in order," Vandren said when she stood before them.

"Unnecessary." Caldera's voice was hollow.

"Are there any questions before we continue?"

Yeah, hundreds, Caldera thought, looking into the eyes of the most powerful people on the planet. "What will happen to my position?" It was the most pressing question she could think of.

"Your position?" Vandren repeated, looking down at her. "You mean your captaincy?"

"Yes. I served the Vanguard for nine years," Caldera replied shortly. "I care about who takes my command." The reality of the statement washed over her. Despite her recent ill-will toward the king and his 'missions', the Vanguard had given her purpose following the death of her parents. In many ways, it had saved her.

Vandren sighed. "You'll make an official statement tomorrow, but considering the circumstances, you can tell the crew under your command that everyone has been promoted. It will be simpler that way." He paused before adding, "But I'm afraid as the new queen of this sector, you can't go back."

The air left Caldera's lungs as the realization hit her—it was as if someone had punched her in the gut. She was most likely never going to see her colleagues again, her friends—Ren.

"Now can we—" Vandren began.

"I have to make a call."

"There will be time for that later."

Caldera was overcome with a fierce and sudden panic. "Today, I was seemingly abducted in front of my friends and they haven't heard anything from me since..." She let the sentence trail off, gauging the Council's reactions.

"What's your point?" Vandren snapped, glaring down at her.

"Let me call my partner to let him know I'm okay."

Vandren didn't respond.

"It's just a call," she pressed, staring unwaveringly up at him.

"Now see here!" The representative from Natioh stood, the oversized sleeves of his silver robe billowing. His teal skin and external gills, the telltale sign of a natare, shimmered under the fluorescent lights. The white dotted tattoos that ran down the center of his face in two parallel lines shifted as he moved.

Vandren lifted his hand, cutting him off. "That's enough, Randis." He turned back to Caldera. "You have five minutes."

Without hesitation, Caldera ran back into the hallway, already typing Rennick's number into her communicator.

"Callie, what the fuck is going on?" he asked frantically, picking up on the first ring.

"Ren," she whispered, suddenly not sure what to say or how to tell him what had happened. *Where do I even start?*

"Markarian and I are outside the palace. Do you need help?"

Caldera smiled. "No, I'm fine, and let Sear know I'm all right, too," she said, her voice shaking. The silence on the other end was so abrupt that Caldera thought she had lost the connection.

"Hello? Are you still there?"

"Callie... Are you sure you're okay?" Rennick asked carefully. "What's—"

"I'm the new Queen of Tellis," she blurted out, interrupting him. "King Quill is dead. I assume he died suddenly, and in his will, it says that I'm his heir." She paused to catch her breath. "The tests confirmed it."

The only thing she could hear on the other end was his breathing.

"Ren?" She gripped the communicator so hard she thought it might break. "Rennick, come on." She checked her watch. *One minute left.* "Say something!"

"Are you serious?"

Caldera's thoughts whirled. The people in the palace most likely either resented her, hated her, or didn't trust her. *I need someone on my side.* She glanced at her watch again. *Thirty seconds.*

"Caldera, talk to me! Please!"

"Ren, you said you'd follow me into commandership... Are you still with me?" she asked, cupping her hand around the mouthpiece of the communicator.

He sighed heavily, voice ragged. "Yes, of course."

"I swear I'll explain everything to you as soon as I can," Caldera promised, hanging up as she walked back into the conference room, a plan hatching in her mind.

CHAPTER 6

Caldera strode back inside, shoulders back, head held high. Taking a deep breath, she glanced over each council member until her eyes fell on Vandren.

"If you're quite done with all the interruptions," he said, meeting her gaze, "we're going to move on to the coronation ceremony."

Caldera froze. "Right now?"

"There's no reason to wait," Vandren replied, laying his hands flat on the tabletop. "You are Quill's heir, and Tellis needs a sector leader."

Her head swam. "How am I related to the late king?" Caldera asked, unable to stop herself. "I can't be his daughter... I just can't."

"You're not Quill's child," Vandren agreed, swiping through the results on the holopad in his hand. "You're his niece." He paused and lifted his eyes from the screen, his lips pinching into a thin line.

I thought both of my parents were orphans. A pang of heartache stabbed through her at the thought of them—wishing she could see them one last time. "Which one of my parents was Quill's sibling?" she asked, forcing herself to focus.

"Your father was Quill's brother," Vandren answered. He handed the holopad to Randis, who quickly scrolled through the test results before passing it back.

Caldera watched as each council member reviewed the results of her DNA tests, their expressions ranging from simple disbelief to flat-out disgust.

"Now, Caldera Keane, is Your Majesty ready to take the oath?" Vandren boomed when the holopad returned to his hands. His voice took on a new air of authority as it reverberated through Caldera's body.

Your Majesty. The title sounded strange to her ears. She wasn't a queen. "Just one more question," Caldera replied, squaring her shoulders. "How do you know my father was King Quill's brother?"

Vandren narrowed his eyes. "Do you doubt the legitimacy of our tests?"

Caldera shrugged, barely able to contain a smirk at the intentional inconvenience she was causing the council members. "I'm curious."

"It wasn't difficult to obtain your parents' medical records," Vandren explained, his voice clipped. "We track descendants through genealogy. It's very simple. Now shall we move on?" He grimaced, observing Caldera as if she were a test subject.

My father was royalty? She nodded, unable to speak. Her newfound confidence drained rapidly.

"Let's continue." Vandren snapped his fingers again.

Justle reappeared through the side door, presenting Vandren with a new holopad.

"Here's how this will work," Vandren said. "I will read the oath to you in the form of a question. Since you will have no idea how to respond, Justle will prompt you with what you must say. Do you understand?" He scanned his hand and passed the holopad to his right.

"Yes," Caldera muttered, her chest tightening as each of the other council members scanned their hands and passed the holopad back to Vandren.

"At the end, you will approach, sign your name on this document, and scan your handprint," he continued.

"I understand," Caldera said bitterly as her breathing quickened. *The plan,* she reminded herself, trying to focus on anything but her shaking hands. *As soon as I'm officially sworn in, I can—*

"Caldera Keane, are you willing to take the oath?" Vandren asked.

Justle leaned in, whispering into her ear.

"I am willing," Caldera echoed past the knot in her throat.

"Will you solemnly promise to govern the peoples of Sector One, Tellis?"

More whispering from her right. It took every ounce of self-control she could muster not to step away from Justle. "I solemnly promise to do so," she replied.

"Will you, with your newfound power, promise to uphold law and justice? And to provide mercy in judgments when it is apt to do so?"

Her eyes darted from side to side as if she were a trapped animal. "I will."

"Now repeat after me," Vandren instructed as Justle bowed and stepped away. "The things which I have before promised, I will perform and keep."

Caldera repeated his words with shaky breath, wringing her hands together behind her back.

"Now approach and sign the royal decree." Vandren pushed the holopad toward her.

She obeyed, then scanned her hand while holding back the bile in her stomach that had almost found its way into her mouth.

Justle stepped forward, stamping the outline of the planetary emblem over her signature.

"Congratulations, Your Majesty," Vandren announced, letting Justle take the holopad away. "You are officially the new Queen of Tellis."

All the council members stood up and bowed.

"Justle will show you to your new living quarters and—"

"Actually," Caldera interrupted, "I have a request before you adjourn."

Vandren stared at her in disbelief. Kex *whirred* under her breath, her thin tongue flicking in and out of her mouth. Her yellow eyes narrowed into slits. The other three council members blinked down at her, uncomprehending.

"What is it, Your Majesty?" Vandren finally replied, glowering at her.

Caldera met his gaze. *Here we go.* "Well, considering the circumstances, I feel—exposed."

"How do you mean?" Cleo asked softly, her emerald cat eyes bright with curiosity.

"Simply put, I feel somewhat unsafe," Caldera continued, her heart finally settling down into a more normal rhythm.

"Unsafe?" Randis questioned. One of his white dreadlocks fell over his shoulder as he leaned forward. "What would make you think such a thing?"

"Everyone in this palace swore loyalty to Quill, not to me. I'm a stranger, and I can't blame them for not trusting me."

"Get to your point!" Kex hissed.

Caldera smirked, the spark inside her chest finally igniting. "I want a personal bodyguard."

The council members exchanged glances.

"That's very unorthodox," Vandren replied, placing his hands in the sleeves of his robe. "The palace is secure. The windows are sealed. Guards are stationed at every door—"

Caldera cut him off, determined not to lose this debate. Her mind flashed to Justle and Aloriea. "I understand. What I'm saying is, I'm not worried about who might break in. I'm worried about the people who are already here."

She held Vandren's gaze.

"That's a very serious accusation," he said, his voice low and rumbling.

"I'm not accusing anyone of anything. All I want is peace of mind."

Skepticism flickered across the council members' faces.

Randis sighed deeply. "Should we vote on this matter?"

Caldera's eyes widened. *They'd vote on such a simple request?* Her heart rate rocketed as the room spun under her feet. *This isn't going to work.*

Vandren turned toward his compatriot and nodded, a vein pulsing at the side of his neck. "All those in favor of the request from Her Majesty, Queen Caldera, for a personal bodyguard, raise your hand." His voice was steady and commanding.

With almost no hesitation, Cleo and Randis raised their hands confidently.

One more, please! Caldera cried out internally, suppressing the shock that they voted for her at all.

Thael's hand rose slowly, his amber eyes downcast as if he was doing something wrong.

Caldera let out a sigh of relief.

"The vote is three to two in favor of Her Majesty's request," Vandren said tightly. His eyes shifted to glare at Thael. "We'll appoint you a bodyguard tomorrow."

"I already have someone in mind," Caldera said. The relief that flooded through her body propelled her forward.

"Who?" Vandren asked, his eyes blazing.

"My former partner, Rennick Silvera."

"And what would make him different from any other guard we would appoint?" Thael asked, looking at her with a modicum of respect instead of like she was an insect he wanted to crush under his foot.

Why did he even vote in my favor?

"We've been partners in the Vanguard for years. We started together and came up together. Who better to help watch my back than someone who has been doing exactly that from the moment we met?" She paused. "He's someone I can completely trust, which was the basis for this request in the first place."

The room fell silent, as if the air had been sucked out of it. A shadow passed over Vandren's face as he stared down at her, his gaze cold and unflinching.

"Grant her request so we can adjourn this meeting," Kex rasped as she pulled her hood over her head. "I must get to Sedrolla. I'm already running late."

"Very well," Vandren replied. "This meeting is dismissed. Justle, please have Sol and Saro inform mister Silvera about his new position." He stood, followed by the other council members. "But first, take Her Majesty to her new living quarters," he added as he shuffled toward a door hidden behind the dais.

Justle nodded and hurried Caldera out of the conference room.

Caldera bit the inside of her cheek, her mind racing. Justle's gait was much slower than Sol and Saro's, which gave her ample time to memorize the various bland hallways of the palace that were lined with closed doors and alcoves. As she trundled behind him, her boots echoed off the marble floor.

"May I speak freely?" Justle asked after a few minutes of walking in silence. He looked back at her before turning to climb a staircase that could have fit an entire transport between the two stone railings.

"Sure. Why wouldn't you be able to?"

He sighed, shaking his head. "What you did back there was extremely...ill-advised."

"What do you mean?" she asked as she glided her hand along the railing.

Justle's face was grim as he paused their ascent. "You have a lot to learn. No one talks to the Council like that, not even the sector leaders. *Especially* not the sector leaders."

"I didn't do anything."

Justle shook his head at her over his shoulder. "You asserted your will, and that's enough."

"Enough for what?"

"I can't say here," Justle whispered. He glanced toward the

ceiling as they continued the climb, the dark circles under his eyes black-rimmed and heavy.

Caldera followed his gaze but saw nothing.

They passed another large, uncovered window as they reached the top of the stairs. Light from the two moons, Atria and Arlune, beat down on her.

They stopped at a closed door toward the end of the hall and Justle motioned for her to go in.

"Your quarters."

Caldera opened the door and stepped inside the giant room. A gasp escaped her lips as the grandness of it overwhelmed her. The size of the room was nothing compared to its beauty.

The marble floor swirled in gray and white arcs. Sheer, golden curtains draped over the windows. Toward the middle of the room, a lone chair and small table sat a few feet away from an ornate fireplace, with an oversized wardrobe pressed against the same wall. A side door to the right of the bed led outside to a large balcony.

Her head swiveled to take it all in.

"I will tell you this—" Justle grabbed the door before it closed behind her. "You were right about needing a bodyguard."

A chill ran down Caldera's spine as she walked over to the canopy bed. Sitting on its edge, she continued to take in her new surroundings. "What do I do now?" she whispered to the empty room.

She closed her eyes and rubbed her temples. When a knock echoed off the walls, she gasped, jumping to her feet.

"Coming!" she called, closing the distance to the door, and pulling it open to find Aloriea standing there. "Oh," she said as the woman breezed past her. "Please, come in."

Aloriea stood in the middle of the room with her arms crossed, looking around critically.

"Can I help you?"

"No," Aloriea replied shortly, her dress swirling against her legs.

"Then why are you here?" Caldera said, forcing a tight-lipped smile across her face.

"To inform you of the opinions of the royal court—Justle and I, and what's left of the palace staff," Aloriea said.

Caldera frowned. "Oh, really? And what are they?"

"Mixed," Aloriea replied, walking over to the glass doors that led out onto the balcony.

"Go on."

"Well, as I'm sure you've noticed, there aren't many people in the palace now."

"I have noticed that."

"That's because most of them have resigned," Aloriea said, her back still to Caldera. "Why do you think that is?"

"That's an asinine question," Caldera replied. "And one you already know the answer to." She paused. "So why are you really here?"

"I'm your advisor now," Aloriea snapped. She whirled around, her cheeks flushing red. "So, I'm here to advise you."

"In what way?"

"Hopefully, in a way that helps everyone." She paused, squaring her shoulders.

Caldera raised a curious brow.

"Make your motivations known, that's all I'm saying," Aloriea continued as she wrapped her arms around herself, her body going rigid.

"Why didn't you quit with the others?"

"I have my reasons."

Caldera watched silently as Aloriea walked toward the door.

"Your bodyguard should be here within the hour," Aloriea added. She glanced over her shoulder, then disappeared into the hallway.

What is her problem? Caldera sighed, walking to the doors that led out onto the balcony. She pulled them open and stepped outside, letting the chilly air fill her lungs and blow through her hair. "What am I doing here..." she muttered, looking up into the night sky. *How could I not have known about this—being royalty.*

What signs did I miss? Yeah, we weren't poor, but we weren't rich, either.

Leaning against the thick stone railing, she gazed down at the beautiful flower beds of the back courtyard. Tears stung her eyes.

They were never secretive about their lineage. Orphans, both of them. And the cycle continues, I suppose. No siblings. No family.

Has it really been eleven years?

A ball formed in the pit of Caldera's stomach. "I miss you guys," she murmured aloud, looking out over the glittering lights of Astrum.

Her father's kind face swam in her vision. She could almost hear his boisterous laugh as he threw open the door to their house. Could almost see her mother rolling her eyes from the patio as she watered the flowers.

They had said goodbye that day. Had promised they'd be back. She winced. The remnants of the transport collision exploded in vibrant color in her memory.

Caldera gasped, wiped her eyes, and slammed her hands down on the railing, jolting herself back to reality. *I need to figure out how to get out of this.*

CHAPTER 7

There had to be an escape clause somewhere—after all, she was completely unqualified to be queen. And she was about to drag Ren into her mess.

A soft knock at the door made Caldera wipe the dried tear trails off her cheeks and look at her watch. *I've been standing out here for an hour?* She made her way over to the door and flung it open.

Sol and Saro were standing in the doorway, shoulder to shoulder, staring down at her with their unusual eyes.

"Your Majesty," Sol said, bowing. "Your bodyguard is here. He demanded to speak with you—"

"Callie!" Rennick pushed between the two men and stepped into the room. Grasping her arm gently in his hand, he took another small step forward, as if he were going to hug her.

Her face flushed as the warmth from his palm met her skin, sending goosebumps up her arm.

He blinked, releasing her. A soft smile spread across his

face as he straightened his brown bomber jacket. "You okay?" he whispered, tilting his head to the side.

Caldera nodded, relief flooding through her at the sight of him. "Thank you!" she said, then slammed the door between them and the twins. Taking a step back, she took him in, not quite believing that he was really there. His face was etched with concern as his eyes met hers, hair disheveled. He had obviously been running his hand through it like he always did when he was worried.

"Those two told me I'm part of the royal court now or something?" he said, beginning to pace back and forth.

Caldera sighed heavily at his familiar compulsion. "I don't know anything about that," she said, wrapping her arms around herself.

He paused in the middle of his ramble, his eyes meeting hers—never wavering, never flinching. "Tell me what you do know...please."

He was the only one who ever really saw her, who could slice through her doubts like a knife, who could calm her down with a simple smile or an understanding look.

It was why she trusted him, and why she needed him more than ever.

She bit the inside of her cheek. "Everything I told you over the communicator is true. I'm the Queen of Tellis." She swallowed hard and turned away, walking toward the chair by the fireplace.

Rennick followed her. "How is that possible?" he asked, his gaze flicking around the extravagant room.

"My father was Quill's brother. I never knew." She collapsed into the plush chair, forcing back tears. "How, you ask, could I not know that my family was royalty? Another good question," she continued, careful to keep her voice steady.

Rennick prodded the ground with the toe of his boot. "We'll figure this out. Even if I still don't fully understand what the hell is going on." He took a step forward and sat on the floor in front of her. "Are you sure you're all right?"

She stared down into his turbulent eyes, flecked with green. He was clearly trying to hide his own distress, but she knew him too well. Her chest roiled with the urge to release her emotions, to scream, and cry, and lash out—which would only add to his discomfort.

"I'm fine, Ren," she muttered, forcing a smile across her face.

Rennick sighed. "If you say so." He pushed away from the ground and stood. "Callie, I've known you a long time." He walked halfway to the door, then took a breath and turned around to face her. "In case you've forgotten, you can talk to me."

Light filtered through the windows from Bersama's twin moons and littered the room in crisscrossing shadows, bathing them both in silver light.

"I know," she said quickly, trying to conjure a more genuine expression. "Don't worry." She stood and took a small step toward him.

He nodded, turning toward the door as a heavy silence set in.

"Where are you going?" Caldera asked.

Rennick let out an exasperated sigh, contemplation clouding his expression. "I have to go meet with Justle to figure out where I'll be living, I guess. Maybe figure out exactly what this 'new job' entails?" he replied with a forced chuckle.

I'm sorry, Ren, she thought, casting her gaze to the floor.

"Try to get some rest, okay? I'll see you tomorrow."

Caldera nodded as he walked out, guilt rising in her gut.

THE LIGHT OF the next morning shone through the windows, bathing the room in shades of rose gold and pink. Knitting her brow and clenching her eyes shut, Caldera pulled the silk covers over her head as her communicator chimed. When it was clear they weren't going to hang up, she reached across the bedside table with a groan, answering on the fourth ring.

"H—hello?"

"Did I wake you up?" Rennick's voice echoed through the speakers.

"Yeah…" Caldera cleared her throat and rubbed her eyes. "I was hoping to hide out here all day until I can figure out what the hell happened." *And how I can get out of it.* "Maybe stay in bed until someone forces me out of it?"

"I wouldn't plan on that." Rennick chuckled. "Justle knocked on my door this morning to say that I still need to be officially sworn in. He's probably going to pester you next."

"You're getting sworn in? That means you'll get to meet Councilmember Vandren. How fun for you—he's a real treat," she said, rolling onto her side and shielding her eyes.

"Wouldn't you be the one swearing me in? Since you're, you know…the queen."

"Before I got here, I might have said yes." Caldera sat up and swung her legs over the edge of the bed. "But the Council seems to be in charge of a lot more than I thought." She stood, letting the coolness of the marble flow into her feet and up her legs.

A knock sounded on her door.

"Someone's here. I'll talk to you later."

"Okay, okay, see ya."

She started across the room, then paused midway there, looking down at herself. *Shit—I probably shouldn't answer the door in my bra and underwear.*

Another, more forceful knock resounded off the walls.

"Hold on!" Caldera called. She grabbed the blanket off the bed and wrapped it around herself, then opened the door to see Justle standing there. His thick blond hair was perfectly combed and styled, and there wasn't a wrinkle to be seen in his tailored blue suit. The perfect image of a palace representative.

"Good morning, Your Majesty," he said with a bow, smiling brightly. "May I come in?"

Caldera moved so he could walk past her.

"I apologize for not getting your belongings to you in a timely fashion," Justle said, eyeing her makeshift toga before taking a seat in the chair by the fireplace. "Sol and Saro will have dropped it off by the time you get back." He crossed his legs and peered out the window—respectfully not looking in her direction.

Caldera frowned, clenching the blanket tighter to her chest. "Get back?"

Justle's blond head tilted. "Aloriea didn't tell you? Damn it," he said, slapping the armrest of the chair. "She was supposed to brief you about this last night. Did she even talk to you at all?"

Caldera scoffed. "Let's just say it wasn't pleasant, and she definitely didn't mention I had to go somewhere."

"Well," Justle said with a sigh. "You have a speech today."

Caldera's heart jumped into her throat. "What?"

"It's an introductory speech, along with some other announcements—nothing major. You're basically going to introduce yourself, explain your relation to Quill—briefly—and promote your former Vanguard crew accordingly," he said, circling his wrist in the air.

"That actually does sound major, especially for someone who didn't prepare," Caldera countered as her pulse continued to quicken and the hair on the back of her neck stood up. *Public speaking...I can't.*

"Don't worry. You'll be reading from a teleprompter."

Breathe.

"The speech is already written by the Council, I'm guessing?" she asked, taking slow, deep breaths.

In through your nose and out through your mouth.

"Councilmember Vandren, to be precise, but, essentially yes," he replied. "You'll be in the conference room, and it will broadcast live to every holoscreen in Tellis, as well as a direct, private broadcast to each of the sector leaders and council members."

In through your nose and out through your mouth.

"Why just Tellis—shouldn't this be broadcast to all of Bersama?" Caldera asked, shivering. "Shouldn't everyone know about the change in power?"

"The Council prefers to keep individual sector affairs confined to that specific sector," Justle explained. "I'll give you a few minutes to change." He stood and walked back over to the door, his black dress shoes clicking across the marble. "I'll be waiting in the hall. Come out when you're ready."

In through your nose and out through your mouth. Done.

Caldera bit her lip as confusion and relief flooded through her. Councilmember Vandren himself wrote the speech, and at least she wasn't going to be speaking to the entire planet.

Her mind shifted to Aloriea as she made her way to the bathroom to change back into her clothes from the day before. *This is ridiculous. The last thing I need right now is someone trying to sabotage me.* She grimaced, brushing the tangles out of her hair with her fingers.

Aloriea needed to learn that Caldera wasn't someone to fuck with.

"That was quick, Your Majesty," Justle said as they started walking down the hall.

"I don't have any other options, clothing-wise," Caldera told him, pulling down on her black shirt to try to hide the wrinkles. "And I'd prefer it if you'd just call me by my name. Caldera, or Callie—whichever. No 'Your Majesty' required."

He glanced at her quizzically. "Really?"

"Why not? From what I can tell, that's basically the only thing I can control right now," she said, letting a small smile spread across her face.

"That's...unorthodox." Justle returned her smile, his blue eyes shining. "But I suppose if that's your request, I can try to honor it."

"It's not an order or anything, just a preference," she replied, still not sure what to make of him. *This is the guy that gave me the RB, a device no other Vanguard captain has. Why?*

"I can briefly go into more detail about your speech if you'd like. We have extra time since we have to get Sir Silvera from his temporary quarters," he said, stepping onto the ground floor.

"Yes!" Caldera said, her stomach rolling. "Wait. *Sir* Silvera—temporary quarters?" She raised an eyebrow. "And why are we going to get him at all?"

Justle laughed, his constantly dignified persona dropping for an instant. "That's his title, since he's part of the royal court now, and he's your bodyguard. It's his job to go wherever you go. As for the temporary quarters, after he gets sworn in, he'll be moving into the room next to yours."

"Why?" Caldera asked, hoping her face wasn't as red as it felt as they rushed by a few members of palace staff.

"It makes sense," Justle replied matter-of-factly. "After all, how can he protect you if he's nowhere near you? I told him all of this earlier," he added, almost as an afterthought.

Caldera nodded. "Right. So, the Council mandated all of this?"

"Not exactly," Justle said quickly, not meeting her gaze. "The rooming situation was my idea. You never know what could happen around here ..."

"Oh..." Caldera muttered, falling out of step with him and rubbing her forehead. "Anyway—about the speech."

"Right," Justle said with a sharp nod, handing her the holopad that had been tucked under his arm. "Take a look."

Her unease grew as she scrolled through the preplanned pages.

"*Councilmember Vandren* wrote this?"

Justle squared his shoulders, averting his gaze. "That's correct."

"But."

They stopped in front of Rennick's door and Justle rapped his bony knuckles on the outside.

"Justle, I can't say these things," she said as Rennick stepped into view wearing the same clothes as the day before.

Justle stared at her. "You have to—"

"No!"

"What's going on?" Rennick asked warily.

Caldera met his eyes. "This speech. Councilmember Vandren wants me to say things that I don't believe. Things that won't help Bersama or its people at all—only hinder them!"

"What's it say—"

"Listen to me," Justle interrupted, his voice low and controlled. "This is something you must abide by... We all have to." He took a step back, his gaze never wavering. "Just give the speech."

She set her jaw, her eyes flicking from Rennick's confused face to Justle's stoic one. *What choice do I have?* "Fine."

CHAPTER 8

The trip to the conference room was silent, tense, and awkward. Their shoes clicked off the marble floor, the noise echoing back into their ears as it bounced off the empty walls. Justle walked in front of them, never breaking his stride, his shoulders square and straight. Rennick's hands were shoved into his jacket pockets and his brow was furrowed, curiosity dancing behind his eyes.

Caldera glanced sidelong at him as they approached the ornate door, wanting to know everything he was thinking—to hear his advice, even if she might not agree with it. Her legs were leaden as they stepped into the room. The dais was empty, and the seats seemed to stare down at her.

"Sit in the middle chair," Justle said, breaking the silence. "I'll release the camera and teleprompter when you're ready."

Silently, he pulled two objects out of his pocket. The first was a small, round, silver orb that fit neatly in the palm of his hand—the camera. The second was a black square that, with the push of a button, expanded into a twenty-by-twenty-inch screen—the teleprompter.

Caldera climbed the short staircase to the walkway behind the connected counter and sat at the center of the high-rise dais. Rennick smiled reassuringly at her and she nodded, which Justle took as the sign she was ready. He released the camera and teleprompter, and they floated up, stopping a few feet in front of her face.

As the teleprompter clicked to life, a red dot above the camera lens caught her attention.

Taking a deep breath and swallowing her apprehension, she began reading the pre-written words as they appeared on the screen.

"Citizens of Tellis. My name is Caldera Keane and it is my unfortunate duty to inform you that King Quill has passed on to the universe."

Caldera paused as the blunt information left her mouth, but the teleprompter didn't slow its progression. The words stammered out of her, the weight of their meaning immeasurable.

"I am his niece—his sole heir—and I have accepted the role and responsibility as s-sector leader. I... I am your new queen.

"Those of you who knew me might be aware that I was formerly a Vanguard captain. Not to worry, headquarters has already been notified and they have taken care of my former crew... Which brings me to my next announcement—"

Caldera stopped, her eyes glazing over at the words. The red dot above the camera blinked as if to remind her that she was still on air. The teleprompter scrolled effortlessly onto the next part of the speech, but the statement was burned into her mind.

"The Vanguard will be further defunded."

She forced the sentence out of her mouth, the words tangling in her throat, and glanced down at Rennick, whose eyes went wide. The words seemed to move faster with each passing second as she turned her attention back to the teleprompter. She wanted to throw up.

"Unfortunately, the Vanguard is not producing the results we require in terms of finding the resources Bersama desperately needs. We must redirect our efforts and money elsewhere. But do not worry—the layoffs will not be substantial, and affected employees will receive a severance package in accordance with their years of service."

That's a short-term solution! Some people literally just joined—most people!

The teleprompter rolled its last line: 'Thank you all for welcoming me as your new queen and thank you for your understanding'

Caldera cleared her throat, indignation rising in her chest. *Screw that.* "Thank you all for welcoming me as your new queen... and rest assured, I will be looking into ways to re-fund the Vanguard as soon as possible. Thank you."

The red light shut off as the camera and teleprompter lowered themselves back down to a stone-faced Justle. He blinked, offering a forced, unconvincing smile which she assumed was his way of telling her off and turned to leave.

"So much for a good first impression." Caldera sighed, leaning her head back and rubbing her temples.

The surrealism of her being the one sitting at the high-rise dais, looking down at a would-be audience instead of the Council, continued to make her head spin.

"Callie, what the hell?" Rennick said, walking up the stairs and leaning over to look into her eyes. "The Vanguard's getting defunded?"

"Not if I can help it," she muttered, swiveling her chair to face him. "I added that last part. Now all I have to do is figure out how to save it."

Rennick extended his hand.

Caldera let him help her to her feet. Then she stretched her arms toward the ceiling, sighing heavily as tension piled onto her shoulders. The speech continued to rattle around in her head as they walked down the steps and away from the dais.

"I want to call Markarian and Sear," she said abruptly.

Rennick held the conference room door open for her. "I'm sure they were watching."

"I know, I'm just..."

"Anxious?"

"Exactly," she said, as they started down the hallway. "Don't you think they're at least owed an explanation for that bullshit I was forced to say? Wouldn't you want one?"

"I'm still waiting for an explanation, actually."

Caldera froze, letting Rennick trail a little ahead of her as her stomach cinched into a tight ball. He turned around to face her, his expression unreadable for once.

"Councilmember Vandren wrote that—"

"I'm not talking about the speech Callie, I'm talking about this whole situation." Rennick shook his head, placing his hands on his hips. "You uprooted my life, Cal... My brother is in university, and with our father being gone, that job in the Vanguard was supporting us both."

Caldera's heart sank, as a fact that she had completely overlooked about Rennick's life ran through her head. The full weight of her hasty actions crashed through her body, crushing her. They didn't allow students to have jobs while attending university—their entire focus had to be on their studies, or they'd get kicked out.

Usually, only the rich could attend university. Another thing that was wrong with Bersama. Something she had to try and change.

"What can I say... I'm sorry." She paused, forcing the tears that stung her eyes not to overflow. "You can go."

Rennick's shoulders slumped as he took a step toward her. "I don't want to leave you Callie... I'm not going to. I just need to know that my brother will be taken care of."

She met his gaze eagerly at the affirmation that he would stay, and nodded emphatically. "I'll do whatever it takes," she whispered, trying to smile. "I promise."

"Thank you," he said, matching her expression and shifting to a more lighthearted tone as they continued down the hallway.

"Anyway, we should be able to call Sear and Markarian later, once they're off work."

"I just... I want them around. Some weird shit is going on here. I want them to be in the loop." Caldera glanced up at Rennick. "Don't worry, I'm not going to ruin their lives, too."

"Callie, come on, that's not what I meant," Rennick said with an exasperated sigh, following her back up the main stairwell. "I don't think you ruined my life."

Their silhouettes stretched down the steps and across the open room as the afternoon sun bathed them in warm light.

"Just changed it drastically without asking, that's all," he continued with a shrug, a genuine grin appearing on his face.

Caldera rolled her eyes. "And I said I was sorry—and I'll apologize every day for the rest of my life," she said, continuing up the steps.

"What are you going to do while you wait to contact them?" Rennick asked as they reached the top. "According to Justle, it turns out you were right about Councilmember Vandren being the one to swear me in, so that's where I'll be for about an hour."

"I'm going to see Aloriea to clear up a few things." *I need to know what her motives are. She didn't tell me about the speech for a reason.* "I want to figure out why she's being such a bitch."

Rennick chuckled, slowing his pace. "Okay, well, I'll be back to guard you as soon as I'm 'officially' sworn in," he said, his expression soft. "Try not to start an all-out brawl." He waved lazily before turning to walk back the way they came.

"No promises." she replied, knocking on the door with Aloriea's name next to it.

With a rush of wind, the door opened. "Oh, it's you," Aloriea said, raw anger flashing across her face before dissipating. Her short black hair was pulled back into a tight bun at the base of her neck, fully revealing her horns.

"Can I come in?" Caldera asked, looking up at the lanky akar.

Aloriea glared down at her, then motioned for her to enter, the sleeves of her light pink silken robe billowing.

As Caldera stepped inside and looked around, she was surprised to see that the room looked almost identical to her own, if only a little smaller.

Without another word, Aloriea walked out onto the balcony, the breeze erratically blowing her nightgown and robe around her thin body.

Caldera followed Aloriea outside, unable to hold in her emotions any longer. "All right—what's your problem?"

"My *problem* is that until yesterday you were... What, again?" Aloriea asked, drumming her fingers on the concrete railing and turning her head to look up into the evening sky.

"A captain of the Vanguard," Caldera said, her voice low.

"Right. You don't know the first thing about the world you just blindly stumbled into. And even worse, you brought another unqualified person into the palace. For what?"

"Protection."

"From who?" Aloriea demanded in a scathing voice, fingernails scratching across the stone.

Caldera held her gaze. "You? Justle? I don't know yet."

"You don't know anything."

"Then tell me," Caldera countered. "You're my advisor, aren't you?"

Aloriea's face flushed red, but she didn't answer.

"And why didn't you tell me about the speech?"

Again, Aloriea didn't respond.

"Okay. Then at least answer this—why the fuck do you hate me so much?" she pressed.

"Because you're here and Quill isn't!" Aloriea screamed as she spun around to face Caldera, tears welling in her eyes. She exhaled in short, shallow gasps. "I didn't tell you about the speech because..." She turned away. "I don't know... I wanted you to mess up."

Caldera inhaled sharply and took a step back. "Fine. I get it," she said. She turned to leave, not knowing what else to do.

"Damn it," Aloriea whispered, exasperation coating her voice. "Wait."

Caldera stopped.

Aloriea collapsed into a chair as if her energy was suddenly drained. "I'm sorry I intentionally didn't prepare you. That was extremely unprofessional."

"I'm not your enemy, Aloriea. I'm basically here against my will. Surely you can tell I didn't want this job."

Aloriea rubbed her forehead. "Yes, I can see that."

"Listen," Caldera continued carefully, not wanting to break the delicate truce, "for what it's worth, I know what it's like not to want to let someone go."

"Who—the bodyguard?"

"His name's Ren."

"Is he your boyfriend or something?"

"Umm—no, he's just my friend," Caldera replied, blushing.

"Right," Aloriea scoffed, finally meeting her eyes.

Caldera crossed her arms, desperate to change the subject. "So, you and Quill were close, then?"

Aloriea sighed. "Yes." She glared at her. "I don't want to talk about this—especially not with you."

Caldera took a deep breath. "Why don't you trust me?"

"Because you don't deserve it. Would you trust someone that you just met?"

Caldera sat down. "Maybe, maybe not," she said. *Screw it.* "The fact remains that something is going on in this palace."

Aloriea's shoulders tensed as she glanced sidelong at Caldera. "What makes you say that?"

"You heard what Councilmember Vandren wrote. What I had to say. It's strange." Her mind flashed to Justle's obvious unease and cryptic warning. "You can trust me, even if you don't realize it."

Aloriea chewed on a fingernail, her body rigid. "All right. But if I get arrested tomorrow, I'll do everything I can to take you down with me."

"Fair enough," Caldera said, crossing her arms.

Aloriea sighed. "Do you know how Quill died? Did they tell you?"

"No. I'm assuming it was unexpected."

Aloriea grimaced, a mirthless chuckle escaping her lips. "Extremely. So unexpected, in fact, that it doesn't seem natural."

"What are you saying?"

"What I'm about to tell you...you could have me charged with treason just for thinking," Aloriea whispered, meeting Caldera's gaze, her body shivering. "I believe Quill was murdered."

Caldera's heart pumped in her ears.

"By someone very powerful—if you catch my drift. I'm hoping that you're not involved," Aloriea added.

"Of course I'm not," Caldera said, still not completely sure what she'd just heard. "Why would I kill the only family I had left. Even if I had known about them," she finally managed, taking a deep breath. "Why do you think Quill was murdered?"

"Justle and I knew him better than anyone," Aloriea didn't take her eyes off Caldera. "His actions and mannerisms. I understand that death can sometimes happen out of nowhere, but the week leading up to his passing," she punctuated her point by jamming her finger onto the glass-topped table, "he was acting strange, secretive...withdrawn." She caught her breath. "They wouldn't even let me see his body. Not even the autopsy report. They wouldn't let any of us in the palace," she continued, clenching her hands tighter as a tear rolled down her cheek.

"I'm so sorry."

Aloriea wiped her face and turned away. "Pretty cold comfort."

"I'm sorry. That's all I can offer."

Aloriea nodded as they both fell silent, watching the transports crisscross through the sky. Nightfliers cooed as other nocturnal animals flitted through the trees and tall grass on the other side of the palace wall. The bright lights of the inner city shone like a miniature sun on the horizon.

"Can we just start over?" Caldera said after a few minutes. "I think you need someone to talk to. Since I'm not involved in this conspiracy of yours—"

Aloriea shot her a look.

"I'm not!" Caldera repeated, holding up her hands. "Let's start fresh."

"Okay," Aloriea agreed, eyeing her skeptically.

"Good," Caldera said, clearing her throat. "Hi, my name's Caldera Keane—my friends call me Callie. " She offered her hand.

Aloriea took it gingerly. " Will you help me find out who murdered Quill?"

Caldera sat back in her chair, mulling over the situation. If Aloriea's theory was true, it could mean that Caldera's life was in danger, too. "I'll help you, but to do this, I have some people I think you should meet."

"You want to bring more under qualified individuals into the palace?"

Caldera nodded. "Their names are Sear and Markarian. I'm sure we'll all be friends in no time."

"I didn't say I wanted to be your friend—or anyone's," Aloriea said, scowling.

Caldera smirked. "No, I guess you didn't—but I think I'd like to be yours."

CHAPTER 9

t took three days to convince Aloriea to meet with Sear and Markarian. After continually swearing to her that she'd had nothing to do with the king's death, Caldera was able to sway her, if only partially.

Caldera and Rennick hurried through the halls to the meeting place after retrieving a holopad from her quarters.

The library was located in the left-most tower, Circular in shape, the space was smaller than Caldera expected, though still stunning. A continuous window, no more than twelve inches in height, stretched around the entire room above the shelves, letting in glimmers of sunlight from all angles. The shelves themselves filled the entire space, lined with digital books whose spines glowed a soft white. In the far corner, a single computer terminal sat dormant. A small, round table stood in the middle of the room where Sear, Markarian, and Aloriea waited.

Caldera couldn't hold back a smile. The memory of her mother bringing her to Astrum's public archives flashed across her mind. How she snuggled on her mother's lap, holding the thin metal children's book she had picked out. The magnetic seal that had resisted ever so slightly as she pulled it open, and how the holographic words and images popped into the air.

"I'm having serious second thoughts about this," Aloriea said when they walked in. Her dark green pantsuit and white blouse looked strikingly formal against everyone else's casual wear.

"What's that supposed to mean?" Markarian asked with a grin, leaning back in his chair.

Caldera sighed. "How many times do I have to tell you that you can trust them?" she said, glancing over at Rennick as the door closed behind them. With a huff, she placed her holopad on the tabletop and slumped into a chair.

"I hope you're right," Aloriea said as Sear yawned lazily.

"Can you two please at least pretend to be interested in what's going on?" Caldera asserted, glaring at each of them as her agitation swelled, creeping up the back of her neck.

Markarian flipped curly hair out of his eyes, kicking his boots up onto the table. "I am."

Caldera sighed and rubbed her eyes, thankful that there wasn't anything stuck to the bottom of his shoes.

"I am an astronomer—a scientist," Sear chimed in, his golden fur bristling. "Not a politician. I cannot help it if political issues bore me."

"Oh, this bores you, does it?" Aloriea snapped. "Caldera, do they even know why they're here?"

"You asked me not to tell them anything until you met them," Caldera clipped. "Don't I get points for keeping my word?"

Aloriea shook her head, looking up at the ceiling. "Really, universe? These are the people that are going to help me?"

"It's all right," Rennick said, pushing Markarian's feet off the table. He sat down next to Caldera, his voice soft. "Just tell them."

Aloriea bit a nail. "Obviously, you can't tell anyone about this," she said, looking each of them in the eye, then cast her gaze to the floor, her shoulders visibly stiffening. "I—I think Quill was murdered."

"What!" Markarian said, almost tipping backward in his chair.

"That is a very serious accusation," Sear added, his ears perking up.

"I am aware. I have no proof at the moment, but something doesn't add up," Aloriea persisted, gripping the edge of the table. "Caldera and Rennick vouched for both of you, and seeing as I don't exactly have any other options..."

"That's why you called us here?" Markarian asked, turning his attention to Caldera.

Caldera met his eyes. "Yes. I know it's hard to believe. That's why we need people we can trust to help us work through it. If we don't figure this out, my life could be in danger, too."

"This is crazy," he whispered.

"If this is what you have been dealing with since you got here, why did you send out that order to all the flight consultants?" Sear asked.

Caldera shook her head. "What're you talking about?"

"I just received orders yesterday for every Vanguard flight consultant to gather all of their flight plans chronologically and submit them to the Council. Plans that date all the way back to ten years ago," he said, scratching thoughtfully behind his ear.

"I didn't send out anything." Caldera's chest tightened. "I've only been queen for a little over four days."

"It had your name on it."

"They're orders from the Council," Aloriea interjected. "Or Vandren, rather."

"What?" Sear questioned, his yellow eyes gleaming in the low light. "If that is true, then we must assume this is going on in every sector."

"Maybe that's why Quill was murdered," Caldera muttered. "He decided he didn't want to comply anymore."

"It may not correlate directly to the king being 'murdered,' but the timing is eerily convenient," Sear said with a nod.

"Markarian, have you or any of the other captains received new orders since I've been instated?" Caldera asked.

"Not yet," he replied, shaking his head.

A dull headache started in her temples. Councilmembers weren't supposed to bypass the sector leader and send orders out in their name. "All right, how can we stop them—"

"You can't," Aloriea interjected. "Trust me."

"But I'm the queen, right?"

"In case you haven't noticed, that doesn't mean anything around here," Aloriea snapped.

"Then what's the point? What do I even do?"

"You're a mouthpiece. You do what the Council tells you to."

"Then what's the point of a monarchy?" Markarian cut in.

"To maintain an air of perceived order," Aloriea answered. "Kings, queens, and rulers can pass minor, sector-specific laws, but they're not in control—not really. The Council has the final say on everything substantial. Caldera couldn't even instate a bodyguard without their approval."

"So, it's all a front?" Caldera asked.

"It is now," Aloriea said, chuckling mirthlessly. "But according to old records, it wasn't always this way."

Sear took a deep breath, his ears half flat against his head. "I refuse to be complicit in possible political disintegration that could lead to warmongering." His eyes flicked from Caldera to Aloriea. "I will help you."

"Markarian?" Caldera met his green eyes.

He grinned. "I was almost laid off because of the Council's order to defund the Vanguard. Of course I'm gonna help."

Rennick cleared his throat and turned his attention to the holopad. "What's this for?"

"To help Caldera learn the history, and more importantly, the policies of this sector," Aloriea said as she fished her own holopad out of her pocket and placed it on the table. "I'll transfer the most important files over to you."

Caldera made a face.

"You can't help me if you have no idea how things are done,"

Aloriea pointed out, catching Caldera's gaze. Her eyes were turbulent. "None of you can."

"I believe I have looked through most of the documents that you are about to present, and I have to agree with Callie," Sear said. "If she cannot do anything, then what exactly does she need to learn to help you? How to back down?"

"Possibly," Aloriea muttered, placing her hand on the holopad screen. White light illuminated the device as it scanned her fingerprints, and the screen turned a bright blue as it unlocked.

"That's not gonna happen," Rennick and Markarian said at the same time.

Caldera grinned. "I guess I should learn this crap—even if this position is mostly just for show. Maybe it will help us understand what's going on."

"Plus, we're fast learners," Markarian added with a mischievous wink.

"Fine," Aloriea said, tapping her slim fingers against the screen at lightning speed. She flicked her wrist toward the ceiling, causing the contents she had looked up to float in the air between them as a holographic image.

Caldera quickly unlocked her own holopad, readying it to receive information.

"All right," Aloriea said. "Let's start simple. There are five sectors and five species on Bersama—"

"We need to know about how the government is run, not basic children's knowledge," Markarian interrupted.

"The first sector is Tellis," Aloriea continued, pointing to the floating image, her voice tight. "The main inhabitants are tellins, but some other species live here as well—"

"Clearly," Rennick interjected, looking from Sear to Aloriea.

"—mostly because they either grew up here or moved to this sector before the border shut down. That particular point is the same for all the sectors."

"Why were the borders closed in the first place?" Caldera

asked, leaning forward. "They've been shut down for over ten years, just before any of us entered the Vanguard."

"You don't remember?" Aloriea asked, exasperation creeping into her expression.

Caldera's mind flashed to the sudden loss of her parents. "We learned a little about it in the academy, but I don't really remember. I had a lot going on at that time."

"Something about the desolate section?" Rennick offered.

Markarian shrugged. "Honestly, I just wasn't paying attention."

"Sear?" Aloriea asked, a pleading note entering her voice as if she were begging for someone—anyone—to be on the same page.

"The official statement that the Council released is that they are continuing to hold out hope that the original planets from the first, or, 'desolate' section of the galaxy will begin spinning again," Sear answered, his tail flicking nonchalantly behind him.

Aloriea gave a small, satisfied nod.

"That's never going to happen. We've been to the desolate section, and nothing can live there." Caldera shivered at the memory of the monster she and Rennick encountered. "At least none of the species living on this planet."

"That's the point," Aloriea continued, looking at Caldera quizzically. "All the sector leaders know it's bullshit. There's no scientific proof to support the Council's theory, but they still claim that it'll be easier to relocate everyone if they're not completely split up between sectors." She paused, tucking a strand of hair behind her horn. "There's also the nagging question about why they waited so long. The cataclysm happened one hundred years ago, but they shut the borders down only ten years ago. Why?"

"And if what you say is true—that the sector leaders have basically no power—then they had no choice or say in the matter."

"So that's why there's so much unrest," Rennick concluded, tapping his forefinger against his chin.

"Right, that's the byproduct, but what's the Council doing about it?" Markarian asked. "The border shutdown was their order, and everyone knows it was, but now all the sectors are pissed off and on the brink of war. King Quill's death could be the breaking point."

"Or the excuse." Caldera leaned her head back and closed her eyes as purple evening light filtered in through the thin windows. She blinked. The sun had almost completely set since they began their conversation. "Aloriea, what would have happened if there had been no one to take this throne?"

"It's not really known. I assume the corresponding council member would take over."

"You think that's why the Council needs to get the sector leader out of the way?" Rennick asked.

Caldera met his eyes. A worried expression passed between them as unanswered questions bit at her mind, causing her jaw to ache from clenching her teeth.

"What exactly do flight consultants do?" Aloriea asked, turning back to Sear. "It has to be important, otherwise they would have never sent out those orders."

"We take the flight plans that the Vanguard members receive, compare them to their actual flight logs, and comprise a comprehensive map of their trip," Sear replied. "Essentially, we make sure that they go where they are ordered to."

Aloriea nodded slowly. "You map the galaxy?"

"I suppose that is one way of looking at it," Sear said, scratching his chin. "If all the data from every trip were to be compiled."

"What are they up to?" she whispered, absently twirling a strand of black hair around her finger.

Why would they need the sector leader out of the way? The words swirled in Caldera's head as the room fell quiet once more, the past few days blurring together.

You've been summoned by the Council...

King Quill is dead...

Surprising for all of us...

Caldera's eyes widened. "Surprising for all of us," she repeated aloud.

"What?" Rennick asked, tilting his head to the side and angling his body to face her.

She swallowed hard, her throat threatening to constrict. "When I was first summoned by the Council, Vandren said my appearance there was 'surprising to all of them'."

"I am sure it was," Sear said.

The week leading up to his passing..."Aloriea, when did Quill die?" Caldera asked. "The exact date."

Aloriea blanched.

"I'm sorry to ask." Caldera didn't break eye contact. "It's important."

Aloriea wrapped her arms around herself, gripping her elbows tightly. "Twenty-four days ago."

"You've only been queen for four of those days," Markarian said. "Why would they wait so long to look for you or announce Quill's death?"

Rennick furrowed his brow. "Callie, what does this have to do with—"

"What were we doing twenty-four days ago, Ren?"

He paused, his eyes widening at the realization. "Our last mission... We were shipping out."

"Exactly. We got that order toward the end of the day too."

"Immediate deployment..." he murmured.

Sear, Markarian, and Aloriea were all staring at them, waiting for an explanation.

"Don't you see?" Caldera said, looking at each of them in turn. "We supposedly got the orders from Quill, but he was already dead."

"Are you saying Councilmember Vandren sent you guys on that dangerous mission on *purpose*?" Markarian whispered.

"Maybe Quill sent out the order, and Vandren forgot to revoke it. Or maybe he did not know it was dangerous," Sear tried, his ears flat.

Aloriea rapidly flicked through the holopad in her hand. "Sector Leaders can't send out orders to any agency without their corresponding council member signing off on it," she said, her voice barely audible. "And there's no record of Quill ever sending out a mission request the day of, or before, his death. Vandren sent you on that mission. He knew about you."

"That is speculation," Sear said.

Caldera opened her mouth to reply when a gentle knock on the library door cut her off.

"Good evening," Justle said, peeking his head inside. "My, you all look like you've seen a ghost. Am I really that frightening?"

"Justle! What are you doing here?" Aloriea asked cautiously.

Justle chuckled, tilting his head to smile at Aloriea. "I'm looking for Her Maj—Caldera—and it seems I've found her," he replied, gazing at them all curiously. "And who might you two be?"

"This is Sear and Markarian," Caldera said, motioning toward them. "They worked with me when I was still a captain of the Vanguard. They're my friends."

Sear nodded a greeting while Markarian flicked his wrist in a quick wave.

"Nice to meet both of you," Justle said with a nod before turning his attention to Caldera. "Now then, I'm very sorry to interrupt, but I have something extremely important to tell you."

Caldera stood, the chair scraping against the floor. She flicked her eyes from her friends to Justle as her ears throbbed with each heartbeat. "What is it?"

For a split second, his smile wavered. "Councilmember Vandren feels that a more...hands-on approach to learning the ins and outs of sector control is necessary. To that end, he's sending you to each sector to meet and learn from the leaders individually." He paused. "Queens Eldra and Fenry of Sector Two have offered their expertise first. Lady Morin and Sir Silvera will accompany you, of course."

Caldera's mouth fell open. "What about you?" she asked, trying to gather her thoughts and reclaiming her seat.

"Unfortunately, I won't be going," he said with a smile, clasping his hands behind his back. "I'll be looking after the palace until you get back."

Vandren might've tried to kill me and now he wants me to go somewhere... Fuck... "This is, umm..." She trailed off as her mind raced.

"This is sudden," Rennick said, coherently finishing her thought and taking a stand.

Aloriea's eyes narrowed. "She needs to stay here."

Justle sighed. "Lady Morin... Aloriea, you know as well as I do that it's nearly impossible to appeal a council member's order."

Caldera bit her lip, forcing herself back to her feet. "It's fine," she finally replied, looking from Aloriea to Justle. "How long is this trip going to take?" *And how am I gonna make it out of this in one piece?*

CHAPTER 10

The soft golden light of the next day streamed into Caldera's quarters. The balcony doors were wide open, letting in a cool, early morning breeze. It whispered through her hair, rustling it against her shoulders. Taking a deep breath, she slammed her suitcase closed, a hard frown settling across her lips.

"Are you listening?" Aloriea asked from behind her.

"Yes." Caldera grumbled. *"Don't provoke Councilmember Vandren in any way today.* Got it." A gasp from behind her made her jump. She whirled, her shoulders tensing. "What!"

"You truly have no sense of fashion," Aloriea said, her hands on her hips as she stared into Caldera's open wardrobe. "I guess I'll have to run out and buy you something before we leave," she muttered, shaking her head.

Caldera closed her eyes, pinching the bridge of her nose. The temptation to push Aloriea out of her quarters and slam the door behind her was almost impossible to resist. "Is that really necessary?"

"You're royalty now," Aloriea said, motioning toward Caldera's brown, long-sleeved crop-top and denim jeans. "If you want to dress like that around the palace, fine, but not when you're visiting other sector leaders."

"Just do whatever you need to." Caldera waved a hand in the air. "This meeting with Vandren probably won't last that long though, so hurry."

Aloriea smirked as they headed toward the door. "It would be ill-advised to leave without me."

"Ready?" Rennick asked as they stepped into the hallway, his hands shoved into the pockets of his jacket.

Caldera closed the door to her quarters, giving a quick nod before starting toward the stairs. Her stomach roiled, twisting itself into a tight knot. The empty echo of the palace intensified her dread.

"All right, I'll be back soon," Aloriea said as they reached the bottom. "Remember what I said," she added before veering off toward the palace entrance.

"Callie, what's wrong?" Rennick asked, trailing behind her.

Caldera averted her gaze. "Nothing."

Rennick raised an eyebrow. "Okay, even if I didn't know you, that was the most obvious lie I've ever seen. What is it?"

Caldera sighed heavily. "I honestly don't know what I'm doing here."

"What do you mean?"

Caldera came to a halt. "I'm not a queen, Ren. I have no idea what I'm doing... What I'm *supposed* to do," she said, staring up at the high-rise ceilings.

"I don't think anyone really knows what they're supposed to do." Rennick offered a small smile. "We only know what we can do in the moment—and usually that's enough."

Caldera gazed into his warm eyes, the tension of her body relaxing. *How does he always know what to say?*

Sunlight from the large picture window shone off his copper hair and skin, casting a halo of light that seemed to glow around him. Her stomach fluttered as the knot untwisted the slightest bit. Smiling, she looked down at the floor. "Is that advice or something?" She chuckled, letting hair slip in front of her eyes.

"Hmm...I guess it's not great. How about, 'just be yourself'? Except for the reckless part, of course," he said with a wink.

She laughed. "That's better, I've never thought of that before."

"Come on, we're late for the meeting." He glanced at his watch and tilted his head in the direction of the conference room.

"Let's get this over with," she agreed with a nod, and they continued down the hall, confidence springing back to life in her chest.

Letting comfortable silence fill the air between them, they navigated down the hallway until they got to the familiar, ornate door of the conference room.

"Ready?" Rennick asked, his hand on the door handle.

"Yeah—oh! Before I forget, I talked to Aloriea... Your salary from being my bodyguard—part of the royal court—is definitely going to provide enough for your brother to stay in university."

His face lit up. "When did you—"

"It was important to you, so I made time."

Rennick placed a soft hand on her shoulder and squeezed, his eyes glimmering. "Thank you so much, Callie."

She forced herself to stay still—to resist the urge to wrap her arms around his neck and hug him.

With a soft, reassuring smile, he pulled the door open, ushering her inside.

"Welcome, Your Majesty." Vandren looked down at them from the middle of the dais. His hair was combed back, clearly displaying the deep wrinkles around his eyes. The sleeves of his golden robe billowed as he took his seat. "I assume you know and understand why you're here?"

"I do," Caldera replied as evenly as she could, clasping her hands tightly behind her back. She forced herself to look at Vandren straight-on as Rennick took his place behind her and to the left.

"Good, we'll go into specific details in a minute. First, I'd like to introduce you to Olivare Seren. Along with Lady Morin and Sir Silvera, he'll be accompanying you to each of the sectors," Vandren said, snapping his fingers.

The side door opened, but instead of revealing Aloriea and Justle, the most muscular tellin Caldera had ever seen stepped into the conference room. His black hair was slicked close to his head, and his ill-fitting suit stretched a little too tightly through the shoulders. A multitude of small scars adorned his neck.

"After you get back, he'll become a member of palace security, alongside Sol and Saro," Vandren continued.

Caldera silently examined him as he stalked to the front of the dais, positioning himself to the right of Vandren. The knot in her stomach returned full force as his emotionless gray eyes met hers.

"If you're adding additional security for this trip, shouldn't there be a team?" she asked as her unease grew, spreading throughout her entire body.

"Sol and Saro must stay here to guard the palace, and Olivare is more than capable," Vandren said, casting his gaze to the giant man in front of him. "He was a captain of the Tellin Militia, Special Forces."

"In other words, the real military," Olivare said, his deep voice resonating through her skin, down to her bones. "The type of soldiers the Vanguard wishes they were."

Caldera narrowed her eyes as heat rushed through her, culminating in her cheeks. "We don't wish we were soldiers," she insisted, struggling to control her voice. "We're explorers."

"Enough," Vandren clipped. "The visits will be fairly simple. One day and night at each sector—you'll stay within the sector leaders' palace grounds, meet with them, learn as much as you can about their style of rule, and move on."

Something flitted across his expression that Caldera couldn't place, causing her to shiver.

"You'll be traveling by private shuttle, so the entire trip

shouldn't take over ten days." He reached into a pocket of his robe and handed a holopad down to Olivare.

"What's on that?" Caldera asked, eyeing the holopad as Olivare held it in his huge hands.

"The invitations from each of the sector leaders," Vandren explained. "Present them to the guards at the entrance of the coordinating palace and they'll scan you in."

She nodded, the hairs on the back of her neck prickling. "How long does it take to get from one sector to the next?" she asked, painfully aware that even with all her years in the Vanguard and flying into space, she had never so much as traveled to another sector, even before the borders shut down.

"I'm sure Lady Morin will be more than willing to answer any further questions you may have," he said, standing.

She stood straighter. "Why can't you answer them?" The question escaped her lips before she could stop it.

Vandren went rigid, his glare striking. "If I were to answer all your questions," he countered, leaning forward, "we'd be here all day." He cleared his throat and turned to leave. "Fair travels, Your Majesty," he said over his shoulder before disappearing through the door behind the dais with Olivare.

Caldera scoffed and rushed out the door Rennick held open for her, making her way back to her quarters as quickly as possible.

"You almost knocked me over, you barreled out of there so fast," Rennick said once they were inside her room.

"Sorry," Caldera muttered, sitting on the edge of her bed. "Can you believe that bullshit, though? He wouldn't even answer one question."

Rennick sat next to her. "Yeah, he's an asshole. But you know you kinda antagonized him, right?"

"What happened to 'just be yourself'?" She buried her face in her hands, the irritation slowly subsiding.

"Touché," he said, sighing heavily and leaning back on his hands. "The trip just got a lot more interesting. Ten days with that sunshine of a man—great."

"Olivare's definitely grumpy, and irritating, and aggravating...but he was special forces of the militia. He's probably pissed that he somehow got relegated to 'palace security guard'."

A knock sounded at the door just before Aloriea burst through with a large rectangular clothing box in her hand. She paused, glancing between them. She dropped the box on the table by the fireplace with a *clunk* and untangled a piece of black hair from her horn. "Am I interrupting something?"

"No!" Caldera got to her feet as her face flushed.

Aloriea pointed to Rennick and then to the door. "Get out," she said, before removing the lid from her purchase.

Rennick held up his hands in mock surrender. "Okay, okay. I have to get changed myself." He slid through the door and into the hallway, chuckling.

"Aren't you even going to ask how the meeting went?" Caldera asked.

"I can hazard a guess," Aloriea replied, pushing a bundle of perfectly folded clothes into Caldera's arms. "Now put this on. The shuttle takes off in forty-five minutes."

Caldera slipped into the attached bathroom to change into the outfit Aloriea had bought for her. The navy-blue blouse and black blazer fit snugly around her slim body, and the black slacks hugged her legs from the hips down, tapering at the ankle. She sighed, running a brush through her hair until it shone in a platinum sheet around her shoulders before walking back into the room.

"Is this what fashion means?" she asked, as Aloriea chucked a pair of black high-heels in her direction. "Being immensely uncomfortable?"

To Caldera's surprise, Aloriea laughed. "Sometimes, but you look great. Now let's go."

Smiling wearily, Caldera slipped the shoes on and followed Aloriea out of the door.

"You've got to be kidding me," Aloriea said as Caldera closed and locked the door with a scan of her hand. "What's the deal with you people? Have you seriously never worn formal wear before?"

"Not often enough to know how to tie one of these things," Rennick replied with a chuckle.

When Caldera turned around, her eyes widened. Rennick stood before them in the official dress code of the palace guard—a black suit with the planetary emblem embroidered in gold thread over the right breast pocket. Aloriea frantically fixed the black tie that hung loosely around the neck of his white dress shirt as he ran a hand through his hair. His bronze skin glimmered in the light of the setting sun, sending heat instantly rushing to her cheeks.

Their eyes met, and he smiled, sending her heart rocketing against her chest.

"There," Aloriea said as she finished straightening the tie, jolting Caldera back to reality. "We have to get moving." She gave her a half smile. "Everything all right?"

"Yes. Of course." Caldera tore her eyes away from Rennick and followed Aloriea down the hall. She took a deep breath, forcing her mind to focus on the journey ahead.

"This way," Aloriea said, veering into an alcove just before the start of the stairs and opening a hidden door.

"I didn't even know this was here. Where're we going?"

"The shuttle," Aloriea replied, tilting her head to the side.

Caldera raised a brow in confusion.

Aloriea sighed, shaking her head, "Quill..." She cleared her throat. "*You* have a private shuttle. It's on the roof."

"How did we not notice this before?" Rennick asked as he followed Aloriea up the new staircase toward the roof, looking over his shoulder at Caldera.

"This palace is huge," Caldera said, her heels clicking with each step as she ascended. "Who knows how many rooms we still haven't been in."

Aloriea pushed the door open at the top of the stairs, and, as promised, the shuttle was waiting for them on a landing pad.

Its long rectangular frame stretched one hundred feet across the flat area, the tall peak of the palace roof making it impossible to see from the entrance. The shiny metal exterior of the shuttle reflected their images as they walked up to Olivare, who was waiting next to the descended ramp.

"You were almost late," Olivare said as Aloriea and Rennick passed him. His voice was gruff as his empty eyes landed on Caldera.

"Almost is the keyword there," Caldera clipped, returning his glare with one of her own. Rennick glanced over his shoulder and motioned for her to follow. She hurried up the ramp into the posh interior.

The inside was split into two parts by a transparent plexiglass wall with a sliding door. On the side they entered, sturdy, cream-colored half-tables lined with gold trim sat in front of a white plush couch and chairs anchored into the soft carpet-lined floors. A holoscreen directly across from the couch spread half the length of the wall. On the other side of the partition was a long, rectangular, wood-plated table with high-back chairs surrounding it. The entire ceiling was transparent, the early evening clouds drifting far above them.

Caldera blinked as she absent-mindedly sat on the couch, her body sinking into the soft cushions. "Shit..." she muttered under her breath, still taking in the luxury of her surroundings.

Olivare latched the door behind them. "We're ready," he said, speaking into a communicator he pulled out of his pocket. Without another word, he walked through the door that split the sections and sat down at the table, ignoring them as the shuttle jolted into the air.

The motion made Caldera ache for her ship—for the Vanguard. She bit her lip as Aloriea sat in a chair on the far side of the shuttle, her attention whole-heartedly on her holopad.

"What's on your mind?" Rennick asked softly as he sat beside Caldera.

She gave him a halfhearted smile. "This is pretty surreal."

"You can say that again," he replied. His gaze pierced through her. "The answer is three, by the way."

"Three?"

"It'll take about three hours to get to Sector Two," Rennick said, leaning back heavily against the corner of the couch.

"How do you..." Caldera began. "Oh, right. Your dad lives in the capital of Natioh—Mirstone, doesn't he?"

He nodded, casting his gaze to the floor. "Haven't seen him since the borders shut down, though."

Something flitted across his eyes that made her want to comfort him—to reach over and take his hands. "At least your brother still lives here," she offered, lacing her fingers together and placing them firmly in her lap. "How's he doing?" she continued, letting a small smile spread across her lips.

"Will's in the top of his class!" Rennick said with obvious pride.

Caldera grinned, thankful that his mood was lifting. "That's great!"

Aloriea looked up. "We should go over some specifics before we get to Mirstone Palace."

Caldera closed her eyes, exhaling sharply. "Like what?"

"The general itinerary of our visit," Aloriea replied, holding up her holopad. "Now listen up."

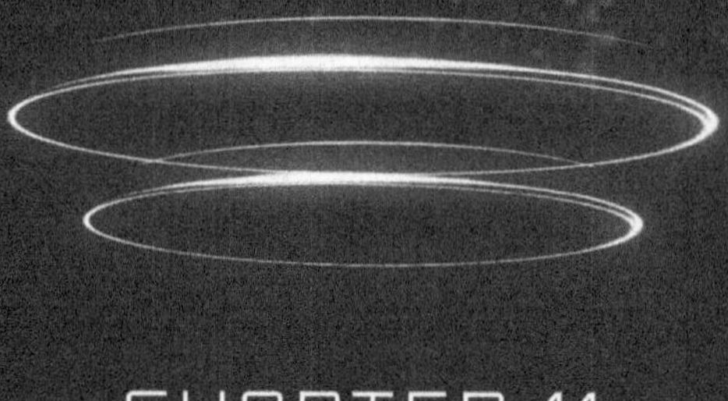

CHAPTER 11

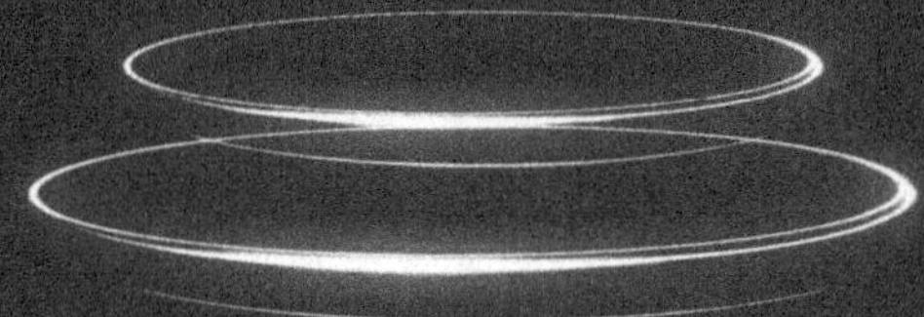

Caldera leaned her head against the window, unable to take her eyes off the vast ocean of Natioh. Whitecaps crested over various creatures as they came up for a quick breath before diving into the shimmering depths. A quickly advancing stretch of land caught her eye, contrasting harshly against the miles of uninterrupted sea.

The speakers crackled to life inside the shuttle. "We're approaching Mirstone Palace," the pilot announced. "Five minutes to touchdown."

Uncut grass rolled with the wind as the shuttle landed gently on the thick, circular concrete platform precariously perched on an outcropping of a cliff about half a mile behind the palace.

Caldera stepped off the ramp onto the lush green grass, filling her lungs with fresh air as a salty breeze blew through her hair. Warmth clung to her skin as the sun glimmered off the waves crashing against the rocky cliffside. Despite her jittery hands and racing heart, she couldn't help but smile. She felt sharp and alert as she gazed out over the water. Its vastness seemed never ending.

"What a beautiful sector," she breathed, turning to Rennick as he walked up beside her.

He nodded in agreement. "Beautiful," he whispered, looking out over the horizon as he slid his hands into his pants pockets. The breeze rustled his hair and suit, causing the edges of his jacket to flap against his body and his tie to blow over his shoulder.

The pounding in Caldera's chest intensified. The fear and agitation regarding the upcoming meeting completely diminished for the moment as her gaze lingered on Rennick. Folding her arms across her body, she closed the distance between them until her shoulder touched his bicep, her body leaning against his.

He went rigid, as if surprised by the sudden contact, before gently relaxing into the touch—leaning back against her with equal pressure.

"Will you two come on!" Aloriea called, forcing Caldera to turn around. Olivare was already halfway to the palace as Aloriea waved them over, her purple dress whipping around her slender frame. "Queens Eldra and Fenry are waiting for us in the great hall," she said, guiding Caldera and Rennick toward the palace.

The towering, stone-lined metal walls curved up toward the sky, forming a perfect dome. The palace was large, but from what Caldera could tell, it seemed to be all one level except for a single connected tower.

She swallowed hard. "Is it true that the queens are...severe?" she asked, her breath catching in her throat as she voiced the question that had been plaguing her the most.

"Eldra is sweet." Aloriea re-tightened her bun and flattened her flyaway hairs as the party came to the large metal door of the palace entrance. "Fenry, on the other hand, is...forthright."

Great... There's no way I'm making a good impression. Caldera bit the inside of her cheek as Aloriea approached the tall bald man guarding the scanner for the door. His fin-like ears pointed straight up as they got closer.

Olivare stood waiting, his thick arms crossed over his chest. "It's about time," he grunted, narrowing his eyes.

"Nobody told you to run ahead," Caldera snapped.

Aloriea stopped in front of the guard. "Dathan—I mean, *Sir Gar*, it's nice to see you again," she said, bowing her head in greeting.

The man smirked. "Likewise, Lady Morin," he said, mimicking her motion and stepping to the side. The external gills on the sides of his neck flicked open and closed in the blink of an eye.

"Queen Caldera Keane and party here for Queens Eldra and Fenry Ione," Aloriea continued, her voice crisp. "We're expected."

Dathan nodded. His bright green eyes contrasted sharply with his stone-gray skin. "I've already reviewed your invitation—scan your hands for entry, please," he said, motioning toward the device on the wall.

Caldera placed her hand on the scanner after Aloriea. When it lit up green, she stepped to the side, waiting for Rennick.

"You're the new sector leader for Tellis?" Dathan asked, his gaze quizzical.

"That's right," Caldera said with a nod, watching as Aloriea cast her eyes to the ground.

To her surprise, Dathan's expression softened. "You have some pretty big shoes to fill. I suggest you listen to everything this one has to say," he added, pointing at Aloriea.

Caldera caught Aloriea's gaze. "I'll try."

Dathan bowed, motioning them inside as the doors swung open, and then followed behind them before they closed.

Caldera's mouth fell open when she stepped through the inner archway into a large, open, multi-tiered area. Bare floor-to-ceiling windows ran the entire length of the right wall, providing a perfect view of the ocean behind the palace. Her heels clicked against the pale-blue agate floor. The translucent bands that ran through polished, gleaming stone swirled in a multitude of different directions. Two arched hallways flanked the back wall.

The second tier consisted of two large walkways on either side of the room, encased by thick, swirling stone banisters. From what Caldera could see from the lower level, small tables and pillowy chairs were interspersed throughout the walkways, as if placed there solely to gaze out at the ocean below.

Eldra and Fenry stood at the head of a large white stone table surrounded by a dozen uncomfortable-looking stone chairs. They were both waiting patiently for Caldera and her group to approach, clad in long, beautiful dresses that hemmed the floor.

"Aloriea, my dear," one of the women said, the long sleeves of her cream-colored dress fluttering as she gripped Aloriea's hand in her cerulean one. "I'm so sorry to hear about King Quill."

"Thank you, Your Majesty. That's much appreciated," Aloriea replied as she bowed her head. She moved to greet the other queen, whose long hair obscured her face as she spoke to Aloriea.

A pang of irrational jealousy shot through Caldera's chest at the fact their condolences weren't directed at her. It made her lack of flesh-and-blood family even more pronounced. *I didn't know Quill—had never even met him,* she reminded herself as the first queen approached her.

"It's nice to meet you, Queen Caldera," she said, gripping Caldera's hand. A line of parallel white dots ran underneath both of her gleaming arctic eyes, down to her jawline. Her blue skin glittered in the setting sun. "I am Queen Eldra."

"We must start the proceedings!" the other queen interrupted, her voice booming off the walls.

Eldra sighed, running a hand over her smooth, hairless scalp. "And that's my wife, Queen Fenry."

"Nice to...meet you," Caldera said, looking over Eldra's shoulder at Fenry.

The queen scoffed, her hard navy eyes almost blending in with her dark, indigo-blue skin. Her thin-strapped, silver sheath dress fell gracefully over her lithe body, and grooved, fin-like ears stuck out from snow-white locks, which almost fell to the floor. Shifting the mass of hair to the side, she took her seat, returning her attention to Aloriea.

Eldra smiled wearily, returning to the head of the table and sitting next to Fenry.

Caldera bit her lip as a palace assistant pulled her chair out for her before quickly returning to the edge of the room. She glanced over at Aloriea, who was smiling and laughing with the queens, then reluctantly eased into the stone chair closest to Eldra. It was just as uncomfortable as it looked.

Olivare stood watch at the foot of the table with Dathan, their hands resting on top of their blasters as Rennick was directed to sit across from Caldera.

"So," Eldra said, facing her, "you're Quill's...niece?"

"Yes," Caldera replied as all eyes turned to her. "Although, I didn't know it, or him," she added, her stomach quivering.

Eldra bowed her head. "That's a shame. He was a great man."

"Great. But foolish," Fenry said, her blue eyes narrowing.

"Fenry..." Eldra said, her voice on the edge of a warning.

"Quill's death didn't need to happen," Fenry continued, ignoring her.

Aloriea's carefree expression vanished, gaze glued to the tabletop. Caldera stiffened. "What makes you say that?"

"Isn't it obvious? He went against the Council—didn't do what they wanted," Fenry said, crossing her arms.

Eldra slammed her hand on the table. "Fenry! That's enough."

"Do you do everything the Council tells you?" Caldera muttered. Her nails dug into her palms as she clenched her hands under the table.

"Yes," Fenry replied definitively.

"And you're okay with that?" Caldera snapped, her gaze catching Rennick's worried eyes as she forced herself to stay in her seat.

"Of course we're not, but you're either on the Council's good side or...well." Fenry motioned toward Caldera. "Here we are."

Caldera shook her head, trying to keep her voice calm as rage continued to boil in her gut. "I won't be the Council's puppet—"

"Like it or not, we're all their puppets," Fenry interrupted, her voice suddenly low and controlled. Her eyes darted to the corners of the room. "You'd better come to terms with that right now." Her glare held Caldera's. "You are in no position to question us about our rule."

"Actually, that is why I'm here—to ask questions," Caldera countered, glancing at Aloriea. "The invitation we received stated that this was going to be a 'learning experience'. A chance to observe sector leaders that have been in power for a while," she concluded. "According to Councilmember Vandren, you offered for us to come here."

Eldra and Fenry exchanged confused glances.

"Dathan?" Fenry asked sharply.

He looked confused. "I have a copy of the invitation. It appeared legitimate."

"We're happy to host any sector leader at any time—but we sent no such invitation," Eldra said, her expression troubled.

The hairs on the back of Caldera's neck stood on end. "Then why am I here?"

"Callie!" Rennick yelled as he lunged across the table.

Caldera's ears rang as her back crashed against the hard stone floor, air ripped from her lungs. Screams rang through the hall as a blaster shot echoed off the walls. Rennick's body completely covered hers as she gasped for air through his clothes. "What's—" she choked out.

"Protect the queens!" Rennick yelled over his shoulder, his arms tightening around her.

"Get. Off. Me," Caldera muttered, forcing her throat to let the words out.

A crash sounded next to her ear.

Rennick lifted himself off her, shifting into a seated position. His back was against the now-overturned table, his blaster at the ready as Olivare rushed to his side.

"Thanks for the cover," Rennick said, blindly firing over the top of the table.

Olivare nodded as he aimed his blaster at the upper level of the room, triggering shots in quick succession.

Slowly, Caldera rolled onto her side, trying to ignore the

aching in her stomach as she crawled next to Rennick. She leaned against the table and looked around, her neck stiff. "Where's Aloriea?"

"She was closer to Queens Eldra and Fenry," Rennick said, quickly glancing over the top of the table. "Dathan got them out."

"Give me a blaster," Caldera commanded.

"There aren't any spares!" Olivare shouted. "Get her out of here," he growled. "I'm going after the would-be assassin."

"Wait!" Rennick protested, but Olivare was already around the table and running toward the far stairwell that led to the upper level. "Damn it," he muttered, turning toward her.

"What is it?" Caldera asked as her heart continued to pound. Sweat poured down her back.

"We don't know if there's more than one assailant," he said, outstretching his free hand toward her. "We're gonna be exposed, running out in the open with hardly any suppressing fire."

"Sounds familiar." She gripped his hand as tightly as she could.

"We're running toward that hallway," Rennick said, pointing to an opening behind her to the left. "Ready?"

Slipping off her heels, Caldera nodded. "Ready."

She pushed off the ground as hard as she could, forcing her body into an instant sprint. Unlike when they were running from the rock monster, Rennick wasn't holding back. The grip on her hand was vice-like as he dragged her along beside him while firing in the general direction of the unknown assailant.

Another shot echoed through the air as they reached the hallway. Stone blasted off the corner, showering them in dust as they passed it. They ran through the curved hallways of the unfamiliar palace, not slowing their pace until they reached an alcove. Turning into it, Rennick pressed Caldera against the wall and held her behind him while he peeked around the corner, his body completely blocking her view.

"Okay, I think we're safe for now," he said. His chest quickly rose and fell as he took short, shallow gasps.

Caldera took a deep breath and glanced out the small window next to her. The ocean breeze still rustled the green grass, and an animal she didn't recognize through the dying light of the setting sun flipped in and out of the water in the distance as if nothing had happened. "How did you know…" she whispered, clenching her shaking hands together. Dust fell from her hair. "How did you know I was about to be shot?"

Rennick shook the debris out of his hair and holstered his blaster. "I saw the dot of the laser sight," he replied, swallowing hard.

"You could have been killed."

"But you'd be alive," he replied with a shaky smile.

Tears welled in her eyes as she threw herself against him, wrapping her arms around his body. "You idiot!" she cried into his shirt as his arms closed around her. Warmth cascaded through her body as the faint smell of mint hit her nose. She inhaled deeply, then wiped her eyes and pressed her cheek against his chest.

Fast footfalls echoed through the hallway.

Rennick jumped back and instantly drew his blaster, blocking her with his body again. He aimed at the opening of the alcove.

"Where'd they go?" a familiar voice asked.

"Sweep the palace," another replied. "We have to find them now that it's safe."

"Olivare? Dathan?" Rennick called, lowering his weapon.

The two barreled around the corner, lowering their blasters as they did so. "You're all right!" Dathan exclaimed, his green eyes shining as he stared over Rennick's shoulder at Caldera.

She nodded, stepping out from behind Rennick. "Are Aloriea and the queens okay?"

Dathan nodded emphatically. "Olivare found the assailant, so the queens and Lady Morin are waiting back in the great hall." He paused. "It may not be my place to say but, considering the circumstances, you might want to cut your trip short and return home."

"That's absolutely what we're doing," Caldera agreed, "but first I want to question the assassin."

Dathan's gaze fell to the floor.

"He's dead," Olivare cut in, blinking down at her. "I killed him."

"What!" Caldera and Rennick exclaimed together.

"There needed to be an interrogation," Rennick snapped, taking a step toward Olivare. "Now we won't know who orchestrated this."

Caldera put a hand on Rennick's arm, never breaking eye contact with Olivare. "You had no right to do that."

"What's done is done," Olivare said with a shrug. "The only thing you need to know is that they were natare—it seems like someone from this sector wanted you dead," he added over his shoulder as he walked away.

Dathan motioned them out of the alcove, shooting a sideways glare at Olivare's back. "Follow me."

They hurried down the hallway, past the chunk taken out of the wall by the blaster shot, and returned to the great hall. Eldra, Fenry, and Aloriea were huddled together, talking in hushed whispers around the righted table, the top of which was pitted with blaster craters.

Aloriea's eyes lit up when she saw Caldera. "Thank the universe," she said, her voice quavering. She took an awkward step toward Caldera before stopping short and wrapping her arms around herself.

Caldera smiled softly before joining the small circle.

"This situation is regrettable," Fenry shook her head, which caused her white hair to swish against her ankles.

"I'm glad to see you're unharmed," Eldra said. "But you must leave as soon as possible."

"Gladly," Caldera agreed, "but before we do, do either of you know anything about what happened?"

Fenry's dark blue eyes shot over to Caldera. "You'd better not be suggesting that we had anything to do with this."

"Of course not! It's just... One of my guards killed the assailant," she said, glancing at Olivare. "So we can't question him."

Fenry tilted her head, locks of hair falling across one of her eyes. "We know nothing other than someone wants you dead. You must leave before you continue to endanger our lives." She looked lovingly over at Eldra, the only emotion besides irritation she'd shown all evening. "Now please go."

"You got it." Caldera gave them a quick nod before heading toward the door, followed by Rennick, Aloriea, and Olivare.

"The shuttle should be ready in a few minutes," Olivare said once they were outside.

Aloriea sighed. "Good. I need to lie down."

Caldera slowed her progression, letting Olivare and Aloriea gain distance on her. The chill of the steps bit into the soles of her feet, reminding her that her shoes were still somewhere in the great hall.

As she stood there, the sun set over the ocean, causing a lilac and teal glow to settle over the land. She sighed, glancing down at her bare feet, then over to the gravel-covered ground that led to the shuttle.

"Want me to carry you?" Rennick offered, outstretching his hand, a smile breaking across his tired face.

Caldera's lips quirked up. "I won't say no to that." She placed her hand in his, her fingertips resting against his palm. Their eyes met and she never wanted to look away.

A voice called from behind them, "I'm glad I caught you."

Caldera sighed, let go of Rennick, and turned around to see Eldra shuffling toward her. She held a small holodeck in one hand and Caldera's black heels in the other.

"Your shoes," Eldra said, handing them to Caldera. "And..." She paused, her grip tightening around the holodeck before holding it out in front of her.

"What is it?" Caldera asked as she reluctantly slipped on the heels and took the black box.

"Councilmember Randis has our great hall monitored,"

Eldra whispered, lacing her fingers together. "All our meetings are recorded and sent to him for review."

Caldera blanched. "Is that why Queen Fenry basically denounced Quill earlier?"

Eldra nodded, meeting Caldera's eyes. "She's only trying to protect us. That's a copy of the recording from this evening," she said, pointing at the holodeck. "We can't go against the Council. But if you need us, we'll try to help in any way we can."

"Thank you," Caldera whispered, unable to say anything else as Eldra hurried back inside.

"Hopefully this'll give us some answers," Rennick said, nudging Caldera's arm. "Now let's get out of here."

Caldera nodded, closed her hand around the holodeck, and followed Rennick to the shuttle, a fire ignited inside her chest.

CHAPTER 12

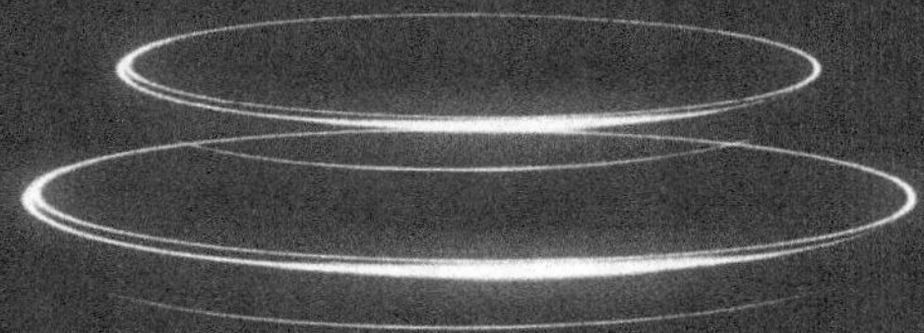

aldera sat at the foot of her bed with her knees pulled up to her chest while Rennick, Aloriea, Sear, and Markarian stared at her in silence, waiting. A warm afternoon breeze from the open balcony doors blew through the golden silk curtains as she gripped the holodeck from Queen Eldra. Taking a deep breath, she lowered her legs, pressing her booted feet firmly against the floor.

"I honestly do not want to watch this," Sear said from his seat by the fireplace, lacing his fingers together as his ears twitched back and forth.

Markarian nodded, his green eyes clouding as he adjusted his flight jacket. "I still can't believe you were almost …" he let his sentence trail off with a huff.

"You don't have to," Caldera replied as she attached the holodeck to her holopad. "Although I'd appreciate it. If we do find something, it'd be nice to have a purely logical eye looking over the facts," she added with a smirk.

Sear grinned, a sharp canine tooth poking out from under his lip. "You just want me here to hack into the cameras in the great hall." His fur bristled around the elbows of the rolled sleeves of his button-up shirt. "If your speculations are correct and there are indeed cameras there at all."

"And for company," Rennick added with a chuckle, leaning against the bedpost closest to Caldera. His faux leather jacket stretched across his shoulders as he crossed his arms.

Aloriea brushed her hands against her slacks as she walked over to the table next to Sear, placing her hands on her hips. "Let's just watch it already."

Glancing at each of her friends, she lifted the image off the holopad to float in front of them, then pressed play. The events of the previous day unfolded just as she remembered them. The heated conversation between her and Queen Fenry, the look of confusion from both the queens about the mysterious itinerary, Rennick tackling her to the ground, and the blaster shot.

"Who's this?" Markarian paused the video and pointed to the foot of the table.

"Olivare," Caldera replied. "He's a new member of palace security."

"You didn't see him when you came in?" Rennick asked.

"No, Sol and Saro were the only ones there to greet us," Sear said.

Markarian pulled his hair into a loose bun. "Well, something's off about him."

"What are you talking about?"

"Look," Markarian said, glancing from Rennick to Caldera, his eyes bright. "There's literally something off about his stance. Rewind the video."

Caldera complied, glancing over at Rennick, who shrugged.

"There. Dathan is looking straight ahead like Olivare should be doing—but he's not," Markarian said. "Zoom in. See? His body's turned."

Caldera held up a closed fist to the image and opened her hand to zoom the image in. Her eyes widened. "Analyze line of sight," she commanded the holopad. An overlay of blue dotted lines appeared, showing the direction of everyone's eyesight in the frame.

"He's looking in the exact direction that the blast came from before it went off!" Aloriea gasped, covering her mouth with her hand. Her hair rustled around her horns as she took a step back.

Sear pushed himself out of his chair and walked over to the hovering image. "The only logical conclusion would be that he saw something," he said. As he continued to examine the dotted lines, the black slits of his pupils expanded until the gold of his irises were small rings.

Caldera's heart throbbed in her ears, drowning out the frantic conversation of her friends. Rennick and Markarian pointed at the image, their lips moving too fast for her to comprehend what they were saying, while Sear and Aloriea nodded emphatically. Her throat burned as she tried to swallow the bile that rose from her stomach.

"We were right... This was all a setup," she whispered, standing and placing the holopad on the bed. She walked toward the door.

"Callie, where are you going?" Rennick asked, grabbing her arm.

She blinked over his shoulder at the wide eyes of her friends. "I'm going to go talk to Olivare."

Markarian shook his head. "That isn't a good idea."

"I agree," Sear and Aloriea said at the same time.

Rennick released her arm. "Let's think about this for a minute. What if he's involved?"

"Why would he be involved? He just got here," Caldera snapped. Rennick took a step back, his brows furrowed, and she attempted to regain her composure. "I need to talk to him to figure out what he saw. It could help us," she added, meeting Rennick's eyes. "It's not like we asked him anything in the moment—we were too frustrated that he killed the assailant."

"You figure he could help us?" he asked, tilting his head to the side.

She nodded. "Maybe he'll give us some concrete evidence that we can use to—to ..." she looked over at Aloriea. "I don't know, arrest someone—the perpetrator who orchestrated it? Where's Justle? He'd know, legally, what to do."

Aloriea bit her nail. "I don't know. I haven't seen him since we've been back."

Caldera took a deep breath. "Well, that's still the plan."

"We'll come with you," Markarian offered, taking a step forward.

"No," Caldera said, her voice stern. "You, Aloriea, and Sear head down to the great hall and see what you can find out about the cameras. Ren and I will head over to Olivare's quarters. Meet back here as soon as you can."

They followed her into the hallway and split up.

Caldera waited until her friends were around the corner before she stormed down the hallway in the opposite direction, her boots clunking against the floor.

"All right, have you figured out what you're gonna say to him specifically?" Rennick asked, hurrying to keep up.

She reluctantly slowed her pace. "I'll just ask him what he remembers about the assailant," she said as they rounded another corner to the block of rooms meant for the palace guard. They passed two doors with Sol and Saro's names beside them.

He nodded. "Maybe he just needs someone to jog his memory."

"Exactly," she said, smirking.

Rennick winked. "Happy to be of assistance, *Your Majesty*."

Caldera came to a stop in front of Olivare's door. She raised her hand to knock, but paused as light filtered out through the open crack of the doorway and voices met her ears. Something pulled at the back of her mind, and she pressed her ear as close as she dared, motioning for Rennick to do the same.

"We were close," Olivare was saying.

An indistinct voice replied to him from the other end of a communicator.

A crash sounded throughout Olivare's quarters as if he had thrown something, causing Caldera to jump. Her heart leapt in her chest.

"Damn it, Vandren! It's not my fault the bitch won't die!" Olivare roared as another crash sounded from inside. "If you couldn't kill her with that bogus mission while she was still a captain of the Vanguard, what makes you think I can do anything—especially since she has a 'bodyguard' now."

Caldera's hands shot up to cover her mouth. She clenched her jaw shut, forcing herself to keep quiet as Olivare continued his rampage. Hot, frustrated tears pricked her eyes. She looked across the doorway at Rennick, his eyes wide and jaw slack as his gaze met hers.

"As far as I know, the attorney's as good as dead," Olivare continued, his voice so low Caldera could barely hear him. "But I haven't had a chance to go through his things yet..."

They sprinted back down the hall, away from Olivare's quarters, their footfalls echoing in her ears.

Vandren was trying to kill us—me—with that mission, before they had to announce that Quill had an heir.

The attorney's as good as dead.

The thoughts raced through her mind as she ran.

Justle...

She ran down the hallway past her own quarters to the main stairwell, down a flight, and around a corner to Justle's room.

"Justle!" she yelled, banging on the door. "Justle!"

No one answered.

"Callie..." Rennick gasped, breathless from their mad dash. "We can't get in." His eyes fell on the locked scanner pad next to the door.

He could be hurt in there! She took a step back and surveyed the area, forcing herself not to hyperventilate. "There's gotta be a way in..."

After a few seconds, her eyes fell on a large picture window a few feet down the hallway.

Rennick followed her gaze and immediately shook his head. "Callie, no—no way. We need to get help!"

"No time," she replied as she ran over to the window and peered out. *Perfect, a ledge.* "Are you with me or not?" she asked over her shoulder, trying to pry the window open.

"Damn it..." Rennick muttered. He walked up behind her and unholstered his blaster, aiming it at the window. "Move."

"What're you doing?" she snapped, pushing his arm toward the floor.

"These windows don't open."

Caldera tapped her chin thoughtfully. "All right, how much time will we have before Sol and Saro are alerted?"

"If they don't hear the blast in the first place? It depends on how often they check their holopads for any inconsistencies throughout the palace. And if they have every single point of entry monitored. If they do, we'll be caught immediately."

"Can I really be reprimanded for breaking into my own palace?" Caldera quipped.

"That's a question for Aloriea or Justle." Rennick re-aimed at the window. "Are you sure you want to do this?"

She nodded, taking a step back. "You heard what Olivare said."

The blaster shot was quick and loud, combined with the noise of the window shattering. The pieces clattered onto the floor and out the window into the garden below. Caldera walked up to the new, gaping hole in the palace.

"Give me your jacket," she said, reaching her hand out. "I need to break the glass out completely."

Rennick took it off and handed it to her.

Wrapping it around her hand, she broke out the rest of the glass as Rennick glanced anxiously down both sides of the hallway.

"Okay, let's go," she said, shaking out the jacket, which sent tiny pieces of glass shimmering through the air, before handing it back to him.

Stepping up to the windowsill, Rennick stuck his head out of the newly formed hole before ducking back inside. "Why don't you go first?" he offered as his chest began to rise in fall rapidly.

"Ren, you don't have to come."

"I'm not letting you go in alone."

She smiled. "Don't worry, we'll be back inside in no time."

"Just a few hundred feet—no big deal..." he said with a sharp nod.

Caldera grabbed Rennick's hand for balance. She stepped out the window gingerly and climbed onto the ledge. Hair whipped around her face as she gazed down at the thirty-foot drop to the ground below. Her lips curled into a smile at the thrill that rushed through her body. She slid along the wall, wind constantly blowing through her clothes as she made her way to Justle's window. When she reached it, she turned her head to Rennick, who was pressed as close to the wall as possible, deliberately not looking down.

"Blaster please," she said. She held out her hand, careful not to lose her balance.

"No balcony?" he muttered, closing his eyes as he held the weapon out to her with a shaky hand.

Caldera grabbed the blaster out of his grip before it tumbled to the ground. "Nope."

She pointed it at the window and fired. Breaking away as much glass as possible with the barrel of her blaster, she crawled into the room, then quickly helped Rennick inside before taking in her new surroundings.

Rennick flinched as a stray piece of glass cut his hand.

"Are you okay?" Caldera asked.

"I'm fine. This is Justle's room?"

She turned around to see a prim, proper, bare-bones room— empty except for a bed, dresser, and desk.

Rennick pressed his hand against his pants to try and stop the bleeding. "Olivare said that he didn't go through Justle's things, right?"

"That's definitely what he said. But maybe *we* should—maybe we can find what he was going to be looking for—something in here that can help us find Justle." She took a deep breath as she opened the bottom right drawer of his desk. "I feel bad about this."

"Breaking into Justle's room and going through his private belongings?" Rennick asked sarcastically.

Caldera hung her head. "Yes. I mean, we heard what we heard but... I just hope Justle is okay... Wait. Look at this," she said as something caught her eye.

"What is it?" He knelt beside her.

She examined the inside of the drawer. "It's a number." A small number five was carefully carved on the inner wall, three inches from the opening, with a short line above it. She pulled open the other three drawers. "There are numbers in all of them," she confirmed.

Rennick's eyes gleamed. "It's gotta be a code of some kind."

"These numbers... They're familiar."

"Are they?" he asked, examining the drawers himself. "Top right is six, bottom right four, top left seven, and bottom left five," he said. "If you rearrange the sequence..."

" It's our Vanguard ship number," Caldera said, finishing his thought. A shiver ran down her spine.

"That could be a coincidence." Rennick stood up and began to pace. "Why would the 'code' have anything to do with us—or you, more specifically?"

"I don't know. Let's line up the drawers in order and see what happens."

"It's worth a shot."

Taking a deep breath and trying to clear her head, Caldera pulled the drawers out until the edge of the desk lined up with the line above each carved number, in order of their ship's identification. When she finished, they heard a soft click.

"Holy shit," Caldera and Rennick whispered at the same time, their eyes searching for the hidden compartment.

She felt around until her fingers found a break just above where a person's knees would be if they were sitting at the desk.

"Here," she said as she worked her fingers into the cracks, then pulled down and out.

The drawer didn't resist.

They looked inside, their heads almost touching, and found an unlabeled envelope and a holopad.

"This is what Olivare was going to look for," Caldera said, grabbing the contents. "What do you think they say?"

"Only one way to find out. We should get out of here first, though."

Caldera nodded, just as the holopad cast their faces with blue light.

"Did it turn itself on?" Rennick asked, alarmed.

"No, I must've done it accidentally. There wasn't a lock on it. Damn it!"

The floating image of Quill's face appeared before them.

"It's a video message," Rennick breathed.

She nodded, mesmerized. With trembling fingers, she pushed the play button.

"Hello. Hopefully, I'm speaking to Caldera Keane—my niece—the rightful heir to the throne. I'm confident that the rail beam technology that I ordered Justle to give to you, despite his protests, has saved your life. It's the whole reason I'm making this."

"Quill and Justle knew about me the whole time?" she murmured.

"And about Vandren's plan to get rid of you..." Rennick added.

"First, I want to apologize to you. For dragging you into this life—I truly wish I could have let you live yours. Second, I'm going to clear up a few things regarding your circumstances. It's the least I can do," Quill continued, voice soft as his blue eyes stared into the screen. "Caldera, you're probably wondering how you didn't know about your heritage and why your parents didn't tell you."

"Yes," she said aloud as she gripped the holopad tighter, her heart pounding in her ears.

"Simply put, they didn't know about it themselves. I'm your father's brother, as I'm sure you know by now, but the age gap between us is quite—drastic." He paused, looking away from the camera as if summoning his courage. "When your father was born, it was back before the Council had complete control, but our parents—your grandparents—saw that was about to change, and they had their first child smuggled out of the palace."

Caldera paused the video and took a deep, heavy breath, her parents' faces flashing through her mind. "They didn't know..."

Rennick smiled softly. "You all right?"

She nodded, then resumed the video with a shaky finger.

"Fifteen years passed. The Council had completely taken over—and then, I was born. A mistake, by all accounts. My mother died having me, and my father couldn't smuggle out another child, let alone cover up their entire existence," Quill continued. "So here we are. I admit I didn't know any of this until right before my father died a few years ago."

His unwavering gaze burned into her own through the camera, and for the first time since the video started, tears stung her eyes. She bit her lip. *Why am I crying? I didn't even know this man.*

Quill cleared his throat and continued. "You must listen to me. The Council's planning something, and I can't let them go through with whatever it is without interference." His gaze was resolute. "They think I have no heir. This is the only advantage we have. Caldera, I've been keeping a close eye on you. You can clearly handle yourself, and I know Aloriea will help you—eventually."

It might have been her imagination, but through the sheen of tears, Caldera could have sworn that she saw a smirk appear across his lips.

"The letter is for Aloriea. Only she'll know how to read it," Quill said. "It contains the location of a secret room that my parents had built during the early years of their reign. The Council doesn't know about it, and you must keep it that way." He blinked, his eyes staring right at her, down to her very soul. "In it is everything that my parents and I have compiled about the past and present Councils' plans. I couldn't completely figure it out, but I got close. I'm sorry I can't tell you what I've found in case this message is compromised, but you will know it when you see it. I promise."

Caldera swallowed hard as the last minutes of the recording played, tears trailing down her face against her will.

"I know I don't have the right to ask such a thing, but my last request is this—find out what the Council is planning and stop them," Quill said with clear passion in his voice. "I'm counting on you all. And Caldera—I can't tell you much, but I will say this. The way to help Bersama—not just the people of Tellis, but everyone—does not lie in war, but in peace." He smiled softly. "And for what it's worth, I wish I could have known you, my brother... my family." He reached out as if trying to touch her face, and the screen went black.

As soon as the recording ended, it immediately began to erase on its own.

Caldera's vision blurred, the weight of the situation pressing against her chest. She dropped the holopad on the ground as if it suddenly weighed a hundred pounds, and a crunch hit her ears as the screen cracked. Burying her face in Rennick's chest, she balled her fists into his shirt as his hands rested on both her shoulders. Her chest heaved, and as she cried, his hand moved to the back of her neck, holding her close. Warmth spread through her body as she blinked up at him, the sobs subsiding.

"It'll be okay," he whispered, his breath caressing her skin and rustling the stray hairs around her forehead.

Releasing his shirt, she placed her palms flat against his chest. She inhaled softly, realizing how much she counted on his strength, and just how much she wanted to get lost in his embrace.

"We've gotta get out of here and show this letter to Aloriea," she said, wiping her eyes. "If what Quill recorded is true, then the fate of Tellis—of Bersama—might be depending on it.

CHAPTER 13

Caldera picked up the cracked holopad, then handed it and the note to Rennick. He tucked them both into his inside jacket pockets.

"Damn it," Rennick muttered, walking to the door. "We still can't unlock it."

"Back outside then," she replied, climbing stiffly through the broken window and across the ledge.

Her boots pounded against the floor as she crawled back into the hallway. When she looked up, her eyes met Olivare's.

"What the fuck are you two doing?" Olivare bellowed. He sprinted over to them and grabbed Caldera's wrists, jerking her forward before she could blink.

The hold was a death-grip. From the look on his face, Caldera knew he would have no problem hurting her—even killing her—if the order was given.

Her heart raced as she took a step back. "Where's Justle, you bastard?"

He didn't let go. "No idea."

"Stop," Rennick said, his voice harsh as he crawled through the window. "Let go of her. Now."

Olivare eyed him and cocked his head to the side, seeming to size him up. "Or?"

Rennick took a step closer, his face inches from Olivares. "I don't need to spell it out for someone like you."

"You may come to regret threatening me—*Sir Silvera*," he rasped.

Clenching her jaw, Caldera jerked her arms away. "That's enough. If you say you don't know where Justle is—fine. Just let me know when you run into him."

"Very well... Your Majesty," Olivare grumbled. "But you didn't answer my question. What were you doing?"

Caldera glanced over her shoulder at the gaping hole in the window and shrugged. "Getting some fresh air."

"They said you'd be trouble," he scoffed.

Olivare shouldered past Markarian, who was coming up the stairs with Sear and Aloriea right behind him.

"What the hell was that about?" Markarian asked, glaring at Olivare's back.

"Ren..." Caldera whispered, placing a hand on his arm, her heart still racing. "Are you okay?"

Rennick's expression softened. "Of course. It's just, he grabbed you and... I just don't want anything to happen to you, that's all," he continued, his eyes piercing into her, his affection undeniable.

Warmth flowed through Caldera's body, culminating in the apples of her cheeks. She didn't move, unable to look away, unwilling to break their connection.

"I suggest we head back to your quarters," Sear said, snapping Caldera out of her trance. His eyes flicked around the hallway. "It seems to me that we have both found something of interest."

Caldera nodded. "Let's go somewhere more private."

SHE USHERED HER friends back to her quarters and locked the door behind her.

"Okay..." she said, sitting at the foot of her bed and glancing over at Sear. "You go first ..."

Sear nodded. "All right, I suppose we can talk about what just happened later," he said, pulling out his holopad. "It turns out there are cameras in the great hall. My initial hack into them was successful—"

"But we didn't get very far," Aloriea interrupted, crossing her arms.

"It seems there is a wiretap on them," Sear said, narrowing his eyes. "It looks like one of the receivers is localized, though." He tapped the holopad. A schematic reading of the camera's internal system floated in front of them. "As you can see," Sear continued, pointing at the image, "the information that the cameras record is simultaneously transmitted to Councilmember Vandren and somewhere else."

Caldera looked around at the confused faces of her friends, knowing she was wearing the same expression.

Sear sighed. "It means that there is a receiver somewhere in this palace that is also connected to all the cameras."

"We have to find it. It could help us get a leg up on Vandren," Caldera said. "Where is it?"

He shrugged, collapsing the image. "I cannot tell. It is en-crypted. Whoever did it was remarkable with computer systems."

"I thought you were good at computers?" Markarian quipped.

"I dabble in many things," Sear said, his ears perking straight up. "That does not mean that I have mastered it all."

Markarian lifted his eyebrows, a mischievous grin spreading across his face. "So what are you a master at again?"

A low snarl sounded from Sear's throat.

"Here we go," Caldera muttered, rubbing her brow.

"Why are you antagonizing him?" Rennick asked Markarian.

"Boys—" Aloriea stepped between Sear and Markarian and

held up her hands. "Now is really not the time." She turned to Caldera. "It's your turn. What were you two doing climbing through that window?"

Caldera met Rennick's anxious gaze. "We…" She paused, biting her lip. "We broke into Justle's room."

Aloriea blinked. "You what?"

Caldera held up her hands. "Let me explain—"

"Explain what?" Aloriea snapped, redness flushing across her face. "That's completely unacceptable! He's—"

"He's missing, Aloriea," Rennick interjected. "That's what the altercation with Olivare was about."

"What…"

"We overheard him talking to Vandren about Justle," Caldera said, standing and taking a step toward her. "He said some things that led us to believe something was wrong," she added carefully.

Taking a deep breath, she explained what they had heard. How they were right that the Council had tried to kill her before she even knew about her royal heritage, what Olivare had said about Justle, and what they had found in Justle's room.

"This can't be happening," Aloriea gasped, letting Sear steer her to a chair.

"It's crazy," Markarian added, a deep wrinkle appearing across his forehead.

Sear reached his hand out to Rennick, his tail swishing against the floor. "Let me see that holopad."

"It's blank now," Caldera replied. "It erased itself after the message played."

"Still," Sear said, grabbing it out of Rennick's grasp. "We need to make sure there are no traces of anything left on it before it is disposed of—I will take care of that."

Aloriea looked up at Rennick, her eyes glassy. "Give me the note."

He obliged, pulling out the envelope and placing it in her shaking hands.

"You don't have to open it here if you don't want to," Caldera offered, staring at Aloriea who gripped the letter so tightly that her knuckles turned white.

She closed her eyes and inhaled sharply.

Caldera walked over to her. "Listen to me," she said, placing a tentative hand on Aloriea's shoulder. "No matter what, we're going to find out why the king was killed." She paused, meeting Aloriea's eyes. "I promise you—I swear to you—we will."

"Thank you, Callie."

Caldera smiled softly, glancing over at the door to her quarters to make sure it was still locked.

With another deep breath, Aloriea worked her thin fingers under the flap of the sealed envelope and tore it open. Unfolding the letter, her gaze clouded. "That's odd."

Aloriea silently handed the letter to Caldera.

"What is this? There's nothing here. Just a jumble of letters and numbers."

"I would like to examine it," Sear said, his fur bristling.

She passed the paper over to him with a shrug.

"You are, by all accounts, correct." He raised a bushy eyebrow. "There is no discernible dialogue in this note."

"It's called a skip cipher," Aloriea replied. She squeezed herself between them and gestured at the lines of random letters. "A way of secretly communicating." She plucked the note out of Sear's grip. "In this version, you start with the first letter and then count out to the eleventh letter, and so on and so on until you make a word," she said, pointing at the writing. "You keep doing that, starting over with the next letter in the sequence and counting out, until you decrypt the entire message."

Markarian peered over Caldera's shoulder. "I'm surprised I've never heard of anything like that. Working in the Vanguard, I mean."

"I don't want to say it's ancient," Aloriea said, taking a deep breath. "But its origins are unknown, and I'm sure it existed before the cataclysm."

"You can decode it, right?" Caldera pressed.

"Yes," Aloriea replied softly. "I'm a little ashamed to say that it was our main way of communicating throughout the palace."

"Why?" Caldera asked.

"This palace isn't exactly the safest place in the world," Aloriea replied patiently. "Researching secret codes was, I guess you could say, a hobby."

"We need to destroy this as soon as you're done with it," Markarian said firmly.

Rennick nodded. "I think we can all agree with that. How long will it take you to decrypt it?"

"It looks like it's only one or two sentences," Aloriea said, clearing her throat. "Maybe five minutes."

Caldera walked back to the edge of the bed and sat down heavily. Sear and Markarian milled around the room, anxiety plaguing their faces. As she looked out at the encroaching night, her mind raced, wandering and swirling. Clenching her hands into fists, she desperately wished Quill was still alive and that she and her friends were still simply members of the Vanguard, and not part of a royal death conspiracy.

"Hey," Rennick said, sitting next to her, jolting her out of her trance. "Are you okay?"

Caldera instinctively scooted closer to him. "As much as I can be, considering how fucked up this situation is."

"Yeah, this was not what I was expecting when I became a palace guard."

"Technically, you're my bodyguard."

"Everyone be quiet," Aloriea called from the table.

"We didn't say anything," Markarian said, nudging Sear, who shook his head and walked away.

"We'll get through this," Rennick murmured, a smile lighting up his face. "Of that, I have no doubt."

"Well, you've always been the optimist," Caldera replied, looking into his eyes, doubts forgotten, and stomach fluttering. "One of the things I like most about you."

"Done!" Aloriea announced, standing and turning to face them.

They all gathered around her.

Aloriea bit her nail. "It's not exactly giving us the answers we need."

"Tell us what it says," Caldera pressed, setting her jaw.

"Quill only gave me half of the information—half the coordinates to this 'secret room' he mentioned in his video message."

Rennick sighed. "Okay, then, who has the other half?"

Aloriea looked up, her eyes cloudy. "According to this... Justle."

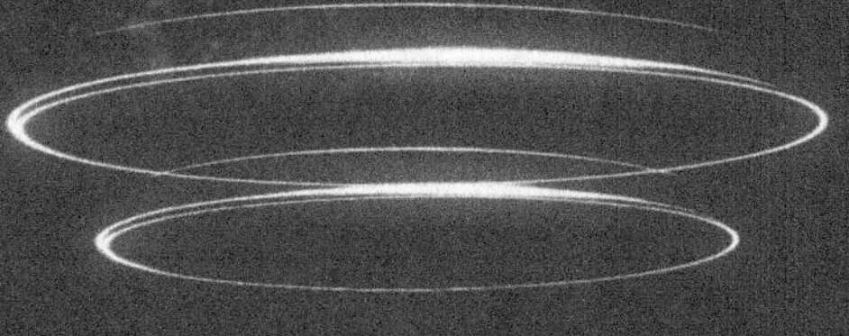

CHAPTER 14

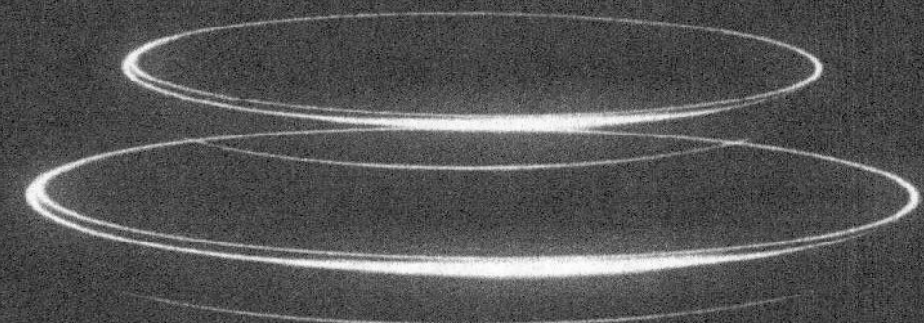

D amn it!" Caldera shouted, punching her fist into her palm.

Rennick took a tentative step toward her. "Callie, just take a breath."

She whirled around, glaring at him as heat rushed to her face. "Ren, don't start with me!"

"I agree," Markarian said. "I think you're overreacting."

"How?" Caldera said, lowering her voice as her gaze caught Aloriea's distraught expression. "Justle is gone."

Sear tapped his chin. "We have half of the coordinates. That is why."

Her anger waned as she relaxed her fingers, letting rationality take over. "Right..." she muttered. "That's something... What are they?"

"Thirty-seven degrees north by thirty-eight feet south," Aloriea read, handing the translated note to Caldera.

Markarian snatched the note out of her hands before she could look at it, skimming the paper himself. "Then that's where we'll start, I'm sure we can somehow figure the rest out—"

"Unfortunately, we have to hold off," Aloriea interrupted, nervously chewing her nail. She took the piece of paper back and slipped it into her pants pocket.

They all turned to her, their faces masked with confusion.

"Why?" Caldera asked, trying, and failing, to not let her frustration show.

Aloriea averted her gaze, a look of discomfort flashing across her face. "The Summit Conference is tomorrow evening, and I need to prepare you. With everything going on, it slipped my mind. It was already on Quill's schedule, so I didn't give it a second thought—"

"What the hell is a Summit Conference?" Caldera interjected, her stomach dropping to the floor.

Rennick, Sear, and Markarian shrugged. Sear looked particularly irritated that he didn't have the answer.

"You wouldn't know about it," Aloriea replied quickly. "It's not something that's advertised to the public."

Sear and Markarian exchanged glances as a tense silence set in. Aloriea tapped her fingers against her arm, clearly unwilling to say more.

"Very well," Sear said with a nod. "We shall take our leave." He walked toward the door, the bottoms of his exposed paw-like feet padding across the marble floor.

"Yeah, that's definitely our cue to go," Markarian agreed, following him.

"Wha—why are you leaving?" Caldera asked. "You're both a part of this. Plus, we'll still need help figuring out the coordinates."

"We will come back tomorrow after the conference," Sear said with a wave of his hand as his tail swished behind him. "Like I said before, political affairs bore me."

"And I have to be at Vanguard Headquarters early tomorrow anyway. Captain and crew evaluation," Markarian added. "It'd be preferable for me not to pull an all-nighter the day before... again." He chuckled. "Call us after 'the event'."

Caldera sighed heavily as the door to her quarters whisked shut. "They deserve to know—"

"They aren't part of the royal court, and as such, they aren't entitled to this information," Aloriea stated plainly.

"They could help—"

"No."

Caldera closed her eyes, tilting her head toward the ceiling. *Breathe in... Breathe out...*

"Callie."

Rennick's voice was there beside her, cutting through her irritation.

"Sear and Markarian understand. Let's just hear what Aloriea has to say."

"Fine..." she muttered. She opened her eyes and rubbed her forehead, trying to push the mystery of the coordinates and the unjust treatment of her friends out of her mind. "Let's try this again—what's the Summit Conference?"

Aloriea retook her seat at the round table by the fireplace, setting her holopad in the middle of it. Motioning for Caldera and Rennick to sit across from her, she pressed a finger on the holopad's center. It sprang to life, casting a blue glow across their faces.

"It's the way government funding is distributed to organizations throughout Tellis. There are ten organizations attending this yearly cycle."

As she spoke, a list popped up from the holopad screen, floating in the air between them.

Rennick squinted up at the names. "Vanguard, Militia, Tellin Transports, the Tellin School Systems and Universities..." He paused, his gaze lingering on the last name. "These aren't just any organizations. They're major—they make up the foundation of Sector One—of Tellis."

Caldera's heart thudded in chest as her eyes fell on the fifth name listed. The Tellin SWS—Social Welfare System.

The image of the homeless person she met when Sol and Saro brought her to the palace invaded her mind—their emaciated body, the fear in their eyes.

I could help.

"Exactly," Aloriea was saying, snapping Caldera out of her memory. "That's why this conference is so important," she said, turning to Caldera.

"How does it work?"

"A representative from each organization, and their families, come here and 'socialize'."

"Like a ball?"

Aloriea shook her head, hair tangling in her horns. "Absolutely not. It's more like a glorified business meeting." She paused. "With cocktails...and hors d'oeuvres." She tapped her chin. "No dancing that I can remember, though."

Caldera massaged her temples. "So what do I have to do?"

"Listen to their pitches."

"What are they pitching?" Rennick asked.

"That depends on the organization. The militia will probably request an increased budget for weaponry, the TSSU will most likely want increased funding for updated holotexts." She shrugged. "It really does depend on who you're talking to. It's paramount that you pay attention."

Caldera massaged the base of her neck. "What do I do with their 'pitches' afterward?"

Aloriea looked away. "You'll take the requests that you want to fund to Councilmember Vandren for review." She took a deep breath. "You can only grant the requests of two organizations this yearly cycle—"

"Out of ten?"

Aloriea nodded reluctantly.

"Vandren's orders I take it?"

She gave her another nod.

"How can I..." Caldera let her sentence trail off, her mind racing. "Have all the organizations ever been funded at the same time?"

Aloriea's mouth pinched. "Not that I'm aware."

That was why people hated Quill—one of the reasons, anyway. But unbeknownst to the citizens, he hadn't been allowed to fund every organization.

How many of the things he'd been hated for were actually his fault?

And now it's my turn. The people are going to hate me, if they don't already.

"Callie?" Rennick nudged her arm.

She swallowed hard. "Aloriea, when are the representatives getting here?"

"Five o'clock tomorrow afternoon."

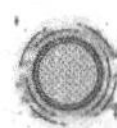

"I CAN'T BELIEVE I'm late!" Caldera huffed as she ran down the hallway to the great hall where the Summit Conference was already underway.

"I can," Rennick said, keeping pace beside her. "It took you over an hour to pick an outfit."

"Aloriea gave me too many choices!"

Her short black heels clicked on the floor as they turned the corner, her hair flying out behind her. As they passed windows, the scenery from outside blurred in her peripheral vision. The black-to-gold ombre dress she wore let her move freely and she was glad she had chosen one that only went down to her knees and not the floor.

"Well, you look very nice," Rennick told her as they slowed their progression. Caldera smiled, smoothing the wrinkles out of her dress and straightening the off-shoulder straps. "Thanks, you too. Have I ever told you that the palace guard uniform...umm... suits you."

"Shut it," he said as he adjusted his jacket and tie. He playfully nudged her shoulder. "Ready?"

Caldera smoothed her flyaway hairs, nodded, and stepped into the open room.

The great hall was bustling with life for the first time since

Caldera arrived at the palace. Two huge crystal chandeliers overhead gleamed with bright light that was supposed to mimic the sun, making the gold inlays of the stone walls shine and glimmer like a gilded ocean. The silk drapes normally covering the windows were thrown open, letting in the light of the rising moons.

Palace staff were bustling around with silver trays of hors d'oeuvres and champagne flutes. All wore either black blazers and slacks or plain black dresses with the Tellin planetary emblem embroidered on the right breast.

"Who organized all of this?" Caldera whispered as she stepped into full view of the guests and patrons.

"Quill," Aloriea answered, walking up to them in a powder-pink, strapless sheath dress, champagne flute in hand. The bottom of her gown haloed the floor. "Nice of you two to join us."

"Not Vandren?" Rennick asked. His wide eyes mimicked Caldera's own amazement at the sheer scale of it all.

"No. I suspect he wouldn't care if the Summit Conference happened at all. Scheduling it is the job of the sector leader. Luckily you didn't have to do anything this year," she said, tilting her head toward Caldera as she tapped the glass of the flute against the tip of her horn. "Nice outfit. I'm honestly surprised."

"I never get to dress up," Caldera said with a wink. "So what do I do now?"

"Mingle. Come on, I'll introduce you to some of the representatives." Aloriea linked her arm to Caldera's. She glanced over her shoulder. "You stay behind us and pretend you're not there."

"Sure." Rennick clasped his hands behind his back and followed them as they meandered through the crowd.

Caldera's ears rang. The lights were too bright. The people were too loud. Children were running around, screaming and laughing. Most of the adults—the reps and their partners—hadn't even noticed she was there, and the ones who did seemed unsure of approaching her. She had no idea who was who, or what organization they represented. She was lost.

Sensory overload was taking over.

Gripping Aloriea's arm as tightly as she could, she glanced behind her and met Rennick's eyes. He gave her a small, reassuring smile.

I can do this. I can do this. I can—

"Ouch," Aloriea said, smacking Caldera's hand. "You're digging your nails into my skin."

"Sorry."

"I'll be right there with you the whole time. You know what to do—"

"No, I really don't."

Aloriea sighed and slowed her pace, bringing them to a halt. "You were a captain, right? You must have made speeches to your crew before. Just pretend you're doing that."

"That's different."

"No, it's not. You presumably ordered people around, listened to them, tried to help? It's the same principle here."

Caldera shook her head, taking Aloriea's arm and pulling her to the side of the room. "You don't understand. I earned my captaincy—that position wasn't given to me. These people..." She paused, taking a deep breath. "They don't respect me."

Aloriea glanced around the bustling room. "You're right, respect and reputation are earned—but it's not impossible to achieve. Do you think it was easy for me, an akar—or Sear, a matan—to come into Sector One and gain people's trust?"

Caldera didn't respond. She rubbed a hand up and down her arm and wished she could fade into the background.

"No, but we did it because we proved we knew how to get the job done."

"That's the problem. I don't know."

"True—but you have me, and friends that support you. We'll help you through it." Aloriea smiled. "So if these people don't respect you...make them."

Caldera grinned. "I... Yeah, I could do that."

"Good. Then let's start with a rep you might actually recognize."

Aloriea turned to a person beside her who was wearing a dark green button-up with the sleeves rolled up to the elbows, and black slacks. She tapped them on the shoulder.

"Mx. Auris," Aloriea said as they turned. "This is Her Majesty Queen Caldera Keane."

They had a smooth, tawny complexion, and wore an unwavering smile. "It's a pleasure to meet you, Your Majesty. I'm Deimi Auris, the representative for the Vanguard." They bowed, silky blond hair falling over their shoulders as they did so.

They look familiar... That name sounds familiar too, Caldera thought, beginning to bow as well. She stopped when Aloriea elbowed her in the side.

Caldera flinched and straightened up, extending her arm. "It's nice to meet you."

"Likewise," Deimi replied in a melodic tone, taking Caldera's outstretched hand.

"Umm—I..." Heat rushed to Caldera's cheeks as she struggled to form a single sentence. She didn't have to see herself in a mirror to know her face was beet red.

"It's all right, Your Majesty," they said, seeming to take pity on her. "I want you to know, I harbor no ill-will regarding your succession." They paused to replace their empty champagne flute with a full one from the tray of a passing server. "The opposite, in fact. You were one of my captains were you not? It's quite amazing."

"Oh—thank you," Caldera said. She followed suit and quickly grabbed a drink, happy to finally have something to do with her hands. "Wait, did you say one of your captains?" *I knew I recognized that name!* "You're actually the head of the Vanguard?"

"I am." Deimi chuckled, taking a sip from their glass. "Not all the representatives here are heads of their respective organizations, but I like to make a point of personally showing up to events like this."

"I can't believe I'm actually meeting you. The Vanguard... It means a lot to me."

"It meant a lot to Quill too, rest his soul," Deimi replied softly, placing a hand over their heart. "Though now I'm not sure if it was genuine interest or to keep an eye on you." They laughed as if remembering a past, heartwarming conversation.

"Well," Caldera said, gaining confidence. "I don't want to discredit my late uncle, but my interest is certainly genuine."

An amiable expression settled on Deimi's face. "Well then, why don't I tell you why I'm here."

Caldera nodded excitedly as she glanced over at Aloriea, who was looking at her with what seemed to be pride.

"Now, from your speech, I know that the Vanguard is being further defunded—" Deimi began, suddenly all business.

Shit. I completely forgot about that.

"—but it seems like you'll be trying your best to put the necessary funds back into it as soon as possible."

"Yes, absolutely."

"Good. Then when the time comes—and if we can possibly get your sign-off after tonight—consider allocating a certain amount to the redesign of the geocode coordinate systems."

Caldera inhaled sharply. *The coordinate system...* "Umm, is there something wrong with it?"

Deimi shook their head. "No, but Quill seemed to be particularly interested in creating a coordinate system where, even if you only have half of the coordinates, you can still be led directly to your destination."

Caldera's ears were ringing again. *Justle. Aloriea. Coordinates. He was anticipating that something would go wrong...for someone to disappear.* She glanced from Aloriea to Rennick who stood beside her, mouths agape.

"I just wanted to follow up on his wishes," Deimi continued, looking uncomfortable. "Of course, feel free to accept or reject it as you see fit—there really is nothing wrong with our coordinate system as is."

They turned to walk away, to mingle with other guests, to let *Her Majesty* move on to the next 'pitch.'

"Wait," Caldera blurted, catching their arm.

Deimi looked down at the sudden grip, not completely hiding their shock.

"I'm sorry," Caldera said, releasing them immediately. "I just... Is it even possible to find a destination without both parts of the coordinate?"

"Of course it is. It would take some time, though."

"How?" Caldera pressed. "How can we—I mean, how can anyone get to where the other half is?"

"I suppose it's not something that you would regularly think about, even being a former captain—"

"I trust my equipment. Malfunctions don't happen." Her mind flashed to the RB. "Not very often."

Deimi sighed. "It's in the very structure of the coordinate system itself. For example, if you have the east to west half, the other half is somewhere in that surrounding area. Hence, it will take some time to find the destination, but it's not impossible."

Another piece of the puzzle clicked into place.

"Thank you! Thank you so much!" She grabbed Deimi's hand and shook it before turning on her heel to make her way through throngs of people to the archway of the great hall.

"Callie—" Aloriea said, gripping her shoulder and turning her around just short of the exit. "Where are you going?"

"To find where the other half of the coordinates lead—"

"You can't leave. You still need to talk to the other representatives."

"But—"

"If you leave, it'll get back to Vandren," Aloriea hissed in her ear.

"She's right, Cal," Rennick added, scanning the room. "Even if the reps don't say anything, Olivare is standing watch at the entrance, and he will."

Caldera wrapped her arms around herself, looking around at well over fifty people populating the great hall. Representatives from Tellis' most crucial organizations were all biding their time until they could talk to her—to try and convince her to fund them.

"That aside, these people deserve to have me listen to them," she said, resignation taking over.

"Exactly," Aloriea agreed with a nod.

"Ren, will you let Sear and Markarian know to get here in about three hours? And tell Markarian to bring his geocode device."

"Sure thing," he replied, pulling his communicator out of his jacket pocket.

"All right," Caldera said, turning to Aloriea. "Introduce me to the next rep."

CHAPTER 15

"Ten organizations. Ten representatives. Ten pitches." Caldera groaned as the doors to the palace closed behind the last guest. "My head hurts."

"Everyone has checked out," Sol said, handing Caldera his holopad for review.

Caldera scanned her hand without looking at the list. "Thank you," she replied, handing it back to him.

"Are we dismissed?" Olivare huffed, his gray eyes flat.

"You are."

"Thank you, have a restful night," Saro replied as he, Sol, and Olivare strolled past them.

"Well?" Aloriea asked, turning to face Caldera after the three guards disappeared around the corner. "Which two organizations are you going to request funding for?"

"Didn't I just say my head hurts?"

"Vandren is about to be on the holoscreen in the conference room."

Caldera glanced at Rennick, who looked just as tired as she

felt. The great hall was eerily empty, and light from the moons shone in through the windows uninhibited.

"I think I'm going to request allocation for the Tellin SWS—"

"Good choice," Aloriea said, nodding her approval. "What else? The TERA? Maybe the TCJS?"

"The Environmental Restoration Agency, and Court and Justice Systems both made compelling arguments." She took a deep breath. "But I think I'm going with the TSSU."

Rennick stopped mid-yawn. "The school systems?"

"Yeah, they want funding for updated holotexts, like Aloriea said, but also for building new campuses for the universities." She smiled up at Rennick. "They want to be able to admit more students as well as keep them comfortable."

"Callie…"

"Plus, if they can admit more students, the cost of tuition will go down," she continued, beaming.

Without a word, he took a step forward, pulling her into a hug.

Caldera stood there, unable to move. Her arms were stuck at her sides and her heart raced in her ears. The sudden, unprompted intimacy sent shockwaves throughout her body.

"Thank you," he whispered. "You didn't have to do that. But I'm glad you did." He took a step back, flashing a smile. "You've helped my brother and I out so much."

"No problem," Caldera mumbled. "It's for everyone that has the dream of attending university but can't afford it. I want to help them, too."

He beamed. "I'd expect nothing less from you."

"We need to get going," Aloriea interjected. She ushered them out of the great hall, down the hallway, and into the conference room.

Taking a deep breath, Caldera pushed through the door, coming face to face with Vandren's image on the holoscreen.

"Your Majesty," Vandren said as Aloriea and Rennick shuffled in behind her.

Caldera bowed her head. "Good evening."

"What are your choices for this yearly cycle of funding?"

Skipping the small talk, I see. "I've decided to fund the Tellin Social Welfare Services and the Tellin School Systems and Universities. They've requested—"

"Hmm... Interesting choices. Not what I expected of you," Vandren interrupted, scratching his beard. He turned his attention back to her. Their eyes met through the screen. "I'm sorry, but I regret that I must decline your requests."

Caldera blinked, unsure if she had heard him right. It was as if someone had sucked all the air out of the room. She looked behind her for support. Aloriea's gaze was firmly glued to the ground, while Rennick's was hurt.

Her blood began to boil.

"What?"

"Fine choices, yes, but I've been reviewing the military operations of the other sectors and have ascertained that our militia needs allocation the most."

"All the organizations need allocation, but the ones I've picked have been ignored for too long! Have you been to Astrum lately?" Her voice was rising. She couldn't help it. "You can't walk down the street without seeing a homeless person! The schools are dilapidated, and the texts are so outdated it's almost impossible to learn anything at all!" She took a step toward the screen. "I can say confidently that the organizations I've picked need funds just as badly as—"

"Queen Caldera," Vandren interrupted. "Please, calm down. My decision is final."

Her body shook with rage.

"Did I even have a choice?" She asked before she could stop herself.

"That was the intention—"

Bullshit.

"So you're going to double-fund the militia?"

"Technically, you are," Vandren replied, his eyes narrowing. "Tellis must be prepared in case of sector war. The conference had already begun by the time I had spoken with the other council members, who are all directing their sector leaders in the same way." Vandren paused. "The prepared speech will be sent to you tomorrow morning. Please announce it to the public by the end of the day."

The holoscreen shut off.

Caldera's breath was coming in short, shallow gasps. Her hands were shaking. "Fuck!" she screamed, turning around to face Aloriea and Rennick.

Silent tears were falling from Aloriea's face.

"What is it?" Caldera asked, regaining some composure.

"It—" Aloriea took a deep breath, wiping tears off her face. "It's always like this. I'm sorry. I should have warned you not to get your hopes up." She averted her gaze.

Caldera took Aloriea's hands. "It's not your fault. Quill knew all of this already—you're still trying to adjust. Just like me."

"I thought..."

"Maybe this time would be different?"

She nodded. "I never learn."

"That's not necessarily a bad thing," Rennick offered. "You want to see the best in everyone. Even someone like Vandren."

The conference room fell quiet.

"Ren, where are Sear and Markarian?" Caldera finally asked.

He checked his communicator. "They'll be here in about thirty minutes."

She dropped Aloriea's hands. "Let's wait by the entrance to meet them. We need to find out where the other half of the coordinates lead. Tonight."

THE FIVE GATHERED in Caldera's quarters when Markarian and Sear arrived. Sear typed half of the coordinates from Quill's letter into Markarian's geocode device. The small screen blinked blue as he keyed the coordinates onto the number pad.

Rennick stretched his arms above his head. "So we're going now then?"

"In the dead of night?" Markarian chuckled. "Why not?"

"I'm still not sure I completely understand," Aloriea said, handing Caldera the decrypted letter. "We don't have the entire sequence."

"Deimi Auris reminded me that we don't need it." Caldera took the paper and ripped it into tiny shreds before throwing it into the recycler.

"Right..." Aloriea stood, the chair legs scraping against the floor.

Sear seemed to pick up on her confusion. "Exact coordinates are a combination of latitude and longitude," he explained, clearing his throat.

"You have the latitude half," Markarian added. " We'll start by finding out where your part of the coordinates takes us."

"Exactly," Caldera said, pulling her hair into a short ponytail as she headed toward the door, happy to be out of her dress and into something more practical.

In the hallway, Markarian held the geocode device in front of him.

"This will lead us to my half of the coordinates?" Aloriea asked, pointing to the unimpressive black and yellow box.

"Yep." Markarian nodded as the screen blinked again. "You can type in any coordinate—or partial coordinate—and the GC device will take you to that location."

"If there is a signal," Sear added from the back of the group. "But it is rare that there would not be. When you are on planet, it bounces off the satellites in space."

Aloriea exhaled sharply as they walked down the hall. "How do you know I have the latitude half?"

"Latitude is north to south," Caldera replied as they approached the staircase, the skylights casting perfect circles of white moonlight onto the floor.

"Longitude is east to west," Rennick added.

The palace was empty as they rounded the corner to the desolate great hall. Light from the moons filtered in from the open curtains, coating everything in a bluish-white light. The entryway was shut tight, and Sol, Saro, and Olivare were nowhere to be seen. The entire area reminded Caldera of a ghost town. If she didn't know any better, she would've guessed the entire palace was abandoned.

"Are you sure you do not have any idea where this will take us?" Sear asked, lowering his voice.

Aloriea sighed. "It looks like we're heading out into the back courtyard—that's all I can guess so far."

Turning one last corner, they came to the back entrance. Caldera followed Markarian out into the bright night, walking down the red brick paths in between perfectly trimmed, bright green bushes. Sweet honey and tangy orange—the smell of Tellis's native flowers—accosted her as a breeze blew through the garden. Blues, purples, and shimmering reds filled her vision. She inhaled deeply, letting herself relax, if only for a moment.

"This is exquisite," Sear said, breaking the silence. "You do not see gardens like this in the city."

"Quill loved it here," Aloriea whispered. "It was our favorite..." She came to a complete stop in the middle of the path.

"What is it?" Caldera asked.

Aloriea's eyes lit up. "I think I know where we're going."

"Where—" Rennick began, but Aloriea sprinted past them.

"Okay, I guess we're running," Caldera said, taking off after her.

"She's going the right way," Markarian added, keeping his eyes on the GC device as he ran after Aloriea.

The group followed her down various stone paths, past raised flower beds, and around a water fountain in the center of the garden, coming to a stop only when they reached the wall that surrounded the palace.

"Well?" Aloriea asked between gasping breaths.

"We're not there yet," Markarian replied as he wiped the perspiration from his forehead.

Caldera inhaled deeply, taking in as much air as she could. "Now what?"

"You said we were not there yet," Sear said, his chest rising and falling in quick intervals as he turned to Markarian.

"Right, we still need to go—"

"Up?" Aloriea finished, pointing her finger toward the star-littered sky.

Markarian glanced upward, his eyes glinting with curiosity. "Yes."

Caldera looked skeptically up at the thirty-foot-high wall in front of her. "We're scaling walls now?"

"It's easier than it looks." Aloriea grabbed a protruding piece of stone and readied herself to climb.

"You climb this?"

Aloriea smirked, pointing. "Look."

Following her finger, Caldera's eyes fell on an even amount of displaced, zigzagging stones, leading all the way to the top.

"It forms a ladder," Rennick said, stepping up next to Aloriea.

"Exactly. Now let's go." She started to climb.

"You sure you can handle this, buddy?" Markarian asked, slinging a playful arm over Rennick's shoulder.

Rennick pushed him off. "Of course."

"He's right," Caldera replied, moving out of the way for Sear to start his climb. "You don't have to—"

"Callie, I'm going up there. If I can climb out a window, I can climb up a wall. I refuse to be crippled by my fear of heights."

"Okay, okay." She held her hands up in mock surrender.

"Don't worry, I'll catch him if he falls," Markarian said with a nod.

Caldera waited until Sear was halfway up before beginning her ascent, exhaling sharply as the sudden coolness of the stones sent goosebumps up her arms. The smell of damp, herbaceous dirt flooded her nostrils as her climb displaced the creeping thyme that grew between the cracks in the real concrete—not metal—mortar. As she reached from one stone to the next, a smile spread across her face. They were finally doing something she was good at.

"See, that wasn't so bad," Aloriea said. She walked across the top of the wall, about thirty feet from where Sear was pulling Caldera onto the wide, flat surface.

"I didn't say it was bad," Caldera countered, grabbing Rennick's hand a few seconds later to help him up. "It's just, I still can't believe that you climb this all the time." She moved out of the way for Markarian. "Especially in your fancy clothes."

Aloriea laughed and brushed the dirt off her slacks. "Well, I haven't lately," she said, sitting down and swinging her legs over the edge.

"This is it," Markarian said, his eyes on the geocode device. "Literally, right where you're sitting." He pointed at Aloriea.

Caldera sat down next to her. "What's so special about this spot?"

Rennick, Sear, and Markarian joined them—Rennick as far from the edge as possible.

"This area marks the edge of the Tellin border and the beginning of Aelmead's," she said, pointing to the tree line. "It's funny... The way the sectors are split up, we're actually closer to Four and Five rather than Two and Three."

"That's true," Markarian started, scratching his head. "I've never really thought about why, though."

"Natares and saurians, the people of Sector Two and Three—Natioh and Sedrolla—have very specific climates and habitats that they have to live in or near," Sear replied. "Tellins, akars, and matans do not." He looked over at Aloriea, who nodded approvingly.

Caldera looked up at the moons, stars, and blinking satellites. "What's the deal with this place?"

"The deal," Aloriea scoffed, "is that, from where I'm sitting, you can just make out the top of the Aelmead Vanguard Headquarters." She pointed to the horizon. "That light—there."

"And?" Rennick prompted, looking over at her.

Aloriea forced a half-smile. "My younger sisters, Neira and Therasia Prax, are a captain and second in command over there."

"You have sisters?" Markarian asked.

"Prax?" Caldera added. "I thought your surname was Morin."

"My mother remarried, and they took my stepfather's name. I didn't."

"I am sorry," Sear said tentatively, "but what does this have to do with the room we are trying to find?"

"I'm not sure," Aloriea said, not taking her eyes off the horizon. "I'm only telling you about the significance of this spot—I don't know why it's part of the coordinates."

"Significance?" Sear whispered. He scratched his beard and stood, pacing back and forth.

"What about it?" Caldera asked.

"Be quiet. I am thinking."

Caldera blew out a breath. "Rude."

"You know, if you spoke your thoughts out loud, we might be able to help you," Rennick said, chuckling.

"Sear letting us help?" Markarian mocked. "That'll be the day."

Sear shook his head, ignoring them.

"What's going on?" Aloriea whispered, leaning in close to Caldera's ear.

She smirked. "He's trying to work out how a significant spot for you would fit into Quill's coordinates for the secret room."

"That's nice, but if I don't know, I doubt he would."

"You'd be surprised at what he can think up."

Sear stopped pacing and motioned for them to stand.

They jumped up, surrounding him eagerly.

"Did you come here first, or did Quill bring you here?" Sear asked, drumming his long fingers against his arm. The bright moonlight made his orange fur shine.

"Quill brought me here," Aloriea replied, biting her lip.

Sear smiled his fanged smile. "In that case, I think it was luck that this spot became special to you."

"What?" Aloriea crossed her arms. "I just told you why it's special."

"Yes, but Quill could have brought you here the first time simply for the view," Sear said. "The fact that it overlooks Aelmead's Vanguard Headquarters is most likely a coincidence."

"What are you trying to say, Sear?" Caldera interjected, glancing toward the back door of the palace. She almost expected to see Sol, Saro, or Olivare charging them.

"It is like a puzzle. I believe that if we want to find the other half of the coordinates, we have to figure out where Quill's favorite place to take Justle was," Sear continued, snapping his fingers. "Significance."

"So we've hit a dead end...again." Caldera closed her eyes.

Rennick shook his head and turned away from the overlook, shivering. "The other half of the coordinates should be somewhere around here, but this place is huge."

"That is true, Ren," Sear said, his ears perking up as he turned his attention to the garden as well. "And we have no starting point."

Markarian crossed his arms. "We'll have to scour every inch of this garden." He gestured at the sprawling grounds. "This is gonna take forever."

An idea formed in Caldera's mind. "Aloriea, how well do you know Justle?"

"Pretty well, I suppose. He worked with Quill for years."

"What're you thinking?" Rennick asked.

Caldera grinned. "I'll explain everything as soon as we get off this wall," she said, ushering them back down the makeshift ladder.

"You'd better go before me," Sear said after Aloriea, Markarian, and Rennick started their descent.

Caldera smiled softly. "Scared you'll fall?"

"I will admit, I was more confident going up."

"Don't cats always land on their feet?"

He chuckled. "I believe that is a myth."

She smirked, making her way back down the wall. She skipped the last two steps and dropped to the ground.

"All right," Rennick said, brushing debris off his arms and legs. "What's your idea?"

"Well, according to Sear, Quill basically picked these spots to specifically correspond with the already established coordinates of this secret room," Caldera replied. "Right?" she asked, looking over at Sear, who was carefully stepping off the last stone step.

"That is the theory," he said.

"So, if we're going by significance, routine, or whatever you want to call it," Caldera continued, turning to Aloriea, "do you know any places in this courtyard that Quill would meet, consistently, with Justle?"

Aloriea placed her hands on her hips, examining the area. "They would always conduct their business out here."

"How come?" Caldera questioned.

Aloriea's eyes glittered with remembrance as she glanced down at her feet. "In case you couldn't tell, Quill loved flowers. He would walk all along these paths with Justle," she said, pointing at the walkways that wound lazily throughout the courtyard and along the various flowerbeds. "He was really quite..." She paused, pressing a finger to her lips. "Gentle."

Caldera smiled at the same time as a pang of guilt swept through her gut. *I can't believe I used to think such horrible things about him.* "What did they talk about?" she asked, suddenly desperate to know more about him.

Aloriea shook her head. "I couldn't say. I'm a political advisor, not a lawyer. There was no reason for me to attend their meetings." Her eyes darted around the garden. Then she pointed to a solitary wrought-iron bench that sat under a tree where the wall wrapped around the right-hand tower of the palace, creating a small recess. "Whenever their meetings would run longer, they'd usually sit over there instead of going inside."

"That's almost directly below where we were on the wall," Markarian said, glancing at the geocode device.

Caldera nodded. "Let's check it out."

The conflicting light of both moons hit the wall, casting a

harsh shadow over the entire courtyard as they approached the bench.

"What exactly are we looking for?" Sear asked as he walked around the bench and tree, his tail twirling in the air.

Caldera shrugged and wandered across a pathway just behind it. "Anything out of place, I guess."

Working in silence, they continued examining the area until the first moon fell below the horizon.

"I hate to say it," Markarian muttered, plopping himself heavily on the bench, "but I don't think there's anything here."

Aloriea yawned and sat next to him. "The sun will rise in a few hours. Maybe we should go to bed."

"I concur," Sear said, stretching.

Sitting on the perfectly trimmed grass across from them, Caldera sighed and pressed the small of her back against the tree, resting her forehead on her knees.

Rennick sat down beside her. "We'll come back and look more tomorrow."

She nodded, falling into his eyes. An emotion that had long been dormant—continually repressed throughout the years—bloomed in her chest.

This is not the time!

She fiddled with her hands as a soft breeze blew through the courtyard, rustling the flowers and leaves of the tree. "Ren..." she said, gazing over at him, his silhouette backed by moonlight.

"Yeah?" The crinkles around the corners of his eyes deepened as he smiled at her.

Her heart jumped, somersaulting in her chest. *Don't do it!* "There's something I want to say" She stopped as an inconsistency along the bricks caught her eye.

"What?" he asked, following her gaze. "What is it?"

"That stone is a different color than the rest. I must've been too close to notice it before. Or the light's hitting it just right."

Caldera jumped up and ran over to the wall, inspecting the stone.

"What's going on?" Markarian asked from the bench.

As soon as they were all gathered around her, Caldera pushed on the stone. It gave way, retracting backward before flipping over and revealing a handprint scanner.

"Holy shit," Markarian said as nightfliers cawed in the distance. "Well, whose hand is it?"

"It's Aloriea," Caldera replied, looking over at her. "It has to be."

Aloriea took a step forward. "Or Justle."

"I think Callie's right," Rennick replied. "Judging from Quill's holopad message, he trusted you more than anyone—it's gotta be you."

Aloriea stood directly in front of the stone and placed her right hand on the scanner. It lit up blue, white light scanning her hand. It blinked red twice and went dark.

"It's not Justle," Caldera asserted after a few seconds of silence. "If it's not you, it's not him."

"Then who is it?" Aloriea said, sounding frustrated

Caldera bit her cheek. "Quill knew about me for years," she said, placing her hand on the scanner. "The code to open Justle's desk was my ship number. It's possible that..."

The scanner lit up blue again as the white light scanned her hand, blinking green twice as it finished.

A soft grinding noise filtered through the air from underground as the scanner flipped back around into a normal-looking stone. The pathway they were standing on shook ever so slightly, sinking below them.

Jumping out of the way, they looked on as a ten-foot-wide staircase was revealed, curving down and to the right, parallel with the edge of the palace. It led into darkness.

"We found it," Caldera whispered, walking toward the first step.

Rennick grabbed her arm. "Hold on," he said, unholstering his blaster and stepping in front of her. "Let me go first. Markarian." He looked over his shoulder and jerked his head toward the entrance.

Markarian gave a quick nod, readied his own blaster, and stepped up next to him.

They began their descent, the stairs lighting up under their feet.

"Let me go next," Sear said, cutting in front of Caldera before she could follow.

"Why?" she asked. "You don't have a blaster."

Sear smirked. "I am a matan," he said, flexing his long fingers to reveal the entirety of his razor-sharp, three-inch claws. "I do not need one."

As soon as he was a few steps ahead, she began walking down the stairs, stopping only when she realized Aloriea wasn't following them. "What's wrong?" she asked.

"What if we don't like what's down there?" Aloriea said, rubbing her arms as if she were cold.

"We probably won't." Caldera chuckled, but stopped abruptly once she saw Aloriea's downcast expression. "Listen, we're looking for evidence of Quill's murder and this place might give us the answers to put whoever did it behind bars. Whatever's down there, we'll deal with it." She smiled, reaching her hand out toward Aloriea. "So, let's go. This is what Quill wanted us to find."

Giving her a half-smile, Aloriea stepped onto the staircase and took Caldera's hand. "Together," she whispered as they began walking again.

Caldera nodded, squeezing Aloriea's hand encouragingly. "Together."

CHAPTER 16

Light flashed under Caldera's feet, illuminating her surroundings for a brief second before she descended into darkness with Aloriea at her side.

From what Caldera could see between the intermittent flashes, the staircase was in pristine condition. The walls blended seamlessly from the underground stone of the castle to smooth metal as they went deeper. There wasn't so much as a jut or groove sticking out of the wall.

Squinting, she forced her eyes to focus through the growing darkness as they continued. Rennick and Markarian were too far ahead for the guide light from their blasters to be of any use, and just a few steps ahead, Sear was only a vague outline. Biting the inside of her cheek, Caldera ran her hand along the icy metal wall as her blurry reflection flashed back at her and disappeared with each bout of light. Aloriea's grip moved to her upper arm, tightening as they continued down the steps together. Swallowing her uneasiness, Caldera hurried the rest of the way to the bottom.

"There's a door," Markarian called, stepping onto a small, square landing. He lowered his blaster and placed a hand against the wall in front of them. "But it's not budging."

Aloriea let go of Caldera's arm and started back up the steps. "We can't leave this open for too much longer," she said, the confidence in her voice returning. "The holopad message said that we needed to keep this secret, right?"

"Yeah," Caldera nodded.

"Look." Rennick directed his blaster light toward the far-left corner. "There's another handprint scanner over here."

Caldera exhaled a shaky breath and pressed her hand on the scanner. "Let's hope this works," she said as her friends crowded in beside her.

It blinked green, and the steps began to quickly and silently rise behind them, trapping them on the landing between the door and a newly formed wall. As soon as the steps completely retracted, a white light flicked on above them and the door opened, splitting in the middle and disappearing into the ceiling and floor.

Raising their blasters, Rennick broke right into the room, while Markarian broke left.

"Clear," Rennick called, holstering his blaster and motioning for the rest of them to step inside.

"Clear," Markarian repeated, following suit.

"Was that really necessary?" Aloriea asked as she stepped past them.

Markarian shrugged. "You never know. There could have been someone down here."

Caldera walked up next to Rennick, her eyes wide. "This place is huge," she said, twisting her head to take in their surroundings as fluorescent lights flickered on above them.

The right side of the room housed floor-to-ceiling shelves that ran the entire length of the enclosure, filled to the brim with leather-bound books. To the left of where they had entered, an advanced computer system was pushed against the stone and metal wall—ten screens, including the main monitor, sat dark.

"This must spread underneath the majority of the palace," Sear said, his feet padding softly against the metal floor as he walked. His thin tail swished at the ground and his ears whipped from side to side. "If not all of it."

Rennick nodded and walked over to a giant laminate table in the middle of the room. "It's the palace basement."

"The basement?" Markarian questioned, jogging over to a closed door halfway down to where the room ended. He opened it and let out a sigh. "At least it has a bathroom."

"That's what you're focusing on?" Aloriea scoffed.

"How was this kept from the Council?" Caldera whispered, walking over to the monitors. Her reflection stared back at her from the black screens mounted on the wall. "I understand the need for secrecy, but this is something else entirely."

Aloriea crossed her arms. "Are you really surprised?" she asked. "The corruption around this place should speak for itself. Not to mention, it's against the law to harbor evidence *or* speak out against the Council," she continued, a small smirk spreading across her face. "Something you don't seem to understand."

Caldera turned to look at Aloriea, matching her expression. "That's something none of us understand."

Aloriea's expression sharpened as she stared down at Caldera. "Let's get started—"

"You are not going to believe this," Sear interrupted.

Markarian walked over to him. "Like this whole thing isn't unbelievable enough?"

"All these journals are handwritten," Sear continued as he put the book he was holding back on the shelf and began frantically flipping through the pages of another.

"Did you think the leather binding was just for show?" Aloriea asked, walking over to the shelves to pull out a book of her own.

Sear chuckled, flipping another page. "Some virtual books are like that—a tribute to the old days." He slammed the volume shut and replaced it on the shelf. "There must be over a thousand handwritten notes here."

"Considering that this place is decades old, of course there is," Aloriea said, staring down the wall. "The sector leaders of the past certainly have been busy. It's considerably safer to physically write things down rather than to save them onto a holopad—"

"Especially with such sensitive information," Sear finished, smiling down at her.

"E—exactly," Aloriea stammered, returning the sentiment with a smile of her own.

"Ren, Markarian, can you help me over here?" Caldera called from the computer, waving them over to her. "We need to get this system on."

Markarian leaned over her shoulder as he positioned his chair, his eyes glimmering with sarcasm. "You need help turning on a computer?"

"No, dumbass." Caldera sighed. "They're looking at books. We're going to look at computer files."

"If there are any," Rennick added, pulling up his own chair. "Which, seeing as how the shelves are overflowing..."

"Exactly," Caldera agreed, pushing the power button and settling into the seat between them. "This might take a while."

"We can't stay too long," Aloriea called from the bookshelves. "You have to get back to deliver the speech that Vandren's going to send over."

"If you think I'm actually going to release the bullshit announcement that the militia is going to be double funded—"

"It'll be worse for you, for all of us, if you don't," Aloriea snapped.

Caldera stared at her.

"I'm sorry, but if we want to keep looking for evidence of Quill's murder, you have to play along. For your own safety, as well as ours."

Caldera nodded as the others fell silent. The thought of endangering any of them with her actions made her stomach churn. "Okay. We'll look until sunrise."

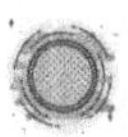

THE HOURS PASSED quicker than Caldera liked, and they hadn't found anything that could be related to Quill's death. Rubbing her blurry, sleep-deprived eyes, she glanced at her watch.

Their time was almost up.

The door to the basement—the only way in or out—was still tightly closed, the scanner waiting for her handprint to release them.

She groaned and leaned her head back in the chair. "We don't have much longer. Find anything that'll help us figure out why Quill was murdered?"

Aloriea and Sear were sitting at the table with piles of books lying open and discarded around them.

"That depends," Aloriea said. "Do you think knowing about how the tariff tax between Tellis and the other five sectors worked eighty years ago will help? Oh, or maybe the intricacies of the sewer system will shed some light on the matter!" She cradled her head in her hands, her elbows pressing down hard on the tabletop.

"Derision aside, Aloriea has a point." Sear closed the book he was reading. "There is no organizational system. We have been down here for hours, but have not found anything related to Quill's untimely death, or the Council's so-called 'plan' from his holopad message—if there is such a thing."

Caldera rubbed her eyes again. "Same here, there are a lot of files, but no real structure to them. It would help if this computer system was connected to the Tellin Informational Network—or anything really."

Aloriea scoffed. "If this place was connected to the TIN, it would have been found years ago."

Caldera glanced at Rennick, who was struggling to keep his eyes open, and Markarian, who was already asleep. "Damn it," she muttered. She stood up and stretched, looking down at her holopad. "As soon as I deliver Vandren's speech, we're coming back."

"I second that," Aloriea muttered, mimicking her actions.

Sear yawned, turning his attention to Caldera as he got to his feet. "Before we go, what is going on with the other nine monitors?" he asked, blinking rapidly as if noticing that they were off for the first time.

"No clue," Caldera replied, sighing heavily. "Couldn't figure out how to turn them on, and we only needed the main one, so—"

Sear bumped her out of the way and took her seat.

"What the fuck!" she snapped, waking Markarian as she stumbled sideways into Rennick, her lack of sleep getting to her.

"I apologize," Sear replied as his fingers flew over the keys until a small window popped up in the middle of the screen. "I had an idea."

Caldera shook her head. "We got that far," she said, pointing at the pop-up screen.

"We know that's how you turn them on," Rennick added. "We just...can't."

"It will only open to a code, but I think I can work around it."

"We know it opens to a code," Markarian grumbled, his voice slurred by sleep.

"Why do you care about this so much now?" Caldera asked. "Why not earlier—you know, when we first got here?"

"I was focusing on the books earlier," Sear replied simply.

"You've got to be kidding me." Caldera shook her head.

Rennick leaned over Sear's shoulder. "So, you think you can turn them on?"

The black narrow slits of Sear's gold eyes focused on the screen. "I believe so." Pages of code popped up in front of him before disappearing just as quickly, and the tips of his retracted claws clicked as his fingers breezed across the keys.

"Are you sure you know what you're doing?" Caldera asked, blowing out a breath as another unreadable page of code opened and closed in front of her. "You're not a computer programmer, you know."

"Good point," Markarian nodded. "You're not erasing all the information, are you?"

Sear scoffed, pressing the enter key. "I got it." All nine monitors blinked to life.

Leaning closer together, they all stared up at the screens, unsure whether what they were seeing was accurate. The nine monitors themselves were segmented into five different screens, each revealing live footage of the palace.

"Holy shit," Markarian said. "They're surveillance cameras."

Aloriea gasped, her hand flying up to cover her mouth.

"Every entryway and exit, most windows—the great hall..." Caldera gripped the back of the chair tighter.

"Almost every main room, too," Rennick said, scrutinizing a monitor to his right, which showed a full view of the library, conference room, and dining area. "Everything except private quarters."

"This must be where the wiretap from the great hall goes," Aloriea whispered.

"Still think this could've waited until later?" Caldera muttered.

"Let me rephrase your question from earlier," Markarian said, turning to Caldera. "How do we know the Council hasn't found this place already?"

"I assume the locks would've been broken."

"And we most likely would have been arrested already," Rennick added, glaring over at Markarian.

Sear tapped an outstretched claw on the table. "I agree. We aired all our suspicions openly in the library when we assumed we were alone. If they knew about this place, we would certainly be in prison."

"Quill really banked on everyone working together," Caldera said under her breath, switching her attention to a different screen.

Aloriea slumped back into her chair. "And no one going missing."

"We have a problem," Markarian said abruptly, pointing to a monitor to the top left of the computer. Olivare stood statuesque with his arms crossed, guarding the door to the back courtyard. "I don't think we're gonna be able to leave now."

"Fuck!" Caldera said, slamming her open palm down on the table. As she hung her head, her eyes fell over the scattered books across the table. "Well, the way I see it, we can either open the door and leave, revealing the location of this room and all its contents to Olivare—"

"Someone we know is working with Vandren," Rennick added.

Caldera nodded. "Or, I skip the speech, we stay down here, and continue trying to figure out what the Council's hiding."

"Neither of which are favorable options," Sear replied.

"We'll all be put in danger if I don't show up." Caldera bit her lip. "But if we go, everything in here will be lost."

"I vote to continue our search," Aloriea said after a moment of silence.

"Really?"

"We can't let the information this place holds go. We'll deal with the consequences of skipping the speech later."

Caldera raised her eyebrows in surprise, looking at her other three friends. "What do you say?"

"I vote we stay," Markarian replied. He stood, tucking curly hair behind his ears. "Aloriea's right."

"I say we go," Sear said, his ears twitching. "There are other ways to find out information besides risking our lives. I firmly believe that if this information is lost, it will not mark the end of our investigation."

Caldera turned to Rennick. "What about you?"

Pursing his lips, he looked back at the monitors. "Sear has a point," he finally said, holding her gaze. "We shouldn't assume the only information that we can get is in here. In the interest of safety—"

"You don't have to worry about me, I can take care of—"

"Callie, this isn't just about you. We're all in danger here."

Caldera blinked, embarrassment rising in her chest and crawling up her neck. "I—I know that..."

Rennick put his hands on his hips, the line of his jaw resolute.

"You made me your bodyguard. So I am responsible for your safety and I do have to worry. I vote we go."

"Two to two," Markarian said, leaning against the computer table. "What d'ya say, boss?"

Ren and Sear have a point...but there's something here.

Caldera squared her shoulders. "Stay."

"Then it's settled," Markarian said. He dragged his chair back to the table, the legs grinding against the floor, and opened a random book.

Without a word, Aloriea joined him, clearly trying to ignore the awkwardness of the situation.

"I shall continue sorting through the computer files," Sear muttered, his voice taking on a low rumble as he sat.

Rennick turned his attention to the monitors. "I'll keep watch. We get out of here as soon as Olivare leaves his post," he said stiffly, looking over his shoulder. "No matter what."

He's really mad at me this time...

Caldera nodded, letting her gaze linger on the back of his head for an extra minute, then took a seat next to Aloriea. "What are you reading about?" she asked, pushing aside her and Rennick's disagreement and gritting her teeth. Her headache from the fluorescent lights intensified.

"Heritage lines," Aloriea answered, turning a page.

"What?" She looked over at Markarian, who had grabbed another book from the pile and was absently flipping through it.

Aloriea turned another page. "It's the way royalty is promoted—if I'm putting it in terms you can quickly understand."

"I think I get it," Caldera said. "The royal family has children, they become the sector leaders after their parents, and so on. Unless they don't have children or a spouse—enter...me."

Aloriea sighed heavily and closed the book but kept her finger on the page. "You're describing the monarchy, and you're correct, for the most part. But I'm talking about the Council."

"Shit." Caldera sat up abruptly. "Let's hear it."

Aloriea smiled and reopened the book. "The heritage line—that's what Quill's parents call it anyway, I don't think there's an actual name for it—is the process of the council members choosing their heirs."

"Choosing?" Caldera asked, tilting her head to the side.

"Right, this was where I left off," Aloriea said, pointing to the text. "It says that the council members aren't allowed to have families." Her voice softened.

Caldera peered over Aloriea's shoulder at the handwritten notes. "Council members are already more prone to assassination attempts and hostage situations," she read aloud. "Having a biological family would put not only the council member, but the family members themselves, at even more risk."

Aloriea took a deep breath and continued reading, "It's not known how they specifically choose an heir, but from my questioning of Councilmember Tomos—that's the council member before Vandren. He had to resign early because of illness, leaving a young Vandren in charge—it was revealed that they essentially adopt an orphan, and raise them in secret. Further investigation leads me to believe that the records are destroyed, that way no one knows who or where they are, until they are publicly announced and take over the position."

"Fuck," Caldera whispered. "So they take a baby, pay off the orphanage to destroy the records, and hide them away?"

"I'm sure it's more nuanced than that," Aloriea said.

"Why would Tomos just volunteer that kind of information?" Caldera asked, crossing her arms. "Especially if it's supposed to be a secret?"

"Quill's parents probably didn't ask him outright."

Caldera chuckled mirthlessly, her mind spinning as she tried desperately to connect the disparate pieces.

"This guy's insane," Rennick said from the monitors, breaking Caldera out of her thoughts.

Markarian looked up from the book he was reading. "Olivare?"

"Yeah, he hasn't moved once," Rennick replied. "Sol and Saro have taken breaks in shifts, but this guy..."

Caldera was barely listening. *If the Council picks their heirs that way, then what would happen if the sector leader had no heir?* She shook her head, refocusing her thoughts. *Would they pick the next in line?* "Aloriea," she said, exasperation creeping into her voice. "Remember what we had talked about in the library? Does it say what would happen if there was no heir for the sector leader? Quill said that the Council not knowing that he had an heir was his only advantage."

"Let me check." Aloriea flipped through the pages. "It doesn't... Wait!" She jabbed her finger into the page. "It's unknown what would happen if a sector leader were to have no spouse, no children." She paused, her eyes flicking rapidly over the text. "Hopefully they would have some family, but it can only be assumed that if none of that is realized, then the corresponding sector's council member would take over, eventually picking a new child so that the royal lineage would start over again." She took a deep, trembling breath. "Whatever Vandren's plan is, it involves taking over the sector completely." She slammed the book shut. "He was never planning to start the royal lineage over. With no one to question him, he could rule without mercy."

"He already does," Caldera whispered, trying to force her hands to stop shaking.

"But it's through the sector leader—they do have a little bit of authority, although not much," Aloriea said, gripping the book tighter. "Can you imagine what he can do unopposed..."

"He could enact even more laws that further widen the gap between the classes in Tellis—he's already shown he doesn't care about the growing homeless population." Caldera blanched. *All he does seem to care about are military affairs.*

"Umm, you guys are going to want to see this," Sear interrupted from his seat at the computer, his voice holding the slightest quiver. "I found something."

"What is that?" she asked, squinting at the circular image in front of her, a knot forming in the pit of her stomach.

"Well, I have a few thoughts—"

Ignoring him, Caldera placed her holopad flat on the table, then walked back over to the computer screen.

Touching the screen with the tips of her fingers, she grabbed the image and flung it over to her holopad with a flick of her wrist. "Go 3D," she commanded.

A holographic image appeared in the air above the holopad. The simultaneous gasp from all five of them filled the space.

Spinning in a slow, clockwise motion was a giant three-dimensional circle.

"What is that?" Rennick murmured, walking over to Caldera.

"Here," Sear said, mimicking Caldera's actions and flicking something over to the holopad.

Numbers appeared in the air next to the floating orb.

"I recognize that arrangement," Caldera said, swallowing the knot that had found its way to the base of her throat. Taking a deep breath, she grabbed Rennick's hand and squeezed. Disbelief clouded her mind. "They're coordinates...of a planet."

CHAPTER 17

"This is it. This is what Quill wanted me to find. He said in his message that I'd know it when I saw it," Caldera said, unable to take her eyes off the slowly rotating orb. The room was silent except for the clicking of keys from Sear rapidly typing on the computer. "But how does this connect to the Council?"

Sear stood, gripping his chin. "And how did they manage to keep it a secret?"

Caldera took a deep breath, looking up into Rennick's eyes as his hands tightened around hers. "Add that to the list of things we need to find out," she said with a sigh, reluctantly releasing her grip.

Rennick took a step forward, scrutinizing the numbers. "The first thing we need to do is figure out if this is a known planet or exo. Just to make sure this isn't old information."

Markarian snapped his fingers. "My Vanguard holopad is connected to the public data servers," he said, fishing it out of his pocket.

"Type in the coordinates," Caldera commanded. She walked up next to him to peer over at his progress.

His fingers flew over the number keys as he looked from the floating image back to the holopad. Finishing and hitting search, he frowned. "Sorry kids, the VH didn't come up with anything."

Aloriea bit her nail. "What about the other sectors' Vanguards? Could they have discovered anything new?"

"Not likely," Markarian said, rubbing the back of his neck. "That kind of information would be in the public servers. Especially since the whole point of the Vanguard in the first place is to find new, inhabitable planets—something they've been failing at for years."

Caldera nodded, forcing the growing agitation down into her stomach. The coolness of the room washed over her as the heat that had been culminating in her body began to subside. "We need a plan," she muttered.

"It looks like Olivare finally moved from his post," Markarian said abruptly. "He's walking toward the front of the palace."

Caldera's gaze flicked toward the screens. Olivare was hurrying down the halls, speaking into his communicator. "He's probably talking to Vandren," she said, motioning her friends toward the door.

"Which means he'll be looking for you soon," Rennick added.

She nodded. "We have to get out of here."

"What're we gonna do with this information?" Markarian asked, jerking his head toward the floating orb.

"We leave it," Aloriea replied tightly.

"Let's transfer everything about this planet to all of our holopads. After we encrypt them, we can try digging a little deeper," Caldera countered as she collapsed the floating image.

"We shouldn't take information out of this room!" Aloriea urged, her eyes blazing. "It's too risky."

Caldera set her jaw. "Aloriea, this isn't what we thought. Yes, Quill was murdered, but based on this, whatever Vandren's planning is so much bigger than that."

Aloriea stood silent, her eyes swimming with tears.

Remorse stabbed through Caldera's chest at the clear pain she was causing her friend, but she continued. "This information could impact the entire planet—not just us, the royal line, or even the sector. In order to investigate it, we need to use everything available to us." She lowered her voice and met each of her friends' eyes. "We don't have a choice. I'm sorry."

The group nodded gravely as they quickly transferred the entire file onto their individual holopads.

Taking a deep breath, Caldera walked over to the scanner and hovered her hand over it. Markarian nodded at her—Olivare was at the front of the palace, talking to Sol and Saro. When she scanned her hand, the stairs descended from the ceiling, allowing them to run up as quickly as possible.

The light stung Caldera's eyes as she reached the top, and she immediately ran to the scanner stone. After everyone gathered themselves around her, she scanned her hand again, causing the stairs to disappear into the ground as if they had never been there.

"All right," she whispered, turning to face her friends. "Just act like everything's normal."

Markarian and Sear's communicators both beeped, causing everyone to jump. They fished the devices out of their pockets to open the messages, their brows furrowed.

"What is it?" Caldera asked.

"All the Vanguard captains got an order," Markarian replied, reading to them from his communicator. "To all Vanguard members, ship out tonight. Objective: Find a mineral known as painite."

"I have never heard of that before," Sear said.

"This substance is extremely rare, but I believe it will be crucial in helping our planet and the other distressed sectors," Markarian continued. "By decree ..." He trailed off and looked up at Caldera. "By decree of the queen."

"That fucking asshole!" Caldera yelled, grabbing Markarian's communicator to re-read the message. Her grip tightened around the device as her signature stared back at her from a decree she had never signed.

"What should we do?" Markarian asked, plucking his communicator out of Caldera's hands.

She looked at the faces of her friends, her gaze lingering on Rennick. She waved her hand in the air as if trying to catch her next thought. "Do what it says—we're pretending like everything's normal, right?"

Markarian nodded, obvious worry clouding his expression as he replaced the communicator into his pocket. "Looks like I'm going on a mission then."

Caldera sighed heavily and turned to Sear, peering over his arm at the communicator screen. "What does your message say?"

"All senior Vanguard scientists are to report to headquarters immediately," he recited as Caldera's eyes breezed over the text.

"What's a planter orb do?" Caldera asked. "The message says it's some sort of new technology that's about to be tested."

"I will fill you in as soon as I can," Sear replied, tucking the communicator back into his shorts.

Caldera frowned. "All right, since we're going to be split up for a while, here's the plan—Ren, Aloriea, and I will keep looking into the planet. Sear, let us know as soon as you figure out what this planter orb is—it could be important. Maybe we could use it." She paused, turning her attention to Markarian. "Markarian, spread the word to as many captains as you can—whoever finds the painite, tell them to bring it to me. Personally."

"Shouldn't be hard," Markarian said. "Since the layoffs, there are only twenty captains left in the entire fleet, but why do you care about a mineral from some random mission that wasn't even ordered by you?"

"I don't, really." She smirked. "But if Vandren wants it, then so do I. If he's going to send out orders under my name, I think I'm entitled to an explanation." She exhaled sharply. "I don't want him to know about this."

He nodded, an amiable grin spreading across his face. "Got it."

"What about Olivare?" Rennick asked. "He's most likely not going to let us out of his sight now."

"Not to mention he has something to do with Justle's disappearance," Aloriea added. "Maybe we should confront him."

"And further risk the wrath of Vandren?" Caldera shook her head. "No way. I'm already anticipating repercussions from missing the speech."

"I agree," Rennick said. "For the sake of our current mission, I think it's best to leave him alone for now."

"All right, we have our plan," Markarian said, shielding his eyes as the sun rose over the wall. "Let's get out of here."

They walked quickly past the gardens, the flowers just opening their petals as the sun's warm rays fell upon them. The green leaves of the trees swayed back and forth with the gentle breeze, glittering with leftover, early morning dew.

The back door of the palace was closed, still unguarded. They made their way through the halls to the front entrance.

"Ahh, Your Majesty," Sol said as they approached. "We were just about to send a search party after you." His tone was jovial, but his eyes were hard as stone. Saro and Olivare stood silently next to him, observing the group with cold indifference.

"You missed your speech—" Saro began.

"We knocked on your door, but you didn't answer," Olivare cut in, silencing him. His rough voice scratched over Caldera's skin.

"Well, did it occur to you that I didn't want to be bothered?" she countered, not breaking eye contact with him.

Something flashed across his face so quickly she didn't have time to register it.

"That may be so," Olivare replied, motioning toward Sol and Saro. "But if you had answered, then this might have been avoidable."

The twins grabbed Markarian and Sear, forcing their hands

behind their backs with a swift motion that said they had done it before.

"What the fuck?" Markarian struggled against Sol's grip as handcuffs clicked into place.

Sear stood silent with his ears flat against his head, his pupils large black pools.

"What do you think you're doing?" Caldera yelled as she clenched and unclenched her hands, unable to keep her voice level. "Let them go!"

Olivare stepped up to her, his gray eyes unflinching and emotionless. "It doesn't surprise me that you don't know the rules," he said, his hands clasped tightly behind his back, which caused his too-tight suit to stretch across his chest and distort the planetary emblem. "Vandren's orders—he's not in the best mood since you disregarded your duties to read the speech he sent."

"Is *that* what this is about?" *He's trying to punish me.* Caldera's ears rang. "Fine, I'll read it. I'll do it right now. Just let them go!"

"Very good. Vandren will be pleased, but that aside, it's against the law for civilians to stay overnight in the palace without clearance," he continued, motioning again to the twins. "I have a job to uphold as well."

"And they did not have clearance," Sol said, his voice holding a hint of displaced excitement that cut straight through Caldera's body to the bone.

Saro blinked at his brother, his brows furrowing. He opened his mouth to say something but clamped it closed as though he seemed to think better of it.

"Thank you" Olivare turned back to her. "They must be detained and searched—it's a simple procedure. We just have to make sure they aren't taking anything with them."

Caldera looked over her shoulder at Aloriea and Rennick, whose faces were a mix of shock and horrified realization. Aloriea's hands were trembling, whereas Rennick's were still. One was on the butt of his blaster, waiting.

"You can't do that," Caldera said, her mind racing. *If they take their communicators, they'll know—Vandren will know. He'll have them killed.*

"Oh?" Olivare replied. He snapped his fingers, causing Sol and Saro to begin leading Markarian and Sear away.

Caldera's heart pounded against the inside of her chest as if it wanted out. She opened her mouth to say something, but didn't know what it was going to be until she had already said it. "You can't take them because they don't need clearance. They're part of my royal court."

"Excuse me?" Olivare growled as Sol and Saro went still.

Markarian and Sear's eyes widened before comprehension set in.

"That's right." She stood straighter, gathering all her courage. "They're part of the royal court so... I demand that you release them."

Sol and Saro looked at her quizzically, their blue and brown eyes flicking from her to Olivare.

Caldera set her jaw. "I apologize for the lack of communication," she said, forcing the words out of her mouth.

"Councilmember Vandren said nothing of this." Olivare glared down at her. "Has he been informed?"

Icy rage spread throughout her body. *You're not taking them,* she thought, balling her hands into fists. *I won't let you.* Sweat poured down her back as she bent her knees, readying herself to fight.

"He doesn't need to be." Aloriea's voice was so sharp, it made Caldera want to instinctively cover her ears as everyone turned to face her.

Olivare turned his attention to her. "What do you mean?" he asked, his voice low and resonating.

"The sector leader is allowed to pick the members of their court without gaining permission from the corresponding council member," she replied, presumably quoting a passage from a law book she had memorized. "Queen Caldera has decided that we are her court," Aloriea continued, casting a sweeping motion across Rennick, Markarian, Sear, and herself. "If she says to let them go—you let them go."

Olivare chuckled. "That may be so, but these two can't possibly be qualified to be members of the royal court."

"That's not for you to decide." Even though Aloriea's tall, lithe figure towered over Olivare's stocky frame, he still seemed massive in comparison. "Sear Arcaro is a brilliant scientist, specializing in many fields of study, and Markarian Ales is a respected captain of the Vanguard," she said, her tone exuding regality. "Her Majesty needs the expertise of both these individuals. The statement that they are underqualified is simply not true."

A tense silence filled the entryway. Fliers chirped in the front courtyard just outside the open doors. Caldera forced air through her throat, which seemed to constrict with each passing second.

"Of course, you could call Councilmember Vandren down here," Aloriea continued, her voice calm and clear despite her trembling body. "Although, I'm sure he wouldn't appreciate making the trip to deal with an issue that, frankly, doesn't concern him."

Caldera watched as Olivare's expression twisted. His condescending demeanor was gone, replaced with what could only be bloodlust. Rennick was next to Caldera in an instant. His blaster was unclipped, pointing at the ground, ready. *He saw it too.*

"I command you to release them," Caldera said again, her voice surprisingly even as she and Rennick stepped in front of Aloriea. Gritting her teeth, she took another step toward Olivare, their bodies now only a foot apart. "Now."

Olivare turned toward Sol and Saro. The twins glanced at him and back at each other before unlocking the cuffs.

"Thanks, asshole," Markarian said, rubbing his wrists and giving Sol a hard shove before walking over to stand next to the open doorway.

Sear was next to him in one quick stride. His fur bristled, tail puffy and twitching.

"We'll talk to you later, Cal—Your Majesty," Markarian said over his shoulder as he and Sear walked down the steps.

Olivare glared at Caldera, Rennick, and Aloriea, his face red. The anger never reached his eyes. No emotion ever reached his eyes. The rage and fear inside Caldera's chest had dimmed with Sear and Markarian's release, but was still there nonetheless. It burned, fighting to get out.

Justle's face flashed across her eyes and without thinking, she grabbed the blaster out of Olivare's holster and shoved it in his face.

"I'm not a politician, so I'm not going to say this diplomatically," she said, catching the gaze of each of them as Sol and Saro turned around, their eyes wide. "Stay the fuck away from my court. My friends."

"Is that a threat?" Olivare asked, a malicious smirk spreading across his face.

Caldera narrowed her eyes and aimed down the barrel. "Absolutely."

To her surprise, Olivare didn't move or attack, but the ruthless smile on his face was a punch to the gut nevertheless.

"Vandren will hear about this," he whispered, leaning in so close that the barrel pressed against his chest.

So much for keeping a low profile. He's never gonna let me out of his sight now.

"I'm counting on it," she replied. Then she discarded the blaster onto the ground and strode down the hall.

CHAPTER 18

The following night, Caldera and Aloriea sat on the balcony overlooking the back courtyard. The red, yellow, and blue flowers were just beginning to close their petals for the day.

"I can't believe Ren had to go to a guard meeting off-site," Caldera muttered, standing up from the glass table and beginning to pace. "We should be sifting through mounds of information in the basement."

Aloriea yawned. "It's a monthly thing, organized by Vandren himself. It helps keep the palace guard in top form while also maintaining the façade that he actually gives a shit about what happens to the sector leader." She leaned forward. "We could go to the basement by ourselves, you know."

Caldera waved a dismissive hand in the air. "I can't focus. Is it normal for the class to be at night?"

"Must've been the only time available."

"Isn't it unsafe for him, Sol, Saro, and Olivare to be gone all at once?"

Aloriea chuckled. "Are you saying you can't handle yourself?"

"No. I'm saying something doesn't feel right."

"I'm sure they'll—"

Caldera's communicator chimed, vibrating against the table-top. The name on the screen read 'Ren'. *That's weird. He only just left.*

"Hey, what's—"

"Cal..." Rennick's breath was heavy on the other end of the line.

"Ren, what's wrong?"

"I don't know—I—I got jumped or something—"

"Where are you?"

"I'm just outside the gates," he coughed.

Fear stabbed through Caldera's body. "I'll be right there. Just stay on the line. Aloriea, you stay here," she managed to call over her shoulder as she sprinted into the hallway.

She raced down the stairs. Shafts of light through the windows mimicked bars reflecting across the floor as she tore through the great hall, skidding to a stop at the entryway where Sol, Saro, and Olivare were standing at attention.

"Your Majesty?" Saro questioned, his brown and blue eyes filled with confusion.

"What the hell?" Caldera panted, her chest rising and falling. "Why are you here?"

Sol glared at her. "What are you talking about? It's our job to guard the palace."

"What about the guard meeting?"

"There wasn't one tonight," Olivare said, his voice gruff.

Caldera's stomach dropped. "Come with me, now!"

"We cannot leave our post," Olivare protested. His normally flat gray eyes held hidden emotion that unnerved her to the core.

She gritted her teeth. "You can if I command it, so let's go!"

As they sprinted down the paved path toward the gate, the flashlight beams from the three guards bounced behind her. Caldera wished she had thought to bring a transport. The mile from the entrance of the palace to the gateway seemed like it went on forever. Her heart increased in rhythm with each footfall as the twin moons of the growing night shone their indifference. Rennick's soft breathing was the only indication that they hadn't gotten disconnected.

When they reached the gate, Sol immediately scanned his keycard, causing the doors to swing open.

"Ren!" Caldera called, barreling out into the road, not stopping to catch her breath. "Ren, where are you?"

"Here!" Saro shouted, shining his flashlight into the ditch. He knelt in the grass and helped Rennick sit upright. Sol and Olivare shined their flashlights on him.

His nose was bleeding and his lip was split open. "Hey, you mind not shining those in my eyes?" Rennick muttered with a cough, raising a bloody-knuckled hand to cover his face.

"Fuck! Ren!" Caldera yelled as she knelt in front of him. She turned to Olivare. "Go get a transport. Now!"

He nodded sharply and started jogging back to the palace. Sol and Saro unholstered their blasters and began searching the surrounding area.

"What happened?" Caldera whispered, taking Rennick's face in her hands and examining his wounds. The first signs of a developing bruise covered his right eye and cheek.

"Good question," he muttered. He attempted a chuckle but only managed to spray his shirt with more blood. "A few guys, maybe four, ambushed me as soon as I closed the gates." He coughed again, wiping blood from his mouth. "The weird thing is, I don't think they took anything."

"It's okay. It's okay," Caldera said, brushing hair out of his face with a shaking hand. "We'll get you help. It looks like you put up a good fight, and your nose isn't broken."

He took her hand in his, lowering it from his face. "Callie. It's okay. I'm fine."

"No, you're not," she whispered, gripping his hand tighter. Tears threatened to overflow, but she pushed them down, forcing herself to reevaluate the situation. She looked around, the surrounding trees seeming sinister in the dark night.

"There's no sign of the assailants," Saro called from across the road.

Was this a setup? If there wasn't a guard meeting—

A transport pulled up and Olivare got out. "Your Majesty, Councilmember Vandren has contacted me. He would like to speak with both of you, in the conference room."

Caldera and Rennick glanced at each other.

"He needs a doctor," Caldera said as she helped Rennick to his feet. "Vandren can wait."

"No, he really can't." The darkness behind Olivare's eyes was back, sending shivers down her spine.

"It's okay, Cal. Let's just get this over with," Rennick said as Sol and Saro helped him into the transport.

Rage simmered inside her chest. "Fine."

The transport ride back to the entrance was short, the scenery darkened by the growing night, breezed by outside as Caldera silently looked out the window.

"Why did Ren get a message that there was a guard meeting tonight if you three didn't?" Caldera grated as the transport slowed to a stop at the bottom of the marble steps.

Ren winched. "Callie—"

She held up her hand to cut him off. "Why?"

Sol sighed, opening his transport door in tandem with Olivare and Saro. "We don't know."

Caldera followed the three men, slamming her door closed as Saro helped Rennick out of the backseat.

"I'm sorry this happened to you," Saro whispered, readying himself to help Rennick up the steps.

"Do you know something?" Caldera asked, stepping in front of him. "Saro?"

He flicked his gaze from side to side before it landed on Caldera.

"We already told you we don't know anything," Sol interjected before his twin could respond.

Olivare hurried up the steps, turning to glare down at her as he reached the top. "Vandren will explain everything. Trust me."

Caldera shook her head and stepped up to Saro, motioning for him to get out of the way. "Move aside." He obeyed and she grabbed Rennick's arm, flinging it over her shoulder, helping him up the steps and through the palace.

No more words passed between the group as Olivare, Sol, and Saro escorted them to the conference room before heading back to their posts. Rennick continued to limp beside Caldera, flinching with every step.

As they opened the door to the conference room, Vandren's face was on the holoscreen on the wall inside, his gold robe on full display.

"What couldn't wait?" Caldera said, her voice clipped. "I need to get Ren to a hospital."

"I wanted to check in," Vandren replied simply, his voice low. "You vetoed my sanctioned arrest of your newly appointed court—I wanted to see what was keeping you from performing your duties."

"You had no right to arrest them in the first place," Caldera snapped. "And if this is about the speech, I'm going to—"

"Sir Silvera, it looks like you had an unfortunate encounter."

Rennick straightened up as much as he could, removing his arm from Caldera's shoulder. "It—it's nothing."

"It would be a shame if it were to happen again."

Caldera's blood froze as she met Rennick's gaze. "What are you saying?" she asked. "Did you—"

"Don't be ridiculous," Vandren interrupted. His hard eyes never flinched away from her, and a clear air of deceit danced in them. "As queen, you shouldn't pick fights with people who are more powerful than you." A subtle grin formed on his lips. "Your bodyguard isn't infallible, and neither are the rest of your friends. Don't disobey me again."

When the holoscreen turned off, Caldera fell to her knees, her legs shaking so uncontrollably that they could no longer hold her up. "That bastard..." Her heart pounded in her ears. "That bastard!" she screamed, hitting the floor with her closed fist.

"Callie..." Rennick said, kneeling next to her and placing his hands on her shuddering shoulders just as the conference room door opened. "It'll be...okay."

"What's going on?" Aloriea gasped, running over to them. "Oh my g—Ren are you okay?"

"It's nothing," he coughed.

"I told you to stay in my quarters," Caldera muttered, sucking in a breath and forcing herself to her feet.

"Saro messaged me and said I should meet you here after I called a doctor."

"Did you?"

Aloriea nodded. "A doctor named Celestin Vareis is on her way. Callie, what's happening?"

Caldera swallowed hard, forcing tears of anger back as she looked at Rennick. A dark bruise had already begun to form under his eye. "Vandren just had Ren assaulted—threatened to kill him...threatened to kill all of you."

Aloriea's eyes widened. "What...he told you that? Blatantly?"

She shook her head. "Not in so many words, but essentially, yes." She met Rennick's gaze. "I can't do this, Ren."

"What?"

"Whatever Quill wanted, it's over. Done. I'm not doing this anymore."

"Callie, you don't mean that."

"Yes, I do," she whispered. "I am not going to put you—all of you—in danger any more than I already have. Vandren wants a puppet, well...he's got one."

"No...Callie, we can't stop now," Aloriea stammered. "Please...you said you'd help me."

Caldera didn't answer. As she turned toward the door, her feet felt like cinder blocks and her chest hollow. Rennick grabbed her arm, forcing her to face him.

"Caldera, stop. Listen to me. Vandren doesn't know you, but I do."

She stared up into his face.

His eyes blazed with conviction as he took another step toward her. Flinching from pain, he took her other arm in his hand. "You've never given up on anything and you can't start now." He loosened his grip. "Yes, we're all in danger here, but rolling over isn't going to help anyone. It'll just make things worse."

Caldera took a shaky breath, clenching her fists. "Ren, I—I'm afraid."

"Me too. But this is proof that we need to act. Now more than ever. Aloriea feels the same, and I know Markarian and Sear do too."

"He's right," Aloriea added, her expression unreadable, eyes misting. "We knew what we were signing up for."

"I can't lose anyone else. You're the only family I have left."

"We'll protect each other—we always have." Rennick took Caldera's hands in his. "Just promise me that you won't bow to *his* threats, no matter what happens. You're better than that."

She smiled, resisting the urge to wrap her arms around him and never let go. "Okay. I promise."

The hollowness in her chest dissipated.

Ren's right. Vandren doesn't know who I am...but he will.

CHAPTER 19

Markarian's mission turned into one week, then two, then three.

Caldera tried to distract herself by burying her head in research regarding the undiscovered planet, but with the constant threat of Olivare swarming her at any moment, the mystery of Quill's death, and Vandren's ridiculous speeches that she was forced to read as her own to the people of Tellis, she was jittery the whole time.

Once a week—since she was 'sufficiently settled' according to Vandren—she would sit on mind-numbingly boring conference calls with the other sector leaders that were designed to create the illusion of working together for the betterment of Bersama.

The discussions varied from pre-written itineraries created by a sector's corresponding council member to simply filling each other in on the minor sector-specific laws or legislations that were passed—if any—that didn't need the Council's approval.

That was Caldera's favorite part.

With every new trade agreement or Tellin business opened,

she saw it as a way to defy Vandren, and even though they had their disagreements, the other sector leaders seemed to be in solidarity over sticking it to their respective council members—which Caldera wholeheartedly appreciated.

As the fourth week rolled around, instead of being a part of the conference call, Caldera found herself marching down the hallway toward the entrance to the palace on her way to meet Jasik Okona, the Ruler of Sector Three.

"Relax, this'll be...fun," Aloriea said, her light-green dress whisking around her feet as she walked beside her.

Caldera's shoulders tensed even more, and her muscles threatened to snap under her black blazer. She was wearing the same outfit she wore when she met Queens Eldra and Fenry, but for some reason she felt underdressed.

They love to remind me on our conference calls that I'll never be the leader Quill was—that I'm simply posing... that I'll never get it right.

"Fun? Jasik hates me."

"No they don't."

"They've literally said, 'you're a horrible leader'. What else could that mean?"

"Well, they hate everyone."

Rennick laughed. "At least you're out of your room," he said from her other side, tucking his hands deeper into his pants pockets. "That's a feat in and of itself."

"I'm just trying to find something—anything—about this mysterious planet," Caldera muttered, rubbing her temples. "Not to mention how that fits into Quill's last message. Which we can't even replay because it erased itself!" She took a breath, stress simmering in her chest and rising to settle into her shoulders. *My tendons are gonna break apart at any moment, causing muscle and blood to splatter all over the walls—*

"Callie," Aloriea said, snapping her back to reality as they came to halt at the entrance.

The palace doors were open and Olivare, Sol, and Saro stood guard. A sleek black transport appeared in the distance, steadily making its way up the paved drive. It came to a halt at the base of the marble steps leading up to the entryway.

The transport door opened, lifting toward the sky, and two guards stepped out first, mimicking the actions of Sol and Saro when they had first brought Caldera to the palace. Their scaly skin and elliptical eyes marked them as saurian, the main species of Sedrolla, Sector Three.

Determining the area was safe, they nodded to the open transport, and Jasik Okona emerged.

Seeing them is different in person. Caldera swallowed hard, trying not to let herself be intimidated.

They were tall and lanky, with an angular, flat face reminiscent of a snake, green-ochre skin, and yellow elliptical eyes that darted from side to side as they slinked up the steps between their guards. Wearing a crisp black suit with an obsidian-colored button-up—the color of their sector—they exuded regality.

As they reached the top, Caldera could see scales covering their forehead, cheeks, and the sides of their neck.

"Introducing Their Majesty, Jasik Okona," Aloriea said with a smile as they came to a stop in front of Caldera.

"It's nice to meet you," she said, reaching out her hand.

Jasik didn't take it, keeping their long spindly fingers laced in front of them.

"Okay," Caldera whispered, dropping her arm. "I apologize for canceling my scheduled visit a few weeks back, forcing you to come here—almost assassinated and all."

They tilted their head to the side, their black hair so short and slicked-back that it didn't move with the motion.

Caldera took a deep breath, motioning behind her. "Well, should we head over to the conference room?"

"Actually, I would prefer an outdoor venue," Jasik said, speaking for the first time in their wispy, thick Sedrollan accent.

"Oh, all right—yeah, we can do that," Caldera replied, glancing over her shoulder. "Please, follow us."

Olivare, Sol, and Saro stepped inside, closing the palace doors behind them.

Caldera, Rennick, and Aloriea led Jasik to the back courtyard, their guards and Olivare bringing up the rear of the procession, with Sol and Saro staying behind to guard the entrance.

"Here we are," Caldera said, pushing open the doors. Walking down the steps into the garden, she couldn't help but glance toward the area where the passage to the secret basement was hidden.

When their feet hit the brick path, Jasik motioned for their guards to stay put.

Caldera did the same, hoping Olivare wouldn't put up a fight in front of a sector leader.

With a sharp nod, he surprisingly obeyed, standing silently at attention next to Jasik's guards.

Aloriea and Rennick glanced at each other, slowing their pace and falling into step a few paces behind Caldera and Jasik.

"So, why outside?" Caldera asked once the silence was too much to bear as they continued walking up and down the perfectly manicured garden paths. The petals of Tellis's native flowers reached up toward the sun without reservation.

"Lesss chance for spiesss," Jasik replied, with a soft hiss, their lips curling upward, accent on full display. "I assume you found the camerasss in your great hall?"

Caldera smirked, finally realizing the reasoning behind their behavior. "Clever—there could be drones though," she said, winking.

"I don't sssee or hear any," Jasik countered, their all-business demeanor dropping.

"All right, I have to ask. Do you really think I'm a horrible leader?"

"I think you're heedlesss when it comes to decision-making. Hotheaded when you don't get your way, and carelesss when it comes to the Council... But do I think you're a horrible leader? No. Councilmember Kex likesss when I say it though."

"Of course she does," Caldera scoffed, averting her gaze.

Jasik stopped walking, yellow eyes gleaming. "In all honesty, at times I wisssh I was more like you."

"You wish that you were constantly on the verge of being killed?" Caldera muttered. Her mind flashed to Rennick, beat up and bloody. Vandren's warning rang in her ears. "Always on your council member's radar? Always being watched?"

Jasik shook their head. "I wisssh I was brave."

Caldera sucked in a breath. *All the sector leaders want is to be free—to help their people on their own terms.* She stepped in front of Jasik, cutting them off. "You can be," she whispered, meeting their eyes. "In your own way, you are."

"I do what they tell me—"

"That doesn't mean anything. You're trying to survive." Her mind flashed to Quill. *The leaders are more scared than ever before because of what happened to him.* "As long as you know in your soul that you want things to be different. As long as you truly want to help the people of your sector, you *are* brave."

As Jasik blinked, their forked tongue flicked in and out of their mouth reflexively. Fliers chirped overhead, expressing their enjoyment at the growing heat as the sun burned in the sky.

"Sedrolla is lucky to have you," Caldera asserted, her gaze never wavering. "I'm sure of it."

"You really want to change thingsss for Tellisss?"

"I want to change things for Bersama."

Jasik smiled, showing their sharp teeth. "Then count me as one of your alliesss—truly." They glanced over their shoulder, including Aloriea and Rennick in the conversation for the first time. "I'll do whatever I can to help you."

They reached out their hand to Caldera.

She grinned, taking it. "Deal."

A HOT BREEZE blew through the open balcony doors of Caldera's quarters the next day, carrying the sounds of chirping fliers and buzzing insects that were all too happy about the turn of the season. The sheer curtains whipped inward as Caldera rested her face against the stone table, letting the coolness of its surface flow into her cheek.

"This is driving me crazy," she said, squeezing her eyes shut.

"The waiting or the heat?" Rennick called from the balcony.

She faced him, opening one eye. He was leaning against the thick stone railing, hair blowing wildly in the wind as he smiled at her between the constant flapping of the curtains. She sighed, sitting up. "The waiting—obviously."

"It's only been a month since Markarian shipped out," Aloriea said matter-of-factly, looking down at her holopad.

"Only?" Caldera stared across the table at her.

Aloriea's hair rustled against her horns. "It's an extremely rare mineral. What did you expect?"

"I don't know," Caldera complained. "It doesn't help that that's the only thing we know about this painite." She ran her hands through her hair, tucking the loose strands behind her ears. "And don't even get me started on how little information we've found regarding Justle's disappearance—despite our best efforts to discreetly search for him—or the unknown planet."

"That's true," Aloriea muttered, biting her nail. "At least we've made another sector leader our ally, and we've had better luck with the planter orb. It's lucky that individuals can keep their jobs after becoming members of the royal court, or else Sear wouldn't have been able to research it."

Caldera leaned forward. "You're still going on about that— what was I supposed to do? Let them get arrested?"

"All I'm saying is that you really backed yourself into a corner," she said, placing the holopad on the table as she met Caldera's gaze. "A thank you for getting you out of it would be appreciated."

"You've got to be kidding," Caldera said, shaking her head in disbelief as a chuckle escaped her lips. "You know I thanked you—"

"Oh, really? Must've slipped my mind," Aloriea interrupted, grinning.

"We are not starting this fight again," Rennick interjected, coming inside to sit down at the table. "What does Sear say the planter orb is?"

"He's bringing the prototype here after he gets off work today, but I'm looking through his notes now," Aloriea said, scrolling through the information on her holopad.

Caldera bit her lip. "Took him long enough to get them to us."

"He didn't want to send anything until he was sure."

"So what does it say?" Caldera pressed. "Is it a weapon, like the rail beam?" Her heartbeat sped up at the thought of another piece of tech resembling the RB.

Aloriea shook her head, looking back down at her holopad. "Although it is only being released to the Vanguard and Militia, according to Sear. Based on these schematics, it's more of a shield, or forcefield of some kind."

Caldera reached her hand out. "Let me see that." Aloriea placed the holopad in her palm. "Attach to your person. Impenetrable. Keeps you grounded," she read, skimming the notes. "It's so tiny. How can it do all of that?"

Aloriea shrugged and plucked her holopad from Caldera's grip. "We'll find out in about thirty minutes."

"What about Justle?" Caldera muttered. "Ren, are you sure your PI friends haven't found anything yet? We're paying them enough..."

"Yes. They're trying, Callie, but having to do all of this off the books is making it difficult for them." Rennick rubbed his forehead. "No amount of money can change the fact that they don't have anything to go on."

Aloriea's gaze fell to the table. "Just like us. The palace records show that he never left while we were visiting Natioh. He just...disappeared."

Caldera massaged her temples, forcing air out of her nose. "The cameras in the Cave didn't reveal anything either," she said, clenching her jaw.

"Ugh," Aloriea groaned. "I thought we agreed to call the basement 'the Vault'."

Caldera smirked. "Cave is more appropriate."

"No, it's not."

"Fine, fine. Vault it is." Caldera laughed as her communicator chimed. She dug it out of her pocket and looked down at the screen. "It's from Markarian!" She let the holographic video float above the communicator so they could all see it.

Markarian's face stared back at them from the bridge of his ship, his green eyes shining. His expression was serious and held a touch of worry. "Callie, listen, I'm sending a message because we're in the desolate section of the galaxy, and, as you know, the light delay is like, twenty-four hours from here to Bersama—"

Cold sweat formed at the base of Caldera's neck as the hairs on her arms stood up. *The rock monster.* "They're in the desolate section!" she yelled. "Why would they go there, it's extremely dangerous—"

"We found the painite—I mean, my crew didn't, but one of the captains did."

"They actually found it," Aloriea said, her eyes widening. Her expression quickly changed from excitement to contemplation. "Now what?"

Markarian's image bounced up and down as he spoke, as if he were jumping, indicating they were under thrust.

"Two newbies found it," Markarian was saying as the image continued to undulate. "A newly promoted brother-sister team—Grey and Sylvie Lasson. They're on their way to you now."

Caldera closed her eyes and attempted to stay calm.

"By the time you get this message, they're only going to be about an hour from landing," Markarian said. "They're leaving their ship in orbit and coming down in a private, two-person, shuttle. I, uh...told them to land in the back courtyard. Sorry 'bout that, but they're expecting you. I'll get there as soon as possible, but..." His amiable smile wavered, or it could have been the unstable message. "Like I said, we're in the desolate section, so it'll probably be about a week before I can get back—even under full thrust. So all I can say right now is, good luck."

The message ended, filling the room with silence. Even the animals outside seemed to quiet down.

"Damn it, Markarian," Caldera whispered, breaking the tense stillness of the room. "How are we going to explain a shuttle landing in the back courtyard?"

"In his defense, we didn't really give him any instructions," Rennick said, crossing his arms.

Aloriea gripped her chin. "He said they're landing in a private shuttle, right?"

Caldera nodded. "Sometimes on longer missions, it's permitted to load smaller cargo shuttles for emergencies or small landing parties."

"All right, then we can say you're expecting a visitor... Someone who doesn't want to be noticed entering the palace."

"And who would that be?" Caldera asked.

"Well...didn't Jasik say that they'd like to help you?"

Caldera's eyes lit up as she reached for her communicator. "We could say that we're negotiating on something in secret."

Aloriea grinned. "Exactly! It would be a good excuse to keep Sol, Saro, and Olivare up at the front entrance, too. Under the guise of 'keeping out prying eyes'."

"I'll fill Jasik in on the plan. Hopefully they'll play along—maybe send out a fake itinerary that I can give to the twins and Olivare."

"Okay, but wouldn't they inform Vandren about the Ruler of Sector Three visiting again?" Rennick asked. "Especially since it's not sanctioned."

"Olivare definitely will," Caldera said, "but it doesn't matter. By the time the message reaches him, we'll have the painite."

She sent the message to Jasik, getting a response less than a minute later. Caldera grinned. "They'll do it."

A knock echoed through Caldera's quarters, causing them all to jump.

"Sir Arcaro for you, Your Majesty," a familiar voice said.

"Callie, let me in," Sear's voice filtered through the door.

Caldera glanced down at the communicator still sitting in the middle of the table. *Sear's already here? How have thirty minutes passed?* "Shit," she muttered, running over and ushering Sear inside. She was about to close the door when Saro grabbed the frame.

Caldera narrowed her eyes, stopping just short of smashing his fingers. "What do you want?"

"I wish to apologize," he muttered, removing his hand from the doorframe.

Caldera straightened. "For what?"

"Almost arresting part of your court."

"That was weeks ago," she huffed. "But...thank you, I guess." She went to close the door, but he blocked it again.

"It was unlawful," he said, blinking as if working up the courage to continue. "My brother knew it, but he was following orders from Olivare."

"Olivare? Are you saying that there isn't a law stating that civilians can't stay overnight in the palace?"

Saro fidgeted with his fingers, lacing them together. "There is, but it's old and outdated. Lady Morin knows of it—that's why she didn't question him, since it was what Councilmember Vandren wanted."

Caldera's mind raced. "If you knew it was unlawful, why didn't you intervene?"

He looked away, his multicolored gaze falling to the floor. "Because Sol didn't ..."

A pang of sympathy shot through her as she examined the surprisingly timid man in front of her. "You know," she said, letting a soft smile spread across her face. "I think you're different than I originally thought. Hiding behind a gruff mask."

Saro met her eyes again. Emboldened. "I have something else to tell you."

"What is it?"

"Sol and Olivare wanted to send the video of you breaking into Justle's room to Vandren. I don't know why."

"Shit!" Caldera snapped, clenching her fist. *So they did catch that on camera. They knew Justle was hiding something for Quill.* "So—"

"But I deleted it before they could," Saro interrupted.

Surprise coursed through her. That's why *I was never questioned or punished.* "Saro..." She glanced over her shoulder at her friends. Aloriea pointed at her watch, while Rennick and Sear raised their eyebrows. "Thank you for telling me," she said, before finally closing and locking the door between them.

"What was that about?" Rennick asked, frowning.

"Saro might be on our side after all," she muttered.

They played Sear the message from Markarian and quickly explained their plan as Sear padded his foot up and down, his tail twitching back and forth.

"This plan of yours could work," he said, a fanged canine poking out from the top of his lip. "But I am against it."

Caldera sighed heavily as her platinum hair blew across her face. "Why?"

"It is a plan for short-term success," he replied, turning his golden eyes to her. "The repercussions will most likely be severe when Councilmember Vandren finds out this was all made up."

"We'll worry about that later," Caldera said, glancing from Rennick to Aloriea.

Aloriea took a step forward. "Thanks to Markarian, we don't have time to think of something better."

Sear grunted in resignation. "Very well."

"I'll send out a message and fake itinerary from Jasik to the palace guards," Caldera interjected with a sharp nod, grabbing her communicator off the table.

"Sear, do you have the planter orb?" Rennick asked. "Aloriea told us you were bringing a prototype. Do you think it could be of any use to us?"

He nodded, reaching into his breast pocket and pulling out the object from the schematic.

Caldera finished her message, hit send, and crowded around Sear to peer into the palm of his hand.

The object was small and simple; a semi-circle the size of a half-marble, with a two-inch prong sticking out of the bottom, tapering to a sharp needle. The tip was protected by a small wax ball to prevent accidental insertion.

"How does it work exactly?" Rennick asked, gingerly picking it out of Sear's hand.

"You quite literally insert it into your body," Sear said, pointing at the needle tip. "The demi-sphere is actually the shield," he continued, pointing at the top. "Once it is attached to you, it activates, covering the body, and surrounding area, in an impenetrable shield."

"Is that safe?" Aloriea asked, her forehead creasing.

Sear shrugged. "I left before the trials started."

Caldera looked down at her communicator. Another fifteen minutes had passed. "We have to get to the back courtyard to meet Grey and Sylvie."

Rennick gently touched her arm before they walked out into the hall. "Hey," he said, dropping the planter orb into his pants pocket.

Caldera swallowed hard, forcing herself not to think about the warmth from his hand on her skin, or the goosebumps flying up her arm. "Yeah?" she whispered, letting the other two gain some distance between them.

"This is terrible timing," he chuckled nervously, "but do you think we could talk later?"

Her heart did a triple-backflip as heat instantly rushed to her cheeks. "Y—yes," she said, silently cursing herself for stammering. "What about?" she asked, clearing her throat as they strolled down the hallway, half-heartedly attempting to catch up with Aloriea and Sear.

"Nothing in particular," he said, eyes gleaming. "I think we could both use a little break, though."

Caldera smiled, her body pulsing with elation. "That was out of the blue."

Rennick grinned. "I've known you long enough to realize when you're about to burst from stress."

"Any word from the twins or Olivare?" Aloriea asked over her shoulder.

Caldera looked at her communicator. "They said, 'understood'."

The sun was setting as they pushed open the doors to the back courtyard. Pink and gold light settled on the flowers as long shadows stretched over the grounds.

"I see them," Caldera said, shielding her eyes and pointing to the sky, where a small silver object steadily advanced toward them.

"Right on time," Rennick said under his breath as they walked down the steps, the wind whipping up around them.

"Right on time indeed," a harsh voice said from their left.

Caldera flinched and slowly turned to face Olivare, who was sitting casually on a short pillar meant for a flowerpot. "Why aren't you up front—" she began, but the roar of the shuttle made it impossible to be heard, forcing everyone to cover their ears as it landed. Even though it was a small cargo shuttle, it still took up over half the courtyard, displacing almost all the flower beds.

The wind whipped Caldera's hair around her face so violently it was like she was being slapped.

Olivare sat there, unflinching as his black hair flew in the gale. "You and your 'court' aren't as sneaky as you think," he replied after the shuttle's engine had powered down. "Negotiations with Sector Three's leader?" He chuckled. "That was the most obvious fabricated lie I have ever seen."

Caldera's chest tightened. The stabilizing clamps of the shuttlecraft caught her attention as they released, descending from four sides and settling onto the green grass.

"Callie!" Rennick grabbed her shoulder and pulled her behind him, simultaneously stepping in front of Sear and Aloriea. His blaster was out, safety off. He pointed it at Olivare.

Caldera peeked around him to see that Olivare had his blaster out too, resting on top of the pillar. His hand curled around the grip, but he wasn't pointing it at anything. *How did I miss that?* Her cheeks burned as she frantically tried to assess the rest of the situation. Sear's ears were flat against his head, fangs bared and claws out, while Aloriea's hands covered her mouth.

"Go find Sol and Saro, they might be able to help," Caldera commanded, trying any excuse to get them out of this situation.

"But..." Sear growled, his voice low.

"Now!" Caldera interrupted, shoving them toward the entrance. They obeyed, running through the open door and down the hall.

"Why are you here?" Rennick asked after Sear and Aloriea had disappeared around the corner, his voice hard.

Olivare hopped off the pedestal and stretched, his blaster shining in the dim sunlight. "I suspect the same reason as you are," he said, taking a few steps forward.

Caldera and Rennick exchanged worried glances.

"We don't know what you're talking about," Rennick said, slightly lowering his blaster so it wasn't pointed directly at him.

"Vandren wants the painite mineral and I mean to give it to him." Olivare never took his eyes off the shuttle, which was fully settled and stabilized.

"Why does he want it?" Caldera snapped. She stepped out from behind Rennick and balled her hands into tight fists, nails biting into the skin of her palms.

Olivare ignored her. His eyes were on the slowly descending ramp and the red-haired girl that appeared at the top.

She followed his gaze. *That must be Sylvie.*

The air rang, vibrating with noise. It took Caldera a minute to register it as a blaster shot.

Sylvie Lasson was no longer walking down the ramp but had fallen off and was lying in a crumpled heap beside it.

CHAPTER 20

Caldera sprinted toward the shuttle, her pounding heart threatening to burst out of her chest. Rennick shouted, but his words were lost as she reached the injured girl. A red, glistening pool was slowly forming under her body, spreading across the grass as it coated her hair and clothes.

With a quick intake of breath, Caldera pressed her hands against the gaping wound in her shoulder.

"What the fuck were you thinking, Callie?" Rennick yelled from behind her. "That was too reckless!"

She didn't respond as she glanced over her shoulder. Rennick had followed her—most likely preventing her from being shot herself. He was kneeling at the base of the ramp, clearly trying to catch his breath, his blaster pointing at Olivare. She turned back to Sylvie, gingerly pressing her fingers against the girl's throat—searching for a heartbeat. After a few seconds, her throat pulsed.

"She's still alive!" Caldera shouted to Rennick as blood seeped through her fingers.

Rennick didn't move—he was a statue frozen in a firing pose.

Olivare hadn't moved from his position either, his stance nonchalant.

"We have to get her back on the ship," Caldera muttered, as footsteps echoed off the ramp.

"Sylvie?" a man questioned from the top, confusion coating his thin voice.

Olivare's attention flicked toward the new interruption.

"Don't you fucking move!" Rennick yelled, swiftly moving in front of the ramp, his blaster never wavering from Olivare. "I don't want to shoot you, but I will!"

Caldera took a deep breath, her full attention again on Sylvie. "Get your sister. Get her hooked up to ECS, and get the hell out of here," she called, meeting Grey's uncomprehending green eyes.

"What the fuck is going on?" Grey yelled as he jumped off the side of the ramp and landed in front of Caldera, his freckled face flushing.

"Hurry!" Rennick commanded. "We'll deal with this."

Grey gasped when he saw his sister's body. He took off his flight jacket, quickly tying it around her shoulder.

The girl whimpered as he tightened the makeshift binding.

Caldera quickly helped him gather her in his arms. Blood smeared across their shirts, trickling behind them as they started up the ramp.

The body in his arms groaned. "W—wait," Sylvie said, her voice weak—forced. Her eyes fluttered open to reveal fading green irises.

Caldera flicked her attention to Olivare. He yawned, and she winced. *Why is he just standing there?* Balling her blood-covered hands into fists, rage boiled inside her gut. *What's he waiting for?*

"Take it," Sylvie muttered. She slowly reached inside her flight jacket pocket and pulled out a black stone with swirling red veins.

Caldera grabbed it out of Sylvie's ashen hand. "Okay, now go!" she said sharply, stepping off the ramp as it retracted.

The seconds ticked by at a snail's pace as Caldera and Rennick waited for the shuttle to lift off.

A breeze blew through Caldera's hair as she eyed Olivare. The seeming disinterest at what he had done pulled at her muscles—wanting to force her forward, to go on the attack. *Something's not right.* She pulled her communicator out of her pocket, smearing it with blood. Stepping completely behind Rennick, she sent a message to Sear and Aloriea. *Stay away from here!*

The rush of air as the shuttle finally ascended caused them to stagger forward, almost knocking them over.

Olivare's joyless laugh filled the empty air. "What do you think you've accomplished?"

"Fuck you!" Caldera screamed, her voice breaking. She was unable to hold in her growing rage any longer, and she wished she had a blaster of her own.

"Why did you shoot her?" Rennick demanded, aiming down his sight and partially stepping in front of Caldera again.

Olivare exhaled sharply, lowering the gun to his side.

Rennick didn't return the favor.

"It was to be the fate of anyone who found it," Olivare said with a shrug, letting out an exasperated sigh. "Regardless, I'll take that stone now—I know she gave it to you," he added, walking toward them.

"Don't," Rennick commanded, taking a step forward. "Put your weapon on the ground. Slowly."

Olivare smirked as he complied, raising his hands in mock surrender.

"You're under arrest," Rennick said.

Olivare laughed. "You really believe you're in control, don't you?"

"Put your hands behind your back," Caldera snapped as she stepped in front of Rennick. Wiping the blood from her free hand onto her pants, she gripped the stone tighter. Her muscles twitched with the anticipation of an attack.

Olivare did as she said, a smug smile spreading across his face.

She approached him slowly, with Rennick at her back. Neither had anything to detain him with, but she couldn't let him get away.

Caldera had almost reached him when a blinding flash and deafening bang accosted her. She fell backward, the rock flying out of her hands as her back slammed into the stone path of the garden.

Before she could regain her senses, Olivare was on top of her, his hands wrapped around her throat.

She ripped at his fingers, kneeing him repeatedly, to no avail. His cold eyes stared down at her, emotionless as he squeezed tighter. Her last voluntary breath escaped her lips as her throat closed. *He's really going to kill me.* Her fingers went numb as she continued, in vain, to try and free herself.

A shot rang in her ears and Olivare's grip loosened as he jerked to the side, letting in the slightest wisp of air, but he didn't let go of her completely.

"Hey!" Rennick's voice seemed far away as her eyes clouded, tunnel vision setting in. "This is what you want, isn't it?"

To her surprise, Olivare let go and stood up, gripping his shoulder. Blood dripped from between his fingers onto the red stone pathway. "You bastard, you shot me."

"The next one will be in your head," Rennick said, his eyes wild. "Now, take it and leave before I kill you."

Caldera rolled over, gasping for breath, as her ears rang. *He shot him?* She looked over at Rennick. He was holding his blaster in one hand and a small, black-and-red marbled stone in the other. *The painite.*

"No... Ren, don't give it to him!" she tried to call out, but it came out as another coughing fit.

Their eyes met as she forced herself to her knees, her heart pounding against her chest in a violent attempt to get her body to its feet. By the time she was standing, Olivare had reached Rennick.

"Hand it over," Olivare commanded. He held out his hand, completely disregarding the flesh wound in his shoulder as if it wasn't there.

Rennick gripped the stone tighter to his chest, taking a step back.

Olivare chuckled, shaking his head. "All right …"

He lunged forward, his fist connecting with Rennick's cheek, which caused him to stumble backward. His blaster flew out of his hand.

"Ren!" Caldera screamed, her voice scratching against her throat. She propelled her legs forward, her feet dragging on the ground. Her lungs were still not filled with enough oxygen to run.

Olivare grabbed Rennick's shirt and threw him to the ground. The stone fell from his hand, bouncing away from them. Olivare stalked toward it. Rennick rolled over and grabbed his ankle, forcing him down.

Caldera forced air into her lungs, making her way over to them when a glint of light caught her eye. *Ren's blaster!* She jogged over to the weapon and grabbed it out of the flower bed.

Gripping the blaster, she aimed it toward Olivare. The men were rolling around on the ground, neither gaining the upper hand. She lowered the weapon. *Shit! I can't get a clear shot... should I kill him even if I could?* Her stomach twisted, a mix of rage and uncertainty roiling inside her. Her hands shook as she raised the blaster again.

Olivare was on top of Rennick, his back on full display as he tried to choke the smaller man. The stone behind them grabbed Caldera's attention. An idea formed. *He wants the painite... Whatever it is, he can't have it.* She shifted the barrel of the blaster over to the mineral—the stone that had already caused so much suffering.

Flicking on the laser sight, she coated the stone in red light. Exhaling slowly, she pulled the trigger. It shattered, releasing wisps of red smoke.

"Bastard!" Rennick growled. Taking advantage of the distraction, he punched Olivare in the nose. The snap of bones was audible from where Caldera was standing. Rennick forced him off to the side and ran over to her.

"No!" Olivare screamed, crawling toward the broken pieces of the destroyed mineral. "Do you know what you've—"

Caldera didn't hear the rest as Rennick wrapped his arms around her, pulling her into a quick hug.

"Are you okay?" he asked, gently pushing her back to arm's length, his hand caressing her cheek.

Caldera stared up into his eyes. His expression was clouded and distraught. She nodded and dropped the blaster to the ground, reaching up to cover his hand with hers. "What about you?" she rasped, examining his swollen face. His lip was split open and blood trickled down his chin.

"I—" he started, but was cut off by a deafening ripping noise, as if something was cutting through the atmosphere itself.

They turned around just in time to see Olivare scrabbling against the stone path, his fingertips leaving bloody smears across the concrete as he was yanked into a swirling red-and-black tear in the sky.

"What the fuck is that?" Caldera screamed as her feet began lifting off the ground, pulling her toward the opening.

"Callie!" Rennick yelled. He caught her hand and pulled her close. Holding her to his chest, he crouched down, the combination of both their weights keeping them on the ground.

She wrapped her arms around his torso, her fingers digging into his back, and looked over his shoulder, unable to pull her eyes away from the churning opening in the air itself. The inconceivable depth of the inside was mesmerizing. The reds, blacks, and metallics swirled and shimmered as the opening grew.

"I'm sorry," Rennick whispered in her ear, digging into his pocket as they started floating into the air again. He let out a sharp breath as a pinprick stung the back of her neck.

The noise around her ceased as she was jerked away from him. A shimmering dome fell over her body, encompassing a circular, three-foot area around her. Caldera reached out, and it fluctuated under her touch. *The planter orb!*

She turned back to Rennick. He held onto the brickwork

of the raised garden bed next to him, digging his fingers into the edges to anchor himself.

Rennick's hair whipped wildly around his head as plants, dirt, and debris flew past them, disappearing into the rip. His mouth moved as he readjusted his grip on the bricks.

She couldn't hear anything. The dome was completely soundproof.

"Ren!" Caldera screamed. Rennick stared at her, unable to hear. She pounded on the dome, but it only shimmered its indifference.

Rennick smiled somberly, holding up his hand.

Caldera touched the outline of his palm, but the dome blocked the contact.

He tried to hold on, clearly using every ounce of strength he had, but the cyclone threatened to pull him away. The knuckles on both his hands turned white.

Caldera looked around. Anything that wasn't anchored to the ground was being sucked into the hole.

Behind Rennick, the spinning circular shape undulated, erratically pulsing and fluctuating. *It's unstable—it's going to close on its own!* Her heart skipped a beat. She looked back at where her and Rennick's hands should have touched—where her hand still was.

The bricks surrounding the raised flower bed gave way.

Caldera couldn't hear anything else, but she heard that. She could have sworn she heard it. The *crunch* as the bricks fell apart.

Their eyes met in a horrific moment of realization.

Rennick was sucked back with such force, it was as if someone had a rope attached to him, jerking him away.

He was gone.

CHAPTER 21

The gardens, flowerbeds, trees—even the stone walkways were gone. Everything was stripped down to the dirt and mud underneath. Only the small, circular stone patch Caldera had been sitting on when the dome fell over her remained after the tear disappeared—a lone disk in the aftermath of the destruction.

"Ren! Ren!" Caldera screamed, her voice beginning to fail completely. She didn't know how long she had been screaming or pounding on the dome, only that her fists hurt. She paused, looking down at her red, swollen hands that were already bruising. *Did I break my wrists?* She blinked, shaking her head as she continued to hit the dome. It shimmered with each impact but didn't falter.

She threw her body against the unyielding wall again. "Let me out!"

Her voice echoed back into her ears as she punched the forcefield with every ounce of strength she could muster, sending shooting pain up her arm and into her neck. She gasped, her knees buckling as she steadied herself against the dome.

Gritting her teeth, she took a deep breath and leaned against the transparent wall as tears streamed down her face. When she reached around to the back of her neck with both hands, she found the circular object.

She probed around the area, trying to find a place to slip her fingers under it—to rip it out. There was none. *No, there's got to be a way. I have to get out of here—I have to find Ren!*

Her stomach rolled in an agony that wasn't entirely from her broken bones, and the heaviness formed a ball of bile that was rapidly finding its way up her throat. She dug her nails into her skin. Ignoring the ache in her fingers and shattered wrists, she grasped the edges of the foreign object. Blood leaked from the wound, making her hand slick. She pulled, and a searing pain shot down her spine and into her legs.

Doubling over, an involuntary blood curdling scream escaped her lips. She didn't let go—even as her vision blurred. Gasping for breath, she braced herself against the dome, leaving shimmering, bloody fingerprints floating in the air in front of her. With a final battle cry, she tore the orb from her neck with a sickening rip, and the dome disappeared.

Caldera looked down at her hand, covered in blood, still holding the orb. A small mass of skin and sinew was attached to the part of the orb that had once been in her body. She discarded it on the ground as her vision tunneled, her heart beating in her ears as she stepped onto the decimated landscape.

Her head spun as she tried to get her bearings. Even though she had been to the back courtyard countless times, she couldn't remember which way the door to the palace was.

Caldera stumbled, tripping on an unknown force as double vision swirled in her eyes. She only managed a few more steps before falling to her knees. Glancing down at her hands, she saw they were red, but she couldn't remember why. Her entire body was numb.

Tunnel vision blackness was encroaching fast, threatening to send her into darkness. The wetness of the blood running down her neck and back made her shiver as coldness seeped down to her bones.

She tried again to clear her mind and think of what her next move should be—to force herself to stand back up and walk—but she couldn't. Her limp body fell against the ground as unconsciousness settled in, causing her to inhale the aroma of musky, long undisturbed dirt. Closing her eyes, the only thing she could think about was what she had just lost.

CALDERA GROANED, STIRRING slightly as her vision filled with bright colors, greens and blues obscuring her field of view. The ringing in her ears was replaced with a continuous beeping that she couldn't place, each sound fighting for dominance as her hearing slowly came back.

The bright color stepped back, revealing its identity as a headscarf and the dark-skinned woman wearing it. A mix of light and dark brown hair curled out of the top and over the sides. The woman wore a white lab coat with an embroidered gold crown over the top of a bright blue blouse and black slacks.

"Ahh, Your Majesty, I'm glad to see you're awake," the woman said. "Pardon my closeness. I was checking your vitals."

"I—" Caldera said, but stopped, her voice so raspy she could hardly speak. As she sat up, the bed adjusted automatically to her movements.

The woman smiled pleasantly and handed her a glass of water. "Please, take your time—there's no need to rush into conversation just yet."

Caldera grabbed the cup, her eyes widening as she realized both her wrists were in form-fitting casts, and that various tubes and wires jutted from her arms. She looked around, just then recognizing what the monotonous beeping was—a heart rate monitor. *I'm in a hospital.* Relief coursed through her.

She gulped the water, downing the contents within seconds. After replacing the glass on the table, she glanced over at the woman, who had moved to the foot of her bed and was examining a holopad.

Caldera inhaled deeply, fighting the urge to gag as the smell of cleaning antiseptic hit her nose. The room was completely white, with a large window taking up almost the entire wall across from her. Outside, shuttles and personal transports crisscrossed the sky in the distance, revealing that they were on one of the topmost floors. She covered her eyes as the sun's mid-afternoon rays coated the room in blinding light.

The woman walked over to a wall panel and typed something in. The room dimmed as the window tinted at the command.

Caldera eyed the woman as she silently typed into a holopad. "Who are you?" she asked, forcing her vocal cords back into action. *If she was sent by the Council...*

The woman looked up. "I'm sorry, how unprofessional. I'm Doctor Celestin Vareis," she replied. "I'm not surprised that you don't remember me, our previous interaction was very brief. I've been your attending physician for the past five days."

"Five days?" Caldera tried to piece together what had happened that would have made her fall unconscious for that long.

"That's correct—we had to induce a coma to reverse the damage you did to yourself," Doctor Vareis said as if reading her mind. "You're lucky we aren't dealing with anything more serious."

"What..." Caldera started, but let the thought trail off as her memories flooded back. *The planter orb. Ren.* "My friend—" she said, trying again.

"Yes," Doctor Vareis interrupted. "Your friend, the palace guard, umm—Saro, I believe, found you in time, so you're lucky."

Saro? Caldera thought, knitting her brows together. "No— not him. My other friend—Ren... Rennick Silvera. Where is he?"

Doctor Vareis's mask of professionalism slipped slightly, a look of genuine confusion spreading across her face. "I'm sorry, he's not here." She finished with the holopad and hung it at the foot of the bed.

Well, he has to be here somewhere. Caldera grimaced. "What do you mean, I'm lucky?" she asked, swallowing the lump that was growing in her throat.

"Well, besides two broken wrists..." Doctor Vareis narrowed her eyes, the mask slipping yet again. "That thing you ripped out of your neck is dangerous. It bonded with some of the neurons from your spinal cord. Ripping them out—to be frank—could have paralyzed you."

Caldera wrung her fingers, unable to speak. Doctor Vareis continued talking.

"It may not be my place to say, but this 'planter orb' should never have been released in the first place," she said sternly. "That little demonstration last week sent four people into this hospital—same as you. And I suspect more will come in time."

"I—I didn't—"

"It was released on your orders," Doctor Vareis interrupted. "It's improperly tested and irresponsible."

A flash of anger welled up inside Caldera's chest. *I didn't release the fucking thing, Vandren did!* she wanted to scream but stopped just short of doing so, realizing she had once held the same sentiments about Quill. She took a deep breath. "You know you're talking to the queen, right?" she said, her anger not completely dissipated. *If I blame Vandren outright, I'll face the same fate as the former king.*

"I do." Doctor Vareis straightened, her brown-eyed gaze hard as stone. "But you're in the hospital of Astrum, and you're my patient. It's my duty to tell you your diagnosis as well as when you're doing something dangerous. I'm treating you like I'd treat anyone else."

The heart rate monitor beeped its indifference as a heavy silence settled in. Doctor Vareis fiddled with a screen that displayed numbers and readouts that Caldera didn't understand. Her body felt stiff with anger and frustration.

"Okay…" Caldera said. "In that case—thank you." She released the blanket, smoothing it out over her legs.

The mask of professionalism dropped, her expression curious. "Thank you?"

"Yeah. Nobody treats me like a normal person anymore," Caldera said, tears stinging her eyes.

"I don't get too many thank yous," Doctor Vareis chuckled—a warm, surprising sound that Caldera's ears welcomed. "Despite saving lives." She smiled for the first time since Caldera had met her, showing off her slightly gapped front teeth.

The door to the room swished open.

Before Caldera could say anything, her friends were around her, almost knocking Doctor Vareis to the floor. Sear's soft fur brushed against her body on the right, while Markarian and Aloriea were on her left, sandwiching her into a hug. She squeezed as tightly as she could, trying unsuccessfully to wrap her arms around all three of them. Tears freely streamed down her face. She didn't want the embrace to end.

"She's only just woken up. You shouldn't crowd her," Doctor Vareis said, her voice muffled against Caldera's ears that were pressed against Sear and Markarian.

Sear, Markarian, and Aloriea took a step back, turning to look at the interrupting doctor. The grimaces on their faces spoke louder than any words could have.

"Doctor Vareis, could you give us a minute?" Caldera asked, flicking her eyes toward the door.

The doctor paused, then blew out a frustrated breath. "Of course, Your Majesty," she replied. The door latch clicked into place behind her as she exited the room.

Caldera's friends turned back to face her, their eyes all shining with tears. "Where's Ren?" she asked before anyone else could speak.

They all exchanged shocked glances, and Aloriea immediately burst into tears, covering her face. Markarian and Sear blinked down at her as tears streamed silently down their cheeks. They all sat around the edges of the bed, almost in unison.

The heart rate monitor increased in frequency with each passing second. As if she needed the confirmation—as if she couldn't feel her heart pounding rapidly, insistent on beating a hole in her chest.

"He—" Markarian began, but stopped as the words caught, tangling in his throat. He reached into his jacket pocket and pulled out a hand terminal.

Caldera took the device with shaking hands. *This is how the Vanguard files official reports.*

When she turned it on, it immediately opened to a completed and submitted report—the way she knew it would. She rapidly skimmed the information, her eyes flying over the words. *Both heat signatures, from past occupation in the Vanguard, to current occupation as personal bodyguard of the sector leader, scanned in all parts of the galaxy. No results.* Her breath caught as she instinctively scrolled through to the bottom and froze.

There was no air. No heat. Only coldness that spread through her body, into her core.

Name: Rennick Silvera.

Occupation: Personal bodyguard to the sector leader.

Status: Deceased—died in the act of protecting the queen.

Caldera threw the terminal across the room, screaming as if it had burned her. It hit the wall, breaking into smaller useless pieces.

"That isn't true, Vandren must have written that! You know he can't be trusted!" she shrieked, not caring anymore if someone heard her as her tear-filled eyes moved from Markarian, to Sear, to Aloriea.

"Callie..." Markarian said, placing a hand on her arm, his voice softer than she had ever heard it. "Vandren didn't write that report... I did."

Caldera jerked away from him like he'd punched her. Her vision blurred from uncontrollable tears. "Why would you do that? You don't know that!" She pushed him away as hard as she could, but from her position, she only managed to make him stand back up from his seat—which he retook immediately.

Aloriea stared at her through bloodshot eyes, her body as still as a statue.

"How could you!" Caldera choked, her voice on the edge of giving out. The knot in her stomach tightened, and she had to wrap her arms around herself to keep from calling out for help. Her body doubled over, forehead pressing against her knees.

"Caldera..." Sear's hands were on her shoulders, forcing her to turn toward him and look into his golden eyes.

She went still, her own name sounding foreign to her ears—she couldn't remember the last time Sear or Markarian had called her by her full name.

"I am... I am so sorry," Sear continued, the tear tracks on his face shining in the fluorescent light.

Caldera lunged forward and grabbed his shirt, feeling the pull of fur under the fabric as she clenched it in her fists. "He's not—he's not dea—" The words dissipated in her throat, making her want to vomit. Tears streamed down her cheeks in waterfalls, her body racking with sobs as she buried her face in Sear's chest. "He's not!" She screamed again into his shirt, between gasping shallow breaths.

Aloriea placed her hand on Caldera's leg as Markarian touched her arm. As much as she wanted to pull away from them—from their touch—she couldn't force herself to move.

Sear wrapped his arms around her, his hands gently rubbing her back, trying to soothe her—even though his own body was trembling.

CHAPTER 22

"As soon as Grey sent out the distress call, Sol and I herded Lady Morin and Sir Arcaro into a safe room. Sol stayed with them," Saro told Caldera. "I ran outside to find everything destroyed."

Caldera tried to imagine Saro stepping out into the decimated courtyard. The gardens that he and his brother had patrolled for years, gone. The emptiness in her heart was the only thing to greet her.

"Send me the footage," Caldera demanded of Grey. Newly released from the hospital, she stood in the doorway to her quarters, hand outstretched toward the red-haired man in front of her. "I know your ship's external cameras caught everything as you flew away."

Grey nodded as Sear, Aloriea, and Markarian crowded in around him. "Y—yes, of course. I just wanted to personally thank you—"

"The footage. Now...please."

"I do not think that is a good idea," Sear said from behind Grey, his ears lying flat against the top of his head, his golden eyes filled with sorrow.

Caldera ignored him. "As queen, I command you," she said, her voice low and flat.

Grey nodded, holding out the holopad, hands shaking.

"Callie!" Aloriea called, right as the door whooshed between them.

Caldera quickly locked it so no one could enter.

She walked to the bathroom, the holopad trembling in her hands, and opened the video. Sitting down next to the toilet, she hit play. The quality was crystal clear. She could zoom in as close as she wanted, and it wouldn't pixelate—the perks of a top-of-the-line Vanguard explorer-class ship. There was no sound, but she didn't need it—she could still hear everything clearly.

They were there, the three of them. Olivare had just stood up after trying to choke her to death, and was walking toward Rennick. Then they were floating, lifted off the ground seemingly by nothing—Olivare had already been sucked in. Then she was sitting on the ground, and Rennick was gone.

Opening a new program, she scanned the planet for Rennick's vitals. It came up blank after a few minutes. Her eyes blurred as her stomach rolled once. Her head was in the bowl, vomiting up the contents of her stomach, the holopad clicking against the marble floor where she dropped it. She took a deep breath, wiping her mouth with her sleeve, then picked up the holopad and hit rewind.

Caldera couldn't remember how or when she had made it back to her bed, finally leaving the bathroom once everything had been completely expelled from her stomach. She *tried* to sleep, but his face was always there, horrified, and knowing that he was doomed—the last look they had shared.

By day five, she had memorized the entire thing. The holopad intuitively knew how to adjust the image, automatically zooming in to the specifications she preferred, without her prompt.

Through scanning and researching every millisecond of footage, she learned that Olivare had cyber augmentations in his ears and eyes that allowed him to be unaffected by the flashbang he had thrown at her...that the brickwork of the raised flower bed had begun to crumble as soon as the tear had opened—Rennick had no chance.

As if being an expert on the footage would somehow change the outcome. The scan for Rennick's vitals was continuous in the background, but she never heard the *ping* of a discovery.

She was numb to the information by the eighth day.

Caldera pushed the memories aside as she wrapped an arm around her stomach, curled into a ball, and hit play for the nine-hundred and forty-second time.

"Callie, open up!" Aloriea's muffled voice called through Caldera's door, her fist banging against the thick metal.

Caldera ignored her, the way she always did. She rolled over and pulled the covers up to her chin, trying to find comfort in the silk sheets. It was a fool's errand—they were wrinkled and filled with eight days' worth of restless nights.

She pushed them away and looked down at the holopad propped up on the bed next to her, the video paused for the moment. Squeezing her eyes shut, she tried to will her stomach to stop growling, unable to remember the last time she'd had anything other than water.

They were still trying to get in. She exhaled sharply. *Leave me alone!*

Her thoughts wandered as she pressed play again. Pieces of the past week wove through her mind as she slipped in and out of consciousness, her stomach continuing its protest.

A clink followed by a whirring noise coming from the balcony met her ears and interrupted her ritual. She hit pause and looked out the glass doors without moving, recognizing the sound as the quick retraction of a grappling hook gun.

Contemplating if she still had the strength to sit up, her eyes never wavered from the balcony. *So this is it then. This is when the Council decides to assassinate me.* She wondered who they were sending. If she knew them. If she'd even try to fight back.

The whirring stopped, and a black-gloved hand reached over the thick concrete railing. Caldera closed her eyes. *Knowing won't do me any good—won't do anyone any good. I can't tell them who killed me once I'm dead, anyway.* She took a deep breath as the door to the balcony quietly squeaked open. *Mom. Dad. Ren... I'll see you soon.*

"Callie?"

Her eyes shot open. "Markarian? What are you doing?" she said, attempting to rise into a seated position.

"You won't open the door," he scolded, scratching the back of his head. Half of his black hair was pulled into a bun, the other half curling above his shoulders.

"So you broke into my room?" she continued for him as a piece of unwashed white hair fell in front of her eyes.

"We're worried about you! Vandren is making shit up to explain your 'disappearance', and the other sector leaders are freaking out!" he snapped. Regret filled his eyes, and he took a step back. "Sorry..."

Caldera waved it off. "It's fine," she said, pulling her knees up to her chest in an attempt to hide the fact that she still wore the same clothes from over a week ago. "What's he saying?"

"'She's mentally unable to perform her duties'. No further explanation. Which is why the sector leaders are losing their minds over this. And despite Aloriea's best efforts to persuade them otherwise, they think you met the same fate as Quill... They think you're dead."

"Did Vandren announce that I was?"

"No, but the leaders think he's covering it up. Until you show your face, they won't believe anything else."

"Is that why you're here? To tell me to go back to my 'duties'?" The question came out harsher than she had intended. She looked away.

"I know you're alive, but... I just wanted to see if you're okay," he said, clearly already knowing the answer as he glanced at her. With a sigh, he walked over to the table in front of the fireplace and took a seat. "And I wanted to explain something to you."

"What?" she asked, meeting his eyes. A soft breeze from the open balcony doors rustled the thin curtains, caressing her skin and jostling her limp, dirty hair around her shoulders. She wanted to get up and slam them shut.

He took a deep breath. "I want you to understand why I filed Ren's death report when I did."

Caldera's stomach lurched, and she was glad it was empty. "Okay," she whispered, resting her chin on top of her knees as she averted her gaze.

"The Council," Markarian said, looking directly at her, "was going to cover this up."

"What!" she shouted, unable to contain herself, knowing she shouldn't be surprised. Outrage filled her chest as she flung her legs off the bed, the sudden movement making the sheets ruffle and her head spin. She fell sideways, dizziness clouding her mind.

"Hey." Markarian's voice was gentle in her ear.

She didn't know how he had gotten to her side so quickly, but his hands were on her shoulders, helping her to her feet.

"Careful, you almost hit the floor," he said, trying to steady her. "That probably would've cracked your skull."

"I can walk." She stumbled forward, and Markarian caught her again before she tumbled to the ground.

"You can't," he countered, his voice stern as he grabbed her arms and walked her over to the chair. "When's the last time you ate something?"

Without answering, she begrudgingly let him sit her down, narrowing her eyes as he sat across from her. "What do you mean they were going to cover it up?" she asked, her voice low, the first new sparks of emotion other than grief emanating inside her chest.

Markarian sighed, more to himself than to her. "In those five days when you were in a coma, Grey and I were summoned by the Council—all of them. They asked us why we were ordering our crews to look for Ren," he explained. "Grey let them listen to his distress call, but he kept the video—the one you have—a secret. They don't know that the situation was caused by a fight over the painite. All they know is that Olivare tried to kill you and the mineral got destroyed in the scuffle, causing that—that *thing* to open."

Caldera's stomach twisted with each word. Her hand shot up to her throat where Olivare's handprints had been bruised onto her neck.

"They ordered Grey to destroy the voice record," Markarian continued, his gaze downcast. "And for us to stop looking for Ren."

"But you didn't do either of those things," she mused, glancing over at the holopad still lying on her bed.

"No," he replied, shaking his head. "The opposite, actually." He looked up at her, the grin that spread across his face saying he had found a loophole in the rules—the Council's rules. "Over the next four days, with the help of Grey, and Sylvie—"

Caldera flicked her gaze toward him.

Markarian's smile softened. "Yeah, she's back in action. Which you would've known if you had listened to Grey before he gave you the holopad," he said, gripping her shoulder. "You and Ren saved their lives."

Her stomach knotted again. "What happened after you scanned the planet for Ren?" she probed.

"I filed the report. It's public record now. The Council *can't* cover it up—or, at least, it'll be harder for them to."

"What'd they do when they found out?" Caldera asked around the lump in her throat.

Markarian's grin was gone. "That remains to be seen. I might have to go on the run...depending on if they want to try me as a traitor."

Shame immediately radiated from her gut for endangering another one of her friends. "That wasn't very smart of you," she said, looking directly at him.

"Yeah, well... I learned from the best," he countered, giving her a forced smile.

Caldera wrung her hands. "If they ordered you to destroy the record and stop the search, how come you and Grey didn't get arrested immediately?"

"That's what I'm getting at," Markarian explained. "That's why I think I'll be fine. It was all off the books, so to speak."

"Their order wasn't a real one?"

He nodded. "I'm guessing it was to scare us into complying. They know they can't make too much more of a fuss around members of your court, *or* people that you're in close contact with. It'll draw suspicion to them, or at least Vandren. It'll make it look like he can't control what goes on in the sector he oversees."

She tapped her chin. "So what have they done now that you've submitted a public report?"

"As of yesterday, they've officially disavowed Olivare and are honoring Ren as some kind of hero," he answered with a flourish. "I doubt that he'd like that, but at least he'll be remembered."

The knot in her stomach unwound slightly. "Thank you," she whispered, tears finally making their way into her eyes.

"Callie, listen," Markarian said, placing a hand on her shoulder again. "I don't want to believe this any more than you—none of us do... But we still have each other. Will you please let us help?"

"Help, how?"

Markarian was silent for a while, letting the breeze from the open balcony blow through his hair. His bright green eyes dimmed as he met her gaze. "Because we can all understand what you're going through in some way, shape, or form. Sear's entire family has disowned him simply for living and working in Tellis instead of Muléus—and now he's stuck here. Aloriea's dealing with Quill's death. And me..."

"You've lost someone, too?"

"Yes."

Her eyes widened. "I know about Sear's situation, and obviously Aloriea's, but how do I not know this about you?"

Leaning his head back, Markarian stared up at the high-rise ceiling. "Because I never told you the story of how I got my scar."

She sat back, waiting for him to continue.

With a sharp inhale, he sat forward. "I was a regular Vanguard tech member, working below decks."

Caldera nodded.

"Remember when recon missions weren't only left to the captains and first officers?"

"Of course."

"Well, a group of techs, myself included, were sent out onto the surface of an exo we had landed on to investigate its condition. Take samples, see if it had harvestable soil, stuff like that. Anyway, the weather got bad, raging winds, impenetrable dust clouds—the works. So we took shelter in a cave to wait it out."

"What happened?"

"A quake. Seismic. Ground opening up, people falling in, the whole shebang."

"Markarian..."

"I managed to grab one person before they fell. They were hanging over the gap, grabbing onto my arm for dear life while I called for e-vac with the other hand."

Caldera gripped the collar of her shirt, never taking her eyes off Markarian. He was no longer looking at her.

"A huge stalactite ended up breaking off the ceiling and slashing my arm. It made me lose my grip. I dropped the person I was holding onto. My sister."

"I'm so sorry, Markarian," Caldera gasped, placing her hand on his arm as tears welled in his eyes.

"After that, I went back to the academy and learned how to be a navigator, a higher-up position, resulting in a transfer to your bridge crew."

"I don't know what to say..."

"You don't have to say anything. Callie, I didn't tell you this so you would feel sorry for me—that's why I don't tell people in the first place. My sister wouldn't want that," he said, wiping his eyes. "I told you because I want you to understand. You're not alone. We know how it feels. Like the world's going to end, right?"

Tear trails streamed down her face as she nodded, glancing toward the door. "Sear and Aloriea are outside, aren't they?"

Markarian smiled softly, sitting back again with a shrug. "Open the door and find out."

CHAPTER 23

"Are you sure you can handle this?" Aloriea asked as she zipped up the back of the black dress Caldera was wearing.

"I told you—I'm fine," Caldera replied, making sure her voice didn't waver.

"It's just…" Aloriea started, fastening the clip at the base of Caldera's neck, just below the scar from the planter orb. "Vandren's going to be there, so…"

"Don't worry, I won't embarrass you," Caldera clipped, turning to face Aloriea.

Aloriea's eyes narrowed. She had pulled her hair into a tight bun, leaving her light brown horns fully exposed and gleaming in the sunlight that streamed through the windows. "I don't care about that," she said, her voice low. "I'm worried about you." She sighed. "You can't break down today."

"I know." Caldera attempted to pull her hair back into a half-ponytail, but gave up almost immediately. "We're burying an empty casket anyway," she continued hollowly, her shoulders slumping. "So why would I?"

Aloriea sighed again as she began braiding Caldera's hair, which had grown a little below her shoulders. "You don't have to go," she whispered as she finished, stepping to the side.

Caldera looked up into eyes that were filled with compounded loss. "I know that, too," she said, reaching out and taking her friend's hand. "I want to—I need to ask *him* a question," she continued as a pang of rage shot through her chest.

"Vandren?" Aloriea asked.

Caldera nodded, tightening her grip on Aloriea's hand.

"What kind of question?"

"I'm going to ask him what painite is, and why the Vanguard's looking for it."

Aloriea shook her head. "That's dangerous—for all of us."

"Actually, I don't think it is. Markarian never got reprimanded," Caldera countered, meeting her gaze. "There are already too many eyes on this palace as it is—with me becoming queen out of nowhere, Justle's disappearance, and now this." She paused, her gaze falling to the floor. "Any word on his whereabouts?"

Aloriea shook her head. "There are still no leads. The private investigators are thinking about closing the investigation."

Caldera gritted her teeth. "Anyway…" she continued, "Vandren can't go around killing us with everything that's been going on."

"Okay, point taken," Aloriea said. "But he won't tell you anything anyway."

Caldera turned toward the door. "I'm not expecting him to."

"Then what's the point?"

"To show him I'm not going to be complicit in whatever the fuck they're doing," Caldera snapped, exiting the room.

Aloriea followed Caldera down the hall, her long, black sheath dress shifting around her body as her heels clicked loudly. "What happened to being secretive?"

Caldera had to repress a laugh as Rennick's words swirled in her mind. "Fuck that," she replied, stalking toward the front entrance. "I've never been good at stealth missions—I'm too reckless for that."

They hurried down the hall and staircase to the doors of the front courtyard entrance. The sun glowed off the marble steps and into her eyes as Caldera paused to squint up at the sky. Then she followed Aloriea down to the private transport where Sear and Markarian were already waiting, along with Sol and Saro.

Markarian's hands were jammed into the pockets of his pants, his black suit jacket contrasting harshly with his solemn green eyes.

Sear clasped his hands behind his back, his plain black button-up pulling across his shoulders. Dressy shorts fell just below his knee.

Caldera cast her gaze to the ground as Saro opened the door for them. She forced the growing hollowness down into the pit of her stomach, containing it.

The ride to the royal cemetery was short. Complete silence filled the entire transport as Sol drove them to their destination. Saro looked back at them periodically through the divider but didn't speak. His eyes were glassy and full of pity. Caldera forced herself to look away.

The scenery blazed by so quickly she couldn't make out any of it. Taking a few deep breaths, she tried to steel herself for what was to come.

As they reached their destination, the transport slowed and drove under a huge archway carved out of stone that was bordered by two pointed towers with filigree carvings adorning the very tips. The wrought-iron gates were held open by a man and woman wearing black suits, like Sol and Saro. After they drove past, the security detail closed the gate behind them—only letting in 'pre-approved' people.

They continued down a long, winding gravel road before pulling to a stop next to a canopy-like structure with a small group gathered around it. Vandren was one of them, his golden robe billowing in the breeze, and in the middle of the crowd was the casket. Caldera's stomach lurched as Sol opened the door for her.

"Are you all right, Your Majesty?" he asked, reaching his hand out to her.

She nodded and steadied herself, then took his outstretched hand. She didn't trust herself to talk. Her friends were beside her in an instant.

"You can do this," Sear whispered in her ear as he walked past, his tail swishing the perfectly manicured, green grass.

Caldera nodded again, thinking that she should have told Sear and Markarian about her plan, but it was too late.

A gentle breeze blew through the trees that rimmed the cemetery and the flowers that lined the headstones. The sky was crystal blue, so clear that she could make out the outline of Bersama's two moons.

What right does the weather have to be so nice today? Caldera grimaced, digging her fingernails into her palms.

As they slowly made their way over to the group, a few older men and women glanced up at them. Caldera surprisingly knew most of them—although not personally, and she didn't want to. Anger welled up inside of her at the sight of his extended relations. *Why are you people even here? Ren hated pretty much all of you.*

Rennick's family glowered at her, bowing as she approached. Her stomach rolled over again. She nodded back at them, pointedly not making eye contact, and started making her way over to Vandren when she was cut off by a young man who looked so much like Rennick that she couldn't hold in a gasp—even though she recognized him. One of the only people in his family that Rennick cared about.

"Your Majesty, can I talk to you—just for a second?" the Rennick clone asked.

She nodded and stepped to the side of the group.

"My name's Willix—Will. I'm Ren's younger brother," he said once they were far enough away to give the illusion of privacy.

"I know," Caldera replied, taking a deep breath. "I've heard a lot about you over the years." The hollowness in her chest deepened. "What did you—"

"I wanted to meet you," Willix interrupted. "I was hoping I could sooner, but..." He paused, searching for the right phrase. "Being sequestered at university doesn't offer a lot of opportunities."

Caldera blinked. "Do you...want to tell me something?" The breeze blew tiny strands of hair around her forehead that were too short to fit into the braid.

"I just...want to talk to the person my brother gave up his life for—the clandestine queen."

Her stomach dropped. "That's what people are calling me?" she asked, desperately trying to change the subject and digging her nails deeper into the skin. "The secret queen?"

"Could be worse," he replied with a wave of his hand, glancing over at the group crowded around the empty casket—his family. "There are plenty of people out there who think you're some kind of usurper."

Her sorrow turned to anger. "That's why you wanted to talk to me?"

"Are you?" Willix asked bluntly, crossing his arms. His stance, hazel eyes, and brown hair made him look so much like Rennick, that she had to glance away.

"No," Caldera replied simply, forcing herself to look at him.

"Well... That's good, then," he said, with a tone that said, 'I don't quite believe you'. "I doubted Ren would be involved with someone like that."

"And what do you think about me?" Caldera blurted, unable to stop herself. She wasn't sure why she asked—or why she even cared...but she did.

He turned back around to look at her, considering the question. "I don't know..." His eyes took on the sheen of incoming tears. "I want to hate you, but Ren... He cared for you deeply, so that counts for something."

The emptiness inside her body dissipated slightly, despite

Willix's proclamations of potential hatred. *That counts for something.* She set her jaw and walked past him, making her way over to Vandren, who was offering his condolences to Rennick's family.

Her blood boiled as the phrases, "my deepest apologies", and, "he died a hero, protecting the queen from a murderous traitor", met her ears.

That 'traitor' was sent by you, you piece of shit! She gritted her teeth, stepping into his line of sight.

"Ahh, Your Majesty," Vandren said, bowing his head. "I wasn't sure you would make it today—after the traumatic events you went through." His gray gaze flicked from the green grass at his feet to her eyes.

"Of course I made it," Caldera snapped as the mourners filtered away, back toward the empty casket. "Surprising as it is that we're having a funeral at all," she continued, forcing her voice to stay level as she stepped closer to him.

"Blame your friend Markarian for that," Vandren muttered, his voice low.

"I don't blame him for anything. In fact, I'm thanking him," Caldera said, standing beside him. "Ren will be remembered now, and the incident won't be swept under the rug. It was your idea to have this half-hearted, empty casket funeral anyway—"

"Does his family not deserve some sort of closure?" he asked, his mouth quirking up into a passive smile as he turned to face her, his hands hidden in his robe's oversized sleeves. "What's this really about—Your Majesty?"

This is it. "I know you sent out the order for the Vanguard to search for the mineral painite," she whispered.

"Oh? That would hardly be secret knowledge to you."

"No, but now I know about the side effects, too."

"Clearly," he said casually. "You're still alive."

She swallowed the lump in her throat and pressed on, her heart pounding against her ribcage. "My question is this. What would the Council want with a mineral that can create black holes out of nowhere?"

"Do you believe you know what's going on?" Vandren asked. A flash of amusement that she wasn't expecting crossed his face, causing the rage in her gut to rise into her chest.

"Yes," she lied, hoping he'd reveal something—anything.

The look of amusement intensified as he leaned in close to her face, his voice a barely audible whisper. "Well, since you already know everything, then you must realize that your friend didn't have to die."

Caldera's breathing slowed as a haze fell over her, a red flower blooming inside her chest—the petals of unchecked grief and rage reaching out to every extremity of her body. She blinked and saw Rennick's face in front of her so vividly it was like she was back under the dome.

She blinked again as the punch connected—her fist against Vandren's cheek.

A snap, followed by a jolt of pain, shot up her arm as Vandren's body fell limp against the ground, the haze lifting just in time for her to realize the severity of what she had just done.

Fuck.

A chorus of screams erupted from the mourners, and in another blink of an eye, Markarian and Sear were around her, grabbing her wrists and yanking her down to the ground. A yelp escaped her lips as the pain from her broken bones shot up her arm. Markarian had his blaster out, pointed at no one in particular as he kneeled in front of her, trying to shield her with his body. Sear wrapped himself around her, pinning her arms to her sides.

"Don't shoot!" she heard Markarian yell, but she couldn't see him—Sear's body obstructed her entire view.

"Sol, Saro. Please, just calm down," Aloriea was saying somewhere in the distance, her voice shaking.

"Callie!" Sear frantically whispered in her ear as his arms tightened around her even more, the bristling fur from his chest scratching against her face. "Why would you do that?"

She didn't have a chance to answer.

"Please, please. Sol, Saro, lay down your arms," Vandren's

muffled voice said. "The poor woman's obviously in distress and acting out," he continued, talking about her as if she were simply throwing a tantrum—and in a way, she kind of was. Subconsciously trying to punish herself for failing to save her friend.

Caldera struggled against Sear's embrace, but he held tight, unflinching.

"She assaulted you, Your Excellency!" Saro said, holding a hint of regret. "We must, at the very least, detain her..."

Caldera stopped struggling to break free as a sinking feeling appeared in her stomach.

"Unnecessary," Vandren replied.

Caldera's eyes widened. *What is he doing?*

"Saro, please direct the family members back to their transports," Vandren ordered.

A few moments later, the outbursts from the onlookers faded as they were herded away from the commotion.

"This is unacceptable, Your Excellency," Sol said once the family was out of earshot. "She must be arrested."

Vandren came into view, shaking his head. "Put the palace on lockdown, don't let her—or her court—leave. If they do, they'll be immediately arrested and tried for treason."

"With all due respect," Sol continued. "What will that do?"

"It will hopefully, finally, make her realize that she's not the one in control here," Vandren whispered, leaning in close to her, his face already swollen where she had hit him. "I am."

Sear sat back without releasing his hold on her.

"This is your last chance. Is that understood, Your Majesty?"

Caldera didn't respond. She glared at him as involuntary tears streamed down her face and dripped onto Sear's arms.

Vandren smirked, waving his hand in the air. "Get her out of here."

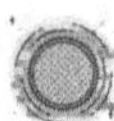

"I ASKED YOU to do one thing—one!" Aloriea shouted as she paced around Caldera's quarters.

Sear sat silently at the table in front of the fireplace with his head in his hands, and Markarian with his boots up—neither one interjecting on Aloriea's tirade.

"I—" Caldera said, from her seated position at the end of the bed. The indigo shades of night seeped into her quarters, only to be fended off by the glowing lamps and overhead chandelier.

"No!" Aloriea interrupted. "You're going to sit there and listen to all the ways you've just fucked us over!" Her eyes blazed with anger as she whirled around to face Caldera.

Caldera balled the blankets into fists beside her, and let Aloriea continue. A new quick-heal cast squeezed the broken wrist of her right hand.

"One—" Aloriea said, counting on her fingers. "You assaulted a council member."

Caldera flinched.

"Two—you cost Sear and Markarian their jobs!"

"What?" Caldera interjected, glancing behind Aloriea at the men sitting at the table.

Aloriea's eyes narrowed. "Yes... Sol informed me before I came up here." She wrapped her arms around her body as if trying to comfort herself. "Even if they didn't interfere with Sol and Saro today, they're still on lockdown. Last time I checked, you can't be a Vanguard flight consultant *or* captain if you can't go into the fucking headquarters."

"I—I didn't..."

"Three—you put all of us in danger, including yourself!" The first sheen of tears appeared in Aloriea's eyes. "The three of you almost got shot today!" she screamed, her voice breaking as tears streamed down her face. "What if you all died? I can't... I can't..." she trailed off, furiously wiping her eyes and turning away.

"I'm sorry," Caldera muttered as the air left her lungs. She was unable to provide anything else, not even an explanation. There wasn't one to offer.

None of them responded. A look she didn't understand passed between Markarian and Aloriea as their eyes met. *Is it despair? Detachment? They're giving up on me. Sear hasn't even looked up from his hands.*

Caldera bit the inside of her cheek, realizing what she had to do, but not wanting to commit. "I know I fucked up," she said, looking at each of them. "I've ruined all of your lives as a byproduct of simply existing."

Her breath caught as Aloriea's expression softened, and Sear looked at her for the first time since they'd gotten back from the funeral. *Maybe I don't have to do this...* She shook her head, dismissing the idea as she took another deep breath. "So, I'm giving you an out."

"What are you talking about?" Markarian asked slowly, clearly analyzing every word.

"Have Sol and Saro summon Vandren back here...and renounce me," Caldera said quickly before she lost her nerve, spitting out the words. The thought of being completely alone made her nauseous.

The look of pure shock that passed between the three of them was partially unexpected, based on the thirty minutes of yelling and screaming leading up to it.

"If you do that, maybe you can return to your old lives," she continued before they could say anything. "More importantly, you'll be safe. You'll never be safe if you're around me," she finished, averting her gaze.

A silent conversation seemed to pass between the three.

"Is that an order?" Sear asked, just as the silence became uncomfortable. Nightfliers continued to chirp outside the open window.

"N—no," she muttered, shame radiating across her entire body as her gaze met Sear's. "I'll never do anything like that. Not to any of you."

"Good," Markarian said, his boots hitting the floor. "Because we weren't going to listen to you, anyway."

"What are you—" The realization hit her as her friends' soft smiles eliminated any lingering nausea she still felt.

"This isn't just your fight," Aloriea said, walking over to sit next to her. She placed a hand on top of Caldera's, the anger gone from her voice.

"You haven't ruined our lives, Cal...and just because we're a little angry doesn't mean we're going to leave you alone in this death trap," Markarian said.

Caldera smiled as tears welled in her eyes. "A little angry?"

Markarian shrugged, an amiable smile beaming across his face.

"And it is a death trap," Sear interjected, laying his hands down on the table.

"Sol and Saro were way too ready to put a bullet in your head," Markarian added, pounding his fist against the table. His face flushed red, smile gone. "Mostly Sol."

"That doesn't mean you should risk your own lives!" Caldera yelled. She jolted to her feet, the happiness disappearing—replaced with an intense urgency to make them understand why she couldn't lose them. She hung her head. "I've lost too many people already—my parents died in a transport accident when I was sixteen, and with no other family, I had no one. I was lost." Her eyes glazed with the sheen of unfallen tears. "And now Ren ..." Caldera cleared her throat, meeting each of their eyes. "You're all I have left."

Before any of them could respond, her communicator chimed the alert for a received message. She furrowed her brow and walked over to her bedside table—the crease only deepening once she opened the message.

"What is it?" Aloriea asked.

Caldera shrugged and handed the communicator to Aloriea. "I honestly don't know," she said, walking over to Sear and Markarian to embrace them. "It's not every day that spam gets through onto a communicator," she continued, turning back around.

"I..." Aloriea paused. "I think I recognize this."

"What are you talking about?" Caldera asked. "It's just a bunch of dots and dashes."

"No," Aloriea replied more definitively, pointing at the screen. "I definitely recognize this. It's not spam. It's a message."

"How do you know that?" Sear asked.

Markarian playfully pushed Sear to the back of the huddle, stepping in front of him so he could see. "Aloriea's our resident code breaker, remember?"

"That I am," Aloriea replied. "This was one type of code that Quill and I thought about using to communicate with—but it turned out to be too conspicuous."

"What do you mean?" Sear asked, leaning over their shoulders so his face was closer to the screen.

"Dots and dashes are a little too obvious. It screams, 'I'm hiding something'," she said with a chuckle.

Caldera grabbed the communicator out of her hands, checking the information. "Who's it from?"

"Well?" Markarian probed, excitement in his voice.

"The information's wiped," she replied flatly. "I don't know."

Sear pointed to the message. "Can you read this, Aloriea?"

"I never learned it—I honestly can't even remember what it's called. There were a lot of options in the book Quill brought to me."

"Would this book be in the library?" Sear asked, scratching behind his ear.

Aloriea shook her head. "No way. I have no clue where he even got it."

Caldera tapped her foot against the floor, contemplating what their next move should be. "I think I have a pretty good idea."

CHAPTER 24

Caldera took a deep breath as she pushed open the back courtyard doors. She hadn't been back since *the incident*. The gasps that followed revealed her friends hadn't been back, either.

A crater of barren ground and remnants of torn and dying vegetation met their eyes. The wall still surrounded the palace, despite new sections of crumbling concrete where a stone façade used to reside.

"Holy shit..." Markarian whispered, his hand shooting up to cover his mouth.

Caldera stepped out into the night, the dewy air clinging to her skin. "Yeah..." she muttered. "Let's go."

"Are you sure that the entrance is still there?" Sear asked. His ears flicked around as if he expected to be attacked, his claws at the ready.

"No," she admitted, not letting herself look around at the decimated landscape. Eerie silence filled her ears. There was nothing for the breeze to rustle, no animals calling out into the night.

An involuntary sense of responsibility for the mess stabbed at her gut.

"Callie?" Sear said, touching her shoulder, which jolted her out of her trance. "Are you listening?"

She shook her head. "Sorry. What did you say?"

"What's the plan if the entrance is toast?" Markarian asked, his hand resting on his hip where the holster of his blaster used to reside. The moons cast opposing shadows across his face, giving him a menacing glare that he didn't actually have.

There isn't one. "Let's hope it's not," she replied without answering the question.

They came to the corner of the palace where the entrance was tucked away, winding beneath the ground. The wrought-iron bench and tree were gone, but Caldera recognized the fake stone that was still there, attached to the palace wall—sticking out like a sore thumb.

It's so obvious, how has it not been found before? She pushed it in, triggering the mechanism that flipped it over to reveal the scanner as if nothing had happened. It lit up when she pressed her hand against it. After a few seconds, it glowed its green light of approval, and the ground sank.

They sprinted down the stairs, closing the entrance without saying a word, and immediately ran to the shelves and shelves of books. Nothing had changed since the discovery of the secret room, almost two months prior. It was as if the portal had never opened.

An hour passed and her knuckles turned white as Caldera tightened her grip on the book she held. As she turned the pages, she could almost convince herself Rennick was still there—still alive. That he would walk out of the bathroom, spouting something about secret codes and rooms. How they were so close to finding the answers they wanted, and how unlikely all of this was in the first place. She bit her lip to keep from crying.

"Here!" Aloriea called, walking over to the table. "I found the book that Quill showed me when we were deciding on what code to use to talk to each other."

"You knew what you were looking for, and it still took you an hour to find it?" Markarian complained, his back cracking as he stretched.

"In case you haven't noticed, there's like a thousand books in here," Aloriea pointed out, taking a seat.

Caldera looked up from the volume she'd been absently staring into. Slamming it shut, she replaced it on the shelf and sat next to Aloriea as she opened the ratty journal and started flipping through the pages.

"There," Aloriea said, pointing to a page. "It's called... Morse code."

"Shit..." Markarian whispered, leaning over the back of the chair. "It's ancient—like, *ancient* ancient."

Aloriea nodded. "Even more so than skip ciphers."

Sear sat down on the other side of her. "How are we going to read it?" he asked.

"There's a translation in here somewhere," Aloriea replied, rapidly flipping through the pages.

"Stop!" Caldera jabbed her finger onto a page, her eyes catching a glimpse of something.

Aloriea turned back to the page she was pointing at. "Yes! Okay, Callie, you read me the sequence of dots and dashes, and I'll decrypt it."

"What should we do?" Markarian asked, clapping Sear on the shoulder.

"Be quiet?" Aloriea suggested, a hint of a chuckle entering her voice.

"You could actually write down the letters as she says them," Caldera interjected between soft bouts of laughter—the first shred of happiness she had felt in a while.

Markarian nodded, his amiable smile never flinching as he sat down next to Sear.

Caldera looked down at the message. "Okay, are you ready?"

Aloriea nodded, her focus already on the book.

"Dash," Caldera said, looking up from the communicator.

"T," Aloriea replied.

Markarian scribbled the letter on a piece of paper.

"Dot, dash, dot," Caldera continued.

"That's R."

"Dot, dash."

"A."

"Dash, dot, dash, dot."

"What was it again?" Aloriea asked, rubbing her eyes.

Caldera repeated the sequence, slower this time, the chill of being underground making her shiver.

"Okay, that's C."

"Dot."

"E."

"That's it," Caldera said, placing the communicator on the table and looking over at Markarian.

"Trace," he said, holding the paper up for all of them to see. "It says 'trace'."

Sear leaned back in his chair, his tail swishing against the floor. "Trace what?"

They sat in silence for a minute before Caldera gasped, her eyes widening. "*This*," she said, standing up so quickly she knocked over the chair. "Trace this." She pointed at the communicator. "The signal!"

Her eyes lit up as an idea shot to the forefront of her mind. Her heart raced. She was almost too scared to say it out loud. "What if it's Justle?"

The room fell silent. Shock from the implication of what she had just said reflected across their faces.

"It... It would make sense if it were," Sear finally whispered, rapidly tapping an outstretched claw on the tabletop. "Thinking about it logically."

"It would explain how he seemed to magically disappear," Aloriea finished.

Markarian placed his hands on his hips. "We don't know if it's him. It could be a wild goose chase."

Caldera gripped her chin as various possibilities of who could have sent the message ran through her mind. "I think we should pursue it." She met his eyes. "Think about it. This isn't random—the message was encrypted, and who else would know about Morse code specifically?" Excitement swelled in her chest. "It's him, and if we can get him back, maybe we'll finally get our questions answered!"

"What do you mean?" Aloriea asked, gripping the collar of her blouse. "You think he knew something about Quill's murder?"

"Absolutely—that's got to be why he disappeared in the first place. If we find Justle, we'll find out definitively why Quill was murdered and who did it!" She punched a fist into her palm. "We have to listen to the message and trace it back to the source—figure out where he is. The only problem is, how?"

"It's too bad we don't know a computer expert," Markarian chimed in, giving Sear a mischievous grin. "Otherwise, we could hack into the Vanguard's state-of-the-art communications system and track the signal that way."

"Yes, it really is too bad," Sear continued, pushing himself away from the table to stand up.

Caldera's expression softened. "Sear..."

Sear gripped the bridge of his nose. "We are wading into dangerous waters, Callie. The systems that we would need to use will all be monitored," he said, fur bristling.

"We have our holopads—"

"Not enough power," Sear interrupted. "The only viable option is through an actual computer connected to the system, and last I checked, the one down here *is* not." He clicked his claws against the table, dappling it with holes. "The one in the library is most certainly monitored by the Council—or at least Vandren. And we must not forget that we cannot leave the palace."

Caldera let out a frustrated sigh. "We're so fucking close."

"What would you need to get this computer connected?" Aloriea asked.

"We have no way of obtaining these items...but...I would need a router and repeater," Sear replied hesitantly. "I could wipe and encrypt them here. You are not thinking..."

"Yes," Aloriea said simply.

"Care to share with the rest of the class?" Markarian asked.

"I'm going to take what we need from the library," Aloriea explained, standing up. "The computer there will have the router and repeater that we need to connect this one to the Tellin Informational Network."

A wave of jealousy and grief washed over Caldera as she thought about how she and Rennick used to finish each other's thoughts and sentences. "Well, you're not going alone," she said, shame flooding her chest.

"Obviously," Sear agreed. "I am going with her."

"No, you are not." Caldera took a step forward. "You need to stay here and get this computer ready. I'll go."

A resigned sigh escaped his lips as he took a seat at the computer. "I must point out that this is not a very well thought out plan."

Caldera knitted her brow. "Markarian, watch the cameras and let me know if anyone's gonna show up and surprise us," she said, holding up her communicator.

Markarian nodded and faced the monitors as they blinked to life.

Caldera walked over and scanned her hand, revealing the stairs. She paused when Aloriea was halfway up. "Sear, if I use the communicator, the signal from the message won't be lost, will it?"

"Of course not," he replied matter-of-factly.

Caldera nodded and started her own ascent. When she reached the top, she closed the staircase and turned to face Aloriea.

"I just realized that you locked them in there," Aloriea said, her voice thoughtful. "Your handprint is the only one that works on the scanners."

Caldera looked from the scanner to where the stairs were hidden. "Huh... We should probably fix that."

Aloriea nodded. "Let's go," she said, running to the doors.

As Caldera followed close behind her, she kept her eyes

trained on the ground, careful not to look around too much. She was still focused on her shoes when they burst through the doors, and she ran into Aloriea's back. "Why'd you stop?" she asked, rubbing her nose.

Aloriea took a deep breath, her shoulders tensing and relaxing before she turned around to Caldera. "How are you?"

"What?" Caldera asked, crossing her arms. Aloriea's gaze didn't waver. "Fine—I'm fine," she answered with a wave of her hand. "Why?"

"Look, I'm just going to say it," Aloriea began. "We all saw you zoning out into that book, and how you won't look at your surroundings when you're in the courtyard..."

"So what?" Caldera snapped, her eyes instantly brimming with tears. She looked away, hugging her arms across her body.

"This is what I'm talking about. You're bottling everything up. Just talk to me."

Caldera hung her head. "I'm trying to move on, but his face... That last look, it haunts me," she whispered, swallowing hard as she avoided Aloriea's gaze. "As soon as I start to come to terms with everything, it's like this—this oppressive force knocks me back down, pushing against my chest until I can't breathe." A tear rolled down her cheek. "No matter how much I resist...it's eventually going to crush me." She dug her fingernails into her arm, her eyes glued to the floor.

Aloriea vehemently shook her head, taking a step forward. "It won't crush you. We won't let it. You're not alone, Callie."

"How did you get past the pain of Quill's death?" Caldera asked abruptly. She wiped her face, eyes burning.

Without hesitation, Aloriea pulled her into a hug. "I didn't—not really," she said, resting her chin on the top of Caldera's head.

Wrapping her arms around the wiry woman, Caldera buried her face in Aloriea's chest.

"I cared about Quill... He was my closest friend," Aloriea whispered, her breath rustling Caldera's hair. "Even so, I'm not going to lie. I still don't have an answer for you." She ended the embrace.

"Well, this has been extremely unhelpful, thanks." Caldera began to head down the hall to the library.

"Callie." Aloriea grabbed her arm. "I may not know exactly what you're going through, but I can understand it. If you ever need to talk to me, I'm here."

Caldera smiled softly. "Aloriea, you're a shitty pep-talker—but, thank you."

She chuckled. "Don't mention it," she said just as Caldera's communicator rang.

"What the hell are you two doing?" Markarian asked after Caldera answered.

"Talking," she replied with a shrug, trying to make eye contact with one of the hidden cameras as she continued to walk down the hall.

"Well, you wasted a shitload of time, and now Sol and Saro are on their way to the back!"

"Fuck," Caldera said as she and Aloriea stopped in their tracks a few feet away from the library doors.

"It looks like they're doing a sweep," Markarian continued. "Going into each room, making sure no one is in it."

"How long until they get to the library?" Caldera asked as she pushed open the doors and dragged Aloriea along behind her.

"It's hard to tell on these cameras. Ten minutes, maybe less."

Caldera turned to Aloriea. "I'll go distract them. You get the router and the other thing."

"Repeater," Aloriea corrected.

"Whatever, just do it."

Aloriea shook her head and peeked out the door. "*I'll* intercept them."

"No—"

"I'll be able to stall them better than you would," Aloriea interrupted. "They're not exactly your biggest fans right now—I don't know exactly what Vandren said to them after what happened at the funeral, but apparently it wasn't pleasant."

"That's true," Caldera muttered. "But, listen, I may not be completely incompetent when it comes to computers, but I don't know what this stuff is—or how to detach it from the integrated system."

"I will walk you through it," Sear said through the communicator.

Caldera gritted her teeth. "Fine. Go!" She hurried over to the computer system and Aloriea ran out the door. "Markarian, keep me updated on Aloriea's interaction with the twins," she said, placing the communicator on top of the desk and crouched down in front of the little black box that was attached to the metal underneath it.

"Will do."

The soft glow of the book spines illuminated the shelves as the fluorescent lights overhead turned themselves on.

"Okay," said Sear, "pry open the box, tell me what you see, and I will tell you what to remove. I can zoom in a little bit with these cameras, but not much. Please be descriptive."

Caldera nodded to herself and dug her fingers into the sides of the small box, ripping it open. "Umm, okay...there are some wires...yellow and green, and then it just looks like a computer chip," she said, sitting back on her haunches.

"Hmm, that is interesting. It sounds like it is upgraded," Sear said, skepticism in his voice.

"So, what do I do?" Caldera asked, blowing out a breath.

"Let me think," Sear snapped. "I was not expecting Vandren to have a library's system upgraded. Quill must have been using this computer behind his back a lot."

"There's a situation," Markarian interrupted.

Caldera grabbed the communicator. "What's happening?"

"Not sure, since there's no sound. I don't know what she said to them but it looks like they're arguing with each other."

"Sear!" Caldera yelled. "How do I detach this thing?"

"If there are yellow and green wires in there, and a computer chip, the router, and repeater are both self-contained inside the box," he replied quickly.

"You know what, fuck this," said Caldera.

"What?" Markarian and Sear replied in unison.

Without responding, Caldera grabbed the knife out of the compartment in her boot, aimed the handle at the top of the box, and brought it down hard. The box snapped off the computer system, landing with a clunk at her feet.

"Well, that is one way to do it," Sear said. "Hopefully it is not broken."

"Go figure out what's happening with Aloriea," Markarian interjected. "They're right around the corner."

Caldera replaced the knife and picked up the box, shoving it into her pocket.

When she ran out of the library, she was immediately hit with muffled shouts. She rounded the corner just as Sol grabbed onto Aloriea's arm, causing her to gasp in a combination of pain and surprise.

Caldera sprinted down the hall, reaching them just as Sol and Saro noticed she was there. Aloriea's eyes were filled with fear, causing Caldera's chest to overflow with rage. Without a word, she grabbed Sol's wrist and dug her fingers into his skin until he had no choice but to let go. As soon as he did, Caldera planted her foot square in his stomach, kicking him back against the wall.

Sol gasped as the air was knocked out of him, and he leaned heavily against the wall in an attempt to regain his breath, his hand over his stomach.

"I thought I told you to leave my friends alone!" Caldera growled, holding her arm out in front of Aloriea.

Sol groaned in response, lowering himself to the floor.

"Are you all right?" Caldera asked, turning back to Aloriea.

She nodded, wrapping her arms around herself. "I just wasn't expecting that," she muttered. Her eyes flicked to the side, narrowing.

Caldera followed her gaze to see Saro pointing a blaster at her head with shaking hands. *He doesn't want to do this.* She was about to say something when Aloriea stepped in front of her, blocking the weapon's trajectory.

"What do you think you're doing?" she asked, her voice surprisingly steady.

"What does it look like?" Saro replied in a low voice. "First, she attacks a council member, and now my brother."

"He attacked Aloriea first!" Caldera snapped, stepping out from behind her. Saro's eyes flicked to her, but his blaster was still trained on Aloriea. Her heart raced, a cold sweat forming on the back of her neck. *If he pulls that trigger...*

"You drew your weapon on the queen, that's more than enough for a treason charge," Aloriea continued, not skipping a beat. "You know that."

Saro bit his lip. "She—"

"It doesn't matter," Aloriea interrupted. "Yes, earlier, you had a reason, but not this time." She glanced over at Sol, who was standing up, brushing the wrinkles out of his suit. "She could arrest him right now, and legally, there's nothing either of you could do about it. He attacked a member of the royal court un-prompted," she continued, motioning to herself.

Caldera blinked, unsure if what Aloriea was saying was the truth. The hardness of her eyes made it impossible to tell.

Saro lowered his weapon.

"Maybe I didn't make myself clear the first time," Caldera said. She pushed forward and grabbed the barrel of his blaster. "If you or your brother ever touch any of my friends again—" She twisted the blaster out of his hands and lowered it against her side, Rennick's smile flashing across her eyes "—consider your-selves dead."

Turmoil swirled behind Saro's multicolored eyes. "You don't need to threaten me," he said, his voice hardly more than a whisper as he took a step back.

Caldera scowled at him, unable to read his true intentions. "Let's go." She ushered Aloriea down the hall, the blaster gripped tightly in her hand.

"How am I supposed to keep the palace safe without a weapon?" Saro called after them, his voice grave.

"Take it up with Vandren," Caldera called over her shoulder as they rounded the corner, her mind racing. *I'm sure he'll issue you another one, in the hopes you'll eventually kill me with it.*

CHAPTER 25

D id I break it?" Caldera asked over Sear's shoulder as he rapidly typed on the computer. The musty, damp smell of the secret room tore at her last nerve.

He paused, tapping on the cracked black box with an outstretched claw. "No, it works," he said, and Caldera let out a sigh of relief. "It is harder to encrypt than I thought it would be."

"Well, you'd better hurry," Markarian said, poking at Saro's blaster that Caldera had discarded on the table. "Someone's bound to notice that thing's gone and report it to Vandren. And if it's not encrypted when he scans for it..."

"He'll find this place," Caldera finished.

"I am working as fast as I can," Sear snapped, his shoulders tensing. "I just finished adding all our handprints to the scanner so we can get in and out of this room individually. I will hook this up, but I can only do one thing at a time."

Caldera took a deep breath, trying to force her excitement

down into her stomach. *We're gonna find Justle. We're finally going to get the answers we've been looking for.*

She glanced over at Aloriea, who was sitting quietly at the far end of the table. With a sigh, she walked over and sat next to her. "Your turn to talk."

Aloriea chuckled mirthlessly. "I've known Sol and Saro for years," she said, gritting her teeth. "They've never acted like this. I mean, Saro has always taken his brother's lead, but Sol has never been this blatant about..." she trailed off, her gaze falling to the floor.

"About what?" Caldera pressed.

"His anger and general distaste toward the sector leader," Aloriea muttered.

Confusion clouded her mind as Caldera frowned. "I thought that Sol and Saro liked Quill, and that was why they disliked me," she said, slowly trying to put the pieces together.

As Aloriea shook her head, the overhead fluorescent lights glinted off her horns. "You could say they liked Quill as much as any other acquaintance, but they were never close."

"What were they saying to you before I intervened?"

Aloriea hung her head. "At first, we were arguing about how ridiculous it was for them to check every room." She sighed heavily. "Then, when Sol grabbed me, he said, 'If you keep hanging around the queen, you're going to get yourself killed'."

Caldera raised her brows. "I could've told you that."

Aloriea laughed softly. "It's a risk I'm willing to take."

Smiling, Caldera's chest flooded with warmth. "Do you think they're loyal to Vandren?"

"Well, they were following orders from Olivare, who in turn was following orders from Vandren," Aloriea replied, pursing her lips. "So, even though Olivare's gone, I'm guessing they are."

Caldera nodded in agreement, her mind flashing to Saro. *What are his true intentions?*

"There's something else," Aloriea said, biting her nail. "When he said I was going to get myself killed, it felt like..." She paused, wringing her hands together. "I don't know. It didn't really feel like a warning, so much as a prediction."

Caldera caught Markarian's gaze.

"Are you saying that you think they know for sure that you're going to be a target of some kind?" Markarian asked.

"I don't know," Aloriea whispered, shaking her head again. Her eyes misted with tears that hadn't fallen.

"Done!" Sear called, swiveling his chair around to face them. Then he saw their faces. "What is wrong?" he asked, his ears perking straight up.

"It's nothing," Aloriea said, turning away quickly as she wiped her eyes.

Caldera offered a small smile before walking back over to Sear. "So, we're connected to the system now?"

"Yes," Sear replied, facing the screen. "On a completely encrypted and secret network, I might add." A fanged smile beamed across his face. "Which was not easy."

Markarian walked over and slapped Sear on the back. "Nice job."

"Now, onto the Vanguard mainframe," Caldera said with a grin.

Aloriea walked up next to Sear and put a hand on his shoulder. "Amazing," she whispered, looking down at him, her eyes no longer glassy.

Taking a deep breath, Caldera let their temporary victory set in. It filled her with newfound motivation. *Finally, we're one step ahead.* "How long will it take you to access the communications server?" she asked.

"No time at all," Sear replied, clicking across the keys so quickly Caldera could hardly keep up. He stopped and extended his hand toward the screen with a flourish. "Here we are."

Caldera's heart beat faster as if she were running a marathon. "Scan it," she said, holding her communicator out to Sear.

He plucked it out of her hand, connected it to the new server, and ran it through the Vanguard's communications system. After a few minutes, he frowned.

"What is it?" she asked, rapidly looking from the screen to Sear.

"It is not...going anywhere."

Aloriea gripped his shoulder tighter. "What does that mean?"

"It looks like it is to me," Markarian countered, pointing to the screen. "It's pinging all across space."

"That is not what I meant," Sear said. "It is moving, sure, but it is not going anywhere in the sense of finding a destination—even though it is going through the Vanguard's omnidirectional signal scanner." He looked up at Caldera and over to Markarian, waiting.

Caldera squinted at the screen. It reminded her of a heart rate monitor with its erratic ups and downs, and then the flatline. The signal was still searching for the source, it just wasn't pinging off satellites anymore. She gasped, unable to believe what she was seeing. "Are you sure this is...right?"

Sear nodded.

"Somebody better tell me what the hell is going on!" Aloriea snapped, patience lost.

"The signal leads out into the void," Markarian answered. "The uninhabitable edge of the Centaurus galaxy and beyond."

"We will not be able to get to wherever this signal leads," Sear said matter-of-factly. "Even if it does find its source—which it will not."

The confusion on Aloriea's face didn't falter. "Why not?"

"The signal scanners would need a massive amount of power to do so," Sear replied.

"It's tech that just doesn't exist," Markarian added, hanging his head. "No signal has ever reached the end of the void."

"But something got through," Caldera whispered, touching the screen and bringing up the signal's schematics.

Her friends were talking next to her, but she tuned them out, laser-focusing on the specs. *I've seen this pattern before...* The realization almost knocked her over. Ripping the holopad out of her pocket, she brought up the video of Rennick's death, her breath catching in her throat.

"Cal?" Markarian said, his voice distant even though he was right next to her.

She frantically launched the specs from her holopad from right when the hole in spacetime opened over to the computer and overlaid the reading on the signal.

"Callie?" Markarian said again, putting his hand on her shoulder. "What're you doing?"

Caldera tried shrugging him off but found she couldn't move. She stared at the screen, the red, green, and yellow spikes of energy output glowing in her eyes. "They match," she whispered.

Sear looked at the screen, his mouth agape. "How did you..."

"I've done nothing but obsess over this video," Caldera replied, setting her holopad onto the table next to the keyboard. "I've studied every aspect of it—I know it like the back of my hand—"

"We get it," Aloriea interrupted. "I'll ask again, what exactly does this mean?" she said, motioning toward the screen.

"Since something came through from the other side," Sear said. "It means that this rip in spacetime is not a black hole at all—"

"It's a wormhole," Markarian interjected. "A portal of sorts..."

Aloriea glanced over at Caldera, placing a hand gently on her shoulder. "So... If I'm understanding you—to jump the tracer through the void and contact Justle we would need to recreate the rip."

Sear nodded sharply. "On a much smaller scale, of course."

"You think we could actually control it?" Markarian asked, his eyes darting from Sear to the computer.

He hesitated, scratching his beard. "I believe it is possible, but we need the catalyst—the painite. Therefore, we would need to get in contact with Grey and Sylvie, as they were the ones who found it."

Goosebumps shot down Caldera's arms and legs as icicle-like coldness prickled the back of her neck. "Leave it to me."

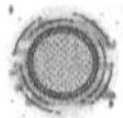

THE TWIN MOONS glowed bright silver in the sky, blissfully unaware of the planet they illuminated. Harsh shadows cast themselves across the obliterated landscape. The courtyard was still painfully empty except for the two figures darting toward the deteriorating wall.

Caldera took a deep breath as she slipped a coil of rope over her head and across her chest like a sash. The plain, black hooded sweatshirt that she had dug out of Rennick's effects hung loose against her body. Aloriea promised she had washed it multiple times, but Caldera swore she could still catch whiffs of him through the fabric. Focusing on securing the rope, she silently cursed everyone—including herself—for not having clothes appropriate for the situation.

"This is a stupid idea," Markarian muttered, folding his arms across his broad chest. "The order's out. If you, or any of us, are seen outside the palace walls, we're to be tried for treason," he continued. "And we'll be convicted, too."

"There's no choice," Caldera said, stretching out her arms and legs. She took a deep breath. "I made a promise to Ren that I wouldn't bow to Vandren's threats. We need more information about painite, and Grey and Sylvie have it."

A chill bit into her skin, causing goosebumps to rocket up her arm and neck as she touched her hand against the stones. She shivered despite herself, examining the wall where Aloriea's secret stairs had once been. Most of the stones were gone, no longer jutting out to create a perfect makeshift ladder to the top of the wall. They had been replaced with crumbling concrete and shallow holes.

Markarian leaned his head back, hair shining in the moonlight. "Vandren's framing this lockdown as protecting you," he said bluntly.

Caldera paused her stretching. "I figured—first it was 'she's mentally unwell'. Now the story's changed to 'it's for her protection'. Not much of a leap considering what I did to him at the funeral." She looked Markarian in the eye. "I don't care what he's saying about me anymore, I want to get Justle back and get my damn questions answered."

He sighed, rubbing his forehead.

"Ren's family hasn't said anything about what really happened at the funeral, then?" she asked as she tightened the laces on her boots, her chest aching.

"No. According to Willix, Vandren made them sign some type of non-disclosure agreement."

She scoffed and stood up, pulling her hair into a tight ponytail.

"I honestly don't understand why he didn't use what you did as an excuse to get you out of the way—to get all of us out of the way," he said, placing a hand on his hip. "It would have been an easy treason charge."

Caldera bit the inside of her cheek. "Vandren's smart," she said. "He's still trying to control the sector through me—trying to limit potential backlash."

Markarian nodded, lacing his fingers together and squatting low.

"Because as much as I hate to admit it," she continued, stepping into the cradle Markarian had created. "I'm Quill's rightful heir, and for some people, that's reason enough to defend me."

"This is still stupid."

Grunting, and using his full strength to stand up as fast as he could, he launched Caldera into the air.

For a second, time seemed to pass slower, as the light from the moons perfectly illuminated where she needed to grab. Caldera reached out as soon as she saw the first of what was left of the protruding stone ladder. Grabbing one stone with each hand, she pulled her body close to the wall to stop the falling momentum.

Her cheek banged off the rocks, which sent a quick jolt of pain through her head. The muscles in her arms ached as she held herself up, her feet searching for purchase.

"You okay?" Markarian called from below, readying himself to catch her if she lost her grip.

Caldera grunted and finally managed to jam her boots into two of the shallow holes left by the stones that had been ripped out when the portal opened. The rope cut into the notch between her shoulder and neck. "Great!" she answered, then focused on climbing the rest of the way up the wall.

She reached the top and crawled over the edge onto the walkway, grateful that Markarian was able to fling her more than halfway up. After catching her breath, she peered back over the ledge.

"Stick to the plan," he said, looking up at her, his hands cupped in a circle around his mouth.

Caldera nodded. All she had to do was lower herself down the other side, run two miles into town, and meet up with Grey and Sylvie at the predetermined location—and hope they hadn't ratted her out. The message that Sear had managed to send Grey over the secure server hadn't said who was coming to meet them, so the likelihood of them reporting it was low.

"Are you sure you don't want me to go with you?" Markarian asked. "This could be a trap."

"You need to stay here and protect Sear and Aloriea if Sol and Saro come looking for trouble."

"All right, but for the last time, this is probably the dumbest thing you've ever done," he said, then sprinted back toward the palace.

No, the dumbest thing I've ever done is put Ren in a situation where he sacrificed his life for mine, Caldera thought bitterly as she watched Markarian disappear inside. "Although, I can't believe I have to sneak out of my own palace," she muttered aloud, tying the rope to one of the wall's protruding merlons. She flung the rope over the side, and without giving herself time to think, began climbing down.

When Caldera's feet hit the ground, the urge to sprint away and never return was almost uncontainable. She closed her eyes, focusing on her friends and how they were all counting on her.

As much as she wanted to get away from the palace—away from Vandren—she couldn't leave them. She wouldn't. *They're all I have left.*

She took a deep breath and opened her eyes, then ran along the side of the wall until she got to the tree line that connected with it, effectively covering her escape.

The road that led up to the palace gates glowed under the artificial lights on the other side. Caldera ran through the trees, keeping up her pace as best she could. After she was off the palace grounds, she emerged from the trees and ran along the side of the road the rest of the two miles to the meeting point.

Caldera was on the outskirts of Astrum, but she could see the glowing lights from the incomprehensibly tall buildings and hear the yelling and laughter of people as if she were in the city's center. The roar of personal transports and shuttles echoed through the night as they took off into the sky.

She shivered and pulled the hood over her head, checking her watch. "Two more minutes," she mumbled to herself as she walked over to the welcome sign, casually leaning against it.

A silver transport pulled up less than a minute later and parked across the street just as Caldera had instructed in the message. She looked sideways without turning her head to face them.

Lights from inside the vehicle flashed once before the transport turned off. She glanced around at her surroundings. The road was completely desolate, and the open field lining the other side was empty—even the skies directly above them were deserted. *Grey and Sylvie either didn't tell anyone, or they felt they could handle the situation on their own if things went sour.*

Smirking, Caldera rushed across the street, opened the door, and jumped into the back seat. She was immediately hit with the smell of artificial leather and lingering cigarette smoke. Before she could say anything, two blasters were shoved into her face.

Fair enough.

"Who are you, and what do you want?" Grey snapped from his position on the driver's side. The transport's tiny yellow ceiling light illuminated him just enough to see.

"We don't have anything for you!" Sylvie added. Her long red hair was pulled into a side braid that fell over her shoulder and down to her stomach.

"That's not entirely true," Caldera replied, lowering her hood.

Gasps filled the inside of the transport as they hastily put away their weapons.

"Your Majesty!" Grey exclaimed, a flash of red spreading across his pale, freckled face. He turned completely around in his seat to face her, hitting his head on the ceiling. "You're not supposed to be outside the palace grounds. The whole sector thinks you're on your deathbed."

"Grey!" Sylvie punched his arm. "W—why did you want to speak with us?" she stammered, her own freckled cheeks flushing.

"I—" Caldera started before clamping her mouth shut. *Can I really trust them?* She swallowed hard, forcing her emotions down. *I don't have a choice.* "I have a favor to ask you," she said, looking from the face of one confused sibling to the other.

"Of course," Sylvie said encouragingly. "Anything you want. I owe you my life!" She paused. "I mean, you and Sir Silvera. I'm so sorry to hear about what happened to him."

A stab of heartache pierced Caldera's body. Emptiness radiated outward, the hollowness returning full force. *Push it away... push forward... Push.* "I need all the information you have on the substance I ordered the Vanguard to bring to me—the painite," she finally said, unclenching her hands. "You two found it, and I need your full report. I need to know where to find it."

Sylvie and Grey both frowned.

"We already gave it to you," Sylvie replied.

"What?"

"Yeah," Grey said, cracking the driver's side window and pulling a cigarette and lighter out of his coat pocket. "Your security detail—I believe their names were Sol and Saro—came to our house about a week after it happened and took it." He lit the cigarette and blew the smoke outside.

"They said you ordered them to collect it," Sylvie added. "And that they were going to give it to you."

Breath caught in her throat as Caldera leaned back against the seat, defeated. *These two are the only ones that knew anything about the painite.* What was she supposed to do now?

"This can't be happening." She chuckled, unable to hold it in, and placed her head in her hands as her mind threatened to completely unravel. *One step forward, two steps back.*

"Are you all right?" Sylvie asked, concern clouding her gaze.

Caldera didn't answer. Her mind twisted, catapulting her deeper into despair. *Justle...whatever happened to you, Sol and Saro were involved. Ren. I'm so sorry...this is my fault! My fault! Ren...*

She covered her face, fighting back the silent tears that pricked her eyes.

Her mind shifted. Markarian's amiable smile flashed across her vision, then Sear's fanged grin, and Aloriea tilting her head before smiling over at her.

"I didn't order them to take anything," Caldera said abruptly, gathering herself. This confirmed that Sol and Saro were definitively working for Vandren.

And that her friends were in more danger than she realized.

I have to get out of here—I have to get back!

"Are you sure you're okay?" Sylvie said, her eyes wide.

"You don't have *any* of the information?" Caldera asked, ignoring Sylvie's question. A pang of inconsolable grief shot through her chest as she came to the undeniable conclusion that, if this didn't work, she was out of ideas to reach Justle.

They paused, an unsure glance passing between them. Eventually, Grey nodded, extinguishing his cigarette and dropping it into a small recycler attached to the cup holder next to him. Sylvie reached into her pocket.

"Here," she said, handing Caldera her holopad. "I copied the original information onto this. It's from the initial scan of the painite mineral. It's not as detailed, but...it's something."

Caldera felt her eyes light up. "Are you serious?" she nearly shouted, snatching the device out of Sylvie's hands. "What made you want to do that?"

Sylvie shrugged. "Instinct? I don't know."

Caldera smiled, the simple act bringing out her exhaustion. "I need one more thing from both of you."

"What is it?" Grey asked.

"Don't tell anyone about this," she replied sternly as she reached for the door handle. She was not looking forward to the two-mile trek back, followed by a rope climb, but she needed to get back as soon as possible. "Consider that a direct order from the queen."

"Of course, we won't tell anyone!" Sylvie swore, her fist over her heart.

"Even if you aren't supposed to be out of the palace," Grey added.

Sylvie glared at him, punching his arm again. "Umm... Your Majesty, if you need us for anything else, we're here."

"Thank you," Caldera said, her voice cracking. "Thank you."

Without another word, she exited the transport and started back toward the palace.

CHAPTER 26

Caldera sat with her knees pulled up to her chest and her back pressed firmly against the wall next to the computer system. Sear was frantically scrolling through the notes she got from Grey and Sylvie three nights before. She glanced over at Aloriea, who was asleep on the mound of blankets and pillows they had snuck into the secret room.

"How's she doing?" Caldera whispered.

Sear's shoulders slumped. "Everyone that she has known for almost her entire life is either dead, missing, or working for a presumed murderer... As such, not great."

Caldera picked at a stray thread on her pants, not knowing what else to say.

"She is also not fond of having to stay down here in the Vault," Sear added, his fingers flying across the keys again, "and I must say, neither am I."

"You don't have to stay down here," Caldera said, frowning. "You just can't leave unless me or Markarian are escorting you."

A low rumble sounded from Sear's throat. "If I wanted to

stay confined within the boundaries of a lab, I would have stayed in Muléus."

"I know, and I'm sorry. I promise this is just a temporary solution. We need to figure out where the twins' allegiances really lie."

Markarian walked over and sat down next to her, leaning in close. "Do you really think Sol and Saro had something to do with Justle's disappearance?" he asked, his hand cupped over his mouth.

Caldera sighed again and leaned her head back against the wall, letting the coolness of the stones seep into her scalp. "It makes the most sense."

She met Markarian's eyes, and her breath caught in her throat as Rennick's face flashed across her mind. Squeezing her eyes shut, she forced his visage away, replacing it with images of Markarian, Sear, and Aloriea.

Markarian patted her shoulder as if reading her thoughts, then joined Sear at the computer.

Caldera forced herself to her feet and over to the computer, focusing on the task at hand. "What's going on with the signal?" she asked quietly, not wanting to wake Aloriea.

"It's in the void," Markarian answered, turning to the monitor that Sear had rigged to continually display the signal's progression. "Still searching, though."

"If we ever want to be able to contact Justle, we need to figure out how to enhance it."

"That would be nice, but this information on the painite isn't great." Markarian yawned. "For being over one hundred pages, it's barely more than we already know." He leaned against Sear's chair, placing his chin in the palm of his hand. "I can't believe it took us three days to sort through all this bullshit."

"Well, it's all we have," she replied, forcing her tone to remain flat. She squinted at the screen, her eyes blurry from the nights of segmented sleep. "At least it lists all the components that the stone's made of."

"It does?" Sear interjected, his ears drooping slightly—the telltale sign that he was exhausted. "What page was that on? I must have missed it."

"Page eighty-five," Caldera replied. "What're you thinking?"

"That we could, in theory, reverse engineer it. If this mineral is at least similar to others I've studied," he continued, scratching behind his ear as he scrolled through the report. "Which is a pretty big if."

Caldera nodded, perking up. "Really? How long will that take?"

Sear hit enter and the components of painite popped up on the screen. "It depends on how readily available these elements are, and if we can obtain them," he said, pointing at the monitor. "If we can, we will be able to artificially create the painite and track the signal."

She leaned in closer. "Aluminum, zirconium, calcium oxide, boron oxide, water, and proxine," she mused. "I can see us getting water, and most of the other stuff..."

"But what's proxine?" Markarian muttered.

"Give me a minute to research how to obtain these materials, particularly that one," Sear said, looking up at them.

Markarian glanced down at him. "What happens when we do artificially create it?"

"We will attach it to Callie's communicator and integrate it with the signal."

Caldera raised her eyebrows, not used to Sear being so polite when he was clearly about to pass out. She looked back at the sleeping Aloriea, and her heart ached for her friend.

"All right," Sear said, tilting his head. "It is all pretty common stuff, except for proxine."

She bit the inside of her cheek. *Where have I heard that word before...* Her eyes lit up as the long-buried information in her mind resurfaced. "Proxine, I know what it is! It should be in the Vanguard data banks. When I became a captain, one of my first missions was to look for that stuff."

Sear clicked his claws across the keys, opening the encrypted files from the Vanguard Headquarters that he had hacked into. "Hmm... Ahh, here we are," he said, squinting at the screen. "You and Ren are listed as one of the teams to find the mineral proxine."

"Mineral?" Markarian scratched his head. "You mean, like painite?"

Sear nodded. "All the materials listed can have a 'mineral' form. That is not uncommon."

"What else does it say about proxine?" Caldera coaxed, leaning over Sear's shoulder.

"You don't remember?" Markarian asked as he gaped at the screen.

She gritted her teeth. "That was nine years ago. Do you remember every mission you've ever gone on?"

Sear nudged her off his shoulder and continued typing. "A request from Councilmember Kex, and backed by all the other councilmembers, had Vanguard members from all sectors clamoring to find this rare mineral."

"I don't remember that," Caldera said.

Sear's ears twitched back and forth. "You would not have. These records, the real ones, were sealed. As far as you knew, it was just another order from King Quill."

Caldera scowled. "Why did they send out this order in the first place?"

"It was not the first time," Sear replied. "This order has been repeatedly sent out to Vanguard members since the cataclysm. Supposedly as a way to preserve something from the planet formerly known as Sedrolla," he continued. "Proxine cannot be found on Bersama."

Markarian leaned in, hair falling around his shoulders. "So, you're saying that this mineral can only be found in the desolate section of the galaxy...on a dead planet?"

Sear sighed heavily. "That is correct. And here is the 'kicker', so to speak. Proxine, given enough time, turns into painite."

Caldera's mouth gaped open. "Are you serious?"

"Extremely," Sear nodded.

"So, what it sounds like," Markarian muttered, drumming his fingers on his arm, "is that the Council has been forming—or trying to form—painite naturally for years."

Caldera bit her lip. "Is the proxine that Ren and I found all those years ago still at Vanguard Headquarters?"

"It is," Sear said, turning back to the screen. "I know what you are about to say... We cannot steal it."

"Yeah, Cal," Markarian chimed in. "There's no way you could get into VHQ."

"I can't—at least not without help," Caldera replied with a smirk, "but I know two people I can ask."

Markarian shook his head. "You want to have Grey and Sylvie help you break into Vanguard Headquarters to steal something that's most likely under guard? I don't know, Cal—"

"They'll help," Caldera interrupted, happy that no one was trying to talk her out of it. "I know they will."

A stark silence fell over them as they weighed their minimal options. Caldera grimaced. The Vault seemed to become dimmer with the realization that there was no choice if they wanted to continue with their plan.

"Very well. You can talk to them later," Sear said, breaking the silence. "We need to turn our attention to the other materials."

Caldera and Markarian nodded sharply.

"The difficult part will not necessarily be acquiring the rest of the substances, it will be getting them to us—within the palace," Sear continued.

Who do we know that could get into the palace without getting questioned or checked? Caldera tapped her chin, an idea forming in her head. "How common are we talking?" she asked. "Like, are all these components something you would find, let's say, in a hospital?"

"Yes..." Sear replied slowly. "What are you—"

"You know what I haven't had in a while?" Caldera interrupted. "A doctor's appointment."

Markarian's and Sear's jaws went slack.

"You're joking," Markarian said.

Sear shook his head. "I highly advise against this."

"Let me know if you have any better ideas." Caldera pulled out her communicator. "I'm all ears."

Markarian glanced over at Sear and shrugged. "Apparently none that either of us can think of right now."

"All right then," she said, pressing the call button. The tell-tale waiting tone of a doctor's office met her ears as she placed the communicator on speaker mode for Sear and Markarian.

"Doctor Vareis's office, how may I help you?"

"Umm, this is...the queen," Caldera stammered, looking at Sear and Markarian, who were shaking their heads. She cleared her throat. "Queen Caldera Keane calling for Doctor Celestin Vareis, please."

The line was silent for a moment before the woman replied, her tone as even and calm as ever. If she thought the situation was strange, she didn't show it. "Voice recognition authorized and approved. Transferring you now."

"Your Majesty," Doctor Vareis's voice came through the line, "what can I do for you?"

"Well," Caldera said, "I'd like to schedule a home visit, of sorts." Her words echoed off the walls, back into her ears. She lowered her voice, hoping the doctor couldn't hear the reverberation.

Aloriea blinked awake, then tiptoed over to them, a look of confusion on her face as Sear put a finger to his lips.

The sigh on the other end of the line was palpable. "Are you injured?"

"Well, no—"

"Then unfortunately, I can't fulfill this request. I simply don't have time."

"What if I said this was an order?"

"My answer would remain the same."

Their past conversation from when she was in the hospital buzzed through her head. "Okay... How about a compromise? That way I get what I want, and you get what you want."

"And what do you think I want?"

"For the planter orb to be recalled."

The line was silent for a minute.

"You can do that?"

"Yes, and I will. I just need you to do this one thing for me."

There was another pause.

"When would you like me to arrive?"

"Now," Caldera muttered, holding the communicator close to her lips.

"Fine. What's the request?"

Caldera quickly told her about the materials that she needed to bring.

"Very well," Doctor Vareis replied, her voice flat. "I'll be there shortly." Then she hung up.

"You know you can't have that piece of tech recalled," Aloriea whispered. "You lied to her."

"I know," Caldera murmured as guilt radiated throughout her body. "But we need these materials. We need to figure out where Justle is."

She replaced the communicator in her pocket before walking over to the handprint scanner. Markarian reluctantly followed her.

"I have a request as well," Sear said before Caldera could scan her hand.

She turned to face him. "What is it?"

"I have some supplies I need from my quarters," Sear replied. "Scales, measuring tools—"

"Your portable lab. Got it," Caldera interrupted. "We'll bring it to you."

"It is a bit messy," Sear added. "My forced relocation to the palace happened rather quickly."

She and Markarian hurried up the steps and into the dim late-afternoon sun, running through the back courtyard and down the palace halls. Markarian broke off to grab Sear's lab supplies, while Caldera came to a stop by the palace's front doors.

"What can we do for you, Your Majesty?" Sol asked, his glare landing on Caldera.

Saro glanced at his brother.

Caldera forced the conjecture about them and Justle out of her mind. "I'm expecting someone."

"Who?" Saro questioned, looking down at his holopad as if he expected the request to be there. His voice was hushed compared to Sol's.

"Let me ask the questions, brother," Sol said, placing a hand on his shoulder.

Saro flinched almost imperceptibly, then nodded before turning back to face the front courtyard.

Clenching her fists behind her back, Caldera narrowed her eyes. "You'll find out soon enough," she clipped, reveling in the scowl Sol gave her before turning back around—vehemently not looking at her again.

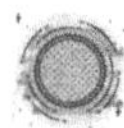

LESS THAN AN hour later, they were back in the Vault with the delivered materials.

"That doctor is all business," Markarian said, handing Sear the elemental components that Doctor Vareis delivered to them, while Caldera closed the stairs.

The silver and white tint of the various chemicals glinted in the fluorescent light as Sear silently examined each container.

"Do you really think she's trustworthy?" Aloriea asked, shooting Caldera a glare. "What do you think is going to happen when she finds out you lied to her?"

Sighing, Caldera placed the small, empty vials on the table. "I don't know, Aloriea. I'll deal with that later." She shook her head and tucked her hair behind her ears, turning her attention to Sear. "Why are they liquid?"

"Because these substances are merely components. Do not forget that they came from a hospital, as well," Sear said, grabbing an empty cup off the table.

Caldera pointed at the small glass vials. "Is that why you wanted those?"

"Yes." Sear picked one up between his thumb and forefinger. "The painite that we create will not be as pure, but that is not necessarily a bad thing."

"What do you mean?" Markarian asked.

"Less potent means it will be easier to control. Now, are you ready?" Sear motioned for them to gather around him.

"Yes! For fuck's sake," Caldera replied, gripping the back of the chair until her knuckles turned white. "What do you need us to do?"

Sear placed his holopad flat on the table and handed her the empty cup. "Fill that halfway up with water," he commanded, pointing toward the bathroom. "We are going to combine all the elements and distribute it into these smaller vials, except the proxine. That is the catalyst, and will go in its own vials, once we receive it."

She nodded, ran to fill the cup to the halfway mark, then ran back out, careful not to spill any.

The schematics and measurements that Sear had predetermined were floating in the air when she returned, and a scale and the measuring beakers were lined up along the table. Markarian and Aloriea each held a cylindrical tube, the cap off.

"It's a regular little lab in here." Caldera placed the cup of water in the middle of the group. "How do you know if these measurements are accurate?" She pointed at the floating numbers in front of them.

Sear grimaced. "I do not. The only thing I have to go off of is the data from the incident."

Caldera grabbed his wrist. "Wait. You don't have to do this," she said, letting go and catching each of their gazes. "None of you do."

"Cal, what are you talking about?" Markarian asked.

Aloriea stood silent, gripping the tube. Tired, black circles rimmed her eyes.

"Instead of combining into an inert substance that we can control, it could open another uncontrollable rip in spacetime."

She winced, remembering Rennick's face before he got sucked through the wormhole. The planter orb scar throbbed on the back of her neck.

"Callie," Sear said, placing his cylinder on the table. "The main component in painite is proxine. And we do not even *have* that substance yet. Nothing is going to happen."

Aloriea nodded, her disheveled hair sticking out in all directions. "And when we do get it, the proxine will be attached separately. We'll be able to control when we break the vials, and when the liquid comes in contact with the mineral."

"And that's what'll create the controlled rip," Markarian finished, clapping her on the shoulder. "Plus, it'll be so small that only the signal will be able to pass through. A 'tear' won't even open."

"Hence, the measuring equipment," Sear added, motioning toward the beakers and scales.

"We don't know if that'll work though!" Caldera gasped. "We could all die..."

Silence filled the room as Caldera squeezed her eyes shut.

"We're all willing to take that risk, Cal," Markarian whispered after a few seconds.

Caldera's eyes shot open to see her friends' smiling, reassuring faces.

"We're doing this," Aloriea said sharply. A glimmer of passion reappeared in her eyes.

Sear pointed at the beakers. "If it will make you feel better, we can measure out each separate component for now, and wait to combine them until later, when we have everything we need."

"Okay..." Caldera said, satisfied with the compromise and picking up a cylinder of her own—her voice was steady, gaining confidence. "After we do this, I'll get in contact with Grey and Sylvie to see if they'll help us get the last piece of the puzzle. The proxine."

CHAPTER 27

The next night, dark clouds intermittently covered the glimmering moons as Caldera lowered herself down the wall, her feet connecting with the green grass of the other side of the palace grounds. Her heart pounded from exertion as she raced to meet with Grey and Sylvie, who had promised to help her break into Vanguard Headquarters.

Their transport was parked in the same place as before, next to the 'Welcome to Astrum, Tellis's Capital' sign. Without a word, she climbed into the backseat, and the vehicle took off into the night as soon as she closed the door behind her.

"Are you sure you want to do this?" Caldera said, poking her head between the two siblings. "The ride there is enough. You don't have to go in."

"What if you get into trouble?" Sylvie asked, her innocent green eyes shining.

Caldera smiled. Sylvie's unquestioning desire to help people reminded her of her own.

"Don't worry about us," Grey added, steering the transport to the right. "We'll get you in and distract any guards we come across, but grabbing the proxine is completely up to you." He paused, flicking cigarette ash out the window. "If you get caught, we'll deny any knowledge about why you're there."

"Grey, we can't do that!"

"You can," Caldera said, placing a hand on her shoulder. "That was actually my idea—your lives come first."

Sylvie crossed her arms and looked out the window, clearly not happy with the decision.

As silence filled the transport, Caldera leaned back in her seat and watched out the window as the bright city lights of Astrum blurred past them. They were unnoticed; indistinguishable from anyone else flying the skies that night.

She closed her eyes and pictured the layout of the inside of Vanguard Headquarters, running their plan through her head.

VHQ had cameras, but Sear planned to take care of that by hacking in and briefly turning them off. They hoped it would cause the guards to walk the halls until the cameras were up and running again—and that was where Grey and Sylvie came in.

"We're here," Grey said, breaking Caldera out of her thoughts as he gently touched the transport down behind the building.

They all exited the vehicle, Caldera keeping the hood of her loose-fitting sweatshirt firmly over her head—messaging Sear to cut the cameras as Grey and Sylvie got out their keycards.

A wave of sentiment, culminating in regret, stung her chest as they approached the door. She had spent nine years working for an organization that was created to help the people of Bersama—a mission statement that she wholeheartedly agreed with—a principle that she'd dedicated her life to. She'd met the head of the organization...and now she was going to steal from them.

The alcoves outside of the tall metal building were filled with the homeless, tossing and turning as they tried to sleep. Caldera found herself wondering if the black-haired person she'd met all those months ago was still around—if they were okay.

Grey and Sylvie swiped their keycards and ushered her in before the door closed behind them.

Caldera lowered her hood and whisked her hair into a short ponytail. "We need to get to the Artifacts Department."

"We've only worked here a few weeks," Grey whispered, glancing around the desolate building. We don't know where that is yet."

Caldera chuckled. "Basement—captains access only." *Why does everything important get put in a basement?* "Which one of you is the captain again?"

Grey raised his hand.

"Okay, get your keycard ready and start thinking up an excuse as to why you were here—regular access into the building could be brushed off as 'you forgot something in your office', but that won't work when it comes to specific departments."

Caldera led them down various identical hallways, past the cubicles of office drones and the locked office doors of the other captains in the fleet. They came to a stop at a dead end where the lift was nestled away from sight.

"This'll take us to the Artifacts Department," Caldera said, motioning toward the keycard scanner. "Let's go—the guards should be making their rounds any minute."

The three rode in silence as the lift dropped them ten levels in as many minutes. A small screen on the wall showed them what their destination looked like beyond the lift doors.

"What's between the main floor and the basement? I mean— the Archive Department?" Sylvie asked, tucking a loose strand of red hair behind her ear.

"The science labs," Caldera replied. "Where they test new tech applicable to the Vanguard crews."

Grey leaned against the lift banister. "If they're down here, it must be secret then? To keep the other sectors from catching wind of what we're up to?"

"Technically, yes, but it's more to keep the information from leaking to the general public before it's ready."

Even as Caldera said the words that she had been told for so long by her ex-superiors, she knew she didn't believe them anymore. They weren't true. *More like, 'it's to keep it secret until the Council is ready to announce it'.*

"But it's mostly because underground labs are more stable than above—fewer variables to contend with, as Sear would say." She took a breath. "That's why it's taking so long to get down here. The lift has to go slow because the slightest atmospheric disturbance—say, the sudden shaking from a lift—could mess up a test."

She grimaced, thinking about their own jury-rigged experiment. *Talk about unknown variables.*

The doors opened into a warehouse-like area. Shelves twenty feet tall lined the space in perfect parallel rows, making aisles just big enough to fit a two-person hover platform through. The spines of the artifact containers glowed, illuminating the names and dates of whatever they contained.

"There's so much..." Sylvie gasped, her eyes widening at the sheer scale of it.

"One hundred years' worth," Caldera said, heading toward the circular hover platform to the right of the lift doors.

Thin metal bars that surrounded the outside of the transporter reached up to Caldera's waist as she stepped aboard. Safety straps hung from the console that sat dark at the head of the platform, ready to wrap around the shoulders and lock across the chests of the people riding so they wouldn't fall off.

"Grey, I need your card."

"One of us should probably go with you."

"Oh! I want to," Sylvie said, raising her hand in the air.

Caldera smiled, seeing so much of herself in the younger girl. "Okay, come on."

"How will you know where to look?" Sylvie asked as she stepped onto the platform and hooked herself in, her head swiveling from side to side.

"I'll type it in. Everything's alphabetical." Caldera scanned Grey's keycard to activate the platform, not bothering with the safety strap.

Lifting into the air, she keyed the artifact she was looking for into the console—proxine. The glowing spines whisked by them as the platform took them directly to their destination, stopping in front of a small compartment.

"Proxine—discovered in the year 3.112."

"Yep...that's when Ren and I found it—nine years ago," Caldera whispered, scanning Grey's card again to open the compartment. A pure, red stone, held in place by four prongs, met her eyes.

"It looks like the stone Grey and I found," Sylvie said, leaning over to look at the item.

"It does, but painite is black marbled with red—this hasn't begun to transform yet."

"Is that good?"

"Yes."

Breaking the prongs, Caldera liberated the small stone from its compartment, and carefully replaced the box on the shelf.

"Why don't you just look for actual painite?" Sylvie questioned, twirling the end of her braid around her finger. "It's bound to be in here."

Caldera grinned. "That's...actually a great idea."

Sylvie beamed as Caldera typed 'painite' into the console. To her surprise, the platform moved backward to the beginning of the P section, stopping in front of another identical compartment.

Yes! Now we won't have to make our own. Excitement crept into her body as she scanned the keycard.

Opening the box, she found it was empty. She gripped the proxine tighter as she glanced at the date.

"Painite—discovered year 3.111."

So painite was first officially logged ten years ago and one year later, we're searching for proxine... The Council must've used it up faster than expected and needed to make more. Why?

"Oh no..." Sylvie muttered. "The sample we found has been the only one for ten years?"

Caldera sighed. "Looks like it." She replaced the empty box on the shelf and directed the platform back to its port where Grey was waiting.

"Did you find it?" he asked.

Caldera nodded and showed Grey the stone, then tucked it into her pocket before handing his card back to him. "Let's get out of here."

The lift jolted into action when the three stepped on. Caldera closed her eyes and leaned against the wall. She was already thinking about getting back to the Vault and starting the next step in the plan when Grey's voice cut through her thoughts.

"We have a problem."

Her eyes shot open, refocusing. He was pointing to the little screen that showed their destination. Two guards were posted right outside the door—waiting.

"Shit."

"What're we gonna do?" Sylvie asked, already preparing to hit the emergency stop button.

"No," Caldera said, grabbing her wrist. "That'll look even more suspicious."

"Then what's your plan?" Grey asked, taking his eyes off the screen to glare at her.

Caldera drummed her fingertips on her chin. The lift continued to rise. One floor, two floors, three. *Damn it, I can't be found here! There's no way I could possibly talk my way out of this.*

Her gaze flicked to the emergency door latch on the ceiling. "Lift me up," she said.

Without a word, they stood on either side of her, bent their knees, and cupped their hands so that she could place her feet into them. As she was fiddling with the latch, the lift rose to the seventh floor.

Fuck!

"Come on, come on," Caldera muttered, pushing her shoulder into the door. The latch gave way.

The door swung back, banging against the top of the lift. The sound echoed throughout the shaft. With the help of Grey and Sylvie, Caldera crawled up onto the top of the box that was beginning to decelerate, its destination in sight.

"Sylvie, come on," Caldera said, reaching her hand back down into the compartment.

"Wha—why?"

"You're not supposed to be here either—captains only, remember?"

She nodded, grabbing Caldera's hand as Grey quickly helped her up.

The lift slowed to a stop. Caldera gently closed the hatch just as the doors *whooshed* open.

Taking a deep, controlled breath, she looked around. The metal tube they were in was almost completely dark, with only the soft white glow of the hydraulic arms of the lift to light their way. Caldera pressed her ear against the cold metal to try and hear the muffled voices on the other side.

"Why were you in the Artifacts Department?" a man's voice demanded.

Caldera glanced at Sylvie, who held her hands over her mouth and nose to try and stay as quiet as possible, her knees pulled up to her chest.

"I wanted to make sure my entry into the archive was logged," Grey responded, without a quiver in his voice.

Wow, he's good, Caldera thought, pressing her ear harder against the hatch door.

"Let us scan your keycard, please."

Silence. Caldera's heart slammed against her chest. She hoped they couldn't hear it.

"Very well, Captain Lasson. Sorry to disrupt you, the cameras aren't working right now, so we must've missed you coming in. Have a great night."

"You as well, officers."

Footsteps of three individuals faded as the door whisked shut. Caldera and Sylvie let out simultaneous breaths, waiting until Grey came back before they opened the hatch.

A few moments later, they heard the door whisk open again.

"Hey, it's safe now," Grey whispered from below. "Let's go, hurry!"

Opening the hatch, Caldera and Sylvie dropped from the ceiling and the three ran out of Vanguard Headquarters as fast as they could, not stopping until they were at their transport.

CHAPTER 28

ere it is," Caldera announced as the door to the Vault opened and the stairs disappeared behind her.

Sear, Markarian, and Aloriea perked up as she entered.

"That didn't take too long," Markarian said, turning to face her. "I'm guessing it wasn't too heavily guarded?"

"It was quite a heist." Caldera decided it was best to leave it at that. She walked over and placed the small stone on the tabletop, where its dull red color contrasted harshly with the wood-like laminate.

Sear's makeshift lab supplies were lined up in perfect order, the liquid materials all carefully measured and sitting calmly in their individual test tubes.

Sear eyed the stone. "First, we need to break off a smaller chunk to attach to the communicator."

Aloriea put her hands on her hips. "How?"

"Easy," Markarian said. He drew a small knife from a sheath attached to his belt, then pressed the stone firmly against the table. He flipped the knife around so the hilt was pointed at it, and in one quick motion, he brought it down hard, striking the mineral. A small sliver of proxine broke loose.

Caldera's heart thudded in her ears, threatening to break her ribcage with each pump. "What the fuck do you think you're doing?" she yelled as Markarian put his knife away. "If there was an adverse reaction—"

"You idiot!" Aloriea chimed in, her hands firmly gripping the back of the chair. "You could have just killed us!"

Realization and shock coursed over Markarian's features. "Holy shit...sorry."

"We were going to have to strike it at some point," Sear said. He picked up the sliver of red material between his outstretched claws and walked it over to the communicator. "Although, a plan of action would have been nice."

"I said I was sorry," Markarian replied, as his face turned red.

Caldera rubbed her forehead, her heart rate beginning to slow. "Okay, what's the next step?"

Sear brought the communicator over to the table. The proxine flake was stuck firmly against the signal amplifier. "Now we finish mixing the materials."

Caldera's hands shook as each separate component was poured together into a single, large beaker, the possibility of their imminent deaths looming over the table.

Sear jotted down notes onto his holopad as each chemical was combined, sweat glimmering off his forehead. His ears twitched back and forth so quickly that a soft breeze emanated from them.

The liquid turned from a soft vermilion to a deep maroon as the last element was poured in.

Caldera let out a shaky breath. Tense silence permeated the room.

"Now what?" Markarian whispered, clenching and un-clenching his hands.

"We trace the signal," Caldera murmured, surprised that she could still speak.

Sear's tail lolled behind him. "I just realized that there is a bit of an issue..."

"What is it?" Aloriea asked, her voice so soft Caldera could barely hear her.

Sear poked a claw at Caldera's communicator, still passively tracking the signal through the void. "Our artificial painite is, for the most part, liquid... It will give the scanner itself enough power to trace the signal, but at the same time, it will fry the circuitry, effectively destroying it—I assume."

Caldera bit her lip. "We only have one shot to get a lock on where the signal came from."

"Exactly," Sear replied.

"Are you even sure that it will trace the signal?" Markarian added.

Sear shook his head. "Again, no, but, if the measurements are correct, the reaction will be contained to the communicator's signal scanner—"

"So this is all on a hunch?" Markarian interrupted, throwing his hands in the air.

Sear's fur bristled. "According to my calculations, the odds of success are about eighty percent."

"And if it doesn't work, we'll lose the signal and everything else," Markarian countered, motioning at the screen. "We'll never find Justle."

Caldera walked over to the monitor, the flatline of the signal staring back at her. *Jumping the signal through a wormhole is the only way we'll ever find out what's on the other side.* She squared her shoulders. "We've come too far," she said, pointing to the communicator. "Do it."

Sear nodded, stirring the contents of the beaker. He carefully filled one of the small, half-inch vials that Doctor Vareis had brought with the components, and attached it to the signal scanner, next to the mineral sliver.

The maroon mixture resembled the color of the painite marbling, reminding Caldera of the portal opening. The reds, blacks, and silvers swirled in her mind again. The vials seemed to twitch as the liquid sloshed inside. She squeezed her eyes shut, attempting to force the undulating tear in the atmosphere out of her mind.

Taking a deep breath, Sear glanced over his shoulder to make sure the signal was active and locked in. He pressed the black rectangle against the vial as if he were simply replacing the back of the communicator.

The snap of glass echoed in Caldera's ears before Sear took a quick step backward.

A single wisp of red smoke emitted from the device—the same wisp she'd seen after she destroyed the original painite. It floated up and disappeared into the air.

Her mind slowed and sweat poured down her back as she waited for the deafening rip. For the blazing wind. For the portal itself to appear and take them all away—to discard them out into space as if they were nothing, like it had Rennick.

The monitor flashed, demanding Caldera's attention. She turned toward the screen to see the signal warping and restarting its scan. It pinged across the satellites again with incomprehensible speed, but this time when it got to the void, it flashed, disappearing. The screen was black.

"What just happened?"

The flash of light lit the screen again and, seconds later, the signal reappeared and pinged off an unknown satellite, finding its destination. Automatic, basic atmospheric scans lit up the screen.

"Oxygen-rich, flowing water, slow but constant axis rotation... It *is* an inhabitable planet," Caldera whispered, unable to take her eyes off the screen. She collapsed into the chair next to her. *It's not conjecture.*

"What the fuck..." Markarian muttered, stumbling backward.

"Is this the unknown object from the notes we uncovered?" Caldera asked, looking over at Aloriea whose hands were covering her mouth in a wordless gasp.

Sear's legs shook as he grabbed onto the back of a chair, the black slits of his pupils widening to completely overtake the gold of his eyes. "It must be."

With shaky hands, Caldera brought up the schematics of the 'unknown object' they had first discovered all those weeks ago. With the signal now able to reach its destination, she reentered the coordinates that they had found.

The Vanguard system ran through the databanks, quickly discarding the known coordinates of the Centaurus galaxy.

"Is this real?" Markarian stammered, making his way back over to her as the system continued its search, now able to reach farther than it ever had.

Aloriea was doubled over with her head resting in her lap, gasping for breath.

"Hey," Caldera said, stumbling over and kneeling in front of her. "Stay with me, Aloriea!"

Aloriea looked up into Caldera's eyes and shook her head, a euphoric smile spreading across her face. "We found the proof..." she said, tears streaming down her face. "We can prove that this is why he was murdered."

"This is where Justle is now." Caldera wrapped her arms around her friend. The tips of Aloriea's horns pressed into her stomach, but she ignored it, rubbing the akar's back. "We'll make Vandren pay for what he did," she whispered. "What he ordered other people to do." *Somehow.*

"Callie," Sear said, turning around to face her. "It is a match—this planet *is* the unknown object, and it is huge."

"How huge?" Caldera asked over her shoulder as Aloriea gently pushed her away, waving her off. She walked back to the screen and had to re-read the number multiple times. "This planet is one hundred times bigger than Bersama!"

"That's not possible," Markarian said.

Sear gestured toward the screen. "You would think not..."

"We should rescan it." Markarian reached for the keyboard.

Sear slapped his hand away. "It does not need to be rescanned," he said, his voice low.

"Why, because you say so?" Markarian scoffed.

"Because there is no reason to waste time."

Markarian narrowed his eyes. "Listen, you genius bastard—"

"Okay," Caldera interrupted, stepping between them to push them apart. "That's enough. If there's one thing that we don't have time for, it's your constant bickering."

Markarian rolled his eyes in the most exaggerated way he could, while Sear shook his head, unbothered.

Caldera took a deep breath. "There's only one thing we can do now..." She let her sentence trail off, mentally preparing for what she was about to suggest.

"What would that be?" Aloriea asked, shuffling over to them, her eyes puffy.

Sear crossed his arms. "We can no longer send a message to Justle."

"We need to try and leak this information to the general public right now," Caldera said. "Now that we know for sure that this is an inhabitable planet, we could expose the Council for keeping it a secret."

"I don't know," Aloriea murmured. "We'd need help— someone who'll back our claims."

Caldera snapped her fingers. "The Queens of Sector Two— Eldra and Fenry. Let's try them. Eldra did say she'd try and help however she could."

Aloriea tapped her chin. "It's worth a shot, but we better wait until tomorrow, it's pretty late—"

"What?" Caldera asked, already hitting send on Aloriea's communicator.

A few moments later, there was an answer.

"H—hello?" The sleep-addled voice of Eldra said.

"Queen Eldra, it's Caldera."

"Caldera!" Eldra shouted, all sleep gone from her voice. "You're all right! Fenry—wake up!"

"Umm, Eldra, I'm sorry I haven't been around lately, and this is kind of awkward, but I need a favor..."

"Let me get this straight," Fenry's voice said. "You disappear for weeks, letting Vandren completely run your sector, wake us up in the middle of the night, and you want a favor?"

"Yes."

"What is it?" Eldra asked.

Caldera took a deep breath. "We—my court and I—found evidence of an inhabitable planet that the Council has been hiding from the people. We want to leak this information to the public, but we need you to back us up."

Gentle breathing on the other end was the only indication that they hadn't been disconnected.

"Absolutely not," Fenry finally replied.

"But—"

"We want to help you," Eldra interrupted. "If what you're saying is true, it could change everything. Do you have indisputable evidence?"

"Well..."

"That's a no," Fenry said. "We're not risking our lives on a hunch. That's final."

"Unfortunately, she's right," Eldra replied. "Call again when you have actual evidence and we'll be behind you one hundred percent."

"Okay," Caldera muttered, hanging her head. "Please don't tell anyone about this conversation."

"Of course," Eldra replied before disconnecting the line.

The air felt heavy as Caldera handed Aloriea her communicator back.

"Well, now what?" Markarian asked, leaning heavily on his elbow.

"We could try another sector leader," Sear proposed. "Jasik, perhaps?"

"No," Caldera said with a sigh. "They'll say the same thing."

"What do you suggest we do?" Aloriea asked.

"We have to go there."

They all stared at her like she had just spoken to them in a different language.

"You're fucking joking, right?" Markarian said.

"That's insane," Aloriea added, her eyes wide. "Despite what Eldra and Fenry say, this *is* enough to expose the Council. This is what they've been hiding, and Quill died for it."

"No," Caldera replied, shaking her head as she pointed at the monitor. "The queens are right. This can be covered up—or denied. We need indisputable proof."

"Going to this unknown planet is out of the question," Sear said, clear irritation bubbling to the surface. "That would be irresponsible and dangerous!"

Caldera tossed her holopad in Sear's direction. After a few seconds of fumbling, he caught it. "Painite can obviously do more than enhance signals," she said, pointing at the device now in Sear's grip. "It can open a wormhole. A portal...and we'd have to go there eventually anyway to get Justle."

"You want to open another wormhole without any testing," Markarian asked, plucking the holopad out of Sear's hands. "The same thing that killed Ren?"

"This isn't about him," Caldera snapped, her heart aching and voice rising. "I'm talking about controlling the portal, making it go where we want it to. I know it's possible—whether he was sent there or just went into hiding, Justle had to get to that planet somehow, right? Quill might've told him how to do it."

"That is indeed an interesting theory," Sear said with narrowed eyes. "But how do you suggest we replicate the process?"

"We have the coordinates," Aloriea offered, her voice becoming stronger. "If we can figure out a way to 'break' the artificial painite within a confined space—one that's locked onto the predetermined coordinates we set, like we did with the signal—the residual effect would be transportation!"

"You mean teleportation," Sear corrected.

"Whatever," Aloriea said, her eyes gleaming. "This could work."

"All right, let us just take a breath," Sear said, patting the air. "We cannot do this—"

"*We* aren't doing it," Caldera interrupted. "I am. Just me."

Markarian grabbed her shoulder. "Have you lost your mind? I'm not letting you do this. Let alone by yourself."

She shoved his hand away. "You think you could stop me?"

"Markarian is correct. Like I said before, stepping through a wormhole onto an unknown planet is extremely dangerous." Sear stepped in between them. "Why would you even suggest going alone?" he continued, turning to face Caldera.

"It makes me uneasy when you agree with me," Markarian muttered, glancing over at Sear. "But thanks."

"It's the only way," Caldera replied, crossing her arms. "Justle sent that message—he has all the answers we've been looking for, and I guarantee he's more than ready to explain everything he knows. We have to go get him," she continued, looking over at Aloriea for support. "Like it or not, it's the most logical thing to do."

"I agree," Aloriea said. "We can test the theory as many times as we need to, to make sure that controlling the wormhole and teleportation is even possible." She looked from Sear to Markarian. "I want answers—and I know both of you do too!"

Markarian narrowed his eyes and drummed his finger over his crossed arms. "Fine..." He met Caldera's eyes. "But I'm going, too."

"No—no way!" she said, shaking her head.

"You don't have a choice," Markarian insisted. He pushed past Sear and grabbed both of her shoulders in his big hands, his gaze never wavering. "I will die before I let you do this alone." He released her, taking a step back.

As a moment of silence passed between them, the weight of the moment settled on her shoulders. Caldera sighed, letting a smirk spread across her face. "You're a pain in the ass, you know that?"

Markarian shrugged, grinning. "What are friends for?"

She chuckled. "Sear? Are you going to help us?"

He gripped the bridge of his nose. "I have already voiced my thoughts, but it seems like it does not matter if I disagree or not," he said, resignation coating every word. "It would be better for me to be involved lest you hurt yourselves... Now, what should the container for this controlled painite break be?"

A smile broke across Caldera's face as warmth radiated from her chest. "It needs to be something that we can easily hold or wear," she said, starting to pace.

"What about a clip?" Markarian suggested, tapping his foot. "We could attach it to our clothes or something."

Caldera shook her head, her eyes bouncing from the monitor to her broken communicator. "Too easily lost."

"Okay, so we should focus on something that's completely wearable, then," Aloriea said, leaning back against the table.

Caldera nodded, forcing the possible repercussions of what they were planning out of her mind. "It would also need to be able to hold vials of the artificial painite and something to lock onto coordinates—maybe a geocode device."

"What about a belt?" Sear said.

Caldera snapped her fingers. "Or a bracelet. That's something we could permanently attach to ourselves without it being too much of a hassle. While still being adjustable in case we would need to remove it."

Sear bared his fanged smile. "A portal bracelet? I believe that could work. We can make them out of any metal as long as I can attach the catalyst to them—the compounds are not radioactive, so it does not matter. The problem is the 'scanning' aspect."

"What do you mean?"

"Well, you saw what happens when painite is not contained—giant rip in spacetime," he said, visibly gauging her reaction before continuing. She stared back at him, unflinching. "Even if it *is* contained, the question is, how are we going to only make it scan your individual bodies, and for that matter, how are we going to get you back?"

"Create a tether *to* our individual bodies through the coordinates and computer system," Caldera replied, her hands on her hips. "We could use a GC device to continually lock onto the coordinates."

Sear rubbed his eyes. "Keeping a person's complete individual biometric composition actively connected to this computer is impossible. It is too much for a single system to handle."

Caldera's heart dropped. "Why?"

"The influx of information would fry the system. It would have to constantly update and connect to all the personal nuances of the specific individual," Sear said, looking from one confused face to the other. "Your heart rate increases and decreases in blood pressure, what food you ate and how it is affecting your metabolism—things like that," he continued. "Outside of a hospital, there is just no way."

"How do you know all of that?" Aloriea asked, a soft smile spreading across her face.

"It is fairly basic anatomy, and knowledge of how the systems work," he replied, grinning.

"What if we made the entire process even simpler then?" she replied.

Sear raised a bushy eyebrow. "Interesting. How so?"

Aloriea took a confident step forward. "Think about it—what are bodies basically made of?"

"Carbon, oxygen, nitrogen, and hydrogen," Sear replied automatically.

"Everybody knows that," Caldera interjected.

Aloriea nodded. "So if we set the system to scan those *basic* elements..." She motioned for Sear to take over her thought process.

"And we limit the area the catalyst engulfs by enabling an internal and external dampener of some kind..." Sear mumbled, pacing back and forth.

Caldera chewed her lip in contemplation. "If we did that, the compact area around the body itself would be scanned."

"Then, it'll work!" Markarian exclaimed, snapping his fingers.

Caldera beamed, unable to keep the smile off her face. "All right, it's settled on how the scan is going to work."

"Theoretically," Sear added, taking a deep breath.

She nodded. "The next question is, how long is it going to take to create one of these portal bracelets?"

"I assume not long once we have the actual items," Sear replied. "You saw how quick it is to mix up the catalyst."

"We're going on a bracelet hunt then?" Markarian asked, taking a seat. "We could always ask Grey or Sylvie to bring us some."

"I actually might be able to help with this," Aloriea replied, motioning for Caldera to follow her. "Come on, let's take a trip up to my quarters."

CHAPTER 29

Sear solidified the coordinates and tested the tether to the other planet over and over. Each time, the brick they were using as a test subject disappeared, then reappeared. After days of testing, experimenting, and calibrating the geocode devices, it was time to put it all to the real test.

They were finally about to leave—to find Justle and the source of the signal.

Caldera took a deep breath as she scrambled into her old vac-suit that Grey and Sylvie had stolen for her. Beside her, Markarian was doing the same.

This is it. Caldera exhaled sharply, fumbling with the strap that held the blaster to her hip. She quickly put on her helmet to check the coms after whisking her hair—which was now well below her shoulders—into a ponytail. "Com-check one. Markarian, do you copy?"

"Loud and clear, Cal."

She chinned the secondary button in her helmet. "Com-check two. Sear, Aloriea, can you two hear me?"

"Affirmative—umm, copy?" Sear stuttered.

"Don't worry about being technical," she said, taking off her helmet. "Answer any way you want to."

Sear nodded, typing in the coordinates. "Five minutes till breach—I am adding the artificial painite to both of your helmets' radio signals, so we will be in constant contact."

"What if we get cut off?" Caldera asked, looking down at the helmet in her hands.

"Since the signal is redirecting through the catalyst, it will not matter. The reconnection will be instant," Sear replied.

"Just like our regular communicators," Markarian said.

"You mean, your communicator." Caldera glanced around at the walls of the Vault and took yet another deep breath. "Mine's still broken."

Markarian flung the pack that held their rations and an extra bracelet for each of them over his shoulder. "You ready?"

His grip was steady on the bag, but Caldera knew he was scared. His other hand was shaking.

She looked down at her own trembling hands and nodded. "Yes."

A geocode device, along with two vials of the inert mixture and two pieces of proxine—contained in their own vials—were attached to the thick silver bracelet that was tightly wrapped around her wrist.

They both carried spare GC devices to attach to the portal bracelets, plus one blaster for each of them.

"Remember," said Sear, his gaze downcast, "your portal bracelets will not be on a timer. You will have to activate them and type the coordinates into the geocode device yourself."

"We know, Sear," Caldera said, turning toward him and Aloriea. "Are you sure you'll be all right by yourselves?" A pang of fear stabbed through her chest at the thought of leaving them alone, at the mercy of Sol and Saro—of Vandren.

"We'll be fine," Aloriea replied. "Grey and Sylvie are on

speed dial, and we won't leave the Vault unless it's completely necessary."

"Plus, I am not as defenseless as you would like to believe," Sear added, his claws glinting in the fluorescent light.

Markarian nodded at Saro's stolen blaster on the table. "Just keep that with you at all times."

"We shouldn't be gone too long...just long enough to find Justle and bring him back," Caldera muttered, gripping her helmet tighter. *If we don't die right now.* Her stomach roiled.

Markarian put a hand on her shoulder. "Let's do this."

"Three minutes." Sear's voice was cold and clinical, a clear attempt to hide his emotions.

Aloriea swept both Caldera and Markarian into a hug. "Good luck," she said, releasing them. She looked at Caldera, her face riddled with fear. "Callie—I'm...sorry."

"Sorry for what?" Caldera asked, shaking her head. Her heart beat so quickly, she was having trouble breathing.

"For believing that you killed Quill."

"Forget about it. Apology accepted." Caldera hugged her one more time before taking a step back.

Aloriea smiled as tears trailed down her cheeks. "Don't die out there, okay?" she said, wiping her eyes. "That goes for both of you." She looked over at Markarian.

"Don't worry," Markarian said with a wink, his voice steady—calculated. "We'll be okay."

Caldera tried to smile, but it came out as a grimace. She wanted to believe him, but there was a chance that they'd die just going through the portal. *Sear was right. It's one thing to experiment with inanimate objects...* She swallowed hard, barely suppressing the urge to gag.

"One minute," Sear rasped, his ears twitching back and forth.

Caldera put her helmet back on. "Communications open," she said, beginning to activate the portal bracelet that was wrapped around her wrist.

"Communications open," Markarian repeated, his voice cracking over the speakers as he mimicked her actions.

"Communications open," Sear said, his voice shaking. "Good luck. Breach in three, two, one."

Caldera gasped as blinding white light flooded her vision. Closing her eyes against it, she instinctively raised her hands to cover her face as the helmet's visor unsuccessfully tried to dim the brightness. A visceral chill washed over her body, and she was falling. Trying to force herself to open her eyes, she found she couldn't, or if she had, then she had gone blind. There was nothing but blackness surrounding her. The freefall stopped—she was floating in the void, her body being pulled in all different directions.

Should I scream? Could I scream? Am I dead? Vaporized instantly because we messed with something we didn't fully understand?

The impact was hard, quick, and instant. Caldera's head banged against the inside of her helmet. Her eyes fluttered open, and she found she had, in fact, not gone blind, but was looking at something tan.

Blinking her blurred vision away, she ran her fingers across the hard ground. *Dirt? Maybe sand?* "H—hey..." she gasped, but was cut off by a coughing fit that she was sure would produce one of her lungs.

"Cal—Callie! Fuck, are you all right?"

"Mar—" another coughing fit gripped her throat as she tried to reply. Gasping for breath, she rolled over to her side, trying to take in her surroundings. Her visor cleared, and a bright blue sky came into view from her horizontal position on the ground.

"I—I see you, don't move," Markarian said, his voice echoing through her helmet, causing her head to pound.

Unable to answer, she attempted to sit up, her entire body shaking with the effort.

"Holy shit!" Markarian's voice broke in and out through her helmet's speakers.

In a matter of seconds, one hand was on her shoulder while the other gripped her arm, hoisting her up and leaning her against something solid.

Markarian's helmeted face appeared in her visor. "Are you okay?"

Chinning another button in her helmet, a scan of her vitals appeared across her heads-up display. It said she was fine. Perfectly healthy, in fact. She nodded once, giving Markarian a thumbs-up, still not confident enough to speak.

He hung his head, letting out a relieved breath. "Thank fuck. Sear, Aloriea? Can you hear us?" he continued, not letting go of Caldera's shoulder.

"Yes," Sear said, his voice sounding uncharacteristically shrill.

"Fuck, yes!" Aloriea screamed. "Did you make it? Are you there?"

"Are we ever," Markarian answered. "Whatever just happened, it was fucking crazy."

"Is Callie okay?" Aloriea and Sear asked together.

Caldera groaned, wanting to answer for herself. "Okay..." she rasped. "Where are we?"

"No idea," Markarian answered. "I'm scanning the surrounding area. Sear, the data should be coming your way. Are you receiving it?"

"Yes, and...it is very odd."

"How so?" Caldera asked, finally able to look around as the nausea subsided.

"The atmosphere is extremely similar to Bersama's," Markarian offered, releasing her shoulder as he looked down at the monitor on his vac-suit.

"That is true," Sear replied, "but that is not what I mean. When I say similar, I mean there is almost no discernible difference, besides a few particulates and minor details."

Caldera slumped against whatever Markarian had propped her up on. "I feel heavy," she mumbled, looking around at the tall, green spiky plants that were interspersed throughout the area—barely resisting the urge to take her helmet off.

"That is one of the subtle differences," Sear said. "That planet's gravity is 0.5 G's heavier than Bersama's."

Markarian grunted, working his shoulders. "That explains it."

"It is not a huge problem, but it *will* take a little time to get used to," Sear continued.

Caldera activated her own suit's scanner, finally able to move freely. Looking behind her, she realized she was leaning against a huge boulder.

Barren land surrounded them for miles. Large bushes, boulders, and the unknown, sharp-looking, stem-like plants surrounded them. The only trees that could be seen stood in the distance on the horizon. The surrounding area rose in places and down in others, making the ground look like it was undulating.

"Mountains," Caldera whispered, leaning forward. "If I didn't know better, I'd say we were in Sector Three—Sedrolla."

Markarian sat back on his haunches, turning his head left and right. "Huh..."

"Sear," Caldera said, "are you sure, we're not still on Bersama?"

Markarian sat down next to her, leaning against the boulder. Sear began frantically typing, the clicking of the keys echoing through her helmet's speakers.

"You are definitely not," he replied. "I can scan the rest of the system, but, if you are in an oxygenated atmosphere—and the planet is not cataclysmic...then you are not even in the Centaurus galaxy."

"Well, there's not much going on, but it's definitely not cataclysmic," Markarian said.

Caldera shivered at the thought of the desolate section of the Centaurus galaxy and the monster that had almost killed her and Rennick. "Well—" she began but was cut off by a tremulous voice coming from behind her and Markarian.

"Put your hands in the air!" It sounded female and had an accent Caldera couldn't place.

"Seriously? Already?" Caldera muttered.

"What? What's happening?" Aloriea's voice chimed through the speakers.

"Looks like we ran into a little welcome party," Markarian answered.

"I'm gonna go ahead and turn off com-two for now," Caldera interjected.

"Wait—" Sear started.

She chinned the button in her helmet, cutting him off.

"I have a weapon pointed at you, so no funny business," the voice behind them continued.

"How do you want to do this?" Caldera asked through the internal speakers in her helmet now that it was just her and Markarian.

"Let 'em get close. Take 'em down," he said, drawing his blaster.

"It's not like we have a lot of options, anyway," Caldera replied, slowly raising her arms at the bequest of the stranger.

"Virtually no cover," Markarian clipped.

"Okay, since we're behind this boulder and can't see them, as soon as our suits scanners say they're close, you grab them, and I'll get them at blaster-point," she said, chinning the area scanner on her HUD. "Since we don't know how big they are, it'll probably be best if you detain them."

"Got it," he replied, holstering his weapon.

The stranger approached, and as soon as they were within arm's length, Markarian whirled to the right and grabbed the wrist of the assailant, forcing the weapon out of their hands. Caldera rolled left, unclipping her blaster and aiming it directly at their head.

"Well, that was easy," Markarian said, holding the shocked woman's arms behind her back.

Caldera looked at her, tilting her head to the side. "We're not on Bersama?" she whispered to herself. Markarian said nothing, focused on holding the struggling woman.

They looked...normal—like any other tellin, only significantly shorter.

Long, jet-black hair that turned brown at the tips was pulled into a tight ponytail, while dark, angular eyes darted around like a trapped animal. The woman's ash-colored skin was turning pink with exertion as she continued to try and free herself. Her white tank top and light denim jeans were stained with dirt, brown boots kicking dust clouds into the air as she stomped the ground.

"Let me go!" the woman demanded, radiating false confidence.

Glancing down at the discarded weapon, Caldera was unable to recognize its design. Its barrel was long and looked like it was made from crude metal with a piece of wood attached to its underside. The stock was plated with wood as well, and the trigger wasn't covered. She took a step forward, her blaster still aimed at the stranger's head.

"No!" the woman screamed at the top of her lungs, struggling harder.

Caldera sighed. "Markarian, can you keep hold of her?" she asked, making sure the external speakers weren't on.

"No problem," he assured her, not even sounding winded.

She opened com-two again. "Sear, you there?"

"Yes, and for the record, that was completely uncalled for, cutting us off like that!"

Caldera raised her eyebrows at his outburst. "Sorry—didn't want you and Aloriea to hear the fight, but it turns out there wasn't much of one," she replied, wiping the dirt off her vac-suit with her free hand. "I won't do it again."

"Fair enough. What is going on?"

"We've detained an inhabitant and—" She paused, looking over at the still struggling woman.

"And?" Sear probed.

"They're remarkably similar to tellins...but never mind that for now. This is the last known coordinate for the message, right?"

"Yes, wherever you are now is where the message to your communicator was sent from. Now, what is this about the inhabitants?"

Caldera nodded. "Markarian, I'm going to talk to her."

"I don't think—"

"She might know something," she continued, cutting him off. "If she's like—like the patroller for this area or something, she might have seen Justle."

Markarian exhaled sharply. "Just be careful. We don't know anything about her, or what she's capable of yet."

Caldera took another step forward. The woman held her ground. Lowering her blaster, she activated her external speakers. "We're not going to hurt you," she said. "Can you understand me?"

The woman stopped struggling. "Y—yes." She sniffed, a breeze blowing through her hair that Caldera couldn't feel.

Caldera breathed a sigh of relief. "Good. I just want to ask you a few questions. Will you answer them?"

The woman nodded silently, trying to regain her composure. "If it means you'll release me."

"Okay, let's start simple. What's your name?"

"Mei—Mei Miller."

"Okay, nice to meet you. Next question."

"Aren't you goin' to tell me your name?" Mei interrupted, narrowing her eyes.

"We'll circle back to that," Caldera paused, contemplating taking off her helmet again. Shaking her head, she took another step forward. "Answer me this—where are we? What's the name of this planet?"

Mei's sudden laughter caused Caldera to jump. Her blaster was pointed at the woman's forehead again in an instant.

"What's so funny?" Markarian snarled, tightening his grip around her wrists.

"You know, you're the second person to ask me that exact question," Mei replied, her eyes trained on Caldera as if she could see through her visor's tinted windshield.

Caldera lowered her blaster slightly. *She's met Justle!*

Markarian's grip never wavered. "Just answer the fucking question."

"Okay, okay," the woman said, a slight smile spreading across her face. "Earth. This planet's name is Earth."

CHAPTER 30

Earth?" Caldera said, putting a hand on her hip. "Never heard of it. What galaxy are we in?"

"I'm not answerin' any more questions until you tell me your names!" Mei replied, glaring at Caldera. When she glanced over her shoulder at Markarian, her entire demeanor had changed. She set her jaw and her eyes flashed with determination.

Caldera sighed. "Fine. My name's Caldera and that's Markarian. Now talk."

Mei's eyes widened. "Caldera... Caldera Keane?"

"How the hell did you know that?" Caldera demanded, instantly readying her blaster again. "Do you know Justle? Where is he?"

Mei raised an eyebrow.

A harsh buzz followed by a thump hit Caldera's ears, filtering in through the helmet speakers as the woman fell to the ground in front of her.

Taking another deep breath, she lowered her blaster while tightening her grip. "What the fuck, Markarian!"

"Calm down, I just stunned her."

"Obviously! Why the fuck did you do that?"

"You stunned an inhabitant!" Aloriea trilled through the speakers.

"She has to have some sort of...mind-reading power," Markarian muttered, eyeing the unconscious woman.

Caldera's head spun. "That—that doesn't make sense," she stammered.

"How else would she know your full name?"

"Because Justle probably told it to her, you dumbass!"

"The inhabitants of this planet can most likely read our minds and use what we want most against us," he persisted, worry seeping into his voice.

"That is a myth. A bedtime story," Sear replied. "You need to control your trigger finger, otherwise we will never get any answers from the inhabitants there."

Caldera's stomach twisted into a knot at the thought.

Markarian sighed. "Fine, let's find out what she knows," he said, scooping up the unconscious woman and leaning her against the boulder.

"I doubt she'll be in any mood to talk to you, now," Aloriea muttered.

Ignoring her, he slid the pack off his shoulder and dug around inside, pulling out a rope.

"Is that really necessary?" Caldera asked, as Markarian tied the woman to the rock.

"Yes, it's fucking necessary," he snapped. "Who knows what she's capable of?"

"All right," Caldera replied, shifting from one foot to the other. The vac-suit's circulation system sent a rush of air over her body to dry the cold sweat that had formed on the back of her neck, sending chills down her spine.

The woman's head lolled to the side. *She doesn't look*

dangerous...but then again, neither do I. "Maybe we should just take her back to Bersama."

Markarian turned around to face her. "Are you joking?" He shook his head, steadying himself against the barren ground. "Please tell me you're joking."

"Maybe this would be enough—"

"Did you just say you wanted to kidnap an inhabitant?" Aloriea interrupted.

Caldera glanced at Mei. "Well..."

"That's insane."

"Speaking of the portal, there is something we need to tell you," Sear said, taking a breath. "We have used up a lot of the catalyst. Apparently, it takes more of the artificial painite to send people through the portal than we had initially calculated."

"What? Why didn't you tell us this before now?" Markarian said, jolting to his feet.

"We were checking to make sure the data was correct," Sear snapped back. "Which it is."

"What we're trying to say," Aloriea said, "is that there's only enough for one more trip through the portal for each of you, including your extra bracelets. We don't have any more on our end. If you bring the inhabitant back here, they have to stay. Same for the two of you. If you come back to Bersama, you can't go back to...what was it?"

"Earth," Caldera muttered. "What about Doctor Vareis? Couldn't she bring us more compounds?"

"No," Sear said, "Vandren has put a huge watch over the palace—probably having something to do with you stealing Saro's blaster—so the doctor would be under extreme scrutiny."

"She wouldn't be able to sneak the compounds in without Vandren knowing. Her entire bag would be scanned by Sol and Saro," Aloriea added.

"According to what we found out about the proxine mineral, it is safe to assume Vandren knows how to make artificial painite," Sear continued. "That means he will know that is what we are doing, too."

"He'd probably storm the palace to arrest us," Aloriea added.

Caldera drummed her fingers against her arm. "What's the plan then?"

"After you find Justle, you need to get hard evidence about the planet before you come back," Sear said matter-of-factly. "Something indisputable, like you said before. Even if you did decide to kidnap the inhabitant, you said they look just like tell-ins, correct?"

"Yeah," Caldera mused. "Only shorter."

"The Council would easily be able to cover that up, along with everything else."

She nodded. "Indisputable evidence," she muttered, turning toward Markarian. "We can do that."

Markarian knelt next to Mei. "And it starts with getting some answers out of her."

"Let's see what she knows," Caldera agreed. "Aloriea, Sear, you two stay quiet."

"Okay," they replied in unison.

"Cal," Markarian said, looking up at her. "Are you sure you're all right to do the interrogating, or do you want me to?"

"Let's just call it 'asking questions'," she replied, taking a deep breath. "I can do it." Markarian nodded, gently patting Mei's face to wake her up. She stirred, and Markarian stepped to the side, drawing his blaster.

"W—what happened?" Mei stammered as her eyes fluttered open, looking from Caldera to Markarian. "Did you...hit me?" She tried to lunge forward, but the rope held tight. "What is this? Let me go!"

"First, you're going to answer the rest of our questions," Caldera said, stepping forward.

"And I didn't hit you. I stunned you," Markarian added. "Big difference."

"I can't believe this! Who do you think you are—"

"Just answer our questions," Caldera said, balling her hands into fists.

"Or what?" Mei countered. "You gonna kill me?"

"No..." she answered, biting her lip. "Of course not."

"Good, 'cause if you really are who I think you are, you wouldn't murder someone in cold blood. Neither of you would."

Caldera furrowed her brow. *What the hell does that mean? What exactly did Justle tell her?*

Mei's eyes flicked from Caldera to Markarian when they didn't answer. "Okay," she continued, glancing to the side. "Ask your questions."

"Cal—" Markarian said, his voice only coming through the speakers inside her helmet.

She held up a hand to cut him off, never taking her eyes off Mei. "You said we're on a planet called Earth," she said, crossing her arms. "What galaxy are we in, then? Centaurus?"

"The Milky Way," Mei corrected, licking the newly formed crack on her lip.

So there's more than one galaxy? "What sector are we in right now?"

"Sector? Do you mean country?" Mei asked.

"Yes, if that's the equivalent," she snapped.

Mei rolled her eyes. "United States, but there are...I guess you could say subsections to each country as well."

"Explain," Caldera commanded.

"Well, for example, we're in Reveille, Nevada, located within the United States. Reveille is a town, Nevada is a state, and the United States is the country."

Caldera exhaled sharply, her head spinning. "What species live on this planet?"

Mei leaned her head back, closing her eyes against the sun, as if she were summoning her strength, her long ponytail falling away from her shoulder. "Humans."

"And?"

"And what?" Mei asked, annoyance creeping into her voice.

"What other species?" Caldera said, struggling to keep her voice steady. "I want to know about all of them."

"Now that," Mei said, straightening her back, "would take a while."

Markarian took a step toward her. "What do you mean?"

Mei hung her head, sighing heavily. "I had this exact same conversation weeks ago."

"Well...reiterate it for us," Caldera snapped.

"We're not like where you come from. There are thousands of different animal and plant species, but as far as others like me—it's just human. That's really all you need to know."

"So are you all the same, then?" Caldera asked.

"Not really," Mei said, taking on a know-it-all demeanor. "Within the human species, there are different races, creeds, and nationalities. For example, my ancestry is Japanese, but my brothers...isn't."

Caldera sighed. *We need to get out of this open area.* "Do you have a headquarters?"

"Umm...no. I guess I could take you to my house. I have a condition though."

"What is it?"

"Stop treating me like a damn hostage and promise not to hurt my brother once we get there."

"This isn't a good idea," Markarian said, his voice booming through the speakers in Caldera's helmet. "This has trap written all over it."

"I concur," Sear added, speaking for the first time in ten minutes. "You should not trust her."

Caldera looked over her shoulder at Markarian. "What if she knows where Justle is? Maybe he's there."

"I'm more concerned about how this is most definitely a trap," Markarian insisted. "We still haven't completely ruled out the mind-reading thing—"

"Yes, we have," Aloriea interjected.

"They could even make us hallucinate, or something worse!" Markarian persisted.

"Remember how easy it was to disarm her?" Caldera countered, making sure her external speakers were off. "If she's a member of the Vanguard—or whatever it's called here—then she's not very good. Maybe the rest of the members are the same," she continued, starting to untie her.

"You're really willing to take that risk?"

Caldera's mind flashed to Justle—about the possibility of getting her questions answered, of saving Bersama. "Absolutely."

Markarian sighed. "Fine, but I'm restraining her the whole way there. Got it?"

She finished untying Mei. "That's not part of the conditions she set."

"Caldera!" he snapped as he grabbed her shoulder, forcing her to face him. "I will not let you put us both in danger. We're restraining her. End of story."

"Fine!" she replied, shoving the rope into his hands, her voice cracking.

"It really is for the best," Sear muttered.

Markarian stepped forward as Mei stood. "Sorry for breaking the truce, or whatever this is," he said, motioning for her to outstretch her wrists. "I'm just not convinced that you're on our side."

"This is so stupid," Mei protested as Markarian tied her hands in front of her. "I'm not trying to trick you!"

"For your sake, you'd better hope you're not," Caldera whispered, her voice low. "Now, which way?"

Mei grimaced. "Straight ahead for now."

To Caldera's surprise, Mei didn't complain anymore, hyper-focusing on the path in front of her.

They walked in silence for a while over the barren ground, with nothing to look at besides rocks in varying shades of brown. The relentless sun promised heat that Caldera couldn't feel, casting long shadows over the ground. Her breath fogged the helmet's visor for a brief second before the circulation system cleared it away.

Markarian kept Mei from tripping when they reached a ragged patch of land.

Caldera cleared her throat, tired of walking in silence. "What was that word you used to describe yourself earlier?" she asked, unable to hold back her curiosity.

"Human?" Mei said, continuing to stare straight ahead.

"Callie," Markarian said, motioning toward her. "Why are you engaging her?"

"This is good," Sear interjected. "The more information you get, the better."

Caldera ignored them both. "No, the other one," she replied, barely resisting the urge to cut the com connections.

"Japanese?"

"That's it," she said, walking up so she was directly next to her. "What does it mean?"

"Do you even care?" Mei muttered, narrowing her eyes.

"I actually do," Caldera nodded. "Our friend sent us a message from this planet, and we need to figure out why."

"Your friend, huh?" Mei said, smiling wearily. "It's a race—like how you look, or the color of your skin."

Caldera blinked. "And there's more than one, right?"

"Oh yeah," Mei replied, nodding sharply.

"But you're separated by both? Species and race, I mean," Caldera asked, desperately trying to understand.

"Umm—kind of," Mei stammered. "It's tough to explain. There are so many nuances. The only thing you really need to know is that humans are the only species that can interact with each other."

"Okay, I—I guess I'm starting to understand." Caldera checked her HUD. It said they had walked a little over two miles. She took a deep breath, the complex nature of the planet swirling in her head. "How much farther?"

"We're close—just over this hill, actually. We live at the bottom of a little valley," Mei said. "And I think you should untie me before we get there."

Markarian caught her shoulder, stopping her in her tracks. "Not a chance."

"I'm just saying," Mei continued, turning away. "This'll go a lot smoother if my brother doesn't see me tied up."

"Fair enough," Caldera said, unable to ignore the irrational excitement growing in her chest. *She's obviously met Justle. Maybe she knows where he is!* Kneeling, she grabbed the knife from her vac-suit boot, cutting Mei loose.

"Are you fucking kidding me?" Markarian's voice yelled into her helmet. "You've lost your goddamn mind, Callie."

"She has a point," Caldera snapped, discarding the rope on the ground. "There's no reason to get into a shooting match if we don't have to."

"We don't know what's over that hill. You're gonna get us killed," he muttered under his breath, the speakers barely able to pick it up.

Caldera closed her eyes, taking deep breaths as they reached the top of the hill. *Markarian's right, this is definitely a trap. But what if it isn't? I'm going to get us killed. But what if—*

"Callie, stop!" Sear's voice was frantic over the helmet's speakers.

She froze and glanced at Markarian, who put his hand on Mei's shoulder to restrain her.

"What is it, Sear?" Caldera asked, her stomach sinking.

"We just received word from Grey and Sylvie," Aloriea said, her voice sounding shattered—she was crying. "The detectives just found Justle's body... He's dead."

Dead? Then who sent the message? The air left Caldera's lungs and her blood ran cold, heart pounding uncontrollably. Gasping for air between the growing tightness in her throat, she stumbled backward and dropped her blaster, falling to her knees. Her legs shook so violently they could no longer hold her up. She had never vomited in her helmet before, but as her mouth began to water, she knew that might just happen. Breathing in and out through her nose, she clamped her mouth shut, her gloved fingers digging into the sandy dirt in front of her.

"I knew this was a trap!" Markarian was shouting, drawing his blaster. "Don't you fucking move!" Then Markarian's voice became close, frantic. "Callie! Hey, Cal ..." He wasn't talking through the speakers.

She looked up to see him kneeling in front of her, his helmet pressed against hers, his voice transferring directly through the contact. One of his hands grasped her shoulder while the other kept his blaster trained on Mei. She relaxed into his hold, trusting his grip would keep her from completely collapsing.

"Okay," he muttered, helping her to her feet. "We have to get out of here—now." He wrapped his arm around her torso, supporting her weight and turning completely back to Mei. "We have no idea what we're up against."

Grabbing onto his arm, Caldera quickly scooped her blaster off the ground, finding her balance.

"Did you think we wouldn't catch on to your scheme?" she nearly spat at Mei.

"What scheme?" she protested, her hands in the air.

"I don't know how you contacted us—or why you wanted to lure us here..." She swallowed hard, ashamed at how easily she was duped. "It almost worked, too."

"What are you talking about?" Mei persisted, her brown eyes blazing.

"Forget about her!" Markarian snapped, trying to force Caldera back the way they came. "Let's go!"

"What the hell's going on up there?" A voice from the bottom of the hill yelled.

Caldera looked down into a shallow valley basin, at the center of which was a small ramshackle cabin surrounded by large bushes and boulders. Two people that she couldn't make out were on the porch. Before she could demand that Mei tell them who they were, one of them stood up and walked down the steps into the open. Caldera could tell he was tall and slender even from one hundred feet away, his blond hair gleaming in the sunlight.

That must be Mei's brother. He's unarmed. Caldera turned

her attention to the other person who had followed him down the steps, her blaster at the ready.

His brown hair was shaggy like it hadn't been cut in a while, and his clothes were a ruffled mess as if he had just woken up. He looked like he hadn't shaved in a few weeks. As he stepped off the porch, he lifted his hand—looking up at them, shielding his eyes from the brightness of the sun.

His golden-brown skin was a shade darker than she remembered.

Caldera dropped her blaster. "Ren?" she whispered, heart thundering against her chest.

Ripping free of Markarian's grasp, Caldera was sprinting down the hill before he could stop her. She yanked off her helmet and discarded it on the ground, her ponytail flying out behind her. The change in atmosphere hit her instantly. No longer protected by the seal of her climate-controlled suit, the heat, and the heavier gravity accosted her, but she kept running.

The closer she got to him, the blurrier he became as tears streamed down the side of her face. She didn't stop, even as her legs ached, the gravity seeming to want to grind her bones together and push her into the ground. Picking up speed, she fiercely wiped her eyes, attempting to clear her vision.

His eyes were wide as he wordlessly reached his arms out to her.

"Ren!" Caldera cried, jumping forward the rest of the way— finally closing the distance between them and wrapping her arms around his neck. They tumbled to the ground together as he unsuccessfully tried to spin them around to break the momentum.

Tears fell in waterfalls down her face as her body racked with sobs. She balled his shirt into fists, repeatedly whimpering his name, her face pressed against the crook of his neck.

Rennick's body shook as he buried his face in her hair, wrapping his arms around her so tightly she could hardly breathe. "Callie..." he whispered, pulling her body even closer into his.

Her heart sang as her name left his lips. She took a deep, shuddering breath, pulling away just enough to see his face. His eyes were red from crying. Tears trailed down his face at the same rate as hers. He sniffled as his fingertips brushed her cheek, making their way to the back of her neck.

"I—" he began, his expression softening, a new tear rolling down his cheek. "I thought I'd never see you again."

Grabbing his free hand, she laced their fingers together, tears still flowing down her face as she nuzzled against his outstretched arm. "I thought you were dead."

A soft smile spread across Rennick's face, his thumb gently caressing her jawline. "You can't get rid of me that easily."

Caldera let out a broken laugh before lunging forward, her lips meeting his. His grip on the back of her neck tightened ever so slightly as he pulled her deeper into the kiss. An explosion happened behind her eyelids as her heart raced—her chest expanding like it was going to burst.

Their interlaced fingers tightened as tears slid down their cheeks, meeting at their lips. She tasted salt as they broke apart, and their eyes fluttered open, their gazes locking onto one another.

Rennick wiped a stray tear from her cheek before kissing her forehead, silently wrapping his arms tightly around her again.

Sighing, she leaned forward, resting her head against his chest and closing her eyes. *If the inhabitants of this planet are making me hallucinate this,* she thought, breathing in as much of him as she could before letting herself give in to total exhaustion, *then maybe they're not that bad.*

CHAPTER 31

aldera's eyes flew open. Early evening light filtered in through the open window directly in front of her as a breeze rustled the curtains. Looking around, she found she was lying on a bed in a room that was barely bigger than a closet. She sat up with a gasp, the heavier gravity instantly trying to pull her back down.

What happened? Did I black out? Shivering, she realized she was no longer in her vac-suit, only the black spandex shirt and leggings she wore underneath.

"Ren!" she called, pulling her knees up to her chest, hoping against hope that her dream was reality. "Ren?" she mumbled again when no answer came, her voice catching in her throat. Her heart dropped. Burying her face in her hands, she gave in to wordless tears.

The door to the small room squeaked open.

"Callie, are you all right?"

Wiping her eyes, Caldera jolted her head up toward the voice. Rennick stood in the doorway with a glass of water in his hand.

Hurrying across the room, he placed the cup on a side table and sat on the edge of the bed next to her.

"Are you real?" she whispered in his ear, wrapping her arms around his neck.

He straightened up, his arms closing around her, chin resting on the top of her head. "I'm real... I'm glad you got my message."

"It was you?"

"Yeah, sorry for being so cryptic, but I knew you'd understand."

They tightened their embrace before separating, letting silence take over while taking in each other's presence. Murmured voices came from a different part of the house, filtering in through the room's closed door.

"I—umm, Markarian's been filling me in on what's been happening on Bersama," Rennick said, rubbing his arm. "I'm sorry to hear about Justle. That's who you thought sent the message?"

Caldera nodded, not knowing where to begin.

"I should have been there," he muttered, turning away from her.

"Ren..." she said, taking his hands in hers.

"I put you, and everyone else, in more danger than ever," he continued as he squeezed her hands, meeting her eyes. "I'm so sorry, Callie."

Caldera cupped his face in her hand. "There's nothing to apologize for. Olivare was going to kill me. If you hadn't done what you did, he would have."

"I meant after that," he replied, a somber smile appearing across his face. "Everything you found out about Sol and Saro."

"Well..." She sighed, lowering her hand with a shrug. "That's all speculation." She paused. "Mostly."

A mischievous grin spread across Rennick's lips. "I heard you punched Vandren. At my funeral, no less."

"He offended me."

He looked down at his hands. "How's my brother?" he asked in a more serious tone.

"Good—I mean, as far as I know. I haven't really checked up on him lately. I'm sorry."

"It's okay." He glanced toward the door. "Can you walk?"

"I think so—the gravity here is heavier, but it feels the same as being on a ship under thrust."

He kissed her forehead, awakening the butterflies in her stomach. "Then let me introduce you to the people who have been housing me," he said, standing and outstretching his hand toward her.

She took it and stood. The weight on her shoulders was immediate. "Although, I guess I haven't been on a ship for a while," Caldera said, stumbling toward the door.

"It takes a while to get used to." Rennick pulled her body close to his, only letting go after she regained her balance.

Taking a few steps forward, she jolted to a stop, a shock of fear coursing through her. "Where's that bracelet I was wearing?"

"The portal bracelet thing?"

"Yes."

"Markarian put them in the pack that you two brought—along with his and the extras," he replied, placing a hand on her shoulder.

Caldera breathed a sigh of relief. "I'm glad we brought extras," she said, gazing up at him.

"Me too." Rennick chuckled, brown hair bouncing over his ears.

As they ambled to the door, the loud, arguing voices of Markarian and Mei, along with a softer voice of the unidentified man she hadn't been introduced to yet, met her ears. Stopping in front of the door, she turned to look at Rennick, her eyebrows raised.

"Yeah... Markarian and Mei aren't getting along too well."

"Well, in her defense, we weren't exactly the nicest of people when we first met," she said, her gaze downcast.

Rennick smiled softly, reaching around her to open the door. "I heard."

The room opened into a large area that appeared to be a sort of living space. Pushed into a corner directly across from her was a black rectangle mounted to the wall, with a couch and chair sitting across from it. Caldera frowned. *Is that their holoscreen?* Two doors were closed on the opposite wall, and directly to her left was the most primitive kitchen she had ever seen.

Markarian, who was also not wearing his vac-suit, sat at a round table right in the middle of the room with the two strangers. "You're awake!" he said, grinning. His black hair was pulled into a bun on the back of his head. "She's awake," he repeated, this time directing the statement to his communicator that was sitting next to him on the table.

"Finally," Aloriea's voice chimed through the speakers.

"Are you all right?" Sear added.

Caldera blinked and looked around the room, expecting to see them pop out from a place she hadn't noticed yet. Her face flushed as she walked over to an empty chair, taking a seat. "I'm... okay," she managed.

"Okay, introductions real quick," Rennick said, putting a hand on her shoulder. "This is John," he said, pointing toward the tall blond man Caldera had seen earlier.

"John Miller," the man said, reaching his hand out toward her, his bright blue eyes shining in the artificial light of the cabin.

She shook it quickly.

"And you've already met his sister, Mei," Rennick continued, motioning toward the small, black-haired woman sitting with her arms crossed, glaring across the table at Markarian.

A small bruise had started to form along her jaw.

She must've hit her head when Markarian stunned her. Caldera nodded, regret filling her body. Rennick sat next to her, his presence still surreal.

"Now that that is over," Sear said through the speakers, "let us get back to the task at hand."

"Love to," Mei snapped. "Like I said before, I don't think staying here is the best option!"

"Did you not hear what they just said?" Markarian said, aggravation accompanying his every word as he motioned toward the communicator. "There isn't another option."

"What's going on?" Caldera asked. "Someone bring me up to speed." The table fell silent as all heads turned to look at her. "What?"

"Well," Sear said slowly, "you already know that there is not enough artificial painite to make more than one trip."

"And with Justle...gone, it's completely up to us to find out what Earth has to do with what the Council's planning," Aloriea added. "We need to bring back indisputable evidence to send to Eldra and Fenry so they can help us rally the people."

Caldera nodded. "Right, so what's the problem?"

"The time here is double the time on your planet," Mei blurted, turning her glare toward Caldera. "So two days here is only one day there."

"Mei!" John snapped.

"I was leading up to that," Sear said, exasperation coating his voice.

Mei turned away from them with a huff.

It wasn't until that moment that Caldera realized how young she must be. Nineteen, maybe twenty. The regret of attacking her returned in full force. "What does that mean?" she asked, forcing herself to focus on the conversation.

"That the time spent here is doubled?" John asked, curly blond hair falling across his eyes.

"Yes. What does that have to do with our current situation?" Caldera replied, flicking her gaze from each person at the table to the communicator.

"We are trying to decide what the best course of action would be in light of this new information," Sear said, the speakers of the communicator crackling.

"Technically, we have more time at our disposal now," Aloriea said. "When you come back to Bersama, it'll basically be like traveling back in time."

Caldera blinked, an invisible force pushing against her chest as she turned to face Rennick. "You've been gone from *Bersama* for twenty-one days..." Her voice trailed off as the realization struck her.

Rennick gave her an apologetic look. "Callie—"

"He's been here for forty-two," Mei interjected. "Basic math, really."

Caldera took a deep breath and closed her eyes, trying to rein in her anger. She attempted to put herself in the shoes of the girl, who had three strangers bombard her home. *Of course, she's angry.* "What was the last thing that was said before I came in here?" she asked, directing the statement at the communicator.

"The three of you should stay there until you can find something to bring down the Council," Aloriea answered.

"And that's where we disagree," Mei said. "I think you should go back to Bersama and formulate your plan there."

Markarian shook his head. "There isn't enough artificial painite to make multiple trips. We need to gather everything we can before we leave for good."

"I think they should stay." John's gaze lingered on Markarian before turning to Mei.

"You can't be serious!" Mei cried.

"This is what we've been dealing with while you've been sleeping," Markarian whispered into Caldera's ear.

"We took in Rennick—" John started.

"Rennick didn't treat me like a hostage when I was trying to help him!" Mei stood up from the table and walked into one of the rooms behind her, slamming the door.

"We have gotten nowhere in the past few hours," Sear said through the speakers. "No offense—John, was it? But I do not think having a child's input on the decisions we need to make is a good call."

"She's twenty," John said with a sigh. "Not a child—she's just angry."

"Rightfully so," Caldera muttered, standing.

"Do you really think that's a good idea?" Rennick said, lacing his fingers behind his head.

"Is what a good idea?" John asked, looking from Rennick to Caldera.

"Yes," said Caldera. "I'm going to try and talk to her. At the very least, it might defuse the situation."

"Umm... I—I don't..." John stammered, raising his hand as if he wanted to stop her.

Caldera was already halfway to the room Mei was in. *We're in the middle of a desolate desert with nowhere else to go and no way to navigate this planet. I have to get her on board with letting us stay here.*

Without knocking, she opened the door and quietly closed it behind her. The room was simple like the one Caldera had woken up in, although slightly bigger. Pictures of various trees and flowers lined the wooden walls. An ancient-looking computer system sat on a table next to the bed.

Mei was sitting in a chair, looking out the window into the growing dusk. "What do you want?" she muttered, glancing over her shoulder.

Caldera sighed. "Mei... I'm sorry."

Mei turned to face her, her eyes downcast as she pulled her knees to her chest. "For what?"

"For this whole situation. It's not fair."

"It's okay..."

Sitting on the edge of the bed, Caldera eyed the artwork as an uncomfortable silence filled in around them. "The pictures on your wall are beautiful," she tried, lacing her fingers together in her lap.

"Thanks, I painted them," Mei mumbled without looking at her.

Caldera's eyes glimmered. "Wow, that's amazing," she said, examining a particularly twisty tree trunk.

Mei swiveled in her chair, eyeing her skeptically.

"I'm serious," Caldera asserted with a sharp nod. "Why plants?"

"It's a tree or flower from each place my brother and I have lived," Mei explained. "I love them. They were always there for me, the way people never were."

"So, you haven't always lived here?" she asked.

A mirthless chuckle escaped Mei's lips. "No."

Caldera smiled softly. "Umm... I haven't thanked you yet."

Mei eyed her quizzically. "For what?"

"For taking Ren in. I honestly could never repay you for that."

Mei wrapped her arms around her legs. "It was nothing."

"Why did you, though?" Caldera asked. "His story must have sounded crazy."

Mei looked out the window just as the sun had completely set below the hills. The growing silence was only interrupted by unidentified animals.

"He was alone," Mei finally whispered, looking down at her knees. "And my brother and I... We know what it's like to be alone." She looked directly at Caldera. "Everyone has a crazy story."

"What's yours?"

Mei bit her lip, picking at her jeans. "The reason we haven't always lived here is because we're foster siblings—do you know what that means?"

Caldera's heart broke for her. "Yes, I do."

"John's five years older than me, but we were always in the same houses, ever since we were kids," Mei continued, her eyes watering. "No one wanted us... So after we got out, we stuck together."

Caldera placed her hand on top of Mei's in an attempt to comfort her. To her surprise, Mei didn't pull away, but smiled. *She's coming around. Good.*

"That's the main reason why," Mei said. "And, it was exciting to learn that extraterrestrials are real."

"What?" Caldera asked, sitting back as she began to relax.

Mei lowered her legs. "Extraterrestrials—aliens... Beings from other planets."

"Oh." Caldera laughed. "Do humans not believe in that?"

"Some don't!" Mei said, excitement in her voice, her words coming out in a rush. "But we're used to weird things happening."

"Oh yeah?"

Mei nodded vehemently, her thin body jittering with enthusiasm. "When you live this close to Area 51, you kinda have to get used to it." She saw the confused look on Caldera's face. "It's technically an airbase, but there are so many conspiracies around what really goes on in there."

"What kind of conspiracies?" Caldera asked. A sinking feeling that she couldn't place appeared in the pit of her stomach.

Mei chuckled. "The most popular one is that there are reptilians living among us and that they're covering it up." She smiled from ear to ear. "Ridiculous, right?"

The sinking feeling grew stronger. "Reptilians?"

"Lizard people," Mei answered with a smirk.

Caldera exhaled sharply. "No way…" She stood and made her way toward the door.

"What?" Mei asked, jumping up to follow her.

"It's not ridiculous," Caldera whispered as she walked back into the other room.

"Nice of you to rejoin us," Markarian said, his brow furrowing as soon as he saw her expression.

"Callie?" Rennick said. "Is everything okay?"

Caldera looked at each face, stopping on Rennick's. "Saurians are already on this planet."

Rennick's eyes widened. "Sector Three knows about Earth?"

"How do you know that?" Markarian cut in.

"What's the Council really up to?" Caldera whispered, ignoring him as she sat back down at the table.

"What are Saurians?" Mei asked, sitting down next to John.

"The lizard people—the 'reptilians' you were just talking about," Caldera replied.

A shocked expression fell over John's face. "They're real?"

"When did you first hear about these reptilians?" Sear asked from the communicator, his voice low.

"What do you mean?" Mei said. "Everybody knows about that conspiracy."

"No—" Aloriea chimed in. "When did the people of your planet first start talking about their existence?"

"I'll look up when people first started reporting reptilian sightings," John replied. He pulled what looked like a black brick out of his pocket and started typing on it.

"Councilmember Kex is a saurian," Caldera said, slamming her hand down on the table.

"It sounds like the Council might be sending some sort of recon team here," Rennick mused.

"All right," John interjected, walking around the table. "I couldn't find an exact date—but the first reports are dated somewhere around one hundred and fifty to two hundred years ago."

Markarian pointed at the brick in his hand. "What's that?"

"Oh, it's a... It's a cell phone," John replied, his face flushing. "Archaic tech compared to what you have."

Markarian smiled. "I wouldn't say archaic—since it can look up information."

Caldera sat back in her chair, the years twisting in her head. "Two hundred years for this planet is one hundred for ours," she whispered to herself. Her face flushed as she worked through the jumble of information. "If they've always known—all the way back to the founding council members...that means..."

"Bersama and Earth were in contact in some form before the cataclysm," Rennick said.

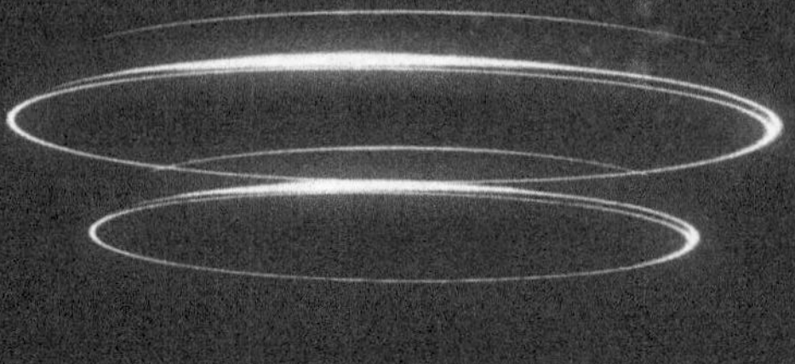

CHAPTER 32

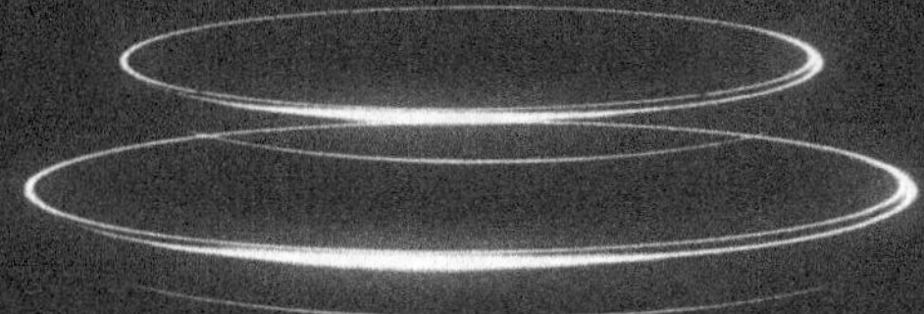

The what?" Mei asked. As she leaned forward, hair fell over her shoulder onto the table.

"Cataclysm." Caldera turned her attention to Mei.

"One hundred years ago, four out of the five planets in our galaxy stopped rotating, nearly killing everyone on them," she said, repeating the words straight out of the old history texts.

"The survivors were taken in by the one remaining planet, formerly known as Tellis," Rennick added, pacing back and forth behind her.

Mei and John stared silently at them, their eyes wide.

"Your planet wasn't always named Bersama, then?" John asked quietly.

Caldera shook her head. "In a show of unity, the planet was re-named and re-split into five sectors in honor of the lost planets." She drummed her fingers on the table, forcing herself to let the history lesson continue.

"Tellis became Sector One, Natioh is the second, Sedrolla

third, Aelmead fourth, and Muléus fifth—corresponding to the population of survivors," Markarian continued somberly.

"And all the sectors contain a different species?" John asked.

"They're not contained in a specific sector, at least, not before the borders were shut down," Aloriea corrected. "For example, I grew up in the palace. But...you're essentially correct."

Mei's eyes grew even wider. "You're a different species?" she asked excitedly.

"We both are," Sear replied.

"Reptilians?" Mei was practically bouncing up and down.

"Saurians," Sear corrected sternly. "And, no. I am known as a matan. Aloriea is an akar."

"Matans have catlike features, like claws, pointy ears—a tail," Markarian whispered to Mei and John when he saw their confused faces. "Akars grow horns on their heads—all different shapes and sizes," he continued, catching their stunned gazes.

Mei's eyes glittered with exhilaration. "Wow, and you grew up in a palace?"

Aloriea's gentle chuckle filtered through the speakers. "Yes, but it's not my family's. It belongs to the sector leader. The kings, queens, or rulers. So—Callie."

Mei's head whipped to the side, her mouth agape. "You're a queen? Rennick never told us you were a queen!" Her voice cracked as it rose another octave.

"Y—yes," Caldera replied, waving her hand in the air dismissively. *Okay, history lesson officially over.* "The *point* is," she snapped, trying to get them back on topic, "that there are, or were, species from Bersama on Earth, so both planets had to have known about each other at some point."

"That's impossible," John said, giving Mei a skeptical glance. "The people of Earth have never known about any other planet—or planets—that hold sentient life."

"Presumably," said Sear.

"Your planet knew about ours," Mei added, "but it has to be a one-way street."

"How do you know that your planet's government is not just keeping it a secret?" Sear asked.

Mei and John looked at each other and laughed. "Trust me when I tell you, something like that could never be kept a secret," John said, leaning on the table.

"Not on Earth," Mei added, crossing her arms. "Someone would definitely leak that kind of information. Out of principle, if nothing else."

John tapped his chin. "Although, they would definitely come off as crazy if they did."

"So why is it a secret on ours?" Caldera whispered as Rennick sat down beside her. A gust of wind from the open window blew through the room and rustled her hair, sending shivers down her spine.

"Maybe it's like Ren said," Aloriea chimed through the communicator. "They could be sending a recon force there."

"It has to be more than that, though," Caldera said, leaning heavily on her elbow. "We found detailed outlines of this planet in the Vault, down to the coordinates and exact size. Quill was able to find out that the Council knows about this planet, but not what they wanted with it."

"Something tells me it's nothin' good," Mei said leaning back in her chair.

Markarian frowned. "What makes you say that?"

"If alien movies have taught us anything, it's that beings from other planets hardly ever drop in just to say 'hi'," Mei replied with another huff.

"Right..." Rennick exhaled sharply. "What could be so special about this planet that warrants a century of secrets on ours?"

"The only logical explanation would be the potential resources the planet itself contains," Sear said. "Bersama is struggling and on the brink of war."

"So, whoever controls the resources controls the outcome," Markarian said.

"Meaning whatever decision we make...if we leak the information or not, there'll still be a fight over this planet," Caldera muttered, her head spinning.

"That has to be why the saurians are, or were, on Earth. I'd also wager members of all the species have been there at some point," Aloriea said. "They were probably sending information about that planet's resources to the previous council members before they were cut off."

"The founding council members must have known that Bersama wouldn't be able to naturally sustain itself—it's essentially an exoplanet. It's too small, even with the dwindling survivors." Caldera tapped her chin with her forefinger. "The saurians, and anyone else, from one hundred years ago obviously wouldn't still be alive."

"If there are recent sightings of them, then the current Council must have known about painite for a while," Rennick continued. "What it does, and how to make it."

"Longer than we initially thought," Markarian said, frowning. "So why would they send out that order to search for actual painite, if they could make it artificially with the proxine they already had?"

"The actual mineral is more potent," Sear said, the sound of his fingers flying over the computer keys echoed through the speakers. "Considering how much of the artificial painite was used just to send Callie and Markarian through once. Perhaps with the actual stone, the portal could become larger and stay open longer."

"I can confirm that," Caldera replied, stomach twisting. Her mind flashed to the immeasurable depth of the unstable rip she had inadvertently created. "I've seen what that stone can do," she whispered.

Rennick and Markarian's expressions softened as they sat in silence around the table, the clicking of keys through the communicator sounding through the room. The wind rushed against the small cabin, rustling the curtains of the open window, causing the ramshackle walls to creak and groan.

Caldera looked out the windows into the black of the night. *We're going to take down the Council, make them pay for everything they've done—everyone they've hurt. They'll do the same to the people of this planet if they get the chance.* She grimaced, forcing herself not to reach for Rennick's hand. *We can't let that happen.*

"Mei," she said, turning to face the girl sitting across the table from her. "You told me you lived near a place where weird things happen all the time, right?"

"Area 51? I mean, we're kind of close to it," she replied, her face flushing.

"We live about an hour away," John amended. "The closest town is Rachel. Why?"

"These 'conspiracy theories', do they all revolve around that place?" Caldera asked.

"Not all of them," John replied. "But I'm pretty sure the ones pertaining to your planet do."

Rennick leaned forward. "What're you thinking?"

"Maybe the general inhabitants of this planet don't know about Bersama, but that place definitely does," Caldera replied, looking from each person at the table, back to Rennick.

"It would make sense," Markarian said.

"I agree," Sear added. "The Council must have a contact somewhere on that planet, to make sure the people that they were sending into the portal got through safely."

"And to cover everything up if needed," Rennick muttered.

Aloriea scoffed. "Now we just need to prove that."

Markarian pursed his lips. "Okay, so how do we do it?"

Caldera bit the inside of her cheek. "We need to get to Area 51. If there's any indisputable evidence that'll expose the Council, it'll be there."

"Hold on everyone, just take a breath," John said, rising from his chair. "Area 51 is not a place you can just go to."

"It's off-limits to everyone that doesn't work there," Mei added.

Caldera glanced from Rennick to Markarian. "How hard could it really be for us to break in?"

"No!" John insisted, raising his voice for the first time. "That isn't an option that can be explored. From what I can tell, you're not equipt to raid Area 51. Trust us, please. You could all get arrested or killed."

A grin spread across Markarian's face. "What do you think we should do, then?" he asked, his voice taking on a suggestive air.

"M—maybe we should start from the beginning," John offered, his eyes bright as his face flushed red. "Figure out why we don't know anything about each other's planets in the first place. What's your solar system called again?"

"Centaurus," Caldera answered, forcing herself not to punch Markarian's arm.

"I can do some research," John said with a quick nod. "Mei, do you mind if I use your computer?"

She motioned toward her room. "Go ahead."

"No offense," Markarian said, waving his hand dismissively. "But I don't think the people of your planet would know anything." He paused, taking in John's agitated expression. "I mean... If we couldn't see you, then I doubt you could see us," he continued, rubbing the back of his neck. A pop of pink met his cheeks before quickly disappearing.

John took a deep breath. "Obviously, but wouldn't you like to exhaust all your resources before writing them off?"

Markarian's amiable smile returned. "Good point. I'll go with you, then."

"Oh—okay," John replied, a shy smile spreading across his face as he walked out of the room. Markarian followed closely behind.

"Bring the communicator with you, please," Sear snapped, his voice crackling. "You will need my expertise."

"Our expertise," Aloriea clipped.

Mei giggled as she scooped up the communicator and followed them into the room, leaving Caldera and Rennick behind.

Caldera smiled, unable to stop herself. "Are they all as kind as those two? The—" She paused, searching for the word. "Humans?"

"I doubt it." Rennick leaned back in his chair and looked up at the ceiling. "The way humans behave is still a mystery to me. I'm sure I just got lucky."

She shot him a questioning look.

He chuckled, holding up his hands in mock surrender. "As lucky as I could have gotten, considering the circumstances."

"Then why don't you know more about them?" Caldera asked, pointing toward the room Mei and John had disappeared into. "They helped you out, but still call you Rennick despite you having lived with them for almost two months in Earth-time. You hardly know anything about this planet. What have you been doing this whole time?"

Rennick averted his eyes. "I honestly don't know. I guess I was holding out some semblance of hope that I would get back to Bersama. To you." He sat up straighter, his eyes suddenly fixating on her. "I didn't want to make friends. I didn't want their kindness."

Caldera's gaze never wavered, her mind flashing to the aftermath of his disappearance. "I understand," she whispered, taking his hands in hers. "When I thought you were dead, I..." Her voice cracked as the warmth of his palms traveled up her arms. "I didn't want kindness either. I felt like I didn't deserve it."

Rennick tucked a stray strand of platinum hair behind her ear, turmoil swirling behind his eyes. "Why would you think that?"

"Because it was my fault that you disappeared in the first place," she whispered. Her heart ached with the pain of the confession. She clutched his hands tighter, using all her strength to force away the advancing tears.

"Callie—" he said, shaking his head.

"*I* destroyed the painite," she interrupted, closing her eyes. "*I* opened that unstable portal... *I*—"

He cut her off. "I know. Callie, don't blame yourself. Neither of us knew what destroying that rock would do."

Her eyes flew open and she forced herself to meet his gaze. "Don't you blame me for what happened?"

"I don't."

Crinkles appeared around the corners of his eyes—the laugh lines she had become so accustomed to over the years. Caldera caressed his cheek, still not quite believing he was there.

"You could stab me in the chest and I still wouldn't blame you for it," Rennick continued as he placed his hand on top of hers, a bright smile beaming across his face.

Quiet laughter escaped her lips. "I missed you," she whispered. "I really missed you."

Rennick leaned forward, engulfing her in his arms. "I missed you, too."

Caldera took a deep breath and a faint, familiar smell of mint hit her nose as she rested against his chest. Closing her eyes, she relaxed into his hold. His heart beat in her ear, strong and rhythmic. *You're here. You're alive. Let's hurry and get back to Bersama.*

CHAPTER 33

allie, Ren, you two are gonna want to see this," Markarian called, his voice booming through the door. "Get in here!"

Caldera and Rennick pulled apart and exchanged questioning glances before running into Mei's room.

John sat at the computer desk with the communicator next to the keyboard, while Markarian leaned over his shoulder, his face glued to the screen. Mei was lying on her bed, staring up at the ceiling.

"What am I looking at here?" Caldera asked, leaning over John's shoulder opposite Markarian.

"A map of our solar system," John replied, tilting his head up to face her. "The universe, as the people of Earth know it."

Caldera shuffled to the side, making way for Rennick to crowd in beside her. "NASA? What's that?"

"It's a space research agency," Mei replied, still staring up at the ceiling.

"We can actually see pretty far out there," John continued, typing on the prehistoric computer system.

They have a space exploration agency, too? Caldera's mind flicked to the Vanguard as she leaned in even closer, her grip tightening on the back of the chair. *Maybe they're not as primitive as we thought.*

"That's not the best part," Markarian said, catching Caldera's gaze.

John grinned. "There are more than just our two galaxies, too," he said, clicking an icon on the screen. "There are billions—trillions, even."

Caldera's eyes widened as name after name—picture after picture—scrolled across the monitor. "How..." she stammered, reaching out as if touching the screen would help her grasp the unbelievability of it.

Markarian smirked. "Still not the best part."

John blushed, clicking another image. "This right here," he said, clearing his throat and pointing to the screen. "This is yours—your galaxy."

"What?" Caldera and Rennick exclaimed at the same time.

"How is that possible?" Aloriea said through the communicator.

"You know about our galaxy, but not about us?" Sear added, speaking for the first time. "Impossible. You need to rescan your results."

"*Tch*," John muttered under his breath, glaring down at the communicator.

Markarian patted his shoulder. "You'll get used to him after a while."

"Can we focus?" Caldera interjected. "The people of this planet know about our galaxy, but not about us. Why?"

"Probably the same reason the people of your planet don't know about Earth," Mei said, rolling onto her side.

John refocused on the screen. "Look," he said, zooming in on the image and pointing to a blurry area. "We can't see through that dust cloud. I'm willing to bet that's where your planet is hidden," he continued, clapping his hands together triumphantly.

"That most likely has something to do with the cataclysm," Sear said.

"It makes sense," Aloriea added. "Four planets stopped rotating at basically the same time. The debris from the destruction sent into the atmosphere had to go somewhere."

"So, it went toward the only planet that still had a gravitational pull," Caldera muttered, tapping her chin. "As the years passed, no one realized anything was wrong, because that's the way it's always been."

"Can someone send me the information that you are all seeing?" Sear asked. "I would like to verify it on our end."

"Umm..." Markarian said, scratching his head. "I don't think so. The technology here is pretty primitive."

"Hey!" Mei and John said at the same time.

"Sorry!" He held his hands up in mock surrender. "But we can instantly transfer data between devices with a flick of our wrists—"

"He's right," Caldera interrupted. "Your tech can't do that."

"Then how are we going to get the information from that planet to this one?" Sear asked.

John's eyes lit up. "How about this," he said, digging through a side drawer.

"Get out of my desk!" Mei snapped, jolting up and reaching over to close the drawer.

"Where's your damn flash drive at?" John asked, attempting to push her away.

Caldera, Rennick, and Markarian exchanged glances, taking a step back from the quarrel.

"Here." John held up a tiny black rectangle and spun around in the chair to face them.

Markarian's gaze clouded. "Okay?"

John smiled, plugging it into the side of the computer. "We might not be able to transfer information to you instantly, but hopefully, this'll work."

"What is going on?" Sear asked.

"Apparently, the way Earth-people transfer information to each other is through a stick," Markarian replied, grabbing the communicator off the desk.

"It's not a stick," John said, unplugging the flash drive and standing. "Okay...technically it is a stick, but you can put information on this." He handed the device to Markarian.

Markarian grabbed the flash drive and turned away quickly, replacing the communicator on the desk. "I'll put this in the pack for safekeeping until we need it," he said, pink blushing across his face.

Caldera sighed. "Is this enough to bring down the Council?" She looked from Rennick to Markarian. "If we don't do something, they'll end up hurting the people of Earth, too."

"My vote's for no. We don't have enough," Markarian replied, crossing his arms.

Rennick drummed his fingers on the table. "This could still easily be covered up."

"All right then," Mei said, standing up from the bed before silence could settle in around them. "What kind of information are you lookin' for, then?"

"Anything and everything pertaining to Earth," Sear replied. "It does not matter, gather as much as you can and I will sort through it here."

John straightened. "That reminds me, I did manage to dig up some more info on that painite stuff you guys were talking about earlier." He pulled a vial with a sliver of painite in it out of his pocket.

Caldera gently took it out of his grasp. "How do you have this?"

"It was how I was able to get that message to you in the first place," Rennick said. "I jammed it into my communicator to hopefully boost the signal."

"And it's here, on Earth," John continued.

"That would explain quite a lot actually," Sear said, his sudden contribution making Caldera jump.

Markarian pressed his fingers to his forehead. "What could that possibly explain?"

"How Ren ended up on Earth without a coordinate system to guide him there, for one."

"So, what are you saying? That the stones are...linked somehow?" Caldera asked.

"It is a working hypothesis," Sear confirmed. "That is why I need all the information you can find."

She shook her head, exhaustion tugging on her mind. *This is too much... I can't think.*

"Are we all in agreement, then?" Sear cut in, his voice ringing out clearly through the speakers.

"About what?"

"You three must stay there until you have enough evidence to prove that the Council is deliberately hiding information to help aid in the upcoming war between the sectors," Sear said, fatigue evident in his voice. "In the right hands, knowing about this planet could help Bersama while not harming Earth."

Caldera looked from Mei to John, who both nodded. Rennick and Markarian did not protest. "All right," she said, "it looks like we are all finally in agreement. We're staying."

CHAPTER 34

Caldera leaned her head back in her chair, its back creaking as she looked up at the ceiling. Her eyes were dry and itchy from lack of sleep. The sheer curtains of Mei's room swished from side to side as a gentle breeze blew through the window, causing her to shiver. She sighed, forcing herself to look at the computer in front of her, its blue glow causing her head to pound.

"I can't believe we've already been here fourteen days…"

"It has only been seven for us," Sear chimed through the speakers of the communicator that was sitting on the desk next to her.

"Thanks for reminding me," she snapped, glaring down at the device. She barely resisted the urge to throw it against the wall. "At least there are no communication delays, since the signal is constantly being jumped through a wormhole."

Rennick walked up behind Caldera, putting his hands on her shoulders. "Maybe you should take a break," he whispered.

"There's so much information about this planet that we still need to uncover," she muttered, leaning her head back until it rested against Rennick's stomach. She looked up at him, knowing her eyes were bloodshot.

"Yes. Unfortunately, there is no time for rest," Sear said.

Caldera scoffed and covered the speakers of the communicator with her hand, trying to ignore him.

Rennick smiled down at her. "Then how about we get Markarian to switch shifts with you?"

"Or Mei," she said, glancing over at the lump that was sleeping in the bed next to her.

"Wasn't she gathering information before you?" he asked as Mei murmured in her sleep, rolling over.

"Oh—right," Caldera muttered, closing her eyes and rubbing her temples. "Okay, Markarian it is." She rolled the chair back as quietly as she could, grabbed the communicator, and stood up from the desk.

Catching a glimpse of the night sky outside the window, Caldera grimaced. Its unfamiliar star systems and single moon glowed down at her. She shook her head at the constant reminder that she wasn't on Bersama.

A weary, knowing smile crossed Rennick's face as they both shuffled out of the room, gently closing the door behind them.

"You're up," Caldera tossed the communicator to Markarian, who was sitting at the table with John, quietly laughing about something.

"Who's on?" Markarian asked, catching the device before it crashed onto the tabletop.

"Me," Sear replied. "But Aloriea and I are about to switch."

"Perfect timing, then," he said, winking at Caldera and Rennick, who both shook their heads.

"You know—" Sear began, his voice tense.

"I'm joking, lighten up," Markarian interrupted. "Although, Aloriea's definitely easier to talk to."

"Well, sometimes I tire of constantly having to dumb things down for you," Sear replied wryly.

Markarian laughed as he headed into Mei's room.

"Make sure you keep it down in there," Caldera said, then turned to face John. "Will you go with him to make sure he doesn't wake up your sister?"

John's eyes lit up as he enthusiastically followed Markarian.

"Shouldn't we discourage a relationship between them?" Rennick whispered into her ear as the bedroom door closed. "Once we leave, they'll never see each other again."

Caldera's exhausted gaze fell to the floor. "I know." She sighed, turning to face him. "But that's not for me to decide." She squared her shoulders. "If Markarian wants to get his heart broken—that's on him."

He made a face. "Wow... Harsh."

"I already told him what I thought," she added, meeting his gaze.

Rennick smirked. "And?"

"He very politely told me to 'mind my damn business'," Caldera said with a shrug.

"Probably should've seen that coming." He chuckled and put a hand on her shoulder. "Can I talk to you outside?"

"Sure."

The night air was brisk against her body as they stepped out onto the porch, the sudden chill shooting goosebumps up her arms. The single circular moon, along with trillions of unfamiliar stars, glimmered in the clear sky, engulfing the landscape in bright white light as they sat on the first step.

Tall, spiky plants—which Caldera had learned were called cacti—seemed to glimmer in the light of the moon, casting long, exaggerated shadows onto the ground where they intermittently dotted the hills and mountains, all the way out to the perceivable horizon.

Caldera let out a soft sigh as the gentle breeze blew through her hair.

"I have to admit, there are worse places to be stranded," Rennick said. He was sitting close enough for their bodies to touch.

Taken aback by the beauty of a place that wasn't her home, Caldera let an involuntary smile break across her face. She swallowed hard, unable to break her gaze away from the moon. Leaning against Rennick, she let his body heat envelop her. "So, what did you want to talk about?"

He shifted, sighing heavily. "It's about Olivare."

Caldera's heart skipped a beat as she conjured up his image in her mind. Her throat began to restrict as she remembered how he had tried to kill her—could almost feel his hands around her neck. "What about him?"

"He's still alive."

Caldera broke into a cold sweat. "What makes you think that?"

"Well..." he said, squeezing her hand hard. "Because I am."

"That doesn't necessarily mean... Y—you didn't see him when you woke up?" she stammered, unable to keep her voice steady.

Rennick shook his head. "We either got transported to two different locations because we weren't locked onto specific coordinates, or he woke up before me and ran away."

Caldera turned to look at him. "Which do you think is more likely?"

"If he did wake up before me, he probably would have killed me in my sleep."

Her stomach twisted in anger as warmth met her cheeks. "If I ever see him again..." she said, her voice low.

Rennick's amiable laugh cut her off, his shaggy brown hair bouncing up and down as his shoulders shook. His golden-brown skin glowed in the moonlight. "Are you going to defend my honor?"

"If I have to," Caldera replied, a smile beaming across her face. The rage instantly dissipated from her chest, replaced with immediate elation. The urge to wrap her arms around him, to pull him in as close as possible—to run her hands through his hair and press her lips against his—was almost impossible to control.

Rennick placed his hand on top of hers and looked up at the sky. "I want you to know something else," he whispered.

"What?" she asked, never taking her eyes off him.

"You're everything to me, Callie, and... I would do it again—attach the planter orb to you. If it meant saving your life... I would," he said, glancing at her from the corner of his eye.

Smiling softly, she caressed the back of his hand with her thumb. "I know." She cupped his face, forcing him to look into her eyes. "But, that just means that you'd send another message, we'd decode it, and basically be in the same spot as we are right now."

He tilted his head into her hold.

Caldera pressed her forehead against his. "Ren, listen to me. There's no planet—no galaxy where we aren't together."

He opened his mouth to reply when the door slammed open, causing Caldera and Rennick to jump apart. They looked up to see Markarian standing in the doorway, communicator in his hands and a smile on his face.

"I was instructed to bring you two in," he said, smirking.

Rennick chuckled, and got to his feet, helping Caldera to hers.

She frowned, as she reluctantly let go of Rennick's hand, following him inside.

"They're here," Markarian said into the communicator as Caldera and Rennick took seats on either side of him. "Have you woken Sear up yet?"

"I am awake," Sear replied, sounding groggy.

"Well," Caldera said, leaning toward the speaker, "don't keep us in suspense."

Rennick looked around. "Where are Mei and John?"

"Sleeping," Markarian replied. "This doesn't really affect them."

Sear cleared his throat. "Now we know for sure that some of the information that you have found about Earth is in direct correlation with things we now know about Bersama," he said, his claws clicking against the keyboard. "Like the dust cloud that we cannot see out of, and they cannot see into."

"I think it's time that we officially leak the information that we have to the other sector leaders," Aloriea cut in. "Mainly Eldra, Fenry, and Jasik—I believe there's enough evidence now."

Caldera bit her lip. "I don't know... You don't have the 'proof' yet."

"That's too dangerous," Markarian said, shaking his head. "You two are there by yourselves."

"Not any more dangerous than you three being on a foreign planet," she countered. "And we can leak the information now, and provide the proof later. It'll take a while to get traction anyway."

"Markarian's right," Rennick said after a few seconds of silence, his foot tapping against the floor. "What if Vandren sends Sol and Saro after you?"

"They wouldn't be able to find out it was us who leaked it in the first place," Aloriea insisted.

Markarian leaned on the table. "How do you know that?"

"Leave that to me," Sear said. "There is no way they will find out."

Caldera stiffened in her chair. "Sear, this is different from hacking into the Vanguard mainframe. They will kill you if they find out." She looked from Rennick to Markarian, their worried expressions feeding the knot in the pit of her stomach. "Tell me you can do this one hundred percent successfully, because if not—"

"I can," he interrupted. "I swear to you, I can—there is too much at stake for the three of you to come back this soon," he added, as if reading her mind.

The hair stood up on the back of Caldera's neck. "All right... If Eldra, Fenry, and Jasik are on board, do it."

"I will send out the information tomorrow," Sear replied quickly, as if he thought she might change her mind.

"In the meantime," Aloriea chimed in, "I need to warn you about something..."

"What?" Caldera muttered, closing her eyes and rubbing her forehead. She was trying to come to terms with the fact that if the

Council did find out what they had done, she wouldn't be able to save her friends.

"Sol and Saro are asking questions about where you are."

Her eyes flew open. "If you're in danger—"

"No," Aloriea interrupted. "We're fine. Stay there. It's mostly Saro who's been asking, anyway."

Caldera pursed her lips. "What does he want?"

"That's the strange part," Aloriea replied. "He wants to know you're okay. Sol's acting like he couldn't care less, but Saro seems genuine."

Justle's face flashed behind Caldera's eyelids—the first person she couldn't save. She shook her head. "Stay away from them," she said, her voice harsh. "Both of them."

Aloriea sighed. "Fine, but it's hard to completely avoid them. We aren't spending every hour of the day in the Vault, you know."

"What's Vandren doing?" Caldera asked abruptly, changing the subject.

The line went quiet.

"Well?"

Aloriea sighed again. "We didn't want to force you to come back too early—"

"Just answer the question."

"He is clearly planning a military operation," Sear replied hesitantly.

Caldera's stomach dropped. "How do you know?"

"I intercepted the order that went out five days ago. All militia members are to report to the palace at the end of the week.'"

"That's tomorrow."

So that's why Vandren was funding the Sector One militia so heavily...the war's starting. Sweat pricked the back of Caldera's neck as she looked around at the disbelieving faces of her friends. "That settles it. We're leaving. Now."

The chirping and singing of wild animals filtered through the open window of the living space where they all sat around the table for what Mei and John called breakfast.

Caldera sighed, pushing away the plate of food that sat untouched in front of her.

"All right, everything's ready," Aloriea said, her voice clipped. "Doctor Vareis is finally here. You can come back now."

"We should have just come back last night," Caldera snapped. Early morning light stung her eyes through the window.

"We were not going to let you come back through the portal without a doctor present," Sear replied. "Once you are here, she is going to monitor your vitals for a while."

Caldera took a deep breath. *We don't have time for that.* "How did she get into the palace with all the extra scrutiny?"

"Because I didn't try to bring in anything that would raise suspicions," Doctor Vareis interjected, her voice sharp. "You're supposed to be 'sick' in your quarters—bedridden, remember? That's what I was told when I was tricked into coming here for the second time."

That wasn't my idea. "Right, " she scoffed. "You had to have known that was a lie from the beginning—"

"Deception aside," Sear interrupted, "the gathering of militia members is going to begin in a few hours. You do need to hurry. More people are going to be coming here than we thought."

Caldera jolted upright in her chair. "Are you two okay?"

"What're they doing?" Rennick added.

"We're fine," Aloriea replied. "But Sear—"

"I intercepted a message from the Vanguard communications section," Sear said, cutting her off. "It was heavily encrypted, but I recently decoded most of it."

"'Recently', meaning about an hour ago," Aloriea clarified.

"Well don't keep us in suspense," Markarian said around a mouthful of eggs.

"It seems that the order was for the militia from every sector to report to the palace—not just Sector One's. And not only is the entirety of every sector's militia going to be gathering here, but all the council members will be in attendance as well."

Rennick pushed his untouched plate away. "All of them?"

"Precisely," Sear continued, lowering his voice.

Caldera pressed her lips together. "They're going to war, but not with each other?"

"Could it be that they've already reached an agreement of some kind?" Markarian asked, taking a bite out of a piece of toasted bread.

"Yes, that's apparent, but we don't know what it is," Aloriea explained. "And the sector leaders themselves aren't invited to the party. Whatever 'agreement' they came to about the war is going to come as a shock to most."

"Why our palace, then?" Caldera asked.

The sound of Sear's fingers flying over computer keys hit her ears.

"It has something to do with the fact that you never had the mess from the initial portal opening cleaned up," Sear replied. "There is a big empty area right out back."

"Big enough to hold all the people that are about to be here in a couple of hours," Aloriea added.

Contemplation clouded Rennick's eyes. "How many people are in the militia these days?"

"Sector One has the most, currently around two hundred and fifty members," Sear said. "With Sector Two coming in a close second, with just under two hundred. The numbers decline from there with each sector, but it is still a lot."

Caldera's face flushed as she looked from Mei to John, who were both sitting quietly across the table from her, picking at their plates. "We have to get there before everyone shows up—is anyone there now?"

"Yes, actually," Aloriea told her. "We can see through the external cameras that there are people building something out there right next to the wall."

"Meaning, we are basically trapped down here," Sear said.

Caldera, Rennick, and Markarian exchanged worried glances.

"You all need to go," John whispered, putting his fork down as he locked eyes with Markarian. "Your friends are in trouble."

"We need to get the information straight, first," Caldera replied. "Since you haven't had time to leak it yet—"

"We're doing that now," Aloriea interjected.

"—once we get back, we'll need to release what we know immediately." Caldera continued. "It could be the only thing that stops the war."

Rennick nodded in agreement. "There won't be time for last-minute organization."

Mei stood up, wordlessly taking everyone's plates—two of which were still piled with food.

The sun shone through the open window, coating them and the table with golden light.

"Okay," Rennick said, leaning forward. "Here's what we know. The Council's been going over the heads of the sector leaders for a long time, passing laws, and sending out orders without the sector leaders' input—probably since its founding."

"The latest of which was to send the Vanguard on a hunt for painite," Markarian said, finishing his toast. "They most likely collected that stone from every sector."

"But before they could get it from ours, I broke it and created a portal to another planet, and galaxy," Caldera continued, her mind swirling.

"A planet which Quill already knew existed, despite not being able to see past the debris cloud that surrounds Bersama," Aloriea said. "He, or his parents, had uncovered old records of it before the cataclysm. He didn't know what or where it was, but he knew it was there."

"Information that got him killed," Caldera muttered.

"Which brings us back to the painite," Sear said. "That is most likely the information that directly corresponds to his death."

Caldera nodded, tapping her chin. "Word of other planets and galaxies could be covered up..."

"But if he had the stone...he could've proved it," Markarian added.

"Why do they want real painite at all?" Mei cut in from the kitchen, the plates clinking together as she placed them in the sink. "I mean, you two got here without it," she continued, walking back to the table. She pointed from Markarian to Caldera. "Why would they even need the actual rock—or whatever?"

"The stone is more potent," Sear said as the noise of shuffling paper filtered through the speakers.

"The artificial amount we have on our end is completely used up," Aloriea added. "According to the oldest records and journals in the Vault, painite used to be fairly common before the cataclysm. Not on Bersama, but on some of the others."

"Of course, we cannot be certain of that," Sear said. "But it *is* mentioned fairly regularly, so that is the most logical conclusion. Regardless, it is obviously how people were traveling to and from Earth."

"Okay, but why would they kill your uncle just because he knew about that stuff?" John asked, facing Caldera. "Apparently, a lot of people from your planet do—I mean...they're here."

"Because he was a person of power," Aloriea muttered. "Someone who could actually change the way the people of our planet perceive the Council."

"When the cataclysm hit," Caldera interjected, steering the conversation back around, "painite became super rare—slowing the travel."

"It's not a coincidence that's when the prosperity of Bersama began to decline," Rennick said.

"Due to that fact and that other species from Bersama are already here, it seems that the planets of Centaurus were always stealing a majority of their resources from Earth, even before the cataclysm," Markarian said. "And Quill found out about that, too."

Mei and John nodded.

"That makes sense," John said. "But it's been one hundred years for your planet since the destruction. Sorry to be blunt, but why'd it take so long for it to become a problem?"

"Because of the dwindling population, which we already discussed," Caldera replied as the cabin walls creaked from the wind outside. "Every species besides tellins almost became extinct—making the resources last a lot longer than they would have otherwise."

"That, and there was a major conservation effort that took place right after the cataclysm," Sear said. "Which made sense at the time, considering the circumstances, but now we know it was mostly because the primary supply source was cut off abruptly."

Caldera's eyes widened, the final pieces of the puzzle clicking together as Quill's final message rang in her head. *The way to help Bersama does not lie in war...but in peace.* "Quill was murdered not just because he found out about all of this, but because he wanted to tell the other sector leaders, and establish contact with Earth in some way. To prevent a war!"

"Yes!" Aloriea said immediately. "Maybe he wanted to create a sort of alliance between the planets themselves."

Caldera nodded sharply. "Then that's what I want, too."

"So, what's your plan when you get back?" Mei asked.

She smirked, looking from Rennick to Markarian. "We're gonna bring the Council down. We're gonna make them answer for what they've been doing—what they've been hiding." She took a deep breath, wishing Sear and Aloriea were in the room with them. "We're going to arrest everyone that had a part in Quill's murder...and Justle's."

Aloriea drew in a sharp breath. "Well, hurry and get back here then," she said as a loud banging noise echoed through the speakers.

"Please do not hit the table," Sear said, his voice farther away than it once was. "You just knocked all the papers onto the floor."

Caldera looked from Rennick to Markarian, and over to Mei and John. A heaviness entered her chest that she couldn't place as she stared into the faces of the two people who had taken them all in. "I... I guess this is goodbye."

She found she could hardly speak the words without her eyes wanting to fill up with tears. Standing quickly, she walked into the room that she had been sharing with Rennick since she arrived and closed the door just as tears started falling down her cheeks.

A few seconds later, the door opened and closed behind her again.

"So..." Rennick sat next to her on the bed, wrapping an arm around her shoulder.

"What's wrong with me?" Caldera muttered, wiping her eyes. "Why do I care about leaving them?"

"Because whether you like it or not, they became your friends?" His eyes were red—he was clearly holding back tears of his own.

"I guess they are," she said, taking a deep breath. "I'm going to miss them."

Rennick pulled her close, resting his chin on the top of her head. "Me too."

They sat in silence for a while. Caldera closed her eyes, letting her breath rise and fall in time with Rennick's. She listened to the sounds of the planet that she had gotten so used to over the past fourteen days. The skittering of animals across the sand outside hit her ears as the push of the wind caused the walls of the cabin to creak. The constant calls of the fliers—which Mei had told her were called birds on Earth—chirped outside the open window.

With a sigh, Caldera looked over at the chair in the corner of the room that had her vac-suit folded neatly across it, the helmet and blasters sitting on top. "You don't have anything to protect you from the transfer," she whispered, desperate to talk about anything else.

"I made it through once," he said, squeezing her tighter. "Plus, there's a doctor on the other side."

"All right. Let me get into this suit and we'll go." She wished it would fit him so she could let him wear it.

Memories of her first day on Earth flooded her mind as she gripped the suit, its ribbed exterior causing her fingers to fluctuate over it as she caressed the material.

"Okay," Rennick said, his voice soft. "We'll be out here."

Caldera changed quickly, the vac-suit forming to her body just the way she remembered. But something was off—something she couldn't put her finger on.

Staring into the darkened visor, a woman she barely recognized looked back at her. *Why do I want to stay?* Gritting her teeth, she tucked the helmet under her arm, grabbed the blasters, and walked back out into the living room.

Markarian was already dressed and embracing John, his face buried in the thin man's blond hair. Rennick and Mei exchanged a quick, tearful hug.

Caldera swallowed hard. "Is everything ready?" she asked into the communicator.

"Yes," Sear answered. "Doctor Vareis is prepared for your arrival. We are ready whenever you are."

Mei wrapped her arms around Caldera's torso. "Bye," she said, her eyes shimmering.

Caldera put a hand on her back. "Goodbye. We'll miss you guys."

John still had his arms wrapped around Markarian.

She shook her head, releasing Mei, and put a hand on Markarian's arm.

He winced and finally pulled away from John, both of their eyes brimming with tears.

"Hey..." he whispered, trying to wipe away the water from John's cheek in vain. "It'll be okay."

John nodded. "Just get home safely, all right?"

"Will do," Markarian said, attempting a smile.

Caldera grabbed Rennick's hand and Markarian's arm. "Let's go," she murmured, gently pulling them toward the door.

"Don't forget these," Mei called, grabbing the helmets off the table.

Caldera and Markarian glanced at each other and over to Rennick.

"You know what..." Caldera began.

"Keep 'em," Markarian finished with a wave of his hand. "A gift from the 'extraterrestrials'."

Mei and John looked at each other, smiles spreading across their tear-stained faces.

Rennick frowned. "What are you—"

"You don't have anything protective to wear," Caldera interrupted, gripping his hand tighter. "So, why should we?"

"It's only fair," Markarian added as he pulled his hair back into a bun.

Caldera whisked her own hair into a ponytail and pushed her back against the screen door, stepping backward onto the porch.

But someone was already out there.

"Hello again...*Your Majesty.*"

CHAPTER 36

Caldera's blood ran cold, the familiar voice freezing her in her tracks. Rennick and Markarian were saying something, rushing past her, but she couldn't understand them. The only thing she could hear was the pounding in her ears.

She forced herself to turn around.

Olivare was standing a few feet away from the bottom step of the porch. He wore a plain t-shirt and denim jeans, his black hair and thick beard shining in the sunlight. Emotionless gray eyes were fixed on her.

Caldera shivered, unable to break eye contact.

"How the fuck did you know we were here?" Markarian was yelling as her hearing came back.

Olivare's gaze lingered on Rennick. "Ahh, the bodyguard extraordinaire," he said, extending his arms. "It's nice to see you again."

Rennick took a step forward. "Answer the question," he snapped, his voice seething with rage.

Caldera shifted her eyes from side to side, trying to see if Olivare had any backup.

The sun was glaring down on him and she couldn't see anyone else that he could rely on for support, but he wasn't trying to take cover. She took a shaky breath. *Is he really by himself?*

Olivare laughed gruffly, raising his hand to shield his eyes from the sun. "Man, this planet is a shithole, isn't it?" he said, looking around. "I see you've made some new friends, too. How cute."

Caldera looked over to see Mei and John had crowded next to them.

Markarian stepped protectively in front of John, blocking them both from Olivare's gaze.

Caldera glanced down at the blaster strapped to her hip. Without thinking, she drew it, stepped out from behind Rennick, and pointed it at Olivare. "Last chance," she said, her voice surprisingly steady. "Answer."

Olivare's eyes bored into her, down to her bones. "I was able to get in contact with the Council," he said simply. "They sent me to a place called Area 51... What a joke."

Anger swelled inside her. She put her finger on the trigger. "How did you know we were here?"

He snickered. "I've always known. It's not exactly subtle when a portal opens—and this 'Area 51' specializes in that sort of thing. If you could call what that place does 'specialized work'." He shook his head. "As soon as you two got here," he said, pointing at Markarian and Caldera, "we knew about it."

"Then why didn't you show yourself sooner?" Markarian demanded. He extended an arm out behind him, making sure John and Mei weren't in Olivare's line of sight.

"Instead of capturing you, the Council decided it would be better to keep tabs on you," he answered, crossing his arms in obvious disagreement. "We've been monitoring your communications and listening to all the little 'theories' you have. You're so close." A look of amusement crossed his face. "And that's why I can't let you leave."

"You were going to?" Rennick asked, his knuckles turning white.

Olivare shrugged. "At first the Council said it wouldn't have mattered if you went back or not... But then you forced their hand when you had your friends send out that transmission to the other sector leaders."

Caldera's breath caught in her throat. "We have to go now! Sear and Aloriea—"

"They're fine," Olivare interrupted, his gray eyes glinting. "For now."

Caldera took a step forward, the blaster pointed directly at him. "I swear—"

"That you'll kill me?" Olivare mocked. "You couldn't before. Besides, I'm not the one that would kill them, it's those twins... Or rather, the dominant one, Sol."

She was about to jump down the steps to attack when Rennick put a hand on her shoulder and gently pulled her back, shoving something into her hand.

"What do you mean we were close to the truth?" he asked, his voice cold and calculating.

Olivare smirked.

"Come on," Rennick coaxed. "If you're going to kill us anyway, at least tell us what the Council's really up to."

Caldera opened her mouth to object when she realized what she held in her hand. The communicator—and that Sear and Aloriea hadn't said a word since the confrontation started. *I could either shoot him now or record what he's saying for the other sector leaders to hear later.* She reluctantly lowered her weapon.

"Oh please," Olivare said dismissively. "If I wanted to kill you, I would have already. I just want a ride. Area 51 can't make painite and don't have any samples that already exist on this planet. I don't want to wait for the Council any longer. I'm sick of being on this planet." His gaze flicked down to the portal bracelets in their hands.

A cold wave washed over Caldera as she realized what he was about to say.

"I'll take those," he said, motioning toward the bracelets. "You're dead either way now, but I'm not in the mood to kill you."

"Then just tell us what the Council is planning," she snapped.

Olivare shook his head, a sinister grin spreading across his face. "The Council doesn't just want this planet's resources. They want the planet itself."

"What the fuck are you talking about?" Rennick questioned, walking down the steps.

Caldera followed next to him as she raised her blaster once more, her finger itching to pull the trigger.

Markarian stayed on the porch, and Caldera caught snippets of muffled protests as he tried to force John and Mei back inside.

"What do you mean they want the planet itself?" Caldera asked through the growing lump in her throat, forcing her hands to stop trembling.

His gaze locked onto her. "Despite all the evidence to the contrary, I assume you have at least half a brain in that head of yours," he said. "But let me phrase this in a way that even you can understand. The Council is going to take over this planet."

Caldera's body shook. She glanced over at Rennick, whose eyes were wide. "It's not a war between the sectors...it's a war against Earth," she whispered.

"Exactly. Bersama needs resources. This planet has them," Olivare answered. "As for the current inhabitants... Well, if they resist—"

"Which they will!" Rennick interrupted.

"—they'll die," Olivare finished with a shrug.

"When?" Caldera asked as her tightening throat threatened to asphyxiate her.

Olivare smiled, looking up at the sky. "It begins today."

Caldera couldn't hold in the gasp as she tightened the grip on her blaster, her legs shaking. "There has to be another way."

"These people won't welcome us," Olivare scoffed.

"Some will," Rennick replied instantly.

"It's that kind of blind optimism that's going to destroy *our* planet," Olivare snapped. "Sacrifices must be made!"

"What about the people of Area 51?" Caldera asked. With Mei and John safely inside, Markarian came down the stairs to stand next to her, his blaster pointed at Olivare. "Why would they help you if they knew this was the plan?"

Olivare laughed. "Those dumbasses thought they'd be protected," he said, taking a breath. "What a joke—but trust me when I say, even you wouldn't want to save them if you knew what they've been doing."

Caldera glanced from Rennick to Markarian. "We won't let you kill this world."

A smug expression crossed Olivare's face. "Like I said, you forced the Council's hand—it's already been set in motion. You can't stop it." In the blink of an eye, he reached behind him, pulled out a weapon from the crook of his back, and pointed it at them. "I'll take those bracelets now."

Markarian's body tensed next to Caldera as he prepared to shoot.

That's when she saw it. A slight shimmer encompassing Olivare's entire body, the faintest glint in the sunlight. "Wait!" she screamed, slapping Markarian's blaster to the side just as he fired.

"What the fuck, Callie?" he yelled, attempting to reposition his weapon.

She grabbed his wrist with her free hand. "You can't shoot him! He's wearing a planter orb. The ricochet could kill you, or any of us!"

Markarian stopped struggling. "How ..."

"Like I said, I've been in contact with the Council," Olivare replied. "The scientists they have working on these 'special projects' really upgraded this thing." He tapped the black band around his wrist. "It's not just an impenetrable shield anymore."

Caldera gritted her teeth as Olivare pointed his weapon in the air and pulled the trigger. The discharge of ammunition passed through the planter orb's shield effortlessly, the sound echoing out into the distance.

"So, you see," Olivare said, taking a step toward them, "I may be outnumbered, but *I* have the upper hand here."

He was close enough now that Caldera could see the black band clearly. It was thick, running halfway up his forearm. A bright light that was emitting from a display screen just out of sight caught her eye. The colors that arced up the band glowed from red to green. She tried to focus through the glaring light of the sun.

Is there a meter or gauge of some kind—a spectrometer, maybe? She squinted harder, but before she could be sure, it flashed off, back to black.

"I'm not going to ask again," Olivare said, his eyes moving over each of them. "Give me the damn bracelets."

They were out in the open—no cover. Their only chance was to get back up onto the porch and hide behind the thick poles that held up the awning.

A blast rang in her ears, and Olivare jerked to the side.

Caldera blinked, glancing over to see Mei shooting a weapon out of the window. "Get back!" she yelled at Rennick and Markarian. Wasting no time, they ran back up the steps onto the porch, taking cover in the entrance to the cabin.

Markarian peeked over his shoulder, his blaster at the ready.

Following his lead, Caldera looked behind her to see Olivare standing and rubbing the side of his head. The black band lit up again.

"Maybe we should just activate the bracelets and go through the portal now?" Markarian yelled.

Caldera shook her head sharply, leaning it against the wooden pole. "We can't leave him here with Mei and John. He'll kill them."

Markarian's body went still. "So what do we do? We can't hurt him."

Shots rang through the air, causing fragments of the cabin to splinter next to them.

She looked over her shoulder again when the shots died. Olivare was messing with the band. "Actually, maybe we can."

Rennick repositioned his body into a crouch. "How?"

"I think that black band on his arm is an energy monitor of sorts—for the shield," she whispered. "The more the shield is used, the less viable it becomes—"

Another bang rang throughout the area.

Mei's still shooting at him—she's trying to buy us time. Caldera looked through the opening between the poles. Olivare stumbled to the side again and let out a frustrated scream, firing three quick rounds in Mei's general direction.

The display pad on his black band lit up yellow.

"So, you're saying we just have to run down the energy on his shield, and it'll dissipate?" Rennick asked.

"In theory..."

"You're forgetting that he has a weapon," Markarian muttered. "And we don't have shields."

"It's not a blaster," Caldera replied. "It must be an Earth-gun. I don't recognize it, but chances are it has a finite amount of ammunition."

"You're right."

Caldera, Rennick, and Markarian turned their heads to see John inching toward them.

"John!" Markarian snapped, his voice frantic. "What the fuck?"

"It looks like a revolver," he continued once he was close, ignoring Markarian. He leaned his back against the pole next to Rennick. "That means that it most likely only has six rounds, and he already shot four."

Markarian glared at him. "Get back inside. Now!"

John matched his expression. "It looks like you need all the help you can get," he countered, pulling out another Earth-gun that looked almost the same as Olivare's. He handed it to Rennick. "Here—safety's off, just pull this trigger, and it'll shoot."

Rennick took the weapon in his hand. "It doesn't need to scan your fingerprints to activate?"

John shook his head.

"That's dangerous," Rennick replied, gripping it tightly.

Another bang echoed in Caldera's ears. "We gotta move," she whispered. "Mei can't distract him forever."

Markarian crawled past Rennick, toward John. Chunks of wood splintered as he passed the openings between posts

Olivare was firing back.

"You need to go back in," Markarian said, grabbing John's arm.

"I can fight after he runs out of ammo. I can help deplete his shield," John replied.

Markarian shook his head. "I don't want you to fight—I want you safe!"

John narrowed his eyes. "I'm not leaving."

"Markarian," Caldera muttered, crouching next to Rennick. "We don't have time to argue. If he wants to help—then let him."

She closed her eyes and took in a deep breath through her nose, then let it out slowly through her mouth. Opening her eyes, she stood up, faced where she thought Olivare was, and began pulling the trigger on her blaster while running down the length of the porch.

Rennick was right behind her, followed by Markarian.

Reaching the opening where the stairs were, she rolled behind another pole just as it was hit with the last round from Olivare's revolver—right where her head had been.

Rennick and Markarian were across from her, their weapons ready as Caldera peeked around the pillar.

"Fuck," Olivare yelled, discarding his weapon on the ground. "Piece of shit!"

"Now!" Caldera screamed, then jumped down onto the ground, firing her blaster at will.

Olivare didn't move, unable to do anything except stand there and let his shield deplete. *We've got him.*

"I'm out," Rennick yelled a few seconds later, discarding the Earth-gun onto the ground.

Caldera didn't look at him, continuing to pull her trigger until it clicked, the energy bolt ammunition that all blasters used, depleted. She gasped, "No, no, no!" she screamed. "I can't be out!"

Markarian yelled in frustration from somewhere next to her. "I only have a few shots left, we shouldn't waste them!"

She looked over to see him strapping his blaster back to his side, trying to conserve what was left.

Olivare laughed. "Nice plan—but I still have some shield left," he said, holding out his arm to reveal a bar that was glowing red on the display.

"That's fine," Caldera replied, throwing her blaster on the ground. "We don't need weapons."

A maniacal smile spread across Olivare's face that made her stomach twist into a knot. They charged at him.

Being the closest, Caldera reached him first. Olivare grabbed at her, but she ducked down, tucked her knees into her chest, then punched him in the stomach. She stood up as he doubled over, bringing her elbow down hard on his back. The shield shimmered with each impact. She tried to kick him in the face as he fell, but he anticipated it and rolled away. Her foot dug into the sandy dirt, causing her to stagger.

Jolting to his feet, Olivare backhanded her before she could regain her balance, causing her to fall to the ground with a gasp.

Without skipping a beat, Rennick jumped into the air and kicked Olivare in the back.

Olivare recovered quickly and punched him in the shoulder, causing him to stumble backward. He threw another punch that Rennick deflected as he crouched, trying to sweep his legs out from under him.

Olivare jumped out of the way of Rennick's leg as Markarian and John both threw simultaneous punches that connected with his chest.

The black band chimed an alert as Olivare skidded backward across the sand.

John ran up to him, throwing another punch that Olivare evaded. He caught John's wrist with one hand and grabbed him by the throat with the other. John grunted, punching Olivare in the face with his free hand, forcing him to let go.

"You really can fight," Markarian said, as soon as John bounced away.

"Krav Maga," John replied, panting.

"What's that?" Markarian asked as he ran forward, head-butting Olivare and pushing him back.

"It's a fighting style—doesn't matter," John replied, wiping the sweat off his brow.

The black band around Olivare's wrist chirped one last time, and the shield dropped, disappearing with a shimmer.

Caldera wiped the blood from her mouth and ran toward them, Rennick at her side.

Olivare fell to his knees, but his grin was back.

"Mar—" she called, but was cut off as Olivare reached up and grabbed the blaster out of Markarian's holster, aiming it at him.

Caldera froze. She and Rennick were still a few feet away—too far to help. Her heart pounded so quickly against her chest she thought it might break her ribs. *No...*

Markarian squared his shoulders as his chest rose and fell. "If you're going to do it—"

Olivare cut him off with a breathy laugh. "Do you really think I'm that predictable?"

Without taking his eyes off Markarian, he switched his target, pointing the barrel at John, and pulled the trigger.

Time seemed to slow as the blast rang out. A bloodcurdling scream reached Caldera's ears. She and Rennick sprinted toward Olivare, her body moving as if she was trying to run through quicksand.

The deranged smile never left Olivare's face. He jumped up and grabbed Markarian by the hair, then threw him to the ground, kicking him in the stomach.

The glint of the blaster caught Caldera's eye, discarded and forgotten.

Rennick continued to run past her. He jumped onto Olivare's back and wrapped an arm around his throat, trying to choke him.

"Getting desperate?" he snarled, flipping Rennick over and stepping onto his chest.

Caldera grabbed the blaster off the ground. "Hey!" she screamed, running toward him. "Get away from them!"

Olivare turned to face her, removing his boot from Rennick's chest. "Are you going to shoot me? The queen herself?" He chuckled, walking toward her, his arms extended at his sides. "Your hands are trembling—you *can't* do it."

Caldera gripped the blaster tighter. She glanced over at Rennick, who was rolling onto his side, trying to catch his breath. Markarian crawled toward John, who lay unmoving as he bled into the sand.

Memories of all the pain, the heartbreak, everything she couldn't control since becoming queen flooded freely through her body. "Yes, I can," she said. She pressed her finger firmly against the trigger, shooting him in the chest.

Olivare staggered back and fell to his knees, a flash of surprise clouding his features.

Caldera discarded the now empty blaster and ran toward Rennick.

Olivare coughed, grabbing her wrist as she tried to run past him. "Missed my heart," he rasped.

"I'm not sure you have one," Caldera said, attempting to free herself from his hold.

"Collapsed my lung though," he wheezed, coughing up blood. "Without assistance, I'll die."

"You're not getting assistance," she snarled, unsuccessfully trying to jerk her wrist away again.

Olivare chuckled, causing more blood to erupt from his mouth. "It doesn't matter—you can't save this planet..." He gripped her wrist tighter, pulling her down closer to his face. "You can't even save your friends."

As she turned to look over at John, Olivare let go of her wrist. Shifting his body, he grabbed the portal bracelet that she had hooked onto the loop of her vac-suit.

"I'm willing to bet you're not as righteous as you pretend to be," he whispered, grabbing each side of the bracelet. "And I'm going to prove it."

"No!" Caldera screamed, lunging at him, but it was too late.

With an animalistic roar, he ripped the bracelet in half, destroying it.

CHAPTER 37

The liquid contents of the vials spilled out, soaking into the sand and rendering the proxine sliver useless. Wind rushed down into the valley, whipping hair across Caldera's face as she fell to her knees and grabbed the broken pieces of the portal bracelet in her hands.

"Time to decide who you want to save..." Olivare said, taking one last staggering breath.

Caldera never took her eyes off him as he fell silent and limp against the ground.

"Callie!" Rennick appeared next to her, clutching his stomach. "What are you—" He stopped when he saw Olivare's lifeless body. "Are you okay?"

She nodded absently, looking down at her trembling hands and turned away from Olivare. "I... I've never killed anyone before." She was an explorer, not a soldier.

"Callie, listen to me," Rennick said, taking her shoulders. "You didn't have a choice."

"You don't think I know that!" She pushed him away abruptly. Irrational anger swelled inside her, fighting to get out. "I'm tired of not having a choice!" Her chest rose and fell in rapid succession as her breath came in short, shallow gasps, her body shaking uncontrollably. "I want—I just want," she stammered, unable to get the words out as tears forced their way down her face.

"What?" Rennick whispered, rubbing his hands up and down her arms, concern flooding his features. "What do you want? Let me help you—please."

Caldera took a deep breath and focused on the rhythmic motion of his hands. Opening her eyes, she looked over his shoulder at Markarian, who was tying something around John's leg. The injured man's chest slowly rose and fell. *He's still alive.*

Olivare's final words swirled in her head. "I—I want to save John."

A worried look crossed Rennick's face as he peered over his shoulder. "We can try, Callie, but—"

"I have an idea," she replied, stepping past him. Tear trails dried on her face as she hurried to her friend's side.

Markarian's hands were covered in deep-red blood. One of the sleeves from his vac-suit was ripped off and tied around John's leg where Olivare had shot him.

"That fucking bastard," Markarian muttered, silent tears running down his face as he continued to apply pressure over John's wound. "Why didn't he just shoot me?"

Caldera and Rennick knelt next to them. She swallowed the lump in her throat as her chest filled with involuntary relief—and instant shame a few seconds later. Clenching her jaw, she forced herself to look at Markarian. "He wanted to prove a point," she whispered.

"John!" Mei screamed. She knelt next to him and gently placed his head on her lap.

John's breathing was slowing drastically, and his skin paled as he continued to lose blood. He stirred, but didn't open his eyes.

"No..." Mei whispered, leaning over until her forehead was almost touching his. Her tears dripped onto his ashen face as she ran her hands through his hair. "You can't die!"

Caldera squeezed her eyes shut, forcing herself not to cry. "Olivare destroyed my portal bracelet."

Rennick reached down to grip her hand. "Are you serious?"

"This can't be happening," Markarian whispered, shaking his head.

Caldera glanced from Mei to Markarian. "Doctor Vareis is with Sear and Aloriea," she said. "We need to use one of the extra portal bracelets to send him through." She swallowed hard, catching Rennick's and Markarian's gazes. "The problem is, if we do use one of the extras, there won't be enough for all of us to go back."

They all stared at her. Tense silence filled the air as the heat and desperation of the day settled on their shoulders.

Rennick squeezed her hand one last time before releasing it as Markarian's gaze fell to the ground. They both nodded solemnly, the unspoken agreement formed.

"Do it," Mei said, hair falling across her eyes as she lowered her chin to her chest.

"You realize it's a one-way trip," Rennick replied.

She nodded slowly, her expression hollow. "I just want him to live."

"Where's the communicator?" Rennick asked, setting his jaw.

"I dropped it by the stairs when the fight started," Caldera said, standing. "Sear and Aloriea must be beyond scared."

"Okay, I'll get it."

"Don't tell them what we have to do," Caldera added grimly as Rennick ran to retrieve the communicator.

Sear and Aloriea's proclamations about the situation became clearer the closer he got.

"Ren, what the fuck is going on?" Aloriea screamed.

"Is everyone—okay?" Sear stammered.

Caldera swallowed hard. "Is the doctor there?" she asked, ignoring him.

"Yes," Doctor Vareis replied. "So, this is what you needed those substances—"

"I'm sending a severely injured man through the portal," Caldera interrupted, looking from John to Mei. "He has a blaster wound on his thigh and is bleeding out."

"Who's injured?" Aloriea interjected, her voice frantic.

"It's John," Markarian said, pressing harder on the wound. Blood continued to seep through his fingers.

"You want to send an inhabitant of Earth here?" Sear questioned.

"Doctor—do you think you can stop the bleeding?" Caldera asked, gripping the communicator tighter. "We're too far away from town to get him to the hospital here."

"I—I'm sure I can rig something temporary, but I'll need to get him to a real hospital right away," Doctor Vareis replied, already fumbling with something on the other end of the connection. "Not to mention, his biology is most likely different."

Caldera nodded sharply. "Ren, I need you to get the other portal bracelets—"

"Sure." Sandy dirt crunched under Rennick's shoes as he ran back to the porch.

"Callie," Sear said, his voice calculating, "how are we going to get him to a hospital? How are we even going to get out of the Vault at all? There are people everywhere in the back courtyard now, with more to come."

"The council members have already shown up," Aloriea added. "And whatever they're building—it's finished."

Caldera winced. *If they just open the door, they'll be detained immediately...but if someone were coming to meet them, it might cause enough of a distraction.*

She snapped her fingers. "Get in contact with Grey and Sylvie," she said. "They'll help Doctor Vareis get John out of the palace."

"They are just two people," Sear argued. "There are going to be hundreds here in less than an hour."

"Then tell them to hurry up," Caldera replied quickly.

Rennick jogged back to them. "Here," he said, handing Caldera the three portal bracelets.

"And then what?" Aloriea asked, her voice tight.

Caldera took a bracelet out of the bag and gently clasped it onto John's wrist. "Damn it, Aloriea, there's no time to explain everything. Just try to keep up! You were recording Ren's conversation with Olivare before the fight started, right?"

"Yes..." Aloriea replied.

"Send that transmission out to all the sector leaders along with a distress call," Caldera continued as she typed the coordinates into the geocode device's interface that was attached to the bracelet's surface.

Looking at each of her friends, Caldera let her gaze linger on Mei. "Are you ready?" she whispered, her finger hovering over the scanner button.

"No," Mei mumbled. She gently laid her brother's head onto the ground and scooted back.

Caldera locked eyes with Markarian, who nodded, a strand of black hair falling across his face. "One."

"Two," Markarian muttered as he released the wound and leaned back so he wasn't touching John.

"Three," Caldera said, pressing the button.

A white light engulfed her vision as a puff of red smoke appeared where John had once been. The bloodstain that coated the sand was the only indication that he had ever been there.

Mei gasped and reached her hand out to touch the air where her brother had once been. Her eyes filled with tears as she pulled her knees up to her chest, sobbing into them.

"Sear? Aloriea?" Caldera said into the communicator.

A banging sound echoed through the speakers in response.

"He is here," Sear called, his voice far away.

"Holy shit," Aloriea said quietly.

"How close are Grey and Sylvie?"

"I just got in contact!" Aloriea said. "They're close, but they won't be able to get here for another twenty minutes."

"And then it's another fifteen to the hospital," Doctor Vareis added from somewhere in the distance.

"Please tell me you can keep him alive until then," Caldera replied.

"I'll try—but I can't and won't promise you anything," Doctor Vareis said.

Markarian took a deep breath and slowly got to his feet, his bloody fists clenched.

Caldera placed the communicator on the ground and typed the coordinates into the remaining two portal bracelets. "Here," she said, lifting them toward Rennick and Markarian.

Markarian grabbed the bracelet, staring at her. "What are you..."

"I'll be fine," she murmured, her voice breaking.

Rennick shook his head vehemently, a grimace appearing across his face. "I'm not going through that portal without you," he said, crossing his arms. "If anything, I'm staying here and you're going through with Markarian."

She got to her feet, forcing her legs not to shake. "Ren..."

"No. Callie, no! I have gone along with your crazy plans before—when you used the RB on that monster, when you didn't know if it would kill you or not. I followed you into the palace, no questions asked," Rennick said, taking a step toward her, his eyes glinting in the light of the sun. "But this is where I draw the line. I'm not leaving you here!"

Caldera smiled wearily, closing the distance between them. "I know you won't," she whispered, taking his hand. A gentle breeze ruffled their hair as their eyes locked onto one another. "That's why I'm not giving you a choice."

With one swift motion, she clasped the bracelet around his wrist, pressed the button to activate the scanner, and shoved him backward.

Rennick's eyes widened as he caught his balance—just as he disappeared into blinding white light and wisps of red smoke.

Caldera's gaze fell to the communicator lying on the ground. Sear and Aloriea's joyful and somewhat confused proclamations came through its speakers almost immediately.

"He is awake," Sear was saying, his voice far away. "Possibly because of his previous bout..."

"Callie," Rennick interrupted, his voice shallow and gasping—hard to hear through the speakers. "Why did you do that?"

She shook her head. "That's a dumb question. I'm trying to save everyone."

"Except yourself!" Rennick snapped, taking a deep, shuddering breath. "You'll be stuck there!"

"Is that true?" Aloriea yelled, her voice breaking.

Caldera nodded before remembering that Aloriea couldn't see her. "Yes," she said somberly. "Markarian's going to take the last—"

A grip on her wrist cut her off, and she looked down. Markarian was about to clasp the bracelet on it. Caldera dropped the communicator and palm-struck his hand, jumping away before he could attach it.

"Damn," he said, rubbing his wrist. "I really thought that would work a second time." He hooked the bracelet onto one of the belt loops of his ruined vac-suit.

Glaring at him, Caldera clenched her hands into fists. "What the fuck do you think you're doing?"

"That's a dumb question," Markarian replied, repeating her words as a sorrowful smile spread across his face. "I'm saving you."

Caldera shook her head, the conviction to get her friend back to Bersama pounding at the forefront of her mind. "You're going through that portal, Markarian," she said, pacing around him.

He matched her strides, not taking his eyes off her. "You're the queen—"

"I don't care," she interrupted, narrowing her eyes.

He stopped pacing and placed his hands on his hips. "The only way you're *not* going through that portal is over my dead body. So what do you say, Callie—are you really gonna kill me over this?"

She bent her knees and raised her arms into a fighting stance. "No... But if I have to break all your limbs and force that bracelet onto your wrist myself, I will."

He smirked. "You can try."

They charged at each other, dust flying up from their sudden footfalls.

Caldera reached him just as he was throwing his first punch toward her stomach.

She sidestepped him, grabbing his arm with one hand and the back of his vac-suit collar with the other, then hoisted herself onto his back.

"You're pulling your punches," she whispered into his ear as she wrapped an arm around his neck.

"I don't actually want to hurt you." With a grunt, he reached behind him and grabbed the back of her suit with both hands. Bending forward, he flipped her off his back and onto the ground. "Despite you saying that you were going to break all my bones."

Unhooking the bracelet, Markarian knelt next to her.

Caldera rolled away, getting to her knees just as he grabbed for her arm. She punched his wrist, causing the portal bracelet to flip out of his grip and land in the dirt a few feet away.

Their eyes locked as they both gasped for breath.

"You could never best me anyway," she panted, angling her body for the next round.

Chuckling, he dug his hands into the sand, readying himself to push off the ground and lunge toward her. "There's a first time for everything."

"Hey!" Mei called, her voice cold. "Sorry to interrupt, but they want to talk to you."

Caldera and Markarian snapped their heads to the side and looked over at Mei, who was holding the communicator as she bent down to pick up the portal bracelet.

"What?" Caldera snapped as she grabbed the communicator away from Mei.

"Tone aside, " Sear said, "I think I might have figured out a way to get you both back here."

She glanced at Markarian. "Really?"

"That's good news," Markarian replied, rubbing his wrist again. "Because I'm starting to think I would've eventually lost that fight." He smiled down at Caldera.

"Obviously," Sear and Rennick replied without skipping a beat.

"Screw both of you," Markarian muttered.

"Anyway," Aloriea chimed in, "we think that if you break the internal and external dampener, it'll scan a much larger area, rather than the space that's just around your immediate bodies."

Caldera's stomach churned. "How much bigger?"

"Well," Sear said, "there essentially will not be any restrictions."

"So, probably about the size of the portal that I initially got pulled through," Rennick finished.

"What about location?" Markarian asked, putting a hand on Caldera's shoulder. "Will the coordinates still work?"

"In theory," Sear replied. "You are not breaking the geocode coordinate system, just the dampeners that control it. Also, considering the small amount of artificial painite in the bracelet, the portal should not stay open very long."

"But we don't know for sure," Aloriea added hesitantly.

Taking a deep breath, Caldera turned to face Markarian, who nodded at her. "We'll try it," she said, turning her attention to Mei. "You're going to want to get as far away from here as possible. Now."

Mei looked down at the bracelet and back up at Caldera. "I want to come with you," she whispered, her gaze unwavering.

Caldera raised her eyebrows. "I don't think—"

"Please!" Mei insisted. "I have nothing here without my brother. I don't have anyone. Please." She glanced away, her eyes filling with tears again.

Markarian shrugged, an amiable smile on his face. "What's the harm?"

"All right," she whispered, reaching out her hand. "Come on."

Mei's eyes lit up as she handed the bracelet over.

"Sear," Caldera said, "I'll let you know when we're about to hopefully come through."

She handed the communicator to Markarian and turned the bracelet over in her hand, removing the back of the power pack that held the artificial painite as gently as she could.

"All right," Sear replied. "The dampeners are—"

"I know what dampeners look like!" she snapped, breaking the first one. The red liquid surged inside the plexiglass container. She took a deep breath. "Both of you, hold on to me," she instructed.

Markarian and Mei nodded, then interlaced their arms around hers.

Caldera swallowed hard, sweat running down her back. "Here we come."

Squeezing her eyes shut, she snapped the second dampener, breaking the vial of artificial painite and destroying the containment field.

They were immediately overtaken by white light.

CHAPTER 38

An unbearable, albeit familiar, stabbing coldness washed over Caldera as if icicles were trailing down her back. Keeping her eyes firmly squeezed shut, she gasped for air as her body stretched in a multitude of different directions before plunging against a hard surface.

Overcome by the sudden warmth, her eyes fluttered open as disembodied hands gripped her shoulders, pulling her upright.

"Callie!" Aloriea came into view as she knelt in front of her, wrapping wiry arms around Caldera's body.

"Hi," she rasped, hugging her tight.

Blinking away the white dots that filled her vision, she took in her surroundings—the dimness of the Vault, Aloriea hugging her so tightly it was approaching the point of choking, and the rest of her friends surrounding her.

We did it. She let a smile break across her face before it instantly faded when she caught sight of Doctor Vareis furiously working on John's wound in a distant corner.

"Is this..." Mei murmured before curling up into a ball on her side. "I don't—my stomach..."

"Markarian, get her to the bathroom before she vomits," Sear said as he gently pulled Aloriea away from Caldera and helped them both to their feet.

Markarian nodded, guiding Mei away.

"I am happy you are back," Sear whispered, the fur from his arms caressing Caldera's face and back of her neck as he hugged her. His embrace tightened for a moment before releasing.

She smiled up into his golden eyes before turning her attention to Rennick.

"Ren, listen, I—" She paused. "I love you."

Rennick smiled. "I love you, too." He pulled her into his chest and rested his cheek against the top of her head. "We should probably stop sacrificing ourselves for each other if we ever want to be together."

Caldera chuckled into his shirt. She pulled away just enough to look into his eyes. "Agreed."

"You need to figure out how to get this man to a hospital!" Doctor Vareis said, snapping Caldera back to reality. "I'll be finished with the makeshift patch in about ten minutes, but it won't hold for long."

"Right," Aloriea replied, jolting to the communicator that sat on the desk next to the computer system. She looked down at the screen. "Grey and Sylvie are here—just outside the entrance of the palace. They want to know what to do now."

Walking over to the monitors, Caldera tried to get a handle on what was going on outside of the secret room.

Several members of the militia were already there, lined up into groups by sector, affiliation, rank, and crew. They faced a raised platform in the back courtyard, their backs turned toward the entrance of the secret room.

All the council members, along with Sol and Saro, were there on the platform, gathered around two semi-circles of thick metal that curved up at least twenty feet in the air, touching lightly in the middle.

"It's a physical portal," Caldera gasped, her hand rising to cover her mouth. "Olivare wasn't lying—they are going to invade Earth today."

"There's got to be at least one hundred people out there already, with more on the way," Rennick said.

John moaned as if to emphasize his point, causing Caldera to wince. "I think we can do it. This distraction could work," she muttered. "Aloriea, tell Grey and Sylvie to meet us at the back courtyard doors."

"The militia members probably have orders to shoot us on sight," Rennick said.

"It doesn't matter. The only thing we can do is open the passage and try to get out," Markarian added. "There's no other option."

Caldera agreed, although the thought of putting her friends in danger made her stomach churn. "Okay, Aloriea, Sear—you two are going with Mei, John, and the doctor," she said. "Ren, Markarian, and I will stay behind to make sure you get away."

Aloriea narrowed her eyes. "We most certainly are not."

"I have to agree," Sear replied, taking a step forward. "We are finishing this together."

"Sorry, but this isn't up for debate—there could be a fight—"

"That is not a problem," Sear interrupted, clenching one hand into a fist as he flexed his claws with the other.

Aloriea placed a hand on Sear's arm. "It doesn't matter. You need us for this."

"How so?" Caldera asked. The tightness in her jaw made it hard to speak.

"We need to shut down that portal out there. Permanently," Aloriea continued, pointing at the monitors. "And Sear and I can." She placed her hands on her hips. "It'll take a little more finesse than ripping a box off a computer system."

Sear nodded, his ears twitching from side to side. "This is true. We can disable the portal so they can never open it."

"You think the Council is going to let you walk right up to it and turn it off?" Markarian asked.

"Once we open that door," Rennick added, pointing behind him, "everyone's gonna see us. There's no way for you two to sneak around unnoticed."

Caldera's stomach twisted into a knot as she realized Aloriea was right. *It won't matter if we get John and Mei help if they don't have a home to go back to.*

"I have an idea," Caldera said, taking a deep breath and stepping into the middle of her friends.

They all looked at her, expectant. "Look." She pointed toward the monitors. "This is where the secret stairway used to be, and where the rope that I used to sneak out of the palace to meet up with Grey and Sylvie still is."

"So what?" Aloriea replied, squinting at the screen.

"You two, along with Markarian, are going to leave with Grey and Sylvie—"

"Why am I going?" Markarian snapped, glaring down at her.

Caldera grabbed his arm, squeezing tight. "Because you're going to help them sneak around the outside wall of the palace, crawl up the rope, and lower them down the wall on the other side," she said, loosening her grip.

He yanked his arm away from Caldera and walked over to where John lay on the floor.

"They will see us," Sear said, his golden fur bristling. "Even though the curve of the wall partially hides that spot—"

"I'm guessing that's where we come in?" Rennick interrupted, looking over at Caldera.

She nodded, pointing at the screen again. "This spot is far enough away that they shouldn't hear you if you keep quiet, and like you said, they're partially turned away from it anyway—we're going to distract them for as long as it takes for you three to disable the portal. We have to stop the invasion of Earth if we ever want to be allies."

"It's risky," Rennick said, heading over to where Markarian, Mei, and Doctor Vareis were readying John for transfer. "The only thing you can do is try to be quiet once you get up to the platform," he added over his shoulder.

"Finished," Doctor Vareis interjected. "We need to move!"

"We'll make as much noise as we can, but you're still going to be in danger," Caldera warned them. "There's no guarantee that this'll work." She swiftly approached the exit, hovering her hand over the scanner.

Markarian and Rennick lifted John off the ground and carried him to the door. Doctor Vareis and Mei hurried beside them, their bloody hands pushing against the patchwork over John's wound.

Swallowing hard, Caldera placed her hand on the device. The white light scanned her hand, flashing green as the door opened and the stairs appeared in front of them. Without a word, she led the group out of the no-longer secret room, and into the stunned gazes of over one hundred members of the militia.

They're not all here yet...good.

A grayish-white sky and sudden chill met Caldera's skin as she took the final step off the stairs onto the exposed dirt of the courtyard, causing her to shiver.

Despite putting off hardly any heat, the sun glared through the clouds, forcing her to squint through the rows of people until she caught Vandren's gaze.

No one's shot us yet.

"There's an injured man that needs passage out of this palace, along with his sister and the doctor that's working on him," she announced before anyone could interject. A barely noticeable cloud of air formed in front of her mouth with every word because of the cold. "As Queen of Tellis, I'm ordering all of you to let them pass."

"Queen Caldera," Vandren said, his voice cutting through the crowd of confused faces, "we were wondering when you would grace us with your appearance." His eyes flicked to the stairs. "Interesting."

"Of course, it would be at the most inconvenient time!" Kex hissed, glaring at Caldera.

Thael matched Kex's expression, while Randis and Cleo looked genuinely surprised.

"And there's a face I thought I'd never see again," Vandren continued, his eyes sliding over to Rennick.

Holding their gazes, Caldera slowly motioned for her friends to move behind her, toward the back courtyard entrance.

Vandren watched silently as they made their way to the doors.

"What are you doing?" Kex jeered. "You're letting them get away!"

Caldera's shoulders tensed with such force, she thought the muscles were going to tear. Her fingernails cut into her palms. *We don't have any weapons. We can't defend ourselves.*

Vandren chuckled, waving his hand in the air dismissively. "Calm yourself, Kex. It doesn't matter what they do."

"And why is that?" Rennick asked, already putting their plan into motion as the other six reached the door where Grey and Sylvie were waiting.

Vandren sighed as the other council members stood in a loose line beside him.

Caldera gritted her teeth, shaking—a mix between the cold and the building anger in her chest. Taking a deep breath, she stepped forward so that she was standing next to Rennick. She fought against the muscles in her body that wanted to rush the platform—to attack Vandren...or Kex.

"I know Olivare told you our plan," Vandren said, his gray-eyed gaze flicking over to Caldera. "Before you killed him."

"News travels fast," she replied, her chest aching at the reminder that she had, in fact, killed someone. "But I'm sure you didn't tell that lunatic everything."

Vandren laughed. "How perceptive."

"Since we can't do anything to stop you," Rennick said, taking another step forward. "Why don't you enlighten us about the rest?"

The closest line of militia members took an equal step in his direction, their hands hovering over their blaster holsters.

Instinctively, Caldera grabbed Rennick's arm, jerking him back.

Vandren chuckled again. "Reverse psychology isn't going to work on me. It's simply as Olivare said—the planet has resources we need."

Caldera held Vandren's gaze, examining the older man standing a short distance in front of her. His hair was slicked back, and his black turtleneck unsuccessfully tried to hide the first hints of wrinkles on his neck. His golden robe rustled in the breeze.

He looks...tired. She forced herself not to feel sorry for him.

"We need to wipe out the current inhabitants so we can take it for ourselves," Kex hissed, her yellow snake eyes shining in the sunlight.

"There has to be another way!" Caldera insisted. The wind whipped her hair around her shoulders.

Vandren held up his hand. "I heard your whole spiel to Olivare," he said, pulling a communicator from the sleeve of his robe and handing it to Sol. "We all did." His downward glare only emphasized the crows-feet in the corners of his eyes. "I used to think that too—but as the years went on, I slowly realized that there's nothing we as a planet can do without expanding."

"But why does that mean death for the people of Earth?" Caldera asked, narrowing her eyes.

"It's them or us," Vandren replied, his voice gruff. "They won't welcome us."

"I don't believe that!" Caldera cried, her voice carrying over the crowd of people.

"What you think about the inhabitants of that planet," Cleo interjected softly as her black fur waved in the wind, "is very idealistic." She averted her emerald eyes, her ears lying flat against her head.

Randis put his hand on Cleo's shoulder, his translucent bluish skin seeming to glitter. "It's necessary."

"It's what needs to be done in order for Bersama to survive," Thael added. His brown-and-tan horns pointed up into the sky, and the black-lined tattoo that ran down his chin and onto his chest shifted with each syllable.

Caldera shook her head. "That's what you're telling yourself, but it's not true!"

"Do you really believe in what the Council's doing?" Rennick asked, raising his voice. He shifted his attention to the crowd of the militia members.

"Absolutely!" a woman from the group yelled almost instantly.

Opening her mouth to reply, Caldera froze when she realized what was around every one of their wrists. Two thick black bands encircled their biceps and forearms on one arm, and one band wrapped around the wrist of the other. *The RB and planter orb shield. These people know everything, and they're still going to kill millions. Once all the militia members get here—and with the combined efforts of millions of robotic attack drones—Earth doesn't stand a chance.*

"If you were half the leader Quill was, you'd be on our side," another male voice added, snapping her back to reality. "But you don't care about this planet—you don't care about us!"

"I do care," Caldera yelled, a cold ball forming in the pit of her stomach. "Quill didn't agree with this! He wanted peace and that's why they had him killed!" She pointed at the Council. "I don't know what lies they've told you, but Quill was against this!"

Rennick grabbed her arm, trying to steady her rapidly shaking body. Blood dripped between her fingers as her nails continued to rip into her skin.

"You may have superior weapons," Rennick added, noticing the same thing that she had, "but the people of Earth have superior numbers. I—we—know firsthand how powerful that weapon is." He motioned toward Caldera and pointed at a militia member's arm. "But, you will be overpowered eventually. Do you really want to die for this?"

Vandren snapped his fingers. All the members jolted to attention, turning back toward the platform. "That's what attack drones are for," he said, a mirthless smile breaking across his face. "They know all of this and still believe in the cause." He glided over to the edge of the platform. "They're on our side." He lifted a hand into the air and snapped again.

Two people broke off from the group, one grabbing Caldera and the other grabbing Rennick, forcing their hands behind their backs.

"So, what about you, Your Majesty?" Vandren continued, fire raging behind his eyes. "Whose side are you on?"

Caldera caught and held Rennick's gaze. "If you go through with this, you're not only making these people, but all the citizens of this planet complicit in mass murder!" She struggled against her captor as she looked up into Vandren's bitter expression. "So I'm on Bersama's side."

Something flashed across Vandren's face as he lowered his arms.

Did I get through to him?

"Councilmember Vandren!"

Her blood ran cold at the sound of Sol's voice. She hadn't been paying attention to where the twins were this entire time.

"Guess who we found messing around with the portal?" Sol continued, his voice harsh but full of glee as he held a struggling Aloriea in his grip.

"Well, bring them here," Vandren commanded, as whatever Caldera had seen in him dissipated.

Aloriea, Markarian, and Sear were led out across the platform.

Sol shoved Aloriea forward, while Saro was barely touching Sear, his multicolored gaze glued to the metal walkway, deliberately not making eye contact with anyone. Markarian was led out by a man Caldera vaguely recognized but couldn't identify.

Vandren snapped again, and they forced her friends to their knees, adjacent to the opening of the portal.

"No!" Caldera shrieked, breaking away from the woman holding onto her, only to be grabbed by two more people.

Caldera slammed her heel down on the foot of the short,

stocky man in front of her. As he jumped back, she grabbed and twisted the wrist of the other assailant that was behind her, forcing them to let go of her arm as she sprinted toward the platform.

Pushing her way through the crowd, her heart pounded like a drum in her ears as she ducked and dodged her way forward. The only goal was to get to the platform.

Glancing to the side, she saw Rennick was next to her, attempting to fight off his own attackers.

They only made it a few feet before being overtaken.

"Let them go!" Rennick yelled from beside her, his arms and shoulders being held onto by two others.

"Please!" Caldera screamed, using all her strength to struggle against the hands that held her at bay. "They were just following my orders—let them go!" Tears welled in her eyes as she pleaded, anger swelling inside of her.

Vandren walked around the three of her friends before turning his gaze back to Caldera. He motioned for her and Rennick to be brought forward.

"Despite what you might think, I'm not unreasonable," he said, looking thoughtfully toward the portal. "I tell you what. I'll make you a deal."

Caldera and Rennick exchanged glances, and Caldera stopped struggling. "What kind of deal?" Aloriea, Sear, and Markarian's eyes locked on her.

"Well," Vandren continued, running a hand over his slicked-back hair, "as your bodyguard so astutely pointed out, we are a little short on volunteers."

Caldera's captors let her go as Vandren waved her onto the platform.

Without a word, he walked over to Thael, who produced a small black box from the sleeves of his scarlet robe.

Caldera swallowed hard as she freely walked up the steps. They pushed Rennick along behind her, forcing him to his knees next to Markarian. "What's your point?" she snapped, rushing toward Rennick only to be stopped by another soldier.

"The deal is this," Vandren replied, taking the box and turning to face her. "Go with the initial invasion force. Use the weapon against Earth, and I'll let your friends live."

A gust of icy wind rushed across the platform, causing Caldera's hair to whip around her face. Her body was still—no longer aware of the cold.

Unable to speak, she looked from her friends' shocked faces back to Vandren. His smile did not waver, nor did it meet his eyes.

He took a step toward her and opened the box, revealing a rail beam. "What do you say?"

"Don't do it, Callie!" Rennick cried, struggling against his captor again.

"I'm sorry," Vandren said, walking toward Caldera until he was only a foot away. "I shouldn't have phrased it as if you had a choice."

He nodded toward the people holding her friends, and they drew their weapons. "If he says another word," Vandren continued, pointing at Rennick, "shoot him."

The captors pressed the barrels against the back of her friends' heads—the one behind Rennick's clicking into action. One pull of the trigger, and he'd be dead.

"Stop," Caldera pleaded.

Aloriea gasped, squeezing her eyes shut. Sear's ears were flat against his head, his pupils so dilated that his gold irises were nonexistent. A low, constant snarl rumbled at the back of his throat. Markarian and Rennick didn't move, their bodies still as statues.

"Why would you even offer me this?" Caldera said, pushing the two members of the militia off her and turning to look at Vandren.

He smirked, shooing the people who had been restraining her back down the stairs. "It's honestly a win-win for us."

"You either help with the invasion and die fighting the humans," Kex explained, her yellow eyes gleaming, "or you don't, and you and your friends die now."

"What if I go through the portal and fight against them?" Caldera replied, pointing out into the crowd.

"Then they'll kill you," Thael said with a snarl. "You know, I initially thought it unfair to have you killed outright—like your predecessor—but this'll do."

"You cannot win," Vandren said, leaning close to her face. "The question is whether you want your friends to die with you or not."

Clenching her jaw, she glanced over at the portal, and the generator beside it, which was almost entirely out in the open. *No wonder they got caught.* She grimaced bitterly, trying to hold back frustrated tears.

Her eyes finally caught Saro's.

"And you're okay with this?" she demanded, turning completely to face him. "Always being under your brother's thumb? Killing innocent people?"

"I didn't kill anyone!" Saro yelled. His blaster shook in his hand.

Caldera took a small step forward. "Then why are you doing this?" she whispered, holding his trembling gaze.

"Enough," Vandren interjected. "Everyone has a weakness. For Sol, it's his twin. For you," he continued, motioning toward Caldera's friends, "it's them."

She shifted her gaze from Saro to Sol. "He offered you the same deal...didn't he?"

Sol's expression softened as he glanced from Saro to Caldera. "I didn't want to kill Justle. He was my friend...but Saro's my brother."

"And what about Quill?" Caldera replied, blinking away tears. "Was he your 'friend' too?"

"I didn't kill Quill," Sol replied quietly, glancing away. "That was Olivare." He took a deep breath before meeting her eyes again, the line of his jaw resolute. "Everything I did was to protect Saro!"

Caldera squeezed her eyes shut, shaking her head before commotion forced her eyes open again.

Saro had removed the blaster from the back of Sear's head, pointing it at Vandren. "Let them go," he commanded as Sol's surprised gaze met with Caldera's.

Vandren released an exaggerated sigh. "You really didn't think this through, did you?"

Without being ordered, four more members of the militia ran up the platform stairs, detaining Saro and Sol.

"That wasn't smart," Vandren continued, evident annoyance creeping into his voice. He walked up to Saro. "I suppose I'll have to punish you."

Vandren unclipped a blaster from one of the militia members' holsters, aimed it at Sol, and pulled the trigger. The shot went straight through his chest.

Caldera gasped as an arch of crimson blood sprayed through the air. Shock coursed through her as she instinctively jolted forward before being cut off by one of the militia members and forced to her knees. Screams of pain filled her ears.

"Sol!" Saro cried, trying to force himself free, his pained voice burrowing into her bones.

Aloriea's eyes were squeezed shut while even more members from the militia forced Rennick, Markarian, and Sear down.

I have to stop this before more people die. Her breath caught in her throat as she looked from the generator to the black bands still sitting in the open box—an idea forming in her mind.

"Vandren," she said, getting his attention before hanging her head in defeat. "I'll do it."

Her friends stopped struggling. Saro was forced next to them, away from Sol's lifeless body where blood continued to pool, dripping off the side of the metal platform.

Caldera was brought to her feet. Vandren handed her the black bands of the rail beam. "How do I know you'll keep your word?" she said, all emotion gone as she slid the first black band up her arm.

"You won't," Vandren replied. He walked over to the generator and powered it on.

"Callie, no!" Aloriea screamed, and a blaster was pressed against the back of her head again.

Sear snarled, his canines bared as his eyes flicked behind him.

"Hey..." Caldera replied, her voice low and controlled, causing the four of them to turn their attention back to her. "I... I know what I'm doing." She flicked her eyes from the black band over to the portal generator, hoping they would understand.

Markarian's mouth gaped open before a knowing grin spread across his face.

Aloriea and Sear both nodded their acceptance almost imperceptibly as tears streamed down their faces.

She held Rennick's stare as a solemn smile broke across his face.

I'm sorry. She turned away, unable to look at her friends any longer, and fastened the second band into place.

The generator whirred. Heavy wind whipped the dust of the exposed ground into the air. The red wisps of smoke appeared and disappeared as the portal itself took shape within the constraints of the metal arms, opening.

Shutting it down will take finesse, huh? Caldera took a deep breath. "Activate," she said. The needles jolted into her arm as the blue symbols appeared, floating in a constant circle around the black band, just like she knew they would. The memory of the rock monster from all those months ago flashed across her mind.

She glanced back at Rennick, whose brown hair was whipping wildly around his head. His gaze did not waver from her. Caldera lifted her arms toward the generator just as the portal stabilized.

"What are you doing!" A militia member yelled, fumbling with his blaster as Vandren and the other council members turned around to face her.

"Saving Earth," she replied, never taking her eyes off Rennick.

Vandren jolted toward her. "Wait!"

"Fire!" Caldera screamed, closing her eyes against the command.

The symbols blazed a bright gold as blinding white light shot from her palm. The explosion resonated throughout the platform, sending her body flying backward as she fell into blackness.

CHAPTER 39

Caldera gasped as pain shot through her entire body, causing her to scream before a coughing fit took over. Distant shouts from all directions met her ears as her surroundings came into focus.

She blinked the blurriness from her eyes. *I'm...alive.*

Red filled her vision as warmth hit her face—the taste of copper filling her mouth. *I'm lying in blood.*

As she tried to sit up, the shooting pain returned.

Caldera dug her fingers into the dirt and screamed, involuntarily drawing her knees up to her chest. A stabbing ache emanated from her cheek which was pressed against the ground.

Taking a deep breath, she slowly reached her hand up to her face, gingerly feeling for inconsistencies. Her fingers found the source immediately. Thick, sticky globules of blood had caked themselves over the wound in an attempt to stop the bleeding.

Starting below her right eye, and stretching to her jawline, was a deep laceration that had almost cut completely through the skin of her cheek and into her mouth.

She punched the ground, trying to ignore the constant ache, then forced herself into a sitting position. Dozens of small cuts across her arms and legs stung at the sudden movement, and tiny blood spots appeared through the new rips and tears of her clothes.

Wet hair, half-coated in blood, plastered itself to the side of her face. She grunted, forcing herself not to scream as another wave of sharp, needle-like pain washed over her entire body, throbbing against the back of her eyes.

Where are they? She scanned the area for her friends, moving her head from side to side as much as she dared as she ripped the black bands off her arm.

Metal pieces of the destroyed platform littered the ground. The gray of the sky deepened as the stirred-up dirt from the explosion blocked the sun. A body, either dead or unconscious, caught her eye, their arm and part of their back peeking out through the swirling dust of the courtyard floor.

With a sharp intake of breath, she turned away, squeezing her eyes shut against the severity of the situation.

"Cal ...dera..."

Squinting through the dust cloud, she searched for the familiar voice, unable to see farther than a few feet ahead of her. "Where—" she rasped before another round of coughs seized her throat.

A soft padding noise met her ears from behind her, as if someone were crawling on their hands and knees.

Saro came into view, blaster in hand.

His multicolored eyes met her dark blue ones. "Caldera..." he tried, as he came to a stop next to her. Deep cuts adorned his face and his suit was ripped and tattered.

"Get away from me," she muttered, her strength rapidly depleting as blood dripped from the deep laceration on her face onto her pants.

"I want to help you," Saro said, quickly tucking the blaster into the crook of his back and placing a hand on her shoulder.

Caldera jerked away from his touch as another indiscernible yell met her ears.

"Fuck!" the voice yelled, followed by a grunt and an exasperated gasp.

"Ren?" she screamed, her lungs burning with the effort.

"Cal—" the voice replied before cutting itself off with a groan.

"He's alive!" Tears streamed down her face, stinging the wound on her cheek. *But what about the others?* She flinched at the thought of her friends possibly being dead. *One step at a time.*

She cleared her throat. "Ren, I'm coming!" she yelled, pushing herself to her knees. Her head spun as she struggled to her feet, the dizziness forcing her back to the ground.

Saro's hands were on her shoulders again as he crouched beside her. "Please, let me help you."

"Why should I?" Caldera replied, glaring up at him. "Sol said you're innocent in all of this, but I don't know what to believe anymore."

The first signs of individual passion glimmered in his eyes. "I don't know if you could call me 'innocent'. I willingly let him dictate my life." He took a deep breath, tears misting his eyes. "Sol was my twin, and I didn't know what he was up to...but I didn't kill Quill or Justle." Grabbing Caldera's elbow, he pulled her to her feet before throwing her arm over his shoulder. "I don't care if you believe me or not. I'm helping you."

A fresh round of stabbing pain shot down her neck. "Fine," she muttered, taking a small step forward. "Just help me find Ren and the rest of my friends."

He nodded sharply, guiding her through the thick dust cloud.

"Ren!" Caldera called, blinking the white dots away from her vision as they stepped over jagged pieces of the wrecked platform. "Keep talking, I can't see you!"

"I think…" Rennick replied, his voice weak—close. "That I might be directly in front of you."

Blood steadily dripped onto the ground as she limped forward, her face throbbing. "Markarian, Sear, Aloriea!" she screamed as she and Saro continued to move.

When they burst through another dust cloud, Rennick appeared in front of them.

His body was propped up against the side of the palace, battered and bloodied. Debris from the explosion had fallen on top of his right leg, just below the knee, crushing it and pinning him there. Damp hair was plastered to his forehead and the sides of his face as sweat dripped down his neck.

"Ren!" Caldera screamed, forcing herself out of Saro's grip and lunging toward him. The sudden movement made her stomach lurch as she collapsed next to him.

"I—" Rennick coughed, blood trickling out of the side of his mouth. "I don't think I'm getting out of this, Cal…" He tried to reposition himself as she gripped his shoulder. His glassy eyes fell over Saro. "Here to help?"

Saro nodded sharply. "Absolutely."

"Good," he said, trying a smile and turning his attention to Caldera. "You're hurt." He reached toward her cheek, his voice catching.

She pushed his hand away as Saro knelt next to them. "I'm fine," she lied, looking down at the giant metal slab pinning him to the ground. "We have to get this thing off you." She grabbed the edge, nudging Saro to do the same.

Saro nodded silently, mimicking her motions.

"I don't think that's a good idea," Rennick gasped, grabbing her arm.

"Why not?" she said, pausing just as they were about to try to lift it.

He grimaced, swallowing hard as his chest rapidly rose and fell. "My leg is mangled under here—I can feel it." He rapped on the metal slab with his knuckles. "As soon as you move this thing, I'll probably bleed out."

"But..." Caldera paused as more shouting hit her ears, filtering through the destruction.

"You three, search over there—the rest are with me. Orders are to shoot on sight if they're not already dead!"

"Vandren," Caldera muttered, meeting Saro's shocked expression. *You've gotta be kidding me.*

Rennick scoffed, wincing as he did so. "That bastard's still alive?"

"We have to get you out of here," Caldera said again, frantically turning back to him.

"Callie..."

"Did you not hear what he just said? We have to move you. We need to—"

"Caldera!" Rennick interrupted, grabbing her arm and pulling her in close. "You need to get out of here."

She shook her head, jerking her arm away. "I'm not leaving you."

Saro shifted his body, his eyes moved from Rennick to Caldera. "He's right, you need to—"

"You," Caldera snapped, turning on him, "do not get to tell me what I 'need' to do!"

Rennick closed his eyes, leaning his head back against the wall. "I can't let you die because of me..."

"That's not your decision to make," she said, gritting her teeth. The dulled pain immediately resurfaced full force. "And neither one of us is going to die if I can help it."

Caldera sat back, examining him again. Her eyes landed on his thigh, which was essentially undamaged. "We need to make a tourniquet," she realized.

"Did you hear what I just said?"

Caldera stretched out her hand toward Saro. "Give me your belt," she commanded as she locked eyes with Rennick.

Saro undid his belt and handed it to her.

She sighed when she saw the skepticism flit across Rennick's face. "Ren, I know it might not work—but it's the only thing we can do." Her voice caught. "We have to try."

"Okay," he whispered.

Caldera pulled the knife from her boot. "We need to expose his skin first," she told Saro as the blackness hanging around the outside of her vision closed in, threatening to throw her into unconsciousness. "I need a slim but sturdy piece of metal." She cut away at Rennick's pant leg until a circle of skin was exposed.

Saro circled the area, prodding the surrounding debris with the toe of his shoe. "Like this?" he asked, bending down to pick up a thin, two-inch metal bar.

Nodding, she looped the belt around Rennick's leg, right above the knee, tightening it as much as she could. "This is gonna hurt," she said, meeting his gaze as Saro handed her the metal piece. "Just...try not to scream." She could hear footsteps through the rubble. They were getting closer.

Rennick squeezed his eyes shut.

Taking a deep breath, she slipped the piece of metal between his skin and the belt. "Ready?"

"As I'll ever be," he muttered.

Caldera turned toward Saro. "Twist the piece of metal around in a circle until you can't anymore. Hold it, and I'll tie it into place." She paused, catching his horrified expression. "I'm injured. You'll be able to get it tighter than me...and that's the point."

Saro gritted his teeth and began the process, tightening the belt even more than it already was.

Rennick let out a bloodcurdling scream before clamping his hands over his mouth. Tears pooled over his fingers and ran down his chin.

Caldera closed her eyes, his scream echoing in her ears as tears of her own streamed down her face.

Saro continued to twist until he couldn't anymore. "All right, go!" he said, holding it in place.

She grabbed the discarded piece of denim that she had cut away from his pants and quickly tied it around the outside of the makeshift tourniquet so it wouldn't unravel.

Rennick's eyes were closed, his chest rising and falling heavily as sweat dripped from his ashen face.

Footsteps echoed in the distance, growing closer with each passing second.

"Ren..." Caldera whispered, her heart throbbing in her ears. "Ren!" She gently shook his shoulder. "We have to try and get this off you now." She grabbed the edge of the metal slab as his eyes fluttered open.

"Okay..." he replied, his voice barely audible.

"Three, two, one," she said, forcing her entire body against the slab.

Taking in lungfuls of air, she forced herself to stay conscious as the sharp edge of the metal sliced into her palms. Blood dripped from her new wounds and she was vaguely aware of Rennick gasping in wordless pain next to her as the slab moved slowly over his crushed leg.

"Stop!" Rennick yelled, his voice hollow. "This isn't going to work." He grabbed her wrist with an exasperated sigh.

Caldera's chest rose and fell heavily as she looked down at their progress. The metal slab had only moved a few inches.

"Fuck!" She punched the ground.

The footsteps were loud—right next to them. It was too late. Now all three of them would be killed.

"Just run!" Rennick rasped. "It was never going to work anyway!"

Wielding a jagged piece of metal, Caldera whirled around, knowing it would be a fight to the death this time.

"You would not have wanted to move it all at once, anyway," a soft, familiar voice said.

"Sear!" Caldera cried, dropping the metal bar and dashing toward him.

He limped forward. Numerous small cuts littered his body and bloody clumps of fur drew her eyes to the larger gouges. A large notch was taken out of his ear, and as he knelt next to her, she saw the ripped sleeve of his shirt tied around the stump of what was left of his tail.

Without a word, she threw her arms around his neck, relief flooding her body.

Sear flinched before wrapping a battered arm around her.

"Are the others with you?" Saro asked, getting to his feet.

"We're here." Markarian came into view, as he helped a staggering Aloriea with one arm while holding a blaster with the other. He had two deep slashes across the bridge of his nose. A blood trail stretched down the back of his neck from a gash on the side of his head.

Aloriea had a broken-off horn and minor cuts all along her neck and arms.

Much the same as Sear, their clothes were tattered and torn, wrapped around the injuries that needed the most attention.

"Saro, good to see ya," Markarian muttered, holstering his blaster.

Caldera sat back, taking them in as her eyes filled with tears. *I didn't kill them. However injured they are—they're alive.* "We have to get out of here," she said, motioning out into the abyss of the dust cloud. "Vandren's still alive, and he issued orders to shoot us on sight!"

"We know," Sear replied, glancing over his shoulder. "I found you as quickly as I could with my sense of smell, but with all this dust in the air, it took a while."

"It's only a matter of time," Aloriea muttered weakly, leaning heavily against Markarian, "They're starting at the far end of the courtyard, doing a full sweep."

Markarian lowered Aloriea to the ground, propping her against the palace wall. "That's why they haven't found you yet, but we could only have minutes, or seconds, left until they do."

"Exactly," Caldera said, her heart pounding furiously against her chest. "We have to get this thing off of Ren." She took a deep breath. "You said something about not moving it all at once?" she continued, facing Sear.

"Yes, we need to lift it gradually, so the pressure in his leg evens out naturally. Otherwise, he will faint," Sear explained , taking a deep breath. "I see you made a tourniquet." A tired grin spread across his face. "Quick thinking."

She couldn't stop herself from smiling. "All right. Ren, we're getting you out of here," she said, bracing herself.

Rennick nodded as Aloriea squeezed his hand.

Sear moved next to her, grabbing an edge without protest. Markarian knelt next to Sear, positioning his hands and settling into a squat. Saro readied himself to push at the end of the jagged platform.

"Three, two, one," Markarian said, lifting.

"Wait," Sear muttered, his voice calculating. "Not too fast." His voice strained as the piece of the destroyed platform slowly rose. "Wait..."

Caldera's vision blurred. She blinked furiously, trying to clear it as she continued to exert all her energy against the metal, its sharp edges digging into her skin once more.

"Now!" Sear yelled. "Push it off!"

With a final cry from all four, the slab moved, tumbling to the side and freeing Rennick. He collapsed onto his side, sucking in air as his fingers dug into the dirt.

Crushed bones protruded from his pant leg, which was soaked in blood.

Unable to hold in a gasp, Caldera moved closer and took his shoulders, forcing him to sit up. "Ren!" she cried, her voice tangling at the back of her throat. Leaning in close to his face, she brushed the hair out of his eyes.

He didn't answer. His chest rose and fell slower with each breath.

"Ren, you have to stay awake," she said, shaking him.

His glassy eyes fluttered open. "Whatever you say..." he muttered, hanging his head.

"We have to go now!" Caldera said. "Sear, do you think you'll be able to carry him?"

"Of course," he replied, nudging her out of the way to kneel in front of Rennick. "Hey," he said, smacking Rennick's cheek. "Stay awake. I am going to carry you on my back, but you need to wrap your arms around my neck and hold on."

Rennick murmured his assent.

"Help me get him up," Sear said, motioning to Markarian and Saro.

"Check the east wall of the palace!" A voice in the distance yelled.

Sear's ears perked up. "They must have heard us—come on."

With Rennick's arms around his neck, he stood up with a grunt, lifting the injured man off the ground.

Caldera staggered forward a few steps, only to fall to her knees again.

"Damn it, Callie," Markarian said, helping her up. "You've lost a lot of blood, too." His eyes met hers. "I'll carry you."

"No," she replied, waving him off. "You need to stay at the front and Saro needs to bring up the rear—you're the only two with weapons." Her head spun.

Aloriea draped Caldera's arm around her neck. "I can't carry you, but I can support you," she said. The circles under her eyes had deepened.

Caldera smiled, ignoring the exhaustion in her own limbs. "Thanks."

Markarian took his place at the front of the group. "Let's get the fuck out of here."

Saro drew his blaster, moving to the back.

Sear wrapped one hand around Rennick's wrists to make sure he didn't let go, then grabbed Caldera's free hand with the other. "So we do not get separated," he said, smiling wearily down at her.

She gripped his hand tighter as they walked, staying close to the wall. Squinting through the dust clouds, she could see frantic movement—shadows everywhere. Everyone was looking for them.

They continued walking alongside the wall of the palace, attempting to draw as little attention to themselves as possible.

"Shit," Markarian muttered. "There's no cover up here."

Caldera gripped Aloriea's shoulder. "Where are we?"

"We're at the edge of the wall. Straight ahead is the fountain," Markarian replied.

"The courtyard doors are about one hundred feet away," Sear added, adjusting Rennick's wrists so he wasn't getting choked.

Caldera took a deep breath, letting her gaze linger on the area in front of her. "We're going to have to run."

"As soon as we step out of this dust cloud, they'll see us," Markarian said, his green eyes frantic. He exhaled sharply. "Saro," he called over his shoulder, "as soon as you're out, start shooting."

"Even if they don't see us?"

"Like I said, they probably will," Markarian replied.

Caldera glanced at each of her friends, lingering on Rennick, whose body hung limp. She could still see his chest slowly rising and falling against Sear's back. "Let's go!" she yelled.

Markarian rushed out into the open, his blaster drawn.

The shots started almost immediately.

Caldera braced herself as Sear plunged through the cloud, jerking her arm, pulling her body forward. She could see the gray sky clearly now as they raced through the courtyard, but she couldn't make out who was shooting at them.

Blaster rounds flew through the air, kicking up the dust at their feet or hitting off the wall behind them.

Saro fired recklessly as he entered the open space, precision and training gone.

Aloriea's hand was a death-grip around Caldera's wrist, her long-legged stride never pausing in their pursuit toward the door.

"I am losing my grip!" Sear yelled.

It took Caldera a second to realize that he was talking about Rennick. If they stopped, they'd be killed for sure.

"We're almost there," was the only thing she could say as the blackness around her vision closed in.

"I am sorry about this," Sear said over his shoulder at Rennick. "It is the only way I will not drop you."

Before Caldera could respond, he flexed his claws, driving them into Rennick's wrists which were wrapped around his throat. Rennick screamed in pain, and blood began trailing from the puncture wounds and down the front of Sear's shirt.

Aloriea yelped and slumped down before regaining her stride, taking Caldera's attention away from Rennick as they almost tumbled to the ground.

"What happened?" Sear yelled, his voice tremulous as they continued to sprint forward.

"I think...something hit me," Aloriea replied tightly.

"We're here!" Markarian cried. Pushing the door open, he ushered them in, then slammed and locked the door behind them.

"We have to keep going," Caldera muttered, letting her body slump against the wall.

Their assailants banged on the door.

Markarian and Saro ran over to Aloriea, looking her over.

"It's just a flesh wound," Markarian said, ripping more of his shirt and wrapping it around her bicep.

"We..." Caldera muttered, then collapsed completely onto the floor.

Leaning her head back against the wall, she could see Sear's legs were shaking uncontrollably. Just as she was about to stand up, he fell to his knees, lowering Rennick to the ground next to her. His bloody claws retracted back into his fingers.

"I am sorry, Callie," Sear said, wheezing. "I cannot keep going."

Aloriea knelt in front of him and caressed his cheek.

Caldera gasped for air, letting the tears flow freely down her face. The salt stung her wound, causing her to flinch in pain.

"Markarian...Aloriea...Saro..." she said, looking at each of them. *We're not gonna make it.* "Take Sear and get out of here." She forced the words out, choking on them as she did.

Markarian sat down next to her, putting his hand on her shoulder. "I think you know we're not going anywhere," he replied.

Quick rushes of footsteps echoed through the hall in front of them as the banging on the door at their backs intensified.

Markarian and Saro wearily raised their blasters.

"Looks like we're going down fighting," Markarian muttered, aiming down the sight.

Caldera opened her eyes to see uniformed security forces running down the hall toward them, coming from the front of the palace. They were completely surrounded. *We tried...and if nothing else, we saved Earth...*

"Please, lower your weapons. Wait... You—you're the queen!" A saurian woman said, her light green skin and scales bristling. Her eyes flicked from side to side.

"And the royal court!" A male natare added, running up next to her. His translucent blue-green skin shimmered under the palace light.

"Who are you?" Caldera asked, forcing herself to stay conscious just a few seconds longer.

The saurian and natare glanced at each other.

"Our sector leaders sent us," the saurian woman said, tongue flicking out from under her curled lips.

Saro shook his head, his blaster clattering against the floor where he dropped it. "I don't believe it..."

"Please," Caldera muttered, her vision almost completely black. "We're being attacked."

"We know," the saurian woman replied, kneeling next to her as she motioned for assistance. "That's why we're here. The perimeter is being secured."

"The queens...Jasik... They must've got my message," Aloriea whispered, leaning against Sear. "They sent a distress call to the other sector leaders."

The natare man nodded sharply. "We're here to help," he said, his external gills quivering. "We weren't expecting all of you to be so beat up, though." He rushed to Rennick and placed two fingers against his neck, searching for a pulse. "This man needs emergency medical treatment right now!" he yelled to someone behind him.

Caldera blinked, letting her gaze linger on Rennick before finally giving in to the blackness.

CHAPTER 40

Caldera opened her eyes to the blinding yellow light of the sun filtering in through the half-closed blinds. All at once, the smell of antiseptic hit her senses, causing her to gag as she sucked air into her lungs. She forced her chest to rise and fall in slower and slower intervals until she was no longer hyperventilating.

As she tried turning away from the light, pressure emanating from the bend in her arm caught her attention. It was an IV. She gingerly sat up and the neck of her white, oversized gown slid off her shoulder.

"You seem surprised," a familiar voice cut in.

"Doctor Vareis." Caldera turned to face the doctor as she entered the room, the door sliding closed behind her. "Where am I?"

"The hospital, somewhat obviously," the doctor replied, walking up next to the bed and gently, yet abruptly, pressing her fingers against Caldera's face. "Not bad for one week—though you'll still have quite a scar."

Pushing her hand away, Caldera narrowed her eyes. "I've been unconscious for a week?"

"Sedated," Doctor Vareis corrected, typing something into her holopad. "You wanted your cheek to heal, didn't you?"

Caldera pressed her own fingers against the soft scar tissue. "I see your bedside manner hasn't improved," she muttered, looking out the window.

The doctor smiled, warmth radiating from her features. "If you're interested, the inhabitants that you brought through the portal are all right," she said, returning the holopad to the pocket of her lab coat. "The man was lucky. If the woman hadn't been able to donate her blood to him, he would have died."

Caldera let a small smile break across her face as sunlight washed over her. "That's good..."

"They need to go back to wherever they came from immediately, though," Doctor Vareis added. "Their biology is similar to tellins, but it's not exact. They're not safe here. If either of them get severely injured, we might not be able to save them."

"I'm sure they won't object to eventually going back to their home planet." Caldera clutched the blankets and looked down for the first time. "Once they're healed and we can get more painite."

Fast-healing casts that formed to her hands were trying to regrow her skin as quickly as possible where she had sliced them trying to move the jagged piece of metal. White, seemingly useless gauze was wrapped gingerly over the top of everything.

The lights of personal transports zoomed by outside the window as silence fell over the room. *Do they know what happened? Whose side were they on?* Caldera shook her head, her friends' faces flashing across her mind. "What about everyone else?" she asked. Doctor Vareis had moved on to silently studying her vitals. "Aloriea, Sear, Markarian, Saro... Ren." She took a deep breath, preparing herself for the worst.

"They're fine," Doctor Vareis replied without taking her eyes off the various charts and monitors of the screen.

Calderas' ears rang. "Even—"

"Yes, even Rennick. He was released from surgery yesterday."

"Surgery?"

A wearied look passed across the doctor's dark face. "His leg—the crushed one. It had to be amputated. He just got his metal prosthetic today." She crossed her arms. "I honestly shouldn't be telling you this, doctor-patient confidentiality and all...but," she shrugged, tucking a dark strand of curly hair behind her ear, "you'll find out eventually, and you're the queen."

Caldera's jaw dropped as tears filled her eyes.

Doctor Vareis sighed heavily as she turned toward the door. "Don't be so hard on yourself. Without that tourniquet, he would have died." She leaned against the doorframe. "In all honesty, the explosion resulting from you destroying that portal wasn't as devastating as it probably seemed to be at the time."

Caldera hung her head.

Looking out the window, Doctor Vareis rested her hands in her lab coat pockets. "Most only sustained somewhat minor injuries."

"Tell that to Ren," Caldera whispered. As she clenched her jaw, the newly formed scar tissue on her face pulled.

"I did," the doctor replied matter-of-factly.

Sighing, Caldera closed her eyes and lifted her chin toward the ceiling as long white hair fell down her back. "We really need to talk about the way you address people."

"There were a few unlucky ones," Doctor Vareis continued as if she hadn't heard her. "Namely, Councilmember Randis."

Shock coursed through Caldera's body. "He...died?"

Doctor Varies lowered her head. "He's a natare. Their skin is a lot...thinner, I suppose you could say, than other species."

"Anyone else?" Caldera asked, hollow guilt rising in her chest.

The doctor's gaze held Caldera's. "There *were* other casualties, yes."

Caldera exhaled sharply, her stomach twisting into a tight knot. Her heart emptied as images of Olivare, Councilmember Randis, and the other faceless victims crossed her mind. "I'm a murderer..."

Doctor Vareis's expression softened. "That's not true," she replied sternly. "And no one's calling you that, anyway."

Caldera raised her eyebrows. "What are they calling me then?"

Doctor Vareis's brown eyes locked onto her. "Liberator."

"What?"

Shaking her head, a small, slightly sardonic smile spread across Doctor Vareis's face. "Do you seriously not realize that you freed this planet from the Council?"

Caldera blinked.

"The secret's out," Doctor Vareis continued. "Everything the Council did, hid, covered up. You name it." She chuckled. "It's been a busy week—you have a lot to catch up on."

Caldera's face broke into a smile. "So everything we did...it wasn't for nothing?"

Doctor Vareis's grin widened. "Absolutely not," she said before turning toward the door, heels clicking against the linoleum floor. "And if you're still not convinced, consider this. If the Council had gone through with their plan, how many would have died on that planet?"

Caldera's chest filled with warmth. "A lot."

"Then actually think about what the facts of the situation mean to you," the doctor added, turning to leave again. "You're a lot of things, Your Majesty, but a murderer is not one of them."

Caldera's heart beat in her ears as her cheeks flushed. *The facts of the situation...* "Wait!" she blurted, causing the doctor to whirl around. "I want to see him. I want to see Ren."

Doctor Vareis sighed. "Then follow me."

Caldera gently lowered herself off the side of the bed, her hospital gown ruffling against her knees. The chill of the linoleum shot up her bare feet and legs as she gathered the IV tubes in her hand, while simultaneously activating the portable machine.

"Isn't this against the rules?" Caldera asked as the doctor held the door open for her. "Shouldn't you be telling me to 'stay in bed' or something?"

Doctor Vareis smirked. "Would you listen to me if I did?"

"Good point." She chuckled, partially stumbling into the hall and grabbing a handrail. She followed Doctor Vareis down the hallway, the IV apparatus floating along beside her, beeping. "What happened to the other councilmembers?" she asked, unable to stop herself.

Doctor Vareis glanced at her. "They were detained by the rescue squad that stormed your palace, and later, in a combined effort, officially arrested by the sector leaders. Along with all the militia members that were following them," she said, steering Caldera down a new branch of the hallway.

"If the sector leaders could do something like that," Caldera said, furrowing her brows, "then why didn't they do it before?"

"You and your friends paved the way for them to stand up for themselves." Doctor Vareis shrugged. "They were living in fear for so long. Fear for their loved ones, their way of life... This whole situation is unprecedented."

Caldera bit her lip. "Do you think this—the arrest—will stick, then?" she asked. "I mean, do you really think they can be convicted of anything?"

"They certainly are powerful people," Doctor Vareis replied, slowing her pace. "I'm sure they have friends in even higher places." Her expression was hard. "Time will tell, I suppose, but you're the queen, not me. So how should I know?"

"That's fair." Caldera shook her head.

She fell quiet as the beeping monitors and distant commands of the staff met her ears. The cacophony of the busy hospital filled the dead air between them as they walked.

"You know..." Doctor Vareis said after a few minutes of silence. "For my part in this—I don't regret giving you those substances...even if you did intentionally lie to me about the planter orb recall."

"Sorry about that," Caldera said, exhaling sharply. "Do you really not regret anything?"

They turned down another hallway, passing nurses and patients who were, unsuccessfully, trying to pretend that they didn't know who she was.

"I don't. Your recklessness saved an entire planet, and let us know another one exists at the same time. Your other friends have been recounting everything to the sector leaders all week," she continued, stopping in front of a door. "I'm sure you two will have to re-explain everything from your point of view again, as soon as you get out of here, though."

"So that's where my friends are," Caldera whispered, pushing the thought to the back of her mind.

"Actually," Doctor Vareis said, opening the door. "They're here."

Four surprised faces turned to greet Caldera as she stepped into the room.

Markarian's hair was cropped close to his head. A long line of stitches, healing a sizable gash, was visible from behind his ear. Two fresh scars stretched across the bridge of his nose and half-way down his cheek.

Small scars adorned Aloriea's neck, chest, and arms, completely on display because of the thin-strapped tank she wore. Her right horn was filed down, awaiting a new prosthetic.

New patches of exposed skin ran down Sear's arms, where fur could no longer grow. His now-short bobtail lolled back and forth as if it wanted to swish the ground like it used to.

Caldera's eyes misted as each of her friends wordlessly enveloped her in a hug. "Why didn't you tell me they were here?" She sniffed, glancing over her shoulder at Doctor Vareis.

"Surprise?" she said with a chuckle before turning to leave. "I knew they were coming your way. You weren't supposed to be getting out of bed yet."

Caldera wiped away tears as the door slid shut.

Hazel eyes met her blue ones as Caldera took a step forward through the group, her breath catching in her throat. "Ren!" She ran to his bedside.

"Hey," he replied, a smile spreading across his face as she wrapped her arms around his neck.

She took a step back, glancing at each of her friends again. "I'm so sorry..."

Tears pricked at her eyes as every word fought to get out of her mouth at once, jumbling at the back of her throat until she couldn't say anything at all.

"We're gonna stop you right there," Markarian said, instinctively running a hand through his short hair.

Aloriea and Sear nodded.

"There's nothing to apologize for," Aloriea insisted, a soft smile spreading across her face.

Sear grinned his fanged smile. "That explosion certainly did a number on us though." He chuckled, scratching behind his half-ear.

"Sorry," Caldera replied, an apologetic grin quirking her lips up.

Sear embraced her again. "No apologies. You saved a planet."

"*We* saved a planet," Caldera corrected, squeezing tight before releasing him. "Where's Saro?"

"Guarding the palace," Aloriea replied. "He has refused to rest."

A relaxed silence fell over the room as Caldera turned back to Rennick. Early afternoon sunlight glimmered through the windows and off his hair as she took his hand.

"We do have to get going, though," Aloriea finally said.

A wave of somberness washed over Caldera. She didn't want them to leave. "Where to?"

"Another meeting with the sector leaders," Markarian explained, exhaling sharply. "Be prepared, because as soon as you two are discharged from the hospital, you'll be in this hell, too," he continued with a smirk.

Aloriea and Sear rolled their eyes.

"Contact us when you're getting discharged and we'll meet you back here. Okay?" Aloriea said, taking a breath.

Caldera nodded, her fingers still intertwined with Rennick's.

"Come on, we will be late," Sear said, ushering Aloriea and Markarian to the door.

"Make sure you visit John and Mei before you get out of here," Markarian added, before strolling out of the room.

"We will," Caldera promised, smiling.

Sear offered his arm to Aloriea, who gently took it, smiling over at Caldera and Rennick before the door slid shut again.

Then it was just Caldera and Rennick. "You're awfully quiet," she said, squeezing his hand.

"I already knew everything they were telling you," he replied with a wink. "Why interrupt?"

Caldera laughed, sitting on the edge of his bed. "Ren... I need to say something."

"Why don't we talk outside?" he interjected, tucking a strand of hair behind her ear.

"Really?"

He nodded. "Why not? I need some fresh air."

Removing the covers, he shifted so his legs dangled off the bed, his metal prosthetic clinking against the floor as his feet hit the ground.

Caldera helped him over to the far side of the hospital room. He pressed a panel on the wall, opening a door that she hadn't known was there.

"You have a balcony in your room?" she asked, releasing his arm and following him outside onto a small, square platform.

Rennick leaned against the railing, a chilly breeze ruffling his hair. "I wouldn't exactly call it that," he said, smiling over at her. "It's meant for the visitors of whoever gets stuck in here."

Caldera leaned next to him, looking out into Tellis's capital city, Astrum. "So... How are you doing?" she asked awkwardly, glancing down at his leg. The prosthetic started below his right knee.

"Managing," he replied, flexing his foot and wriggling his new metallic toes. "What did you want to talk about?"

"I just... I wanted to say that I'm sorry, again," Caldera gasped, tears in her eyes. "I did this. I almost killed you—all of you. I don't understand why you're all forgiving me so quickly—"

"Callie, stop," Rennick interrupted, placing his hands on her shoulders.

"But—"

"After everything that's happened—all the bullshit—we're all here. We forgive you because we believed in what you were trying to do. You're our friend, it's as simple as that," he said, interlacing their fingers and stepping closer to her. "Besides, I was always willing to give my life for yours anyway—you know that." He smiled brightly down at her. "I love you, Callie."

Warmth filled the inside of her chest, branching out to her entire body, as a smile broke across her face. "I love you, too," she said. She pressed her lips against his and wrapped her arms around his waist.

Separating, she rested her forehead against his, keeping her eyes closed and taking in a deep breath. Cold wind rushed through her hair and over her skin, causing them both to shiver.

"What's the next move?" Rennick asked, brushing the hair out of her face. "Because we're with you—no matter what."

Caldera's eyes fluttered open. "I'm not sure," she whispered, turning to look out onto the capital, placing her palms flat against the railing.

"Callie, listen... You may not have been brought up with all of this—politics, royalty, or sector policies—but you were born for it." He paused, placing a gentle hand on her shoulder. "You've always wanted to help the people of Bersama and now you have a real chance."

A smirk spread across her face. "You're right. This is my sector. I *am* the queen... I think it's about time I started acting like it."

ABBY R. LAUGHLIN

is a science fiction adventure author and an ERA at a veterinary clinic. The Cosmic Principle, the first in the Nexus Series, is her debut novel. Future projects include books two and three of the same series, as well as a prequel and two companion novels set in the same universe. Abby is currently living her life in the Midwest with her cats, lizard, and husband.

WWW.ABBYRLAUGHLIN.COM